Circle of Truth

By

Jeffrey C. Dillow

Art: J.C. Dillow

ISBN-10:0996615423

ISBN-13:978-0-9966154-2-6

High Fantasy Publications

FIRST EDITION

www.HighFantasyBooks.com

Other Publications by this author include:

Role Playing Games
High Fantasy
Adventures in High Fantasy
Goldchester
Wizards and Warriors
Murder in Irliss

Fantasy Novel
When Magics Meet

By Jennifer Dillow

The Fifth Chamber

Enchantraen

Weapons

SHORT SWORD ⚔ -O
THREE MAGIC DAGGERS ⚔ -O
FISTS 👊 -2
REGULAR DAGGER 🗡 -1

Ships

☐ CAGO
☐ PERFIDIA
☐ LADY VERAE

Damage

ERASE ALL DAMAGE BOXES WHEN THE NEXT DAY IS CHECKED.

☐ ☐ ☐ ☐ ☐ ☐ ☐ ☐ ☐ ☐

Trial Boxes

☒ ☐ ☐ ☐ ☐

Days

FROM THE 10TH DAY ON ROLL THE DICE. IF YOU ROLL THE NUMBERS INDICATED TURN IMMEDIATELY TO 1003.

1	2	3	4	5	6	7	8	9	10	11	12
									2 OR 3	2 TO 4	2 TO 5

13	14	15	16	17	18	19
2 TO 6	2 TO 6	2 TO 7	2 TO 8	2 TO 9	2 TO 10	(TURN TO 1003)

Manna

ERASE ALL MANNA BOXES WHEN NEXT DAY IS CHECKED.

☐ ☐ ☐ ☐ ☐ ☐ ☐ ☐ ☐ ☐   WHEN THE LAST MANNA BOX IS CHECKED DO NOT CAST ANY MORE SPELLS.

Letters

A B C D E F G H I J K L M N O P Q R S T U V W X Y Z

aa bb cc dd ee ff gg hh ii jj kk ll mm

Equipment

WITH YOU	GONE	
☒	☐	SHORT SWORD
☒	☐	THREE MAGIC DAGGERS
☒	☐	REGULAR DAGGER
☒	☐	SHEFAST
☐	☐	CHARMED WARNING STONE
☐	☐	GEM OF MISSLE PROTECION
☐	☐	5000 GOLD TAMS (IN ELECTRUM)
☐	☐	BOOK OF MAGIC

WITH YOU	GONE	
☐	☐	GEM TO RETURN SHEFAST
☐	☐	INCANTATION OF KNOT
☐	☐	GLASS VESSEL OF CALMING
☐	☐	PEARL GODSTONE
☐	☐	BROACH OF LIFE
☐	☐	IVORY UNICORN
☐	☐	MAGICAL SWORD + 1
☐	☐	STAKE OF CONFUSION

Rogue's Gallery

Find the scene number you are playing. That is your opponent. When the last box here is checked that means your opponent is defeated.

Scene	Name	Damage
38, 76	Wraith	☐☐☐☐☐☐☐☐
86, 274	Mist Demon	☐☐☐☐☐☐☐☐☐
156, 169, 178, 199	Urwurt	☐☐☐☐☐☐☐
237, 292	Eastern Soldier	☐☐☐☐☐☐
247, 295, 399	Slashing Thief/scummy soldier	☐☐☐☐☐
265	Pierl	☐☐☐☐☐☐☐☐☐
296	City Guard I	☐☐☐☐☐
298	Eastern Soldier with blade	☐☐☐☐☐☐☐
311	Laytant	☐☐☐☐☐☐☐☐
321	Mountain Magi (Bar Giant)	☐☐☐☐☐
401, 422, 443	Black Assassin	☐☐☐☐☐☐☐
431	Black Assassin I	☐☐☐☐☐☐☐
431	Black Assassin II	☐☐☐☐☐☐☐☐
431	Black Assassin III	☐☐☐☐☐☐
431	Black Assassin IV	☐☐☐☐☐☐
431	Black Assassin V	☐☐☐☐☐☐☐
419	Penoi	☐☐☐☐☐☐☐☐☐☐
477	Rider in Black	☐☐☐☐☐☐☐
495, 549	Denri	☐☐☐☐☐☐☐☐
611, 615, 618, 631, 649	Dark Lord	☐☐☐☐☐☐☐☐☐☐☐
611	Storm Giant	☐☐☐☐☐☐☐☐☐☐
619	Wolves	1 2 3 4 5 6 Defeated
627	Giant Eagle	☐☐☐☐☐☐☐☐☐☐☐
161, 173	Giant Beetle	☐☐☐☐☐☐☐☐☐☐
1007	Benolic	☐☐☐☐☐☐

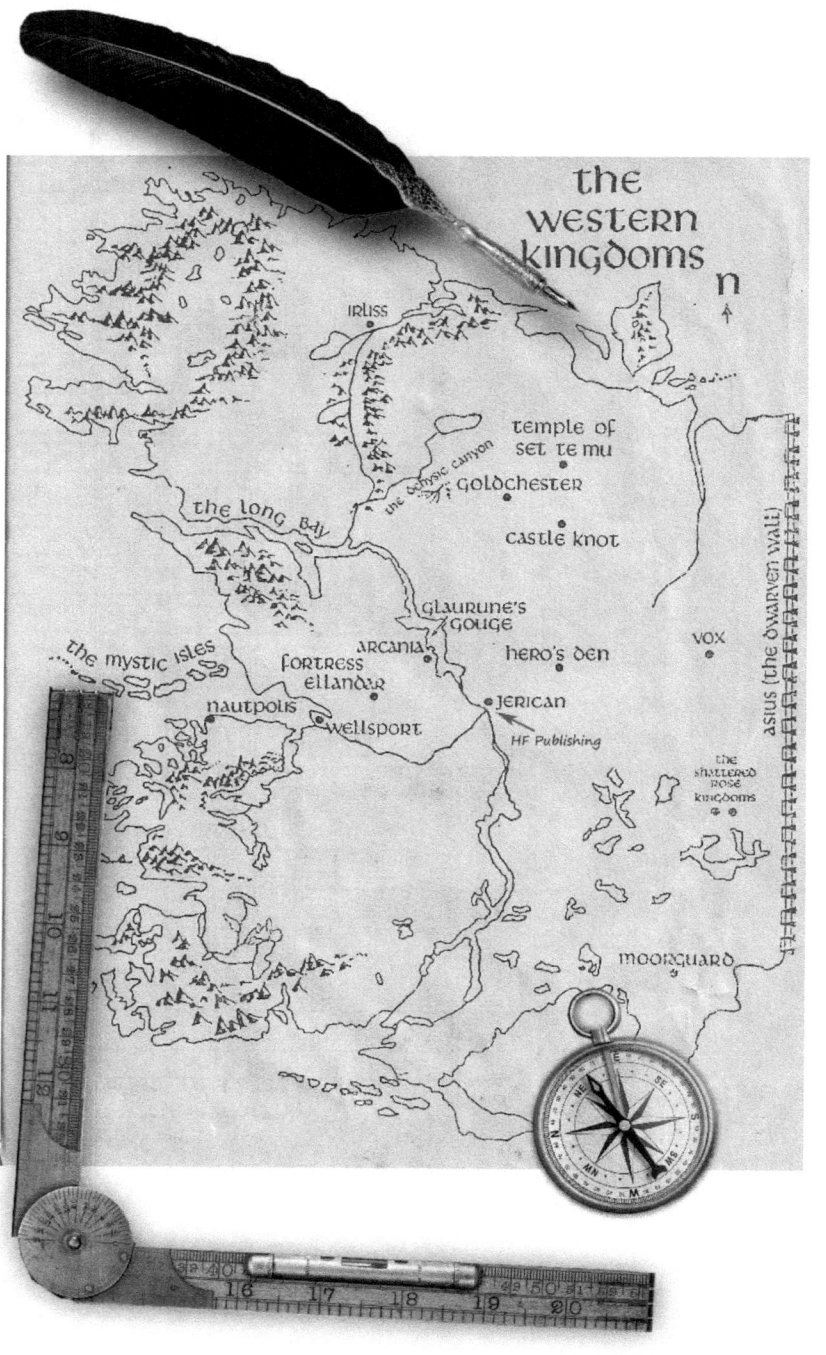

Synopsis

  This book is a point-of-view adventure about a powerful wizard who comes from the Western Kingdoms. The actual person who plays the game can be either a male or female.

  Enchantraen the hero/heroine of the story has long been a rebel fighting against Eastern forces. When the story begins Enchantraen is about to start on a quest across dangerous territory on a venture to the Mystic Isles. You can find the Mystic Isles on the map. The purpose of the quest is to reach the isles and take part in a contest called the *Challengings*. The winners of this contest will be seated as a high authority on a powerful wizard's guild. It is Enchantraen's hope to win one of these positions and to use his/her new influence to fight against the East.

  Enchantraen has a special set of paraphernalia to aid him/her on the quest. One of these items is a magical staff named Shefast. This staff calls lightning from the sky. It also has other abilities but the champion must experiment with the staff during the game to find these properties. Enchantraen also carries a magical book and a charmed warning.

  To start the game find the Character Sheet, the Rogues Gallery, Map, and grab a pair of dice.

  If you do not have dice use 12 coins and count heads as a point.

  You should go to www.HighFantasyBooks.com and download your free character sheet. You can also photocopy the character sheet inside this book. You will need it to keep track of your travels.

Free character sheets and maps at www.HighFantasyBooks.com.

Story Line

Enchantraen the War Wizard

A young mother gently slips the covers up around her child. Blowing the candle out, she turns from the darkened room. The latch on the door slides up quietly as she slips out. In the hallway her husband brushes the tears from her cheek.

"The child will be safe with the nurse," he says softly.

"I know, I know," she chokes in reply. "We've been through it all before."

They return to their own room being careful to step quietly through the straw. He crosses over to the table inspecting the finely-oiled blade of her massive longsword. The edge is true and God knows the metal has been well-proven. She removes the hot coals from the bed warmer and places a last log on the fire that should burn through the night.

Husband and wife slip deep into the covers where they both expect to have another restless sleep. The burden of fear locked in his heart knots his stomach. Tomorrow he knows his wife will march with the legions of Constans. They will both leave the fair city of Nautpolis; she as a warrior of the first rank, and he as a revered armorer. It is possible neither one may return to the child. At least there was a worthy cause for this war, but then again, there always seems to be a worthy cause to take men's lives.

The Eastern Generals, or as the West refers to them, The Dark Lords, have invaded the Western Kingdoms. Somehow five armies have crossed over *Asius*, the great dwarven wall. Establishing a base in the treacherous city of Vox, the five Dark Lords have spear-headed a wave of destruction through the tiny independent kingdoms of the West. One by one the kingdoms have fallen.

The Rose Kingdoms were the first to fall, the castles conquered. Whole cities and towns have been leveled if they dared to resist. Smaller towns like Irliss and Goldchester have been seized and are now governed by the East. As the West crumbles Nautpolis prepares for war!

Suddenly he sits straight up in bed, but she is already halfway down the hall with sword in hand. It sounded like a muffled cry. Stumbling at the door he grabs his big axe and bolts after her.

Looking down the hallway towards the child's room he sees his wife silhouetted in the doorway. A bright light engulfs her as she stands shielding her eyes, frozen in fear. He shoves her aside and blindly swings the axe with every fiber of his massive arms. With the reflexes of a hardened warrior she shoves the blow aside and wood chips fly as the edge of the bed shatters.

In control now they both stand bewildered in the doorway. In the center of the room stands the child. The small babe's body burns like the sun. In the corner, being held at bay by the magical light, are twin asps.

This was your parent's first indication that they were blessed with a "True One." Their child was a wizard!

You are that wizard. Your name is Enchantraen. Your parents returned after this battle, but many more campaigns followed against the East and the formidable Dark Lords. During their absence you were left to study with older wizards as was befitting one of your station.

Over time your parents were soon gone more than they were with you. Your powers grew and it became apparent that you were gifted in the magics. Each time they returned your parents would tell you details of the battles. Your eyes were ever gazing over the walls of the city, trying to trace the movements of the Dark Lords' armies with your mind.

Soon your friends were marching to war and you, a wizard, were left to your studies. Diligently you practiced, a worthy student if an unwilling pupil. In time you declared to your teachers that you too must go to fight.

You still chuckle today remembering the words you said.

"I was born a child of the first rank, and metal runs in my veins. There is an enemy to be fought and I can't waste my powers in this cloister any longer."

Brave words from a young wizard, but in time you would back them up. Strapping one of your father's swords to your side you came of age by your own volition.

Early in your fighting you saw the advantages of joining a society of wizards known as the True Ones' Guild. You finger the hair's-width gold chain around your neck, the symbol of your guild. The guild boasts a membership of 80% of all aether-using wizards from both the East and the West.

The guild is headed by ten wizards known as Elders. The Elders sit at a table twelve times a year. When these Elders gather it is known throughout the lands as the Circle of Truth. From this circle laws are issued that all guild members must live by. The laws change and many are often reversed, yet you always obey the most current declarations of the Elders.

You have talked to many other guild members about the reoccurring changes. The general consensus is that the Elders are extremely varied in their backgrounds; some are Eastern, and some are Western. As time changes so does the proportion of Easterners to Westerners and therefore the laws. It's a turbulent world but you still hold true to the guilds' original meaning. By following their laws you feel that you are contributing to their true purpose; the betterment of the world as a whole, the betterment of the people in both the East and the West.

Your purpose since leaving Nautpolis has been to fight against the East and all their injustice. In the beginning you fought in small ways; stopping barroom brawls, thwarting over-ambitious soldiers, and all things that young first plane wizards can do. Later you organized with a small party of adventurers and, together, your small pranks turned into serious offenses against the East.

The Dark Lords began to issue warrants for your arrest. Large prize money was offered and both Eastern and Western bounty hunters were sent to find you. You always proved to be the *Will-o-the-Wisp* and remained free and defiant. One of your greatest triumphs in your early years was the completion of the *Quest for the Temples*. During this quest you used your powers to locate four mystic temples whose history interlaced with your home city of Nautpolis. Drawing on the power of these ancient temples you constructed a magical defense that today keeps the Dark Lords from using their full force against Nautpolis, the one last stronghold of the West.

Thinking back, you remember the wrath you provoked from your troubles. The Dark Lords cornered you and your party inside Arcania your tower retreat. There you watched from the ramparts as great pieces of the ground gave way. Not wishing to fight you directly they called on demonic allies instead. From the bowels of the earth an army came forth. The battle that ensued is one that neither side likes to remember. In the end you liquefied the demon commander. As his corpse seeped back into the ground you scattered the rest of the troops with great blasts of lightning from Shefast, your magical staff. You put a glamour on your tower to hide it once more. The Dark Lords still search knowing the general area where your tower should be, but they cannot find you. Still, they manage to meddle in your affairs, but always indirectly.

Today during one of the few quiet moments in your career you sit in the comfort of your tower conversing with Jenevan, your familiar. Jenevan is a giantess with huge wings. Being a high-level wizard your familiar is also a powerful creature. In mid-conversation you feel a change coming around you.

Slamming your fist on the table you shout to Jenevan, "It's time again! Quick, come with me to the top."

Using the special traveling devices you built in your tower you and Jenevan teleport to the top of the tower. The cold night air strikes your robe and whips it tightly to your body.

"Do you feel it Jenevan," you shout. "It must be time. I feel the aether! I feel the charge!"

"There," you shout pointing to the northeast, "its Rainolic."

Rumbling like thunder upward the hooves of the seven horses leave the spotted trail of a rainbow. As the chariot dips and disappears to the west the rainbow remains etched into the night sky, so close you could almost touch it. The maddening feeling surges through your veins.

"Do you feel it Jenevan?" you gasp! "The Circle of Truth is in council and it's time for the *Challengings*."

Taking one last look at the night sky you teleport back inside and nervously pace the floor.

The Time of the Challngings is a time when any member of your guild may challenge one of the Elders for a place on the Circle of Truth. At random times the aether (magic energy) will increase. The wild surge of power sends many wizards into sleepless, irritable moods. When the Elders feel it, they immediately send out Rainolic, the True Ones' messenger. He makes the rainbow as a signal for the beginning of the challenges. Any wizard who feels capable, may travel to the Mystic Isles and lay his challenge before the Circle of Truth. There on the isle the contestants compete in friendly tests. More than this you do not know.

You rustle the scrolls in your study and fiddle with the burning lamps.

"Don't even think it," Jenevan's voice slices through the nervous silence.

"You are only fourth plane, master. You know the challenges are meant for the most skilled fifth plane wizards."

Smiling lightly up at her you remember how closely your minds are linked.

"But I am a war wizard Jenevan. I leaned my craft first hand. I am not like those book-learned theorists. Besides, with me on the council I could give the Circle of Truth real meaning and direction again."

"They will stop you, you know," Jenevan flatly states.

"Who?" you reply.

"The East will never let you sit amongst the ten. You have proven your hatred for them many times. Besides, the council members are supposed to be neutral towards the politics of the Kingdoms. They are supposed to be looking out for the welfare of the land."

"Jenevan, that is pure propaganda handed out for first plane wizards. The East sends every wizard they can to the contest for one reason. They want to warp the Circle of Truth to their will."

"They will stop you," Jenevan repeats.

"Thank you for your concern. Be good about this and pack my traveling things. Bring me the maps. I need to plot my course to the Mystic Isles."

As Jenevan goes about her business you move to the secret panel. Pressing the correct combinations of stones the slab slides up revealing Shefast, the staff of lightning. As the wood presses against your palm you feel the power of the metal chards hidden inside it. The increase in the aether has supercharged the staff. Sliding your hand down the length of it you recall its major property.

Shefast can summon the lightning from the heavens to strike your enemies. The staff however seems to have a mind of its own. Sometimes the staff sends out a single powerful blast. Other times the staff will fork out and strike several victims with lesser blasts. The greatest feature about the staff is that it doesn't use up any of your manna to activate it. This saves you energy for your spells.

Using the special teleportation devices in your tower you blink up to the floor where Jenevan is packing.

Seeing the extra pack you say, "No Jenevan; I'm afraid you won't be going this time. I'll need you to stay here and guard Arcania. Since you are my familiar our minds are linked. I need you to stay here and to warn me if any trouble comes to Arcania."

"But master!"

"Silence! On this subject there will be no discussion."

"The guild is the single most powerful magical force in the land. It has been docile and blind to the suffering of the people long enough. I have heard of their great magical storehouses. I have listened to the tales of glistening castles, cloud beasts, and the far-reaching eyes that await the command of the Elders. They need a strong leader with a purpose. There is so much to be gained. I can do things from that seat of power that I could never accomplish sitting here in my tower. The time is now. Lay the maps out before me!"

Your voice seemed to be high and frantic sounding even to you. You pass it off as being caused by the nervous energy built-up inside you.

Looking at the maps (see map of Western Kingdoms) you decide on one of the following ways to begin your journey to the Mystic Isles.

You could travel alone and go west towards Fortress Ellendar. You believe the fortress to be occupied by Tancred, the original owner and a friend of the West. From there you may decide to go to Wellsport to catch a small ship, or go on towards Nautpolis to visit old friends.

Then again, a trip alone might be extremely dangerous at this time. You could backtrack slightly and go to Jerican the ancient merchant's capital. There you could find a much larger war-galley to take you down the river and then to the Mystic Isles. You could even hire troops to bodyguard you if you wished to walk the distance.

"Hmmm," you think. Large numbers of Westerners tend to attract large numbers of enemies. Maybe you should go to Jerican and purchase a few magical items in the plentiful shops.

Then again, time has to be considered. No one knows when the *Challengings* will be over. At any time the phenomenon could end and your chances could be lost.

Well, this will only be the first of a good many decisions you must make. Rolling up the maps you give Jenevan her final instructions on how to guard Arcania. Teleporting down to the front gate with Shefast, your magical book, and your traveling pack with your charmed warning stone you say good-bye.

Leaving the tower you must now turn to scene <u>9</u>.

This Story is Now
Your Story
Make your own way

---

2   Roll the dice. If you roll:

2 to 10, Turn to <u>76</u>.
11 or 12, Turn to <u>58</u>. The staff fails!

3   Roll the dice. If you roll:

2 to 11, Turn to <u>46</u>.
12, Turn to <u>14</u>.

4   <u>Mark off 4 manna points.</u>
The faint light of the moons and stars bend and form around you. At the end of your enchantment you look yourself over and find that you are well-concealed from the normal eye.

Listening intently, you hear something rushing through the foliage towards you. Turn to <u>34</u>.

5   The mist makes breathing difficult. When you hit the ground the air bursts from your chest. Reflexively you inhale, sucking part of the green mist into your lungs. As the mist solidifies you begin to gag. Twirling above you is a scaly green demon. As it laughs you feel its tail ripping at your lungs.

Not an easy end to such a glorious career!

Well, enchantingly, mark it off to experience. The game is over this time and I'm afraid you have been stopped.

Beware, wizard, it is a dangerous world!

If you wish to play again, you must erase all marks and return to the beginning.

6   Roll the dice. If you roll:

2 to 6, Turn to <u>13</u>.
7 to 12, Turn to <u>48</u>.

7   The light is faint at first but soon it flares and brightens the woods. You carefully move the light so that you are just outside its edge, standing in the darkness.

There! A large man with a bow runs for the cover of nearby bushes. He is giving hand signals to a ... to a jaguar! The beast is immense. Stealthfully they move your way. Do you:

(A) Cast a *binding* spell to trap both man and beast?
     Mark off 2 manna and turn to 75.

(B) Cast a *fly* spell to hide among the tree tops?
     There you will be out of reach of the jaguar.
     Mark off 3 manna and turn to 8.

8   Roll the dice. If you roll:

2 to 11, Turn to 21.
12, Turn to 50.

9   The clear night air feels good around you. The fantastic rainbow glimmers in the sky and the stars look like gems set around it. Briefly reviewing the map while you are still in the forest, you plot the quickest route. Midway through your examination of the map you notice that your charmed warning stone is glowing. A strong intruder is near! Not more than three minutes from Arcania and there is trouble already! Judging by the intensity of the glow, you guess the intruder to be within 200 feet of you. Roll one die. If you roll:

1 to 3, Turn to 39.
4 to 6, Turn to 19.

10   Roll the dice. If you roll:

2 to 10, Turn to 20.
11 or 12, Turn to 50.

---

11   Roll the dice. If you roll:

2 to 11, Turn to 7.
12, Turn to 50.

12   "Wait, Almon! I am here in your presence. Quickly, man, tell me what evil beset you."

Almon whirls and slashes the air with his dagger. Suddenly he stops and throws his dagger in your direction. Then he covers his eyes and falls to his knees.

The dagger easily flies over your head but you do not notice it landing. Do you:

(A) Run to Almon's side? Turn to 56.

(B) Stay, wary of the old farmer, and try to talk to him from a distance? Turn to 23.

(C) Turn around to explore the woods and possibly retrieve the dagger? Turn to 41.

13   The familiar light-blue shimmer of light forms around your hands and leaps across the void towards the wraith. You guide the magical cord to wrap tightly around the wraith's invisible arms and legs. Nicely wrapped and sealed, the wraith falls to the ground shrieking. Climbing over the obstacles that separate you, you kneel at the wraith's side.

"Show yourself, dead one," you say as you lift the creature's faceguard.

As the creature's form faintly materializes, you pull back in amazement. You recognize the creature to have once been a local farmer.

(Continued next page)

(13 cont'd)

"Damn the East!" you think to yourself; they are taking the innocent people of the land and turning them against each other.

It would take a wizard with more skill than you to transform such a man. You know that wraiths are often created by high level wizards and then sent on specific missions. Unluckily for Almon this wraith was coming for him.

Pulling a magic dagger you end the creature's unnatural life. As you replace the dagger, you realize how dangerous this trip will be. If indeed there is a high level wizard out there, he could send these wraiths after you ... in groves.

Just then Almon groans with pain. Turn to 47.

14   The light blue light forms, then fails. Attempting to cast the spell again, you are stopped.

A gruff voice shouts from below, "There's a *death* arrow aimed at your throat. Do not move!"

You know that you have extra protection from missiles but this missile sounds like it is magical. Unable to locate the voice, do you:

(A) Talk, asking the man what his business is on your land? Turn to 99.

(B) Brave the arrow and attempt to cast a spell? Turn to 61.

15   The spell sputters and fades. You must be more rattled than you thought. Quickly stepping back into the shadows, you watch Almon run by. Do you:

(A) Yell at Almon to stop? Turn to 12.

(B) Wait and see a moment longer? Turn to 59.

16 The crashing sound alters and changes direction. It seems determined to find you. Just then a farmer comes crashing through the woods. You recognize the man to be named Almon.

Almon runs blindly towards you. His clothes are torn and he is bleeding profusely. You step to the side to keep from being run over and grab the farmer with one hand. Turn to 12.

17 Giving instructions to Jenevan to care for the farmer, you leave. The man will simply have to understand that what you are doing is for everyone's benefit, not just his.

Walking on into the night you are relieved to discover the first few rays of morning light streaming over the horizon. Turn to 98 and mark off N.

18 Mark off 4 manna points.
The spell dies away before it has a proper chance to take hold. Before you have time to try again, turn to 34.

19 There! Just off in the distance you catch a glimpse of a black shadow jumping over a bush. What was that! Whatever it was, it was moving very fast and directly towards you. Do you wish to take the defensive immediately, and:

(A) Cast a *fly* spell to fly directly up into the tree tops?_Turn to 8 and mark off 3 manna.

(B) Fire Shefast to try and scare off whatever it is? Turn to 10.

(C) Cast a *light* spell 100 feet off in the direction the creature is coming from? Mark off 1 manna and turn to 31.

20 First the lightning forms and rips through the air. Plummeting down it strikes the staff and bounds off into the woods. The forest trembles with the rolling thunder. A magnificent display of wizardry, you smile. It's too bad it didn't frighten the jaguar.

(Continued next page)

(20 cont'd)

Sitting slightly off in the bushes, the jaguar stares you down. Resting on its haunches, it is ready to strike, but something is causing the cat to hesitate.

Slowly lifting your eyes you see a large man with a shining arrow pointed at your forehead. The distance between the two is too great to attempt a spell that might affect them both! Do you:

(A) Boldly stand your ground and ask the man who dares trespass upon the lands of Enchantraen? Turn to <u>114</u>.

(B) Attempt a *fly* spell? Escaping could be your only choice left, turn to <u>84</u>.

21   The spell takes hold and you feel the familiar weight loss. Leaping directly up you are soon lost among the top of the tree branches.

Looking back down you see that the spell worked none too soon. Below you is a black jaguar sniffing the ground. The creature is unusually large and seems to have your scent. Protected among the top of the trees, do you:

(A) Wait to see if the jaguar leaves? Turn to <u>57</u>.

(B) Cast a *binding* spell on the creature? Turn to <u>3</u> and <u>mark off 1 manna</u>.

22   Reaching out mentally with your mind, you make the familiar link with Jenevan.

"I am on my way," comes the reply as soon as your mind forms the message. Quietly you wait for Jenevan to report.

"Master, look through my eyes."

(22 cont'd)

The dark night fades around you as your perspective shifts. You see a farmer named Almon running through the woods. He is coming your way. His clothes are torn and he is bleeding badly.

Wait!

Directly behind him comes a wraith! Its black cloak whips and the wind whistles through its platemail. The only part of the wraith's body that is visible is its red glowing eyes.

Do you:

(A) Step to the side and let the farmer run past you? When the wraith appears cast a spell.
Turn to 44.

(B) Cast a spell now? The illusion of a dragon at your side might send shivers even through a wraith!

Roll the dice and mark off 4 manna.

2 to 11, Turn to 35.
12, Turn to 15.

23   "You rave, Almon," you begin.

Just then a hot blade sharply stings in your back. Turning and twisting you see glowing red eyes over your shoulder.

Go to the Enchantraen table that follows and roll one die.

(Continued next page)

(23 cont'd)

Check off the damage boxes on your score card.

ENCHANTRAEN

Roll		Damage
1	--------	0
2	--------	0
3	--------	0
4	--------	1
5	--------	2
6	--------	3

If you expire turn to 25. If you live you tumble forward trying to get away from your assailant.

Successfully doing so, you turn to see the glowing red eyes of an evil wraith. "No wonder," you dimly think, "a wraith can see through your spells."

Standing up you try to shake off the pain and gather your thoughts. As you do so you see the black gauntlet of the wraith tracing out an intricate pattern in the air.

Roll the dice. If you roll:

2 to 7, Turn to 54.
8 to 12, turn to 67.

24   Roll the dice. If you roll:

2 to 6, Turn to 13.
7 to 12, Turn to 58.

25   Sorry, Enchantraen, but when you expire so does your familiar. The wraith simply closes the earth around you and you are forever lost from the sight of men.

(25 cont'd)

In the realm of high magic it is not usual to lose it all so quickly and so easily.

If you wish to play again, erase all your marks on the character sheet and return to the start.

26   Roll the dice. If you roll:

2 to 6, Turn to <u>33</u>.
7 to 12, Turn to <u>48</u>.

27   Dashing into the forest you scramble through the foliage. After a time you discover that the wraith did not follow you. Stopping to catch your breath, you try to determine the best thing to do at this point. As you are thinking, a startling sound causes you to turn to <u>74</u>.

28   Yes! The wraith lets out a death cry as you cause the dragon-illusion to spout its fiery breath. The power of one's own mind is awesome, you think to yourself as you watch the wraith burn away. Simply because it believed the fire was real, the fire was capable of destroying it.

A moan turns your thoughts from your powerful illusion to the wounded farmer. Turn to <u>47</u>.

29   As you begin to lose consciousness you hear the earth rumble. Fighting off the overpowering need to sleep, you find yourself on your hands and knees gasping for air. Glancing up you see that the wraith has tumbled into your newly-made hole.

As you both stumble to your feet to square off, once again a streak plummets behind the wraith. With one mighty swing of her scythe, Jenevan slices through the protective plate of the wraith and sends its soul searing to the underworlds.

"Really, Jenevan," you say as you brush yourself off, "that

(Continued next page)

(29 cont'd)

wasn't necessary. I had everything under control."

"Sorry, Master, but you know how I hate to be closed up in tight places," Jenevan answers with a smile.

A groan from above sends you flying to Almon's side. Turn to 47.

30   Roll the dice. If you roll:

2 to 11, Turn to 4.
12, Turn to 18.

31   Roll the dice. If you roll:

2 to 11, Turn to 7.
12, Turn to 50.

32   Jenevan reports back that she will take care of it.

Moving a little further, you can hear the creature crashing towards you. Altering your course you slip on through the brush until the noise recedes behind you. Holding to your determination to start this quest, you continue on through the night until...

Roll the dice. If you roll:

2 to 8, Turn to 74.
9 to 12, Turn to 16.

33   As your hands weave the last intricate pattern to the deadly spell, you hear the wraith begin to wail. The horrible pitch of its voice increases to one agonizing screech as its cloak and armor melt and form a bloody puddle. Walking to the puddle, you know that you have only temporarily stopped the creature. When the spell wears off the creature will re-form to menace you once again. If it were a normal man that you just trans-mutated, you could solve the problem by taking your boot and

(33 cont'd)

splashing the puddle. That way the man would be scattered and would re-form as bits and pieces. However, a wraith could re-form. To solve the problem you simply place a magical dagger in the center of the pool. Then when the body re-forms, it will have the deadly blade inside it.

Gibbering in the bushes causes you to turn and there you find Almon. Turn to 47.

34　　There is no need for searching as you watch a frightening form come crashing through the underbrush. It is Almon, a local farmer. He appears to be badly hurt. His clothes hang in shreds and blood flows freely from open wounds. He runs by you heading towards your tower. Do you:

(A) Yell and stop him before he reaches the door? Turn to 12.

(B) Wait and see a moment longer? Turn to 59.

35　　The illusion begins to form. Carefully you shape the image, scale by scale, of a full-grown gold dragon. Its scales glisten and shimmer off the leaves. As you pay attention to the last detail, Almon breaks through the foliage and collapses. Behind him comes the wraith who stops dead in its tracks.

You move the dragon forward. If only you could see the wraith's face! You are certain it is shocked, but does it believe the illusion is real?

Roll the dice. If you roll:

2 to 9, Turn to 28.
10 to 12, Turn to 80.

36　　With all the speed you can muster, you jump straight up. Soaring as fast as you can you climb to 110 feet, stop and look

(Continued next page)

(36 cont'd)

down. Hovering just out of spell range, you watch the cursing wraith spirit away into the forest.

With Almon groaning at your doorstep, do you:

(A) Fly after the wraith? Turn to <u>51</u>.

(B) Dip down to comfort the old farmer? <u>Turn to 47 and mark off W</u>.

37 Roll the dice. If you roll:

2 to 10, Turn to <u>38</u>.
11 or 12, Turn to <u>48</u>.

38 The clouds overhead rumble once with a thunderous war cry. From the heavens a lightning bolt leaps and plummets directly at you.

Holding Shefast high you deflect the bolt towards your adversary. With a loud crackling noise the wraith's invisible flesh burns.

Go to the Enemy table that follows and roll one die. Check off the damage boxes on the Rogue's Gallery score card.

ENEMY

Roll	Damage
1	2
2	3
3	4
4	5
5	Die
6	Die

(38 cont'd)

If you have destroyed the wraith, turn to <u>47</u> and run to Almon's side.

If the wraith lives, turn with horror to <u>54</u>!

39 Alerted to the possibility of danger, do you:

(A) Cast an *invisible* spell on yourself and investigate? Turn to <u>30</u>.

(B) Warn Jenevan mentally and tell her to go to the top of the tower to look? Turn to <u>22</u>.

(C) Leave the area, warning Jenevan so that she can take care of it? Turn to <u>32</u>.

40 "Behind you!" shouts Almon.

Whirling you see a black wraith coming at you. Its cloak and black platemail seem to walk on their own. The red eyes tell you that it has seen through your spell. Turn to <u>44</u>.

41 Turning, you catch the glint of moonlight off a dagger as it descends towards your throat. Not taking the time to look further, you leap and roll to the side, landing on your feet again. Looking closer you see a black cloak and "empty" black platemail.

The glowing red eyes in the headless hood cause you to utter one word, "Wraith!"

Cursing the five gods of the Rose Kingdoms, you watch the wraith weave a spell.

You know that the wraith could be casting any spells up to third plane. You also know that you are faster and you can cast your spell first. Turn to <u>44</u>.

42   Roll the dice. If you roll:

2 to 11, Turn to <u>43</u>.
12, Turn to <u>62</u>.

43   The wraith's spell fails to utilize the aether. Turning to <u>55</u>, you are quick to make good on his mistake.

44   Do you:

(A) Cast a *binding* spell so that you may question the wraith later? Turn to <u>6</u> and <u>mark off 1 manna</u>.

(B) Blast it with Shefast? Turn to <u>37</u>.

(C) Cast a *transmutation* spell and melt him away? Turn to <u>26</u> and <u>mark off 2 manna points.</u>

45   Your worst fears are realized as you hear the earth rumble. In answer to the wraith's mystic chant the earth moves as if to heal the gaping wound caused earlier.

As the walls of earth close in with crushing force, you scream, "No! Not here so close to my home!"

In an instant you are sealed away from the sight of man. Yet you live, if only for a few brief moments. As dirt replaces air and as the weight of the earth threatens to crush out your last remaining breath, you think of one last chance.

With twitching fingers and dying breath, you chant the words to the spell that could re-open the earth.

If you roll:

2 to 11, Turn to <u>29</u>.
12, Turn to <u>25</u>.

46   The light blue light forms around your hands and leaps across at the jaguar. Striking it, the blue strands securely bind it. The jaguar growls out in protest, but a louder protest comes from the bushes behind the beast.

"Don't hurt her!" yells the deep voice. "I have a *death* arrow aimed directly at your throat."

Searching the bushes you can't seem to find the man. You know you have extra magical protection from missiles, but the man said "*death arrow.*" That means a magical arrow! Your missile protection might not be enough. Do you:

(A) Talk, asking the man what his business is on your land? Turn to 99.

(B) Brave the arrow and attempt to cast a spell? Turn to 61.

(C) Attempt to fly away? Turn to 71.

47   "Almon, what is it?" you ask, bending over the badly wounded farmer.

"They're ready for you, wise one. Somehow they anticipated the *Challengings*. They are prepared. The East has set traps and blockades for all the Western wizards. You, friend, are at the top of the list," gasps the farmer.

"Jenevan," you shout through your mind link, "come immediately. We have a visitor."

Jenevan appears and the farmer is quickly taken into the tower and cared for.

When his strength returns, Almon begins his grim tale. "They are taking the farms. My neighbors fell without even a sword being drawn. They are setting ambushes along the roads to waylay traveling wizards. I would not let them do it to my farm and that's when the fighting broke out."

(47 cont'd)

Knowing Almon's farmland you know that he lives in a veritable fortress. His farm hands are armed and well-versed in combat.

"My whole family is trapped inside the doors of their own home. The Eastern dogs will take the place in less than a day. I was the only one who could break free," he continued. "I came here to warn you not to go to the Mystic Isles and to plead for your help. We will all be slaughtered if you do not come."

Exasperated, you calculate that such a sidetrack will slow you by at least one day. That one-day delay could easily doom your chances to reach the Mystic Isles on time. Do you:

(A) Thank him for the warning but explain how important it is for you to reach the islands? <u>Mark off N. Turn to 17</u>.

(B) Tell him that the least you could do for so valiant an attempt is to try to save his family? Turn to <u>85</u>.

48   Your magic glimmers once but quickly fades. In horror you watch the wraith's spell taking shape. Roll the dice. If you roll:

2 to 7, Turn to <u>54</u>.
8 to 12, Turn to <u>67</u>.

49   Roll the dice. If you roll:

2 to 11, Turn to <u>20</u>.
12, Turn to <u>58</u>.

50   The magic fails miserably and dies away.

Before you can finish that string of curses about your bad luck, you hear a light growl from the bushes. Staring you eye-to-eye is a big black jaguar! It is sitting on its haunches ready to strike. Something, however, is causing the large cat to hesitate.

(50 cont'd)

Slowly lifting your eyes you see a large man with a shiny arrow pointed at your forehead.

The distance between the two is too great to attempt a spell that might affect them both. Do you:

(A) Boldly stand your ground and ask the man who dares trespass upon the lands of Enchantraen? Turn to <u>114</u>.

(B) Attempt a *fly* spell? It's slim but the situation is desperate. Turn to <u>84</u>.

51   By flying you can easily outdistance the wraith. You see its shade-form pass in and out of the shadows. The wraith has come here alone and is now headed back to where it came from. Almon, the farmer, could be dying even now at your doorstep. Do you:

(A) Fly down and attack the wraith? Turn to <u>44</u>.

(B) Fly back to the tower to look after Almon? Turn to <u>47</u>.

52   The man searches the top of the trees but is unable to locate you.

"I mean no harm," he shouts. "I am here to see the Great War Wizard. I warn you that I will not stop until I have accomplished my goal."

You increase the spells sound until it seems as if the men are about to break through the woods at any moment.

"You will give no threats on the land of Enchantraen. Drop your weapons and tie your beast to the tree before we let the wolfhounds loose," you shout out.

(Continued next page)

(52 cont'd)

Frightened, the man immediately obeys. Watching carefully you are certain that the jaguar is securely bound.

You have always liked a grand entrance.

Shouting, "Silence!" you lower the volume of your sound spell. As quickly as you can fly, you dive to the ground with Shefast glimmering in your hand.

"Speak, trespasser and tell me what business you have on my lands."

"I am here to speak with Enchantraen and I will not speak my purpose to anyone else," he replies.

Do you:

(A) Cast an *Aura* spell that will cause your body to burst into flaming light and shout, "Fool, it is I. Now speak before I blast your soul asunder!"? Turn to 83 and mark off 1 manna.

(B) Attempt to bind both man and beast? Mark off 2 manna points and turn to 75.

53   With a few words and a quick flick of the wrist you attempt to bind the man. Roll the dice. If you roll:

2 to 11, Turn to 73.
12, Turn to 65.

54   As the wraith's black gauntlet finishes the last design, you recognize the spell -- too late! The earth trembles violently and splits to open a wide chasm. Down you tumble.

(54 cont'd)

Go to the Enchantraen table that follows and roll one die. Check off the damage boxes on your score card.

ENCHANTRAEN

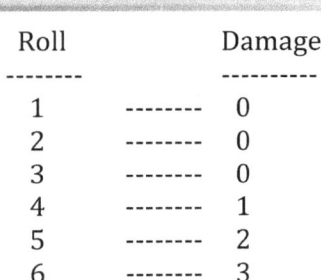

Roll	Damage
1	0
2	0
3	0
4	1
5	2
6	3

If you expire, turn to 25.

If you live, you attempt to stand and collect yourself.

Glancing up you see that the wraith has already begun to form his next spell. If the wraith is clever enough, he could negate his own *tremor* spell and seal you up for good. The freshly cracked earth begins to take on the aroma of a crypt. Turn to 55.

55   Do you:

(A) Cast a *binding* spell so that you may attempt to question the wraith? Turn to 24 and mark off 1 manna point.

(B) Blast it with Shefast? Turn to 2.

(C) Attempt to fly out? Turn to 68 and mark off 3 manna points.

56   Roll the dice. If you roll:

2, 3, 5, 6, or 7, before you can take the first step, Turn to 23.
4, 8, 9, 10, 11, or 12, Turn to 40.

57   The jaguar begins to circle the area confused about which way you could have headed. A whisper from the bushes brings the jaguar over to it quickly. You can now make out the dim image of a man with a huge bow in his hands. The jaguar is certainly under his control. He is too far away for you to make out what the man is saying. Do you:

(A) Immediately go on the offensive and attempt to bind both man and jaguar? Turn to 75 and mark off 2 manna points.

(B) Attempt a much more subtle approach that involves 3 manna points and the use of a *sound* spell? Turn to 79.

(C) Call down to the man and ask what he is doing on your land? Turn to 99.

(D) Let the man and beast pass on by? Turn to 70.

58   Your magic flickers, begins to take hold, and then fades! Gasping, you turn with terror to see the wraith finishing his enchantment. Roll the dice. If you roll:

2 to 5, Turn to 42.
6 to 12, Turn to 66.

59   Following close behind Almon is an evil shade. Cloaked in a black robe with black plate armor comes... comes a wraith!

With no visible body you catch a glimpse of its red eyes glowing underneath its empty hood. The wraith stops dead in its tracks and squares away to meet you. Even invisibility cannot shield you from a creature such as this. Turn to 44.

60   Indeed a face forms in the gruesome whirlpool.

"Not here, little one," comes the voice tauntingly. "We will meet later at my convenience."

The air rips with the explosion of bursting fireballs. The heat from the burning mist singes your robe. The mist burns away into the quiet night.

<u>Mark off M</u>. Looking around, you see there is nothing left to do now but to continue your quest.

Walking on through the night, nothing else happens fortunately. Turn to <u>98</u>.

61   The man immediately sets loose an arrow. The branches of the trees and your own missile protection will make its chance of hitting you very difficult. Roll the dice. If you roll:

2 to 5, Turn to <u>91</u>.
6 to 12, Turn to <u>118</u>.

62   A tinted blue light leaps across the chasm and securely binds your arms and legs. The wraith slides down the side of the hole and begins to work its way towards you. Picking up Shefast the wraith's voice is full of glee.

"In a few short moments, great one, this little hole of mine will collapse around your ears." "Ah-ha-h-h....," comes the deep laughter. "I envy the worms that will eat your flesh."

As he turns to go back up you feel the wraith's binding spell wearing off. Quick calculation leaves you with one hope. If the walls come in around you, your hands might be free for one last attempt.

Shefast is gone! <u>Check the "gone" box</u> on your character sheet. Remember you cannot use Shefast after this point.

(Continued next page)

(62 cont'd)

The *binding* spell begins to fade freeing your hands, but not before... turn to 45.

63   Concentrating on your *fly* spell, you are able to regain enough control to land lightly. The mist is burning deeply into your lungs and your insides are about to burst.

Everything is a blur around you. You realize that you are dying. With a supreme effort your concentrate on the words of another spell. It is an outside chance but it is all that is left to you. The spell is a body-control spell. It is your only chance to fight off this kind of magic.

Your chances, however, of completing the spell are hindered by the mist. Roll the dice. If you roll:

2 to 9, Turn to 106.
10 to 12, Turn to 88.

64   A little surprised you watch the man obey.

"Now," he says, "I have done as you have asked. Take me to the great wizard."

Do you:

(A) Cause your body to burst into flaming light and shout, "Fool, it is I. Now speak!"? With that you close the distance between you. Turn to 83.

(B) Use the old *binding* spell and mark off 1 manna? Turn to 75.

65   The spell flickers and fades at your fingertips.

"Please, Master, I speak true. Don't harm me."

(65 cont'd)

Still on his knees before you, do you:

(A) Try to kill him once again? <u>Mark off 1 manna point and turn to 53</u>.

(B) Decide to trust him to wait for you in Arcania under Jenevan's supervision until your return? Turn to <u>69</u>.

(C) Decide to end the confrontation by sending the man off to the Mystic Isles? After all if he can meet you there you should really have something to talk about. Turn to <u>77</u>.

66   Roll the dice. If you roll:

2 to 7, Turn to <u>45</u>.
8 to 12, Turn to <u>43</u>.

67   "No," you shout at the wraith.

Confused, the wraith's spell sputters and dies. Do you:

(A) Run for the woods trying to escape? Turn to <u>27</u>.

(B) Attempt to magically attack the creature once again? Turn to <u>44</u>.

68   Roll the dice. If you roll:

2 to 11, Turn to <u>36</u>.
12, Turn to <u>58</u>.

69   Giving the man specific instructions, you send him towards Arcania to wait for your return.

Mentally warning Jenevan of his coming, you add some special instructions. He is not to be allowed to roam freely about the tower and he is always to be carefully watched.

(Continued next page)

(69 cont'd)

With that taken care of you finally can get the journey underway. Luckily the rest of the night is quiet. Mark off T and turn to 98.

70   The man and animal race off into the woods. He will never be able to find your tower with all the enchantments surrounding it. Still he was lucky to come this close. Probably an accident.

Turning back to your mission, you travel off once more and luckily you are not disturbed for the remainder of the night. Turn to 98.

71   The man immediately lets an arrow fly. The tree branches, your magical missile protection, and the fact that you are flying at night make his chance of hitting you very slim. Roll the dice. If you roll:

2 or 3, Turn to 91.
4 to 12, Turn to 118.

72   The spell fizzles once more. The jaguar is on you!

Even as a fighter you are nothing to brush aside. The jaguar does however. Its claws sink deeply into your side. Its descending fangs change drastically. The jaguar transforms into a demonic creature!

"Enchantraen! Your power will make me great. Already I feel my strength triple."

With a superhuman effort you struggle to throw this creature off. It is useless. This creature is much more than superhuman. Its fangs ease into your neck. Luckily you won't be around to have to combat this powerful demon. For you, Enchantraen, the game is over!

If you wish to play again erase all the marks on your character sheet and return to the start.

73   Virtually helpless in front of you, the man cries, "No, please, I mean only good!"

Too late. You have made up your mind. The dagger arcs and the man crumbles.

Frantically clawing at the air, the jaguar attempts to reach you. A quick blast from Shefast and the jaguar's growls are silenced, followed by a clap of thunder.

If K is marked turn to 94. Otherwise, roll the dice. If you roll:

2, 3, 5, 6, or 7, Turn to 94.
4, 8, 9, 10, 11, or 12, Turn to 105.

74   A death cry curdles the air from behind you.

"Jenevan, what has happened?"

Through the eyes of your familiar you see the butchered body of a local farmer.

"Don't just stand there, Jenevan," you shout in your mind, "get him inside!"

As Jenevan scans the body you see that it is hopeless to turn back and try to heal the poor man.

"What killed him, Jenevan?"

"I don't know, master. I could not see it."

"Be on guard, friend. I want a nice place to come home to when this is through."

As you go further into the night, Jenevan reports that all is quiet. The rest of the night passes quietly. Mark off the A and N on your character sheet and turn to 98.

75   Roll the dice. If you roll:

2 to 11, Turn to <u>128</u>.
12, Turn to <u>61</u>.

76   The clouds overhead rumble once with a thunderous war cry.
From the heavens a lightning bolt leaps and plummets directly
at you. Holding Shefast high, you deflect the bolt towards your
adversary. With a loud crackling noise the wraith's invisible
flesh burns.

Go to the Enemy that follows and roll one die. Check off the
damage boxes on the Rogue's Gallery score card.

ENEMY

Roll		Damage
1	--------	2
2	--------	3
3	--------	4
4	--------	5
5	--------	Die
6	--------	Die

If you have destroyed the wraith, run to Almon's side and turn
to <u>47</u>.

If the wraith lives, turn with horror to <u>66</u>.

77   "Look, friend," you begin, "I have no need for menial servants.
If you wish to be of some use to me, you must first prove
yourself. Meet me at the Mystic Isles. If you can make it there,
you can act as my squire during the *Challengings*."

The man's mouth drops open. "But few ever make it to the
islands alive," he protests.

(77 cont'd)

"Few are worthy to be my servants," you reply. "If it is too grave an undertaking, return to your father with my blessings. Either way you decide does not concern me at this time. If you value your soul, you will leave now."

The man obeys by running off into the woods, his jaguar at his heels. The rest of the night is a quiet and peaceful journey. Turn to 98 and mark off X.

78 The spell fails. The man nocks an arrow with lightning speed. Turn to 71.

79 Be sure to mark off the 3 manna points. Roll the dice. If you roll:

2 to 11, Turn to 82.
12, Turn to 78.

80 "Silly wizard," the wraith hisses. "Do you attempt to scare me with pretty pictures?"

As the wraith's gauntlet traces an intricate pattern in the air, you dispel your illusion. Seeing what the wraith is doing, you realize how much trouble you are in. Turn to 48.

81 The arrow flies towards you! Roll the dice. If you roll:

2 to 9, Turn to 118.
10 to 12, Turn to 91.

82 The spell is cast and you are most careful to make it sound as realistic as possible. You begin very subtly and increase the noise making it sound as if there is a large number of men approaching with dogs. The man whirls towards the noise.

(Continued next page)

(82 cont'd)

Do you:

(A) Shout at him to stop or he and his jaguar will be slain where they stand? Turn to 52.

(B) Let him run off into the woods chased by the ever-increasing volume of your make-believe soldiers? Turn to 70.

83   Falling to his knees, the man says, "Enchantraen, forgive me. I am but a simple animal master named, Benolic. I am the son of Gerl. It was you who saved the life of my father during the Quest for the Temples. I have traveled far to offer my aid to you in repayment. When I saw the rainbow I was afraid that I was too late and that you would be gone."

Thinking back you cannot remember saving a man named Gerl, but then again there are many Western lives you have saved but cannot remember.

"How did you find Arcania?" you question. "Arcania is well-concealed and its location is not common knowledge even among Westerners?"

"Oh, great one, my father knew the general location. I have been searching these woods for months. It is you who have found me. I still have not seen Arcania."

His story has some credibility. Questioning further, you ask him specifically what he wants from you?

"We are a proud family. My father wishes to repay his debt with the service of his son. It is not what I want of you but what do you want of me?"

Great, you think to yourself. This man cannot possibly keep up your pace to the Mystic Isles.

(83 cont'd)

Do you:

(A) Kill him for trespassing by casting a *binding* spell? <u>Mark off 1 manna and turn to 53.</u>

(B) Tell him to wait at Arcania until your return? Jenevan will instruct him until then. Turn to <u>69</u>.

(C) Tell him to meet you at the Mystic Isles? If he is good enough to get there, he will be worthy enough to serve you. Turn to <u>77</u>.

84   You begin the first motions of your spell when the man lets his arrow fly. Roll the dice. If you roll:

2 to 6, Turn to <u>96</u>.
7 to 12, Turn to <u>116</u>.

85

<u>Mark off the next day and replenish all manna and erase all damage.</u>

Almon refuses to stay behind. You walk through the night supporting him as best you can. It is daybreak by the time you reach his farm. Almon is exhausted. Standing by the side of a stream, you are well-hidden behind the bushes. Looking across to the other side of the stream you can see the lands of the farm. The land has been cleared all the way to the farmhouse.

"Almon," you whisper, "the land is clear, they have left."

Supporting himself on his elbow, he says, "No they haven't. Listen!"

(Continued next page)

(85 cont'd)

The popping sounds of arquebuses can be heard. Looking back at the farmhouse, you can now see the puffs of smoke bellowing from the barrels of the guns. It looks as though the Easterners have broken through the outer defenses. Almon's family must be making a last stand inside the farmhouse itself.

Looking the complex over, you see the central farmhouse sitting on top of a knoll. Around the house are several outer buildings; several barns, coops, and storage bins.

"What kind of attack are you under?" you question Almon.

"Mostly common Eastern soldiers mixed with a few odd creatures like the wraith that chased me."

Looking carefully you see only a glimpse of Almon's men darting in and out of buildings. You will have to get closer.

Before crossing the river do you wish to:

(A) Cast a *shield* spell? That will <u>add 4 damage boxes temporarily</u> to your score card? Turn to <u>104</u>.

(B) Save all your manna until the situation becomes more certain? Turn to <u>125</u>.

86   Roll the dice. If you roll:

2 to 10, The mist demon takes damage on the following table. If the demon lives, turn to <u>60</u>. If the demon dies, turn to <u>93</u>.

11 or 12, Shefast fails to ignite the air. Turn to <u>60</u>.

Go to the Enemy table that follows and roll one die.

(86 cont'd)

Check off the damage boxes on the Rogue's Gallery score card.

ENEMY

Roll		Damage
1	--------	2
2	--------	3
3	--------	4
4	--------	5
5	--------	Die
6	--------	Die

87   It's an illusion! Your spell must have disturbed the wizard that was operating it. When you broke the wizard's concentration, his mindless creations stopped.

The illusion fades and the soldiers are gone. The wizard must be close! Turn to <u>122</u>.

88   Sorry, Enchantraen! You were slain by an unknown assailant. Actually the man was on your side but neither one of you knew it.

The game comes to a quiet conclusion. If you wish to play again, you will have to start all over. Erase all the marks on your character sheet and begin again.

89   Magic! There is a spell working in this area.

Almon screams, "Hurry! They will be running over the place any minute."

Looking where Almon is pointing, you see only arrows and gunshot coming from the farmhouse.

(Continued next page)

(89 cont'd)

"What do you see, Almon?" you question. "There!" he points again. "Can't you see them? They are swarming the place for a final charge!"

"That's it," you whisper to yourself. "The people are under attack by an *illusion* spell."

The power of their own minds is killing them. An *illusion* spell is harmless if you don't believe it, but the creature that cast the illusion can prove to be very harmful. An *illusion* spell of this size is 4th plane so the chances are that there is still a high-level wizard or creature nearby.

Do you:

(A) Attempt to negate the *illusion* spell? Mark off 4 manna and roll the dice. If you roll:

2 to 9, Turn to 108.
10 to 12, The spell fails. You may attempt to negate it again, but it will cost you more manna points. If you wish to try, roll again and mark off 4 more manna points. If not, make another choice.

(B) Save your manna and race on ahead to try to warn the farmhouse inhabitants? Turn to 141.

(C) Decide it is useless to put yourself in this kind of danger and turn and walk away? Turn to 90.

90 "Look, Almon, this is dangerous. Go tell them to quit killing themselves. It is all in their minds. Bye."

As you turn to walk away, Almon yells, "Coward!" and runs towards the farmhouse. Roll the dice. If you roll:

2, 3, 5, 6, 7, Turn to 102.
4, 8, 9, 10, 11, 12, Turn to 153.

91   The arrow seems to burst into a green powder when it strikes a tree limb. You are more than a little surprised when it continues towards you. Your missile protection charm crackles but seems to have no effect. The green powder transforms into a mist and hisses when it strikes your robe and face.

Crying out loud, "No, no!" you feel yourself falling, the green mist encircling your body as you plummet to your death!

Roll the dice. If you roll:

2, 3, 5, 6, 7, Turn to <u>63</u>.
4, 8, 9, 10, 11, 12, Turn to <u>5</u>.

92   The side of the barn explodes outward. A red mist tumbles out and begins to settle low to the ground. Soon a black figure emerges from the center of it.

"Ah, a lich," you say to yourself.

So this is the high-level wizard who has been causing the problem. A lich is a powerful wizard who has learned to preserve his life force by some unnatural means. The lich's skin is drawn taut over its bones. The situation is going to be touch-and-go to say the least. The lich could have a *reverse* spell around him. That would cause a problem if you cast a spell directly at him. Do you:

(A) Attempt to talk rather than start this wizardly dual? Turn to <u>109</u>.

(B) Cast a *transmute* spell at his feet and turn the ground to 30 cubic feet of mud? Turn to <u>132,</u> and <u>mark off 4 manna</u>.

(C) Go for an instant kill? Throwing caution to the winds, you resort to the familiar *binding* spell. Turn to <u>146</u>. <u>Mark off 1 manna</u>.

93   The lightning flashes and runs across the sky obeying your summons. Down it comes, striking the staff, rolling off its tip and exploding directly on the demon. The demon's body begins to glow.

"No, you devil!" it screams. Like flint on dry kindling the demon's body flares and burns.

As quickly as he came he is gone.

The woods resumes its nightly noise. The brilliant rainbow shines overhead luring you on. Through the rest of the night nothing disturbs your progress. The morning quietly comes and its rays are welcome. Turn to <u>98</u>.

94   At the end of the bodies' death throes, the man's eyes begin to glaze and a smile passes over his face.

From death the man speaks. "I have been wronged, great one. I sought only to help."

The spirits of the man and the jaguar can be seen forming a short distance off into the woods.

As the last air escapes the lungs, the voice says, "We will meet again, only next time…"

The air is gone and only the lips move. Looking into the forest you see the ghostly image of the man and jaguar vanish. Perspiring lightly you contemplate what you have done. Realizing there is nothing to do now, you turn and walk off to continue your journey.

<u>Mark off W and turn to 98</u>.

95   The winds answer your command. Coming from all directions, they strike together and begin their dance of death. Around and around they go until they join into one terrific force. With a wave of your hand you send the dancing death into the middle of the soldiers.

(95 cont'd)

The wind hurtles some of the bodies smashing them against the walls of the building. Many more are hurt by the flying debris. With surprising calm the soldiers who are capable turn and begin a headlong rush at you. Odd! They must be well-trained not to panic in a situation like this.

The farmhouse opens up with a new volley of gunshots and arrows. Many more Easterners fall but at least 20 of them will be on you and Almon in one turn. Knowing that this could be the end, do you:

(A) Turn invisible and try to defend Almon as best you can after you have moved out of the way of the charging soldiers? <u>Mark off 4 manna points</u>.

Roll the dice. If you roll:

2 to 11, Turn to <u>145</u>.
12, Turn to <u>121</u>.

(B) Cast a *tremor* spell and split the earth between you and the soldiers? You are sure to kill a few and buy yourself a little time. <u>Mark off 4 manna points</u>.

Roll the dice. If you roll:

2 to 11, Turn to <u>135</u>.
12, Turn to <u>121</u>.

(C) Bring the whirlwind towards you hoping to catch them before they catch you? Turn to <u>155</u>.

96   Concentrating as best you can on the words to your spell, you trust the magic of your missile protection charm to stop the arrow. You hear the charm crackling on your chest. It doesn't sound right! The arrow is magic! It has broken through your

(Continued next page)

(96 cont'd)

defenses! The arrow bursts and a green mist burns your face and robes. You begin to fall backwards.

Roll the dice. If you roll:

2, 3, 5, 6, 7, Turn to <u>5</u>.
4, 8, 9, 10, 11, 12, Turn to <u>63</u>.

97 The spell works! There is definitely a high-powered creature in this area. There, it is more specific now. The power is coming from the barn.

"Inside, you fools!" you shout at the farmhouse. "Almon, get down!"

The barn is large and full of animals. It would be costly to the farmer to try and drive the menace out by destroying the barn. Do you:

(A) Attempt to bluff the creature out? Turn to <u>120</u>.

(B) Sneak around the barn hoping to find the creature? Turn to <u>134</u>.

98

<u>Mark off the next day and replenish all manna and erase all damage.</u>

The morning creeps slowly over the land as you sit on a boulder snacking on the light meal Jenevan packed for you. The spotted rainbow still shines brilliantly in the morning sunrise. Arcania is well behind you now. You feel a little tired after last night's sleep in the woods. Sitting here you begin to slip in and out of peaceful slumber.

The cawing of a crow startles you awake. You must have dozed off!

(98 cont'd)

Looking over your map you must turn to:

(A) 176 if you are going to Jerican, the big merchant capital.

(B) 435 if you are taking the more direct route --- past Fortress Ellendar.

99   "Whose land is that?" comes the reply. Looking, you can zero in on the man's location. Do you:

(A) Answer by saying, "The land you trespass upon is the land of Enchantraen. Prepare to receive the great wizard's wrath!" Turn to 114.

(B) Attempt a spell now that you have a better guess at the location? Turn to 81.

(C) Attempt to fly away? Turn to 71.

100   After toasting you with several mugs of ale, Almon finally draws you off to the side. Roll the dice. If you roll:

2, 3, 5, 6, 7, Turn to 117.
4, 8, 9, 10, 11, 12, Turn to 138.

101   Roll the dice. If you roll:

2, 3, 5, 6, 7, Turn to 123.
4, 8, 9, 10, 11, 12, Turn to 112.

102   "Oh, no," is all you manage to utter before you realized what has happened.

A very strong force has just seized control of your body. What are you doing out here, screaming at a bunch of farmers anyway? The creature has now got you hopelessly under its control. You can feel your legs moving but you really don't

(Continued next page)

(102 cont'd)

know what's going on. You hear yourself speaking but it is as if you were a long way off.

"Do not resist. You should all be glad to give your lives for your masters. Long live the Master of the East. May his birth be as glorious as his kingdom is splendid!"

My, that is an odd thing for you to say. You hate the East. What's that in front of you? It's your hand. What? You are holding your dagger.

"No-o-o-o!" you scream in your mind. The dagger falls and blackness sweeps in.

You were killed by an unknown assailant. You may play again but next time be careful. You should have guessed a powerful enemy was controlling that *illusion* spell.

If you wish to play again, erase all the marks on your character sheet and return to the start. Get him next time!

103　　There! You see them now. They were hidden behind buildings before. There must be at least 100 soldiers preparing to storm the farmhouse. They will attack at any moment! Do you:

(A) Cast a *voice* spell that will give you the power of persuasion over a crowd like this? You could not stop them but you could convince them to wait a little longer. Mark off 4 manna points.

　　Roll the dice. If you roll:

　　2 to 11, Turn to 127.
　　12, Turn to 149.

(B) Conjure up a whirlwind so that you can stop a few of them? Mark off 4 manna points. Roll the dice.

(103 cont'd)

If you roll:

2 to 11, Turn to <u>95</u>.
12, Turn to <u>149</u>.

(C) Sneak up to the other side of the barn? With the protection of the barn, you may be able to cast more spells before they get to you, providing the farmhouse isn't overrun before you can take up a position. Turn to <u>134</u>.

104   Roll the dice. If you roll:

2 to 11, The *defensive* spell takes effect. The invisible force envelopes you in a hard shell. Remember to <u>subtract 2 from the die roll</u> that does damage against you. Turn to <u>125</u>.

12, The spell fails. You must have mispronounced one of the words in the enchantment. You may attempt to try again but it will cost you another 4 manna points. <u>If you wish to try, mark off four manna points and roll again</u>. If you want to forget about it, turn to <u>125</u>.

105   The bodies of man and beast begin to shake violently. A dark green mist issues from both mouths and comes together in a whirling mass.

A voice comes forth. "Fool! Take this warning. We will stop you. You will die on your quest to the Mystic Isles."

Fearing that the mist is transforming into a shape that will harm you, do you:

(A) Attack with Shefast? Turn to <u>86</u>.

(B) Flee off into the woods to prepare a better defense? Turn to <u>60</u>.

106   When you wake you find yourself in a dark room with candles burning. Jenevan is looming over you.

"The healers told me you were dead master. They made me place you here. I knew that you were not. I felt your mind hiding deep within your body."

"It worked!" you say. "Jenevan, I cast a spell to slow my bodily functions down to resemble a death state. That way my body would not be so badly affected by that mist."

"Looking out of the tower window you see the sunlight filtering down through the forest.

"Is the animal master dead?" you ask Jenevan.

"No, master, when I came upon the two of you the animal master was trying to heal you. He told me he had made a grave mistake. He had no idea that you were Enchantraen until it was too late. He has tied his jaguar to a tree and is waiting outside for your recovery."

"What!" you shout, "That man has cost me a great deal of valuable time, not to speak of the discomfort."

Jumping down from the bed, you tell Jenevan that you will deal with this man yourself. After that you will be off once again. Hopefully you will get a little further this time.

With Shefast in hand you leave the tower for the wood once more. As you exit the animal master is standing with his back to you, stroking the head of his jaguar.

Hearing you, he turns quickly to face you.

Mark off K and turn to 83.

107   You swing a small side door open and enter the barn. It is dark. It will take your eyes a moment to adjust. The noise outside stops. Do you:

    (A) Fear you are in danger? If so, you re-open the door and dive back out. Turn to <u>124</u>.

    (B) Crouch low and wait for your eyes to adjust? Turn to <u>140</u>.

108   The firing stops and a cheer comes from the farmhouse. The people begin to file out and Almon runs towards them. Do you:

    (A) Run to the cover of the barn? Turn to <u>134</u>.

    (B) Cast a *detect* spell to try and locate the source of the magic? It will cost you <u>3 manna points</u> and may well prove to be useless. Roll the dice. If you roll:

    2 to 11, Turn to <u>97</u>.
    12, The spell fails. You may attempt to cast it again but it will cost you another 3 manna points. <u>Mark off the 3 manna and roll again</u>. If not, follow Almon and turn to <u>122</u>.

109   "Hold your chants, old wizard. I wish to know why an ancient one bothers with scaring children and simple farmers."

    There are a few silent moments when you are sure your heart has stopped beating.

    Then the lich speaks. "I owe debts to certain creatures, War Wizard. They have asked me to pay those debts."

    "That payment would not happen to be my head, would it?" you ask.

    The parched lips draw tight over its yellow teeth.

    "You and others. Don't worry, I am not expected to kill you

(Continued next page)

(109 cont'd)

here. I will use a much more subtle approach. Turn back, wizard, the time is not right for you to venture to the Mystic Isles."

Before you can reply with word or spell, the lich vanishes. A *teleportation* spell! That's a spell you don't know. The lich could be anywhere now. Somehow you are sure you will see him again. <u>Mark off L and turn to 130.</u>

110 The man begins to weep. "You mean I am here at last? Please, take me before the great wizard."

"Fool!" you shout. "I am that wizard."

"Forgive me, for I am but a simple animal master, named Benolic. I am the son of Gerl. It was you who saved the life of my father during the Quest for the Temples. I have traveled far to offer my aid to you in repayment for this noble act. When I saw the rainbow I was afraid that I was too late and that you would be gone."

Thinking back you cannot remember saving a man named Gerl, but then again there are many Western lives you have saved but cannot remember.

"How did you find Arcania?" you question. "Arcania is well-concealed and its location is not common knowledge, even among Westerners."

"Oh, great one, my father knew the general location. I have been searching these woods for months. It is you who have found me. I still have not seen Arcania."

His story has some credibility to it but there is no way to be absolutely certain. What terrible timing! The man can be of no service to you on this journey, even if he was telling the truth.

(110 cont'd)

Do you:

(A) Kill him for trespassing? Turn to <u>73</u>.

(B) Tell him to wait at Arcania until you can return? Jenevan can instruct him until them. Turn to <u>69</u>.

(C) Tell him to meet you at the Mystic Isles? If he is good enough to get there, he will be worthy enough to serve you. Turn to <u>77</u>.

111   Your eyes have adjusted. Shortly off to your left is a ladder going up the loft. To the right, over a few stalls, is a set of double doors facing the farmhouse. You see little else.

Do you:

(A) Go to the ladder? Turn to <u>123</u>.

(B) Head towards the double doors? Turn to <u>129</u>.

(C) Cast an *invisible* spell on yourself? <u>Mark off 4 manna points</u>. Roll the dice. If you roll:

2 to 11, Turn to <u>145</u>.
12, Turn to <u>115</u>.

(D) Not like what you can't see and go back through the small side door? Turn to <u>124</u>.

112   The lich was successful in casting a *binding* spell. Luckily your magic resistance cancelled the light blue strands before they could wrap you up. Now it's your turn. Do you:

Cast a *binding* spell back at the lich? <u>Mark off 1 manna point</u> and turn to <u>136</u>.

(Continued next page)

(112 cont'd)

(A) Cast a *transmute* spell at the ground at his feet? Turn to 144 and mark off 4 manna.

(B) Try to halt the magic dual by talking, now that you have the upper hand? Turn to 109.

113   The spell takes effect and the lich begins to melt away.

"You hell-spawned devil..." the lich shouts but it is too late for him to cast any real curse.

After the puddle forms, you place a dagger in the center to be certain that the lich will permanently be gone when the spell wears off and the body tries to reform. Turn to 130.

114   The man lowers the tip of his arrow.

"Then at last I am here," he says. "Please, I beg you, take me before the mighty wizard."

Do you:

(A) Shout for him to drop his weapons and tie his beast to the tree? Turn to 64.

(B) Use this opportunity to attack both man and beast while the arrow is pointed down? A *binding* spell should do the trick. Mark off 2 manna points and turn to 75.

115   You really must be nervous for your spell to fail now. Roll the dice. If you roll:

2, 3, 5, 6, 7, Turn to 102.
4, 8, 9, 10, 11, 12, Turn to 111 and make another choice.

116   The man fires his arrow. You concentrate on the words to your spell. The charm hisses and crackles on your chest. Somewhere in the back of your mind you realize that the charm has just stopped a magical arrow. On you chant the spell, trying to ignore the charging jaguar. Roll the dice. If you roll:

2 to 11, Turn to 133.
12, Turn to 72.

117   "Listen, Enchant-t-t-t-raen," says Almon in a slurred voice, "you've been really great. Before I go I would like to give you a special thanks. Th-th-th-anks." With that Almon collapses to the ground in a drunken stupor.

Well, now you have really wasted a lot of time. Looking out the window you see it is nightfall once more.

Quickly leaving you wonder how stupid you can be for wasting so much time. Out the door and down the road you go. Stopping momentarily you are relieved to see that the rainbow still glimmers. Checking your map you make haste in the direction of:

(A) Fortress Ellendar, the direct and more dangerous way? Turn to 435.

(B) Jerican, the more indirect route? Turn to 176.

118   The arrow streaks directly towards your chest. Your charm of missile protection sparks and glitters in reply. From 10 feet away the arrow begins to glitter and turn transparent. You feel nothing as it harmlessly passes through your body. Ten feet out the other side the missile becomes solid once again and burns away in the atmosphere. Looking down at the man you see him standing dumbfounded.

(Continued next page)

(118 cont'd)

As the man reaches for his next arrow, do you:

(A) Attempt to bind both man and beast? Mark off 2 manna and turn to 75.

(B) Shout, "Who trespasses upon the land of the mighty war-wizard Enchantraen?" Turn to 114.

(C) Fly away and hide from the man, hoping he will go away? Turn to 70.

119   There is a brief pause before the next 17 soldiers jump you. If they get to you, you are sure to be dragged down.

With one spell separating you from death, do you:

(A) Cast an *invisibility* spell on yourself to move out of the way? Mark off 4 manna points.

Roll the dice. If you roll:

2 to 11, Turn to 145.
12, Turn to 200.

(B) Cast a *tremor* spell to split the earth in front of the charging soldiers? Mark off 4 manna points.

Roll the dice. If you roll:

2 to 11, Turn to 135.
12, Turn to 200.

(C) Try to run again? Turn to 200.

120   Being careful to guard yourself, you shout towards the barn.

"Come out, trickster, and bring your traveling sideshow with you! Come and bow before your better!"

Roll the dice. If you roll:

2 to 9, Nothing comes out, Turn to 122.
10 to 12, Turn to 92.

121   Roll the dice. If you roll:

2, 3, 5, 6, 7, Turn to 123.
4, 8, 9, 10, 11, 12, Turn to 158.

122   Roll the dice. If you roll:

2, 3, 5, 6, 7, Turn to 123.
4, 8, 9, 10, 11, 12, You may choose one of the following:

(A) Cast an *invisible* spell on yourself.
     Roll the dice. If you roll:

     2 to 11, Turn to 145.
     12, Return to the top of this scene 122 and choose again.

(B) Run for the cover of the barn. Turn to 134.

(C) Cast a *detect* spell once more. Roll the dice. If you roll:

     2 to 11, Turn to 97.
     12, Return to the top of this scene 122 and choose again.

123   A light blue light races towards you. Unfortunately, it strikes and neatly binds you completely. Securely bound you fall like a sack of leaves to the ground. From out of the barn the lich drifts lightly towards you. The ancient wizard is smiling, his lips drawn tightly over his rotting teeth. Looking up, you are

(Continued next page)

(123 cont'd)

powerless against him while bound this way.

"Don't worry," comes the raspy voice, "this will be painless."
The lich stoops down and strokes your hair.

"Dear Enchantraen, do you realize that your pretty little head
will buy me back my soul? It is a worthy death, sweet one."

You can smell his rotting flesh as he props your head on his lap.

The dagger flashes in the sunlight and plunges towards your
throat! Roll the dice. If you roll:

2 to 5, Turn to <u>137</u>.
6 to 12, Turn to <u>150</u>.

124   Before you hit the ground a thunderous explosion rips from
behind you.

Go to the Enchantraen that follows and roll one die. Check off
the damage boxes on your score card.

ENCHANTRAEN

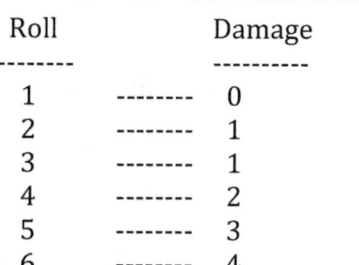

Roll		Damage
1	--------	0
2	--------	1
3	--------	1
4	--------	2
5	--------	3
6	--------	4

If you expire, turn to <u>150</u>. That is what you will see before you
are gone.

If you live, you roll back to your feet and turn to <u>92</u>.

125   You cross the river in a shallow area with Almon in your arms. The water is cold. When you finally reach the other side, you feel a tingly sensation flush over your body. It is the blood rushing through the cold veins of your legs, or is it magic?

Roll the dice. If you roll:

2 to 8, Turn to 89.
9 to 12, Turn to 103.

126   If you wish to gain the farmers' attention, you will have to do something more daring.

Do you:

(A) Fire Shefast to gain their attention? Turn to 141.

(B) Cause an aura of light to burst from your body? Mark off 1 manna point. You shout again while turning to 141.

(C) Retreat back towards the barn to stay clear of the missile fire until you come up with a more concrete solution? Turn to 134.

127   You feel the power of your spell beginning to take effect.

In a loud booming voice you say, "Listen to me. There is death waiting for the first man who goes near the farmhouse!"

Your voice is so powerful that it can be heard over the noise of the battle. All the men stop fighting and look your way. A cheer comes up from inside the house. Your spell seems to have more power than you thought! All the soldiers have frozen as if... wait a minute! Roll the dice. If you roll:

2 to 8, Turn to 87.
9 to 12, Turn to 143.

128 The light-blue light leaps from your hands and wraps neatly around man and beast. The man's arms are pinned to his side and the jaguar is held tightly against a tree.

Do you:

(A) Slay the man and beast with your dagger? Roll the dice. If you roll:

2, 3, 5, 6, 7, Turn to <u>94</u>.
4, 8, 9, 10, 11, 12, Turn to <u>105</u>.

(B) Ask the man to explain why he dares trespass upon the lands of Enchantraen? Turn to <u>110.</u>

129 As you take your first few steps towards the double doors, a voice shouts, "Stop, I give up!"

A wizard starts to materialize in the corner previously hidden by an *invisible* spell.

The wizard is a lich! (Lich -- an ancient wizard who has learned to extend his life. They are extremely powerful due to the years of study they have undergone.)

"I don't know how you do it," the lich continues, "I cast spells at you all the way across the field. You mock my illusions and see completely through my invisibility. You walk fearlessly up to me without the first use of your magic. Truly, Enchantraen, you are the most fearsome wizard I have met!"

"Oh my," you think to yourself. You've really stumbled into this one, but you're not about to let him know that.

"Of course, old one," you begin. "Did you really expect less from a war wizard? Why are you here scaring children and simple farmers? Surely one with your abilities has more useful duties." Turn to <u>160</u>.

130   Soon the remaining farm folk are out and surrounding you with cheers of welcome. You realize that you have done much to increase your legend amongst these people. That is little comfort for the time you have lost from your quest. After you are finished healing the wounded, you gaze up at the sun to discover that the better part of the day is over. As you make ready to leave, Almon comes over to your side.

"I know you have given up much already but I pray you stay a moment longer so that we may properly thank you." Do you:

(A) Say, "No, thank you," and leave regardless of how insistent Almon becomes? Turn to 157.

(B) Decide to stay and suffer a little more lost time? Turn to 100.

131   Roll the dice. If you roll:

2 to 5, Turn to 109.
6 to 12, Turn to 101.

132   The ground at the lich's feet turns to mud! Down the lich sinks as if he were caught in quicksand. He will be totally buried in one turn. Ah, but the lich has already begun his plan to save himself. As he completes his spell, turn to 166.

133   The spell lifts you into the air. The jaguar's claw brushes against your boot. Like a rocket you shoot to the top of the trees. Looking down you see the man has nocked another arrow. Do you:

(A) Shout down asking the man what business he has on your land? Turn to 99.

(B) Brave the arrow and attempt to cast a spell? Turn to 61.

(C) Attempt to fly away? Turn to 71.

134   The barn is large. You can easily find a place of concealment around one of its corners. Do you:

(A) Go inside to find a more suitable position by one of the loft windows? Turn to <u>107</u>.

(B) Cast an *invisible* spell around yourself so that you can maneuver without fear of being hit?
Roll the dice. If you roll:

2 to 11, Turn to <u>145</u>.
12, Your spell fails! You may attempt it one more time but <u>it will cost you 4 more manna</u> points. Roll again or choose another way.

135   The earth trembles and splits in the path of the charging soldiers. Five have fallen victim to your spell. Undaunted, the others scramble to skirt the outer edge. These men are oddly fearless! Well, the men will have to skirt the chasm but your whirlwind won't.

"Back to me!" you shout and obediently the wind shifts and twists your way.

With the whirlwind between you and the soldiers, you begin maneuvering it to cause the most damage.

Suddenly the soldiers stop as if they are being held in suspended animation.

"What," you gasp, "is going on now?"

You do your best to hold the warriors at bay. Roll the dice. If you roll:

2 to 8, Turn to <u>87</u>.
9 to 12, Turn to <u>121</u>.

136   Roll the dice. If you roll:

3 or 4, Turn to <u>146</u>.
All other numbers! Your spell failed. Turn to <u>166</u>.

137   The hand of the lich begins its descent. Suddenly it stops and flies backwards. The lich whirls from view. All you see is Almon, dagger in hand, plunging towards you. Two quick strokes and you are free! Whirling to stand you see the lich facing you.

With a smile he says, "So it won't be now. Let's make it later, shall we Enchantraen? Turn back while you can!"

With that he lifts his hands and teleports away. The last thing you see is his rotting, smiling teeth and Shefast gripped tightly in his hand.

<u>Be certain that the gone box is checked on your character sheet next to Shefast.</u> Thankful to be alive, turn to <u>130</u>.

138   As more jugs of ale are being broken out, Almon takes you over to the side.

"We have a wonderful secret here on the farm," he begins. "It is time that you make good use of it."

As the others are rejoicing he takes you out into the barn. He climbs up a ladder with you closely behind him. At first you hear a neighing sound. You start to question Almon why a horse is kept in the loft. Then you see it!

The loft is open at the top and the sun filters down on the white coat of the animal. It paws the air and stomps the wood planking at Almon's approach. It is a magnificent animal! The creature must stand 25 hands and weigh at least 2200 pounds. Its wings fold and unfold. The sun shines off its coat making the stallion seem even more beautiful to behold.

(Continued next page)

(138 cont'd)

"His name is Constellia. He is one of the bravest Pegasus alive today. What do you think, Enchantraen? Will he be capable of carrying you on your quest?"

"The creature is marvelous, Almon," you reply, patting the creature's neck.

Almon instructs you to climb onto its back.

"When you no longer need him, simply release him and he will find his way back to me," says the old farmer.

A pat on the rump and you are rocketing skyward. "Oh yes," Almon shouts, "tap the neck to signal which way you wish to go."

Do you direct Constellia to head towards?

(A) Jerican, the merchant capitol. Turn to 912.

(B) Fortress Ellendar, the direct route. Turn to 302.

139   "But-but," stutters the lich.

"Be gone, old one. You must repent for your evil doings. I have spoken," you command.

The lich raises his arms and is gone via a *teleportation* spell. You leave the barn congratulating yourself over the cleverness of your choice. Turn to 130 and mark off U.

140   Roll the dice. If you roll:

2, 3, 5, 6, 7, Turn to 123.
4, 8, 9, 10, 11, 12, Turn to 111.

141   "Stop! Can't you see? It is not real!"

Just then a farmer falls over dead. Needless to say the fighting continues. Roll the dice. If you roll:

2, 3, 5, 6, 7, Turn to <u>102</u>.
4, 8, 9, 10, 11, 12, Turn to <u>126</u>.

142   The moment the lich's head goes under, you negate the spell. The earth is solid. The lich is buried alive! Turn to <u>130</u>.

143   Roll the dice. If you roll:

2, 3, 5, 6, 7, Turn to <u>123</u>.
4, 8, 9, 10, 11, 12, The soldiers charge you. There must be at least 20 of them. Do you:

(A) Run for it? Turn to <u>158</u>.

(B) Cast an *invisible* spell and run out of the way? <u>Mark off 4 manna points</u>. Roll the dice. If you roll:

   2 to 11, Turn to <u>145</u>.
   12, Turn to <u>158</u>.

(C) Try your *voice* spell again? Since you have already successfully cast it, it won't cost you any manna. Turn to <u>158</u>.

144   Roll the dice. If you roll:

2 to 11, Turn to <u>132</u>.
12, Your spell fails. Turn to <u>166</u>.

145   The sunlight neatly bends around your body. You start to run but you freeze in your tracks! You can see him now. Standing in the shadows of the barn, wrapped in his own *invisible* spell, is a lich! (Lich -- an ancient wizard who has learned to extend

(Continued next page)

(145 cont'd)

his life. They are extremely powerful due to the years of study they have undergone.) The skin is drawn tightly over the frail bones, making the fact that the wizard is a lich unmistakable.

Wait that must mean....

Turning, you watch the soldiers fade. It was an illusion all the time.

The lich is midway through a spell. There is no way for you to cast yours first. Do you:

(A) Shout, "No, wait, let's talk?" Turn to 131.

(B) Begin your own spell hoping his will fail? Turn to 101.

146   Your spell works! Unfortunately the wizard was protected by a powerful *reverse* spell. The light-blue light leaps towards the lich. As you watch your own *binding* spell turn back against you, you see the lich begin to smile. Turn to 123.

147   The lich fumbles in his robe and pulls out a charm. Simply place this charm next to your body and it will subtract 1 from a roll that does damage against you. Add this to your character sheet.

The lich then stands and says, "You will not be bothered by me again."

The lich vanishes by means of his *teleportation* spell. The charm is an odd-shaped thing. You pick it up and walk back out of the barn. Turn to 130.

148   The lich was unsuccessful! Now, do you:

(A) Negate your *transmute* spell? This will seal the lich in the ground and destroy him. Mark off 2 manna points. Roll the dice.

(148 cont'd)

If you roll:

2 to 11, You are successful. Turn to <u>142</u>.
12, Your spell failed. Turn to <u>166</u>.

(B) Pull the lich out of the mud. Perhaps you could make him talk and tell you why he is here scaring children and simple farmers. Turn to <u>160</u>.

149 Your spell fails! The soldiers are quick to respond. At least twenty of them are charging you. With one spell separating you from the instant death by the soldiers' blades, do you:

(A) Cast an *invisibility* spell on yourself? <u>Mark off 4 manna points</u>. Roll the dice. If you roll:

2 to 11, Turn to <u>145</u>.
12, Turn to <u>200</u>.

(B) Cast a *voice* spell to order the men away from you and the farmhouse? <u>Mark off 4 manna points</u>. Roll the dice. If you roll:

2 to 11, Turn to <u>127</u>.
12, Turn to <u>200</u>.

(C) Turn around and run? Turn to <u>158</u>.

150 You hear a thump and you are surprised to see Almon crumpled on the ground next to you. Apparently he tried to save you. His blood now flows into the rich soil of his farmland. The dagger is down and the lich was right.

Death for you is painless. With your head held high, gripped by your hair, the lich screams in triumph and teleports back to the East. There you are mounted on the trophy case of one thankful Dark Lord!

(Continued next page)

(150 cont'd)

Well, Enchantraen, the game is over this time. That is a tough way to go. If you wish to play again, you must return to the start, and erase all the marks on your character sheet. Until then, since you are mounted on a wall, keep your chin up and keep smiling.

151 You have been careful to place one at the base of the tree. After your nightly preparations are done, you climb the tree and secure yourself above. At last sleep takes you over and you sink quietly into the darkening night. Roll the dice. If you roll:

2, 3, 5, 6, 7, Turn to <u>170</u>.
4, 8, 9, 10, 11, 12, Turn to <u>188</u>.

152 The fairies quickly refuse your offer explaining that they cannot carry such a large gift. They are, however, taken back by your extreme generosity! Turn to <u>227</u>.

153 Running now you find yourself heading back towards your destination. You go as far as you possibly can before the night closes around you. The rainbow is still shimmering brightly as you fall off into an uneasy slumber. Turn to <u>98</u>.

154 You cast the light away from your body. A boulder suddenly flickers then flares. As its illumination begins to engulf the campsite you duck into a shadow.

This trick, you hope, will draw all attention away from yourself. The night goes silent for three heart beats.

From a wide circle you suddenly hear a hundred tiny voices yell, "It's a party!"

In the blink of an eye a ring of dancing nymphs gathers around the boulder. With fluttering wings and high whining voices the tiny creatures jump and tumble around the bright light.

(154 cont'd)

"Fairies," you say despondently. "Now I'll never get back to sleep."

With your sleep ruined do you:

(A) Join in the festivities? Turn to <u>186</u>.

(B) Save time and get an early start on the next leg of your journey leaving the party behind. Turn to <u>196</u>.

155 The whirlwind stalls, gathers its force and darts back your way. Instantly you can tell that you misjudged its speed. The warriors will reach you first! Turn to <u>158</u>.

156 A light trickle of water runs across your leg followed in bulk by slime. Your senses alter and you never get a distinct impression of what exactly the creature is descending on you. In your new beetle form you can fight none-the-less.

It takes 12 damage boxes to kill you in your new form. Subtract from this any damage points you have previously taken and the remainder is what it takes to kill you.

It takes 12 boxes to kill the creature you are fighting. Make note of these new damage boxes on a separate sheet of paper.

With razor jaws you gnash away at the slime and entangling vines.

Go to the Enemy table that follows and roll one die.

(Continued next page)

(156 cont'd)

Check off the damage boxes on the Rogue's gallery score card.

ENEMY

Roll		Damage
1	--------	1
2	--------	2
3	--------	2
4	--------	3
5	--------	4
6	--------	6

If you beat the creature change back to your human form and turn to <u>164</u>. If the creature lives read on!

Striking at the soft, exposed areas of your body the creature manages to by-pass your natural armor.

Go to the Enchantraen table that follows and roll one die. Check off the damage boxes on your new score card.

ENCHANTRAEN

Roll		Damage
1	--------	0
2	--------	0
3	--------	1
4	--------	2
5	--------	2
6	--------	3

If you expire turn to <u>200</u>. If you live go back to the Enemy table and roll again!

157   Turning to leave you hear an odd, neighing coming from the barn. Oh well, you haven't got time. Continuing down the road turn to <u>153.</u>

158   You have failed. Three soldiers are on you instantly. Fight them using regular combat. You strike first and then let all the remaining soldiers strike at you.

If you expire turn to <u>200.</u> If you live turn to <u>119</u>.

159   The flame flickers then flares painlessly on your hand. From there it rockets to the vine and neatly sears it in two. That stopped one vine but the others are closing fast and your equipment is much closer to the marsh. Turn to <u>179</u>.

160   "Oh great one," the lich begins. "They... I mean the Lord Gaoler has sent me. He has promised to wrest my soul from the demon who gave me long life. I would rather have the demon finger my soul than become subject to your magic." Falling to his knees he says, "Do with me what you will but please be merciful. You see I too am a member of the True Ones guild."

His fingers make the hair-width gold chain around his neck clearly visible.

"Great," you think. "What am I going to do with this one?"

Several ideas run through your mind but you may only choose one. Do you:

(A) Tell him to leave a magical token at your feet in payment of his life? Then tell him to run and leave these poor people alone. Turn to <u>147</u>.

(B) Melt the man with a *transmute* spell? Turn to <u>113</u>. <u>Mark off 2 manna</u>.

(C) Order him to return to the Dark Lord Gaoler and slay the decrepit Eastern dog? Turn to <u>139</u>.

161   You breathe a little easier when the spell takes hold. You move forward on your six legs. With jaws powerful enough to tear through hardwood you rip into the sides of your living cell. In a short time you emerge under the stars once more. Your compound eyes make it difficult to see but your antennae give you great sensitivity. Wait, your equipment is still inside!

Do you:

(A) Turn around and rely on your antennae to search out your equipment? Turn to <u>173</u>.

(B) Change your shape back so that you can see and possibly fight your opponent better? Turn to <u>190</u>.

162   As reluctant as you are to fall asleep you must at last give in to your physical needs. As your eyes close you can't shake the feeling that somehow the gods have set you up.

Roll the dice:

2, 3, 5, 6, 7, Turn to <u>170.</u>
4, 8, 9, 10, 11, 12, Turn to <u>188</u>.

163   Your book and all of your equipment lift from the pod answering your call. With your concentration on completing your spell you fall easy prey to the vine behind you.

Go to the Enchantraen table that follows and roll one die.

(163 cont'd)

Check off the damage boxes on your score card.

ENCHANTRAEN

Roll		Damage
1	--------	0
2	--------	1
3	--------	1
4	--------	2
5	--------	3
6	--------	4

If you expire, turn to <u>200</u>. If you live, you find all your equipment securely in your grasp once more. Do you:

(A) Run for it while you can? Turn to <u>210</u>.

(B) Cast a *fly* spell to get above the vines? <u>Mark off 4 manna</u> and roll the dice:

2 to 11, Turn to <u>167</u>.
12, Your spell fails. Take damage again on the table above and choose again.

(C) Start blasting with Shefast, providing you still have it? Turn to <u>184</u>.

164 It doesn't seem to matter that you are covered head to foot in stinking slime. The fact that the swamp ooze threatens to infect your wound is unimportant right now. What is important is seeing your book and equipment safe within the dead pod. Reaching over to gather them you clean and dress your wounds. Tired, but determined you struggle back out. With a change of clothes you are traveling once more. You hope the big city will offer you more comfort than this rugged countryside. Turn to <u>196</u>.

165   Your spell fails and from somewhere below you hear, "Tee hee. I told you the wizard wasn't so tough."

Do you:

(A) Cast a *light* spell? Mark off 1 manna and roll the dice:

   2 to 11, Turn to 154.
   12, Go to the top of the scene and choose again.

(B) Cast a *levitate* spell to get that staff back? Mark off 2 manna and roll the dice:

   2 to 11, Turn to 171.
   12, Choose again.

(C) Jump down and get the staff? Turn to 181.

(D) Shout down, "Who's there?" Turn to 206.

166   Roll the dice:

2, 3, 5, 6, 7, Turn to 102.
4, 8, 9, 10, 11, 12, Turn to 146.

167   Up you soar as soon as your spell takes hold. A few vines slash vainly at your feet but soon you are above them and well out of their reach. They all seem to be heading down into the murky depths of the swamp. You must have risen above the range of their sensors. Do you:

(A) Fly off towards Jerican? Turn to 196.

(B) Start blasting the vines as they recede into the swamp?
   You must have Shefast, and you will have to descend a little to stay within range. Turn to 184.

168   A tiny winged creature tumbles from behind Shefast holding his feet as he rolls laughing.

"That's the stupidest thing I've seen for a long time," wheezes a tiny fairy. "You are one dumb Wiz!"

Do you:

(A) Jump down for the staff? Turn to <u>181</u>.

(B) Now try a *light* spell before he disappears once more?
     <u>Mark off 1 manna</u> and roll the dice:

     2 to 11, Turn to <u>154</u>.
     12, Turn to <u>165</u>.

169   Onward you charge like a raging storm. The thunder threatens to rip the sky apart and the lightning causes big pools of the swamp to boil and splash around you. The vines wither and burn until a large mass begins to surface.

"Ah," you say, "it's an urwurt."

Rising from the swamps' surface comes the foe. It's mass of twitching vines slither up toward you. Your lightning has already badly wounded the creature. You should easily defeat it now.

"No," you whisper under your breath. It seems your lightning has awakened more than one creature from the mossy marshland. Across the top of the water floats many misshapen objects coming like a moving plague.

"How could you have been so foolish as to disturb these troubled waters," you curse at yourself.

Just then a vine lashes up at you and drags you towards the urwurt. With vines slashing around you, you discover that

(Continued next page)

(169 cont'd)

Shefast is useless and your sword is too large to use properly. In desperation you can only use a dagger or your hands.

Down you slash, cutting at the vines of the already badly wounded creature.

Go to the Enemy table below and roll one die. Check off the damage boxes on the Rogue's Gallery score card.

ENEMY

Roll		Damage
1	--------	0
2	--------	1
3	--------	2
4	--------	3
5	--------	3
6	--------	4

If you beat the urwurt turn to 172.

If not read on! Yet another vine lashes out at you drawing you even closer to the bulky mass of the creature.

Go to the Enchantraen table below and roll one die. Check off the damage boxes on your score card.

ENCHANTRAEN

Roll		Damage
1	--------	0
2	--------	0
3	--------	0
4	--------	1
5	--------	2
6	--------	3

(169 cont'd)

If you expire turn to <u>200</u>. If you still live return to the Enemy table and roll again!

170 Roll the dice and add 2 for each symbol you placed.

2 to 7, Turn to <u>198.</u>
8 to 12, Turn to <u>187</u>.

171 The spell takes hold of the staff and you begin to lift it.

You feel the staff being tugged back downward and a tiny voice says, "Lay off *wimpy wand*." Do you:

(A) Tug harder? Turn to <u>194</u>.

(B) Yell, "Who said that?" Turn to <u>206</u>.

(C) Hit the area with a *light* spell so that you can see more clearly? <u>Mark off 1 manna</u> and roll the dice:

2 to 11, Turn to <u>154</u>.
12, Turn to <u>165</u>.

172 The creature goes down under your mighty onslaught but not before the next creature is on you. With thrashing limbs rising high above the marsh you watch the second urwurt descending on you. Flying away will be impossible. You scramble to try and dodge the falling vines. Behind this urwurt there seems to be many more coming. Roll the dice:

2 to 5, Turn to <u>197</u>.
6 to 12, Turn to <u>210</u>.

173   Your feelers reach out and retract. A sharp pain stabs through you.

Go to the Enchantraen table that follows and roll one die. Check off the damage boxes on your score card. Use the damage boxes in the Rogue's Gallery.

ENCHANTRAEN

Roll	Damage
1	-------- 0
2	-------- 0
3	-------- 0
4	-------- 1
5	-------- 2
6	-------- 3

Something thuds against the hard shell of your back but does not do any extra damage. Your equipment has moved. All you sense is a mass of plant life twisting all about you. You sense *one* opening. Do you:

(A) Cancel your spell and revert back to normal? Turn to 190.

(B) Stay in your beetle form and dash for the one opening. Turn to 216.

174   Roll the dice:

2, 3, 5, 6, 7, Turn to 204.
4, 8, 9, 10, 11, 12, Turn to 152.

175   Your spell holds firmly. In aetherial form the vines slash harmlessly through you. Looking around you see no sign of the lich. Disgusted at being so rudely awakened you determine the best thing to do is to continue on in your quest. Amid thrashing vines you calmly walk once more on your way to the big city. Turn to 196.

176

<u>Mark off the next day and replenish all manna and erase all damage.</u>

Jerican is a little less than three days away. The hardest part of the journey will be in the coming day. You will have to skirt a part of the long bay called Glaurune's Gouge. The legend is that Glaurune, the first dragon, fought his last battle here.

Sebastobol, the dragon slayer, fought against him for six months before Glaurune was finally slain by the venomous bite of the great serpent. The battle between the ancient ones gouged this part of the bay out. Ships are careful to always transverse through the middle of the bay. The sides of the gouge are marshy and teaming with misshapen creatures that were said to have sprung from the mixture of venom and dragon blood. Occasionally a creature or two leaves the bay and wanders inland.

The light forest that surrounds your tower is behind you now. As the day progresses you were careful to stay as far from the edge of the swamp as possible without sacrificing much time. Now the treacherous night comes. At last you must succumb to your physical limitations and make camp. This is not your first time out in the wilds. You have picked up many tricks. Looking east you can see the edge of a swamp. You have chosen a campsite where there are several high boulders. You can build your campfire between them and the light will be blocked from anything approaching from the west, south and east. There is also a tree nearby. You picked up the trick of sleeping in trees from a group of elves you traveled with in one of your earlier adventures.

As you start a small fire you think of other precautions you

(Continued next page)

(176 cont'd)

might take. You could surround the area with symbols of fear and paralysis. As a wizard you know how to make these but they will cost you 4 manna points each. Even then there is no guarantee that an approaching creature will see one.

Do you:

(A) Begin making symbols? You can make 1, 2, 3 or 4 symbols. Remember to <u>mark off 4 manna</u> for each symbol you make. Turn to <u>151</u>.

(B) Decide to call it a night and climb up into the tree? Turn to <u>162</u>.

177　Your mount steadily gains on the fleeing soldiers. You feel the great beast's flanks starting to heave. All at once, the fleeing soldiers pull rein and quickly begin to turn and reform ranks.

You think you hear a distant group of horsemen approaching. Reinforcements are coming. That must be why the Easterners suddenly gained courage and stopped to reform.

Do you:

(A) Cast a spell to change shape and fly to safety? You will have to leave your mount behind and it will <u>cost you 4 manna points</u>. Roll the dice:

2 to 11, Turn to <u>466</u>.
12, Turn to <u>470</u>.

(B) Dismount, pull your dagger and fight? Turn to <u>492</u>.

(C) Turn your mount and run? Turn to <u>514</u>.

178   Your spell stops drawing its' power from the aether. Quickly your form reverts back to normal. You are standing at the edge of the swamp. Your equipment is still in a pod not less than 10 feet from you. That 10 feet could well prove to be the hardest journey you'll ever make. Coming down on top of you is a creature called an urwurt. Gasping, you curse yourself for being so hasty to change back. There is no time to cast a spell! The large mass of intertwining vines descends in a sloppy charge. You soon find yourself in a fight to the death with only your hands to help you.

As the vines lash about you, you strike out and try to snap the vines with your hands!

Go to the Enemy table that follows and roll one die. Check off the damage boxes on the Rogue's Gallery score card.

ENEMY

Roll		Damage
1	--------	0
2	--------	1
3	--------	2
4	--------	3
5	--------	4
6	--------	4

If you have killed the creature turn to <u>164</u>.

If not read on!

While you struggle with one vine several others strike at you from behind.

Go to the Enchantraen table that follows and roll one die.

(Continued next page)

(178 cont'd)

Check off the damage boxes on your score card.

ENCHANTRAEN

Roll		Damage
1	--------	0
2	--------	1
3	--------	1
4	--------	2
5	--------	3
6	--------	4

If you expire, turn to <u>200</u>. If you still live return to the Enemy table and strike again!

179   Up from the marsh comes a large bulk of twisting vines. "An urwurt," you whisper under your breath. Your magic book and equipment are soon to be lost in its large mass. You've got to stop it. To lose your magic book will finish your chances of becoming an Elder! Thinking quickly, you surmise what you know about this creature. You are certain the creature has a high magic resistance. Do you dare risk a spell when so much depends on it? You might be able to stop the vine that has your book if you are willing to commit yourself to personal combat.

Do you:

(A) Attempt a *control* spell to force the creature to let go? <u>Mark off 4 manna</u> and roll the dice:

2 to 7, Turn to <u>195</u>.
8 to 12, Turn to <u>220</u>.

(B) Charge and fight the bitter battle? Turn to <u>199</u>.

180   The two vines lash out as you try to get by them.

Go to the Enchantraen table that follows and roll one die. Check off the damage boxes on your score card.

ENCHANTRAEN

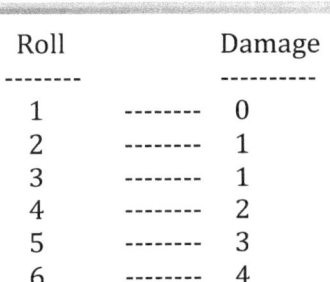

Roll		Damage
1	--------	0
2	--------	1
3	--------	1
4	--------	2
5	--------	3
6	--------	4

If you expire, turn to <u>200</u>. If you live, you find that you are capable of lunging into the pod to get your equipment!

With your magic book and all your equipment in hand do you:

(A) Cast a *fly* spell to get out of reach of the vines? <u>Mark off 4 manna</u> and roll the dice:

2 to 11, Turn to <u>167</u>.
12, Your spell fails. Take damage once more and choose again.

(B) Run for it while you can? Turn to <u>210</u>.

(C) If you still have Shefast you could start blasting. Turn to <u>184</u>.

181   Gathering courage you leap from the tree.

In midflight you hear a tiny voice scream, "Yipes," and you see the scurry of little wings disappear behind the boulders.

(Continued next page)

(181 cont'd)

By the time you hit the ground everything is quiet once more.
Do you:

(A) Cast a *light* spell to see what's going on? <u>Mark off 1 manna</u> and roll the dice:

2 to 11, Turn to <u>154</u>.
12, Turn to <u>165</u>.

(B) Start blasting with Shefast? Turn to <u>213</u>.

(C) Shout at the boulder, "Who's there?" Turn to <u>206</u>.

182   Your spell fails! A vine smashes into your midsection.

Go to the Enchantraen that follows and roll one die. Check off the damage boxes on your score card.

ENCHANTRAEN

Roll		Damage
1	--------	0
2	--------	1
3	--------	1
4	--------	2
5	--------	3
6	--------	4

If you expire, turn to <u>200</u>. If you live, choose again.

(182 cont'd)

Do you:

(A) Try the *aetherial* spell once more? <u>Mark off 4 manna</u> and roll again:

2 to 11, Turn to <u>175</u>.
12, Go to top of this scene and read again!

(B) Cast a *fly* spell to get above the thrashing vines? <u>Mark off 4 manna</u> and roll the dice:

2 to 11, Turn to <u>167</u>.
12, Go to top of this scene and read again!

(C) Start blasting the vines, provided you still have Shefast? Turn to <u>184</u>.

(D) Run for it? Turn to <u>210</u>.

183   A *control* spell would be perfect in this situation. Roll the dice:

2 to 11, Turn to <u>191</u>.
12, Turn to <u>229</u>.

184   Shefast answers your call with mighty shouts of thunder. Each time the lightning strikes, a vine withers and retreats towards the marsh. Occasionally, a vine breaks through your defense.

Go to the Enchantraen table that follows and roll one die.

(Continued next page)

(184 cont'd)

Check off the damage boxes on your score card.

ENCHANTRAEN

Roll		Damage
1	--------	0
2	--------	0
3	--------	1
4	--------	1
5	--------	2
6	--------	3

With the majority of the vines in retreat do you:

(A) Leave this area? It is early morning and you could continue on towards Jerican. Turn to <u>196</u>.

(B) Advance against the vines and rid this area of this nemesis once and for all. Turn to <u>169</u>.

185   If <u>N</u> or <u>L</u> are marked off turn to <u>217</u>.

If not, turn to <u>167</u> if you were casting a *fly* spell, and <u>175</u> if you were casting an *aetherial* spell.

186

<u>Mark off the next day and replenish all manna and erase all damage.</u>

The fairies quickly make room for you in their circle dance. Soon you begin to understand the fairies odd humor and it becomes easy to enjoy yourself. As the morning sun brightens, the fairies offer you a "fàgail" or parting gift. Some fly off but

(186 cont'd)

soon return carrying large flowers. Placing the flowers in a rectangle they ask you to sit upon them. Then each of the fairies grabs hold of a stem and lifts you up. You are soon flying towards Jerican. Your speed is *much* faster than it would be walking. It appears that you will reach the city by nightfall. That's two days faster than if you had to walk!

On the way, you remain vigilant, always looking for danger. You know that in this world there are as many dangerous things with wings as there are creatures on the ground.

Luckily you are close to the world's largest city. If there is such a thing as a safe area in the West, this is it. Soon Jerican comes into view. Somewhat embarrassed by this whole procession you ask your newly found friends to sit you down near the city. No need to arouse attention before it's necessary. Thanking the party for their boon you make your farewells. Although it isn't necessary you think about giving them a parting gift also. You really only have your staff. That would be considered an appropriate gift.

Do you:

(A) Offer Shefast to the fairies as a gift? Turn to <u>174</u>.

(B) Offer no gift but say your thanks and depart friends? Turn to <u>201</u>.

187   A rattling sound wakes you near early morning. Glancing around you quickly spot the source of the noise. The ground is covered with vines. The vines are lined with thorns the size of small daggers. At the end of the vines is a large pod with one large slit for an opening. Behind the pod are red and black berries. One of these vines is quivering at the bottom of the tree. Apparently it was trying to wind its way to you. Other vines are also edging their way up!

(Continued next page)

(187 cont'd)

Do you:

(A) Cast a *fly* spell and soar above the vines? <u>Mark off 4 manna</u> and roll the dice:

2 to 11, Turn to <u>185</u>.
12, Turn to <u>182</u>.

(B) Cast an *aetherial* spell and climb down? In this form the vines can't hurt you, but you can't hurt them either. <u>Mark off 4 manna</u> and roll the dice:

2 to 11, Turn to <u>185</u>.
12, Turn to <u>182</u>.

(C) Start blasting with Shefast, provided you still have the staff? Turn to <u>184</u>.

(D) Run for the best possible opening away from the vines? Turn to <u>210</u>.

188 The roll of thunder and the flash of lightning wake you at early morning. Jumping upright you nearly fall out of the tree from being startled. What? There are no clouds. Looking down you see one of the boulders has become badly charred. At the base of the tree Shefast is leaning. Did it fall? Do you:

(A) Jump down to get it? Turn to <u>181</u>.

(B) Cast a *levitate* spell and bring it up to you? <u>Mark off 2 manna</u> and roll the dice:

2 to 11, Turn to <u>171</u>.
12, Turn to <u>165</u>.

(C) Cast a *light* spell to see the area better? <u>Mark off 1 manna</u>.

(188 cont'd)
    Roll the dice:

        2 to 11, Turn to <u>154</u>.
        12, Turn to <u>165</u>.

189   The walls begin to close, threatening to crush you. Down the tube you squeeze until you come to the half-digested body. Gasping for breath you realize that you are heading down the digestive track of a carnivorous plant. The walls are getting closer. On you slide uncontrollably. There is little room to move but you might have one last chance.

    Do you:

    (A) Cast a spell to change shape into a rhinoceros beetle? <u>Mark off 4 manna</u> and roll the dice:

        2 to 9, Turn to <u>161</u>.
        10 to 12, Turn to <u>214</u>.

    (B) Try to turn yourself aetherial? <u>Mark off 4 manna</u> and roll the dice:

        2 to 9, Turn to <u>193</u>.
        10 to 12, Turn to <u>214</u>.

    (C) Try to slash out with your knife? Turn to <u>214</u>.

190   The spell is canceled and your shape reverts back to its normal form. Your clothes hang in shreds around your neck. Your magic book and all your equipment are left behind. Once your eyes have reverted back to human you see a mass of vines stretching from the swamp.

    The vines are covered in moss and dripping with stench. The stem of each vine is lined with thorns the size of dagger blades. At the end of the vine is a giant pod with one open slit.

(Continued next page)

(190 cont'd)

Slightly behind the pod appears to be a cluster of black and red berries. You were inside one of the pods, but where is it?

There! Off about 10 feet away is the same pod receding towards the marsh. Between you and the pod that has your equipment are two stems. You cry in anguish as the thorns of a stem slash into your back.

Go to the Enchantraen table that follows and roll one die. Check off the damage boxes on your score card.

ENCHANTRAEN

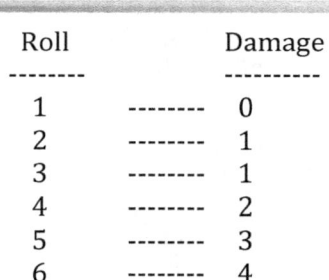

Roll		Damage
1	--------	0
2	--------	1
3	--------	1
4	--------	2
5	--------	3
6	--------	4

If you expire, turn to <u>200</u>. If you live, do you:

(A) Dash towards your quickly disappearing equipment? Turn to <u>180</u>.

(B) Cast a fireball at the stem that just hit you and try to sear it off? <u>Mark off 4 manna</u> and roll the dice:

2 to 11, Turn to <u>159</u>.
12, Turn to <u>209</u>.

(C) Cast a *telekinesis* spell to call back your equipment? Since everything is in your pack you can call it back with one spell. Casting a spell now will leave you open to another

(190 cont'd)

lashing from the nearest stem. <u>Mark off 4 manna</u> and roll the dice:

2 to 11, Turn to <u>163</u>.
12, Turn to <u>209</u>.

191   <u>Mark off F on the character sheet</u>.

You show the guard a dagger and say, "This is all I have to claim and since you have already collected the tax I'm free to go, right?"

Overlooking your staff and book the soldier says, "Certainly, move along now. Take this voucher though in case you are stopped."

The *suggestion* spell works every time, you smile to yourself. Turn to <u>250</u>.

192   The fairies scurry off, obedient to your warning. Before you can gloat over your fearsome bluff you realize you are still tied up.

A day later when you finally wiggle lose you also discover that they have taken Shefast! <u>Mark the gone box for Shefast</u> on your character sheet.

Fuming, you start off again towards Jerican. Turn to <u>196</u>.

193   Your *aetherial* spell takes hold and you feel yourself undergoing a change. Gathering your equipment you simply glide on out of the living plant cell. Outside you see that the ground is covered with vines. The vines are covered in moss from the marsh. Up and down the length of the stem of the vine are large thorns the size of daggers. At the end of the vines are giant pods with an open slit. Slightly behind the pod are a cluster of black and red berries. It was in one of these pods that you were captured.

(Continued next page)

(193 cont'd)

A vine slashes out but easily passes through your transparent form. In aetherial form you are impervious to all normal weapons. Of course you are not capable of using your magic to fight either.

If N or L is marked turn immediately to <u>217</u>. If not, read on.

Do you:

(A) Calmly walk out of this mess unscratched? Turn to <u>175</u>.

(B) Cancel the *aetherial* spell and start blasting the vines, provided you still are carrying Shefast? Turn to <u>184</u>.

194   The staff slowly rises and the tugging becomes stronger.

"Look you frog molester," squeaks the tiny voice. "You better quit using your muscles for brains and put your hands over your head. I've got this thing pointed directly at you."

Glancing over at the charred rock do you:

(A) Put your hands over your head? Turn to <u>219</u>.

(B) Cast the *light* spell? <u>Mark off 1 manna</u> and roll the dice:

   2 to 11, Turn to <u>154</u>.
   12, Turn to <u>165</u>.

(C) Jump down towards the staff? Turn to <u>181</u>.

195   Relying on your magic has often gotten you out of tight situations. This is no exception. The urwurt responds to your wishes. You force the creature to return your book and other equipment undamaged into your hands.

(195 cont'd)

You then force the urwurt back towards the marsh where you command it to fight another of its own kind.

Turning to walk back to safety you listen to the frantic splashing over your shoulder. Feeling lucky and confident in the power of your magic you start walking once more towards the great city. Turn to 196.

196   Jerican is roughly two days away. Even though this should be the easiest part of your journey you are still careful to keep up your guard. You more than anyone else realizes that death can come at any time in the wild Western Kingdoms. You have often thwarted death with no more than quick thought from a clear mind.

Roll the dice:

2 to 5, Turn to 351.
6 to 12, Turn to 342.

197   The urwurt has you. It pulls you close and forces you to fight once more.

If you survive, turn to 172. If you expire consider it a valiant effort and turn to 200.

198   Your eyes flutter open and all is quiet. Too quiet. Looking around you see that the stars, moons, and rainbow are missing. Wait! You're encased in something. It's a plant or something. The walls are closing in around you. You are about to be crushed! Instinctively you punch outward but the walls hold. Looking around frantically you see an opening that heads down a long tube.

(Continued next page)

(198 cont'd)

Confused about what is happening you:

(A) Decide to cast a shape-change on yourself. If you change into a giant Rhinoceros Beetle you could probably dig your way out. <u>Mark off 4 manna</u> and roll the dice:

2 to 11, Turn to <u>161</u>.
12, Turn to <u>189</u>.

(B) Turn yourself aetherial and spirit out of this place. <u>Mark off 4 manna</u>. Roll the dice:

2 to 11, Turn to <u>193</u>.
12, Turn to <u>189</u>.

(C) Push yourself down the tube before you get crushed. Turn to <u>189</u>.

199   Mustering your loudest battle cry you draw your best weapon and charge the mass of misfortune! Cursing it to the six-sided planes of hell you enter combat.

Go to the Enemy table that follows and roll one die. Check off the damage boxes on the Rogue's Gallery score card.

ENEMY

Roll	Damage
1	0
2	1
3	1
4	2
5	3
6	4

(199 cont'd)

If you win turn to <u>164</u> and count your blessings. If not read on!

The vines smash against your body with terrific force.

Go to the Enchantraen table that follows and roll one die. Check off the damage boxes on your score card:

ENCHANTRAEN

Roll		Damage
1	--------	0
2	--------	1
3	--------	1
4	--------	2
5	--------	3
6	--------	4

If you expire consider it a valiant fight and turn to <u>200</u>.
If you live, go back to the Enemy table and strike again.

200 Sorry Enchantraen, but for you the game is over. You were slain and you may not continue. In a world of high magic the end of even your brilliant career can happen with a blink of the eye.

If you wish to play further you will have to return to the start and erase all the marks on your character sheet. Next time don't let them get you!

201 Jerican looms before you in all its glory; the merchant capital of the world, the heart of civilized man. Jerican is special in many ways. It is a neutral city. It does not involve itself in conflicts between East and West. The city is composed of tiny fiefdoms. Each merchant has his own palace guards. The size of these personal guards range from ten or twelve to small armies. It is said that the city itself is run by three key merchants. These

(Continued next page)

(201 cont'd)

three are elected every ten years by the Merchant Guild
members. You know little more about the city's government
than this, after all, you are a wizard not a merchant.

The city is governed by Merchant Council Mandates. One of
these mandates is to register at one of the city's gates before
entering. The city is surrounded by a granite wall with four
major gates. Luckily the lines are not too long.

As you walk through the line you overhear what is going on in
front of you. It seems that the Council has added to its
mandate since you were here last. Along with registering your
name, the soldiers are asking for a list of weapons and magical
items the people are carrying. The people are then given a
choice. They can pay taxes on those items they wish to carry
into the city, or they may leave them with the soldiers and pick
them up when they leave the city. From the size of the tax
being levied the soldiers are obviously trying to disarm the
citizens. There has probably been another outbreak of
violence.

You certainly have the money for the tax but you are uncertain
about what you want to purchase at the magical shops. You
would hate to be caught short of tams if you see something you
like. Looking the soldiers over you feel confident that you can
fool them. The only problem will be if you get caught later. Do
you:

(A) Prepare the beginnings of the spell to fool the soldiers?
Mark off 2 manna and turn to 183.

(B) Decide to pay the tax anyway? Turn to 229.

202   The side of the building begins to glitter then fade. When it
vanishes you simply walk inside. The crowd immediately falls
back against the receding walls.

(202 cont'd)

"Excuse me" you say, "I thought there was a side door. Where can a tired old wizard pick up a few trinkets so that I can go and rest?"

The man who was being waited on tells the shopkeeper to wait on you first.

A little old woman hobbles up to you and whispers, "Hello Enchantraen. You will put the wall back won't you?"

Without even turning you cancel your spell and the wall materializes.

"Sorry El but I'm in a hurry," you reply.

You know the shop's owner whose real name is Eletrianipolical. For obvious reasons you call her El.

Tapping her cane on the floor, she says, "Very well, what will it be today?"

"Well," you say, "I'm about to take a voyage and I'm interested in magical items of some importance. Let's skip the common spell, smoke and flickering light merchandise."

You know that examining magical items is an interesting but time consuming task. You do not have time to examine more than two items.

"This week, El, I believe I would be most interested in."

(A) Nautical magic? Turn to <u>244</u>.

(B) Healing magic? Turn to <u>269</u>.

(C) Combat magic? Turn to <u>273</u>.

203   El rolls the old scroll out on the table. Scrolls cannot be read unless they take on a wizard's life force. To a common man this scroll would appear like a blank parchment, or perhaps he would see faded meaningless words if his eyesight was really good. You can almost see the sea rolling over its' surface. The scroll has power, there's no questioning that.

El leads you into her study and you quickly go to work deciphering the magical abilities. In the end you learn that the scroll can be inserted into your magic book. The spell will cost 3 manna to activate it. The spell has the power to give a ship a burst of speed. The spell will actually cause the water to rise at the stern of the ship and propel it along.

When you tell El you are ready, she comes and quotes you a price of 1000 gold tams. If you want the scroll you must first have the tams. <u>If you have them subtract them from your character sheet and mark off the scroll symbol.</u>

If you think the price is too high or it's an item you don't want simply tell her now and turn to <u>230.</u>

204   Ten little sets of wings flutter forward to pick up the staff. <u>Mark the Shefast gone box</u> on your character sheet. You cannot use any of the options throughout the rest of the book that call for using your staff. The fairies however are taken aback by your extreme generosity! Turn to <u>227</u>.

205   <u>Mark off H</u>.

"Well Enchantraen I'm sorry we couldn't interest you in more. I'm sure you will find the quality of our products as high as ever." El then starts to hand you your merchandise when she glances over your shoulder and stops.

"Well, a, hmmm, your merchandise will be waiting at the city's gate when you leave.

"What," you start to protest!

(205 cont'd)

Looking over your shoulder you see a city patrol group has just entered the shop.

"Oh yes good wizard. It's a new city mandate," says El. She then whispers, "Please humor them Enchantraen. I don't want my shop turned into firewood."

Obliging an old friend you consent to the mandate and leave. Back out in the street you turn to 250.

206   A deep but tiny voice answers, "It's the Eastern Master and his five High Lord Generals. Don't try anything. We've got you surrounded."

"Look," you say, "what do you want?"

"We want you to pull the back of your robe over your head and scream like a chicken," replies the tiny voice. Do you:

(A) Cast a spell to flush them out of the darkness? <u>Mark off 1 manna</u> and roll the dice:

  2 to 11, Turn to 154.
  12, Turn to 165.

(B) Start blasting with Shefast? Turn to 213. (Do not use this if Shefast is on the ground.)

(C) Pull your robe over your head and scream like a chicken? Turn to 168.

207   "Not a bad choice," starts El, "but I'm not sure you will want this one."

She reaches below her cabinet and pulls out a three inch statue of a unicorn. The material of the statue can't be ivory. The

(Continued next page)

(207 cont'd)

statue seems to be snowy white. Taking the statue you go into the back room. There is a wizard's study there where you can better discern the true properties of this statue.

After lengthy study you determine that the statue works by smashing it. Once broken you will release a full-sized unicorn. The unicorn will fight in your place until its defense reaches zero or the combat is over. Then you can step in and finish the combat or turn to the victor's scene.

It's really a nice gadget but it only works once. El explains that it is worth 1000 gold tams. If you want it, subtract the gold tams and reread the scene. Remember how the statue is used because the book will not explain it again. When a scene calls for combat, break the statue and let the unicorn fight first using 7 damage points before it is destroyed, if you don't want the unicorn tell El and turn to 230.

208 If <u>H</u> is marked turn immediately to 392. If not read on.

The Wharf of the Three Rivers comes quickly into view. It looks much the same as it did the first time you saw it except that it is now much later in the day.

The longshoremen are going home and the city guards are beginning to take their positions for the night watch. If you haven't bought your ticket hurry to the window. If you're wanting to exchange go to the other window.

<u>Mark off H.</u> Do you:

(A) Go to the ticket window? Turn to 239.

(B) Go to the exchange window? Turn to 365.

209   Your spell fails as another vine slashes and tears at you.
Go to the Enchantraen table that follows and roll one die.
Check off the damage boxes on your score card.

ENCHANTRAEN

Roll		Damage
1	--------	0
2	--------	1
3	--------	1
4	--------	2
5	--------	3
6	--------	4

If you expire turn to <u>200</u>. If not, your equipment will soon be
on the edge of the marsh. Turn to <u>179</u>.

210   The vines lash out but miraculously miss you. You concentrate
on dodging in a desperate attempt to avoid certain death.
There is no time for a spell. You would be cut to shreds before
you could chant the first few words.

Suddenly the sky seems to explode when a vine rips across
your back.

Go to the Enchantraen table that follows and roll one die.
Check off the damage boxes on your score card.

ENCHANTRAEN

Roll		Damage	
1	--------	1	
2	--------	1	
3	--------	2	
4	--------	2	
5	--------	3	
6	--------	4	*(Continued next page)*

(210 cont'd)

If you expire turn to <u>200</u>. If you live read on.

The vines stop and start receding back into the swamp. You must have made it past their sensors. You fall to the ground breathing in great gulps of the morning air. Tired but determined you wait for your strength to return and start out once more towards the great city. Turn to <u>196</u>.

211   If <u>D</u> is already marked turn immediately to <u>253</u>.

Walking down the bustling street you half dream about the old days when you used to visit this city. You never could afford the nice rooms. You always seemed to end up in a joint where, if you weren't fighting the local rogues, you were struggling against the giant rats who threatened to pull you from your bed. Those were glorious days though. The city had a naïve romance about it. Today you are more familiar with the ugly politics.

<u>Mark off D.</u>

A small boy being playfully chased by his older sister runs into you. Pushing him aside you see your favorite tavern around the corner.

If <u>P is marked</u> turn immediately to <u>234</u>. If not, roll the dice:

2, 3, 5, 6, 7, Turn to <u>308</u>.
4, 8, 9, 10, 11, 12, Turn to <u>386</u>.

212   When spells are combined they must both be successful to work. If one fails, they both fail.

The wizard blushes and stutters, "Ah, well I changed my mind. I don't need to prove myself to you anyway." He then steps back into line with a deepening red blush on his face. Turn to <u>423</u>.

213 The lightning answers the call of the mighty staff. You begin flinging the bolts around like a child would fling stones.

They are on you in seconds. One hundred fairy ropes fly from the darkness and begin to wrap you in a finely woven net.

"This one's nasty! Let's rip up the spell book."

Wrapped this way you and the fairies both know there is little you can do. Do you:

(A) Say, "Look you magical morons. If you are really clever you will leave before you cause any more trouble." Turn to 192.

(B) Say you're sorry about the lightning but as far as you knew they were trolls? Turn to 224.

214 It simply won't work. There is no time left for another spell and the walls are too tough to break through. A little further down the tube and you are wedged tight.

Luckily your oxygen runs out before the digestive juices begin to work. Your brilliant career ends in restful slumber. For you the game is over. If you wish to play again go to the start and erase all the marks on your character sheet. Next time let's try not to end up fertilizing the plants!

215 You hit the floor, roll and bounce up again. The giant runs past you and out the door followed by a tough-looking halfling. A glass smashes on the wall next to you. Looking through the throngs of people you see the innkeeper banging the head of one of his customers on the floor. You'll have to cross the room to get to him that is if you want to.

(Continued next page)

(215 cont'd)

Do you:

(A) Try to stop the whole fight by casting a *sound* spell? A loud ear-shattering boom should do the trick.

Roll the dice:

2 to 11, Turn to <u>361</u>.
12, Turn to <u>321</u>.

(B) Enter the free-for-all to get to the innkeeper? Turn to <u>310</u>.

(C) Leave a note and money on the desk and go take your usual room? Turn to <u>260</u>.

216 You dash towards the opening. It seems as though the vines are thinning out. You receive a vague sensation of wet ground through your six legs. Wait! You're running into the swamp! In seconds the vines are around you. Your feelers gather a sensation of something rising from the water.

Go to the Enchantraen table that follows and roll one die. Check off the damage boxes on your new score card.

ENCHANTRAEN

Roll		Damage
1	--------	0
2	--------	0
3	--------	0
4	--------	1
5	--------	2
6	--------	3

If you expire turn to <u>200</u>. If you live, fight back.

(216 cont'd)

Striking back at the vines you rip and tear until a gurgling sound emit from the swamp. Something large is descending towards you. Do you:

(A) Prepare for battle? Turn to <u>156</u>.

(B) Cancel your spell and turn yourself back into your normal form? Turn to <u>178</u>.

217 Your spell quits drawing on the aether! It simply stops. Caught off-guard a vine slashes into your back.

Go to the Enchantraen table that follows and roll one die. Check off the damage boxes on your score card.

ENCHANTRAEN

Roll		Damage
1	--------	0
2	--------	0
3	--------	1
4	--------	2
5	--------	3
6	--------	4

Diving into a clearing you turn to see the disappearing image of a lich. (A high level wizard who has learned to extend his life.)

As the lich teleports away you hear him laughing.

(Continued next page)

(217 cont'd)

Do you:

(A) Cast an *aetherial* spell and leave this place? <u>Mark off 4 manna</u>. Roll the dice:

2 to 11, Turn to <u>175</u>.
12, Turn to <u>182</u>.

(B) Cast a *fly* spell to get above the thrashing vines? <u>Mark off 4 manna</u>. Roll the dice:

2 to 11, Turn to <u>167</u>.
12, Turn to <u>182.</u>

(C) Start blasting the vines, provided you still have Shefast? Turn to <u>184</u>.

(D) Run for it? It looks possible to get out with just a short run. Turn to <u>210.</u>

218 In the morning you gather your things and move on. The day is cloudy and so are your thoughts. It was a restless night and you are glad to be up and moving. You make good progress by not stopping for lunch. Up and over the last hill and you see it. Turn to <u>201</u>.

219 As soon as your arms go up a blur of tiny wings come at you from both sides. Little hands tickle your sides and fly off.

"Gotcha," comes the voice from below.

Shefast finally answers to your *levitation* spell and flies up into your hands. Below everything is quiet.

(219 cont'd)

Do you:

(A) Pull that darn staff up and ask who's out there? Turn to <u>206</u>.

(B) Cast a *light* spell to see what's going on? <u>Mark off 1 manna</u> and roll the dice.

2 to 11, Turn to <u>154</u>.
12, Turn to <u>165</u>.

(C) Jump down and investigate? Turn to <u>181</u>.

220   "Noooooo," you cry as your magic book is shredded by the creature. The common life force that you and your book share is broken. The damaging effects whiplash back to you.

Go to the Enchantraen table that follows and roll one die. Check off the damage boxes on your score card.

ENCHANTRAEN

Roll		Damage
1	--------	2
2	--------	3
3	--------	4
4	--------	5
5	--------	5
6	--------	6

If you expire turn to <u>200</u>. If you live it is not that great.

Without the book your most powerful spells are gone. You cannot hope to battle a wizard as an equal without them. Someday you will undoubtedly be able to obtain a new book

(Continued next page)

(220 cont'd)

and regain all the lost spells. This however will take time, the one thing you don't have.

The quest is over. Perhaps you simply weren't meant to become an Elder. You will never know until you play again.

221 "Yes," says El, "that is a pleasant little tidbit. Here, let me get it for you."

Wrapped in a cloth is a two foot stake that resembles a dart. You pick the odd object up and take it to the back room where El's study is located. There you can properly check the magical abilities of this item.

After a short while you discern the following. The stake has the ability to blur the object it is placed against. The blur does not seem powerful enough to work against magic but it should aid quite well in hand-to-hand combat. You would use it by throwing it at the ground by your feet. When a scene calls for you to start combat you can do this and it will subtract 1 from any roll of damage against you because your opponent will have a hard time focusing on you. When you are done you simply pick it up and use it later.

El explains that this is worth 1000 gold tams. If you want it subtract the tams from your character sheet. Read this scene again so that you fully understand how to use the magic item. The book will not tell you again.

If you don't want it keep your tams simply tell her no. Turn to 230.

222 Mark off R.

A bottle smashes against the side of the soldier's head. Down he goes revealing the smiling face of the innkeeper standing behind him.

(222 cont'd)

"Remember that good master when you leave your next tip," smiles Dreg the innkeeper. "Now if you will allow me to escort you to your room?" Dreg bows and proceeds up the stairs.

With the crashing sounds of the brawl behind you, you ask Dreg, "What started that mess?"

"I'm not sure master. I think some Eastern soldiers refused to let a Mountain Magi go up to his room using the back stairs. Here we are master," the man says opening the door.

You enter and start to close the door when you see him standing with his palm upward. Do you:

(A) Tip him fifteen gold tams? Turn to <u>280</u>.

(B) Ignore the gesture and shut the door? Turn to <u>254</u>.

223   You glance over your shoulder in faked panic as you retreat. As the group parts the screams become a mass of confusion and you are soon caught up in them and carried away to safety. The city police stream into the area looking for the trouble. They attempt to test for magic but come up with nothing. You guess they probably tried the simple tests for teleportation and invisibility. You continue on thanking the gods that you avoided the trouble. Turn to <u>253</u>.

224   "Sure, and I suppose you have a string of dragons for sale back at Jerican. If your judgement is really that poor we don't think you should be carrying such a dangerous weapon. For the good of mankind we will take it from you."

Before you can protest, the staff and fairies are gone. Once the little creatures are out of sight the ropes melt away. Somewhat confused over the events that just transpired you <u>mark the Shefast gone box</u> on the character sheet.

(Continued next page)

(224 cont'd)

With nothing left to do here you simply decide to get an early start on the next leg of your journey. Turn to <u>196</u>.

225   "Whomph!" The giant gasps and buckles over from the force of your spell directed towards his midsection. His helmet rolls from his head revealing a large horn protruding from his forehead! Turn to <u>307</u>.

226   Again your magic overwhelms those who oppose you. Down the remaining guards tumble, a victim of your might. With the immediate danger out of the way do you:

    (A) Slit the guard's throats so that there will be no one to identify you? Turn to <u>267</u>.

    (B) Drag them out of sight and tie them up in an alley out of harm's way? Turn to <u>285</u>.

227   "Wizard, you are indeed above the common aether-user. It is very rare that a human tolerates our kind, let alone offers them gifts as splendid as yours. We pray you please wear this symbol for us."

The fairy brings out a tiny ring set with a pearl.

"A godstone," you gasp. "Where did you find this?"

They hand you the tiny ring explaining that they must retain some secrets. It hardly matters to you. The pearl is the rarest of all gems. It is the godstone, a representative of wild magic. Some say it is the source of aether. You gladly take the ring and begin to place it in your pocket.

"No," a fairy insists, "place it on your finger."

You take the ring out to demonstrate that it is too small. When the ring nears your finger it expands and fits easily.

(227 cont'd)

"Wild magic," you whisper under your breath. Again exchanging thanks you turn towards the city. <u>Mark off P</u> and turn to <u>201</u>.

228 Roll the dice:

2 to 11, Turn to <u>270</u>.
12, Turn to <u>262</u> because your spell fails!!

229 "First, I have this dagger," you begin.

"I see that. It's magical isn't it? How many more do you have? Wait, is that a wizard's book too. Come on, let's be quick about it. Place it all here on the table," retorts the soldier.

Grumbling to yourself you place your items out in view. You will be charged the following for each item you lay out:

10 gold for each dagger,

20 gold for Shefast,

50 gold for your magic book,

50 gold for your magic ring,

15 gold for a sword,

100 gold for a pearl.

"But these taxes are higher than some of the items are worth," you protest.

"If the price is too high we will be glad to store whatever you don't want to take with you," the soldier replies. "You can pick up the merchandise when you leave."

(Continued next page)

(229 cont'd)

You can now pay the tax for all the items you wish to take into the city by subtracting the amount shown from the gold tams on your character sheet. Anything you wish to leave simply check the gone box on the character sheet next to the item.

Now, going on into the streets of Jerican you once more are overwhelmed by its' enormous size. Unfortunately time is short and you must be very careful about what you do. Turn to <u>250</u>.

230   This is your second and last chance to look at a magic item. If you have already made your second choice turn to <u>205</u> immediately. Be honest and turn there. Come on turn the page.

If this is your second choice do you wish to see?

(A) Nautical magic? Turn to <u>244</u>.

(B) Healing magic? Turn to <u>269</u>.

(C) Combat magic? Turn to <u>273</u>.

231   "Ladies and gentlemen this wizard's papers are in order. Who here accuses this wizard of wrongdoing?"

The voice of a young girl can be heard. She moves toward the front of the crowd. Before she can speak you see the outline of her body begin to glow. Right before the eyes of the crowd the young girl changes into a laytant.

"Spy, informer," shouts a man from the crowd. "This is an Eastern bloodhound. You can't take his word."

"Silence," retorts the guard. "Who else can bear witness against this wizard?"

(231 cont'd)

The crowd is silent. The guard turns to you and whispers, "Be careful in these streets great one. Obviously they are after you."

He turns and orders the crowd to disperse except for the laytant who is asked to show his papers. While the other guards handle the Eastern spy you thank the guard for his warning.

"I wonder what made the spy give up his disguise," the guard muses out loud.

As you turn to leave to continue on your way only the tingling of your godstone gives you any clue. Part way down the street you turn to see the guards dragging the unwilling laytant away. Turn to 250.

232   Taking your place in line you stand quietly and wait. Before long the man behind you tries to strike up a conversation.

"You know," he begins, "I'm tempted to bind everyone and simply go in and take what I want. Where I come from the people are polite enough to move out of my way when they see me coming."

Looking over your shoulder you see a large burly man holding a small book. You know regardless of his boasts that he can't be a very powerful wizard. First, his book looks as thin as the local children's beginning reading book and second, he is speaking of *binding* spells rather than one of the more powerful spells of a high level wizard. You always thought it was disgusting to display your book in public anyhow. Do you:

(A) Ignore the braggart? Turn to 415.

(B) Answer by saying, "Well go ahead and teach them a lesson!" Turn to 258.

233   In a flash you are overcome with the sensation of magic. You have always loved the way the *reverse* spell feels enveloping your body. The two guards with red staffs are trying some type of incantation. Apparently they saw you cast a spell but they must be unfamiliar with the type. Now it is time for your magic versus their magic.

Roll the dice and record this roll on a piece of paper. Then roll again. If you can roll below or equal to the first number you rolled turn to 259. If you roll over the first number turn to 262 knowing that your *reverse* spell was not powerful enough.

234   The pearl godstone begins to heat. You lift your hand to inspect it when a cream colored light leaps from it and strikes the running boy and girl. Shocked, you watch the illusion fade away from the children. Their true form is revealed, a wretched laytant. A bloodhound of the East.

Falling to the ground where the boy stood is your charmed warning stone. Apparently the boy had stolen it from you when the wild magic stopped him. You reach to pick up the stone when a woman screams. The crowd is clearing out in a panic! Do you:

(A) Yell that you had nothing to do with it? Turn to 278.

(B) Run for it and try to lose yourself in the confusion? Turn to 249.

235   Roll the dice:

2 to 4, Turn to 292.
5, Turn to 263.
6, Turn to 247.
7, Turn to 393.
8, Turn to 331.
9 to 12, Turn to 398.

236 You know the spell he is throwing. All you have to do is quietly recite it along with him and add another 2 manna to his spell. <u>Mark off 2 manna</u>.

Roll the dice:

2 to 11, Turn to <u>248</u>.
12, Your spell fails and so does his! Turn to <u>212</u>.

237 The soldier's fist smashes into you and then grasps you firmly. Even a mighty wizard like yourself cannot use your magic when forced into hand-to-hand combat like this. As you and the soldier wrestle on the ground you notice that you have tumbled into the barroom.

You take a wide sweeping swing at the soldier with one purpose in mind.

Go to the Enemy that follows and roll one die. Check off the damage boxes on the Rogue's Gallery score card.

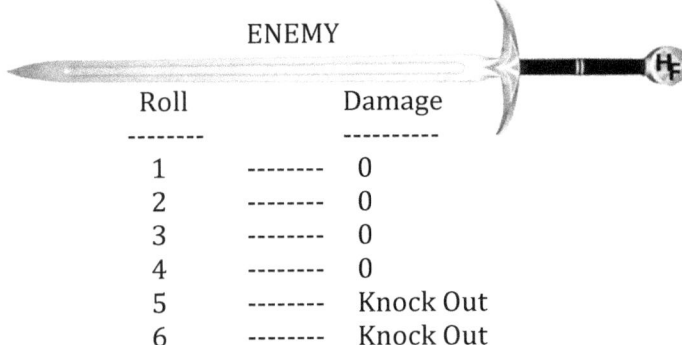

ENEMY	
Roll	Damage
1	0
2	0
3	0
4	0
5	Knock Out
6	Knock Out

If you knock out the soldier out turn to <u>292</u>. If not read on!

The soldier swings back!

(Continued next page)

(237 cont'd)

Go to the Enchantraen that follows and roll one die. Check off the damage boxes on your score card.

ENCHANTRAEN

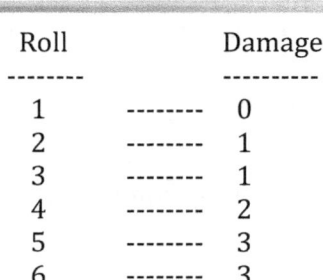

Roll		Damage
1	--------	0
2	--------	1
3	--------	1
4	--------	2
5	--------	3
6	--------	3

If you expire turn to <u>300</u>. If not you find the soldier swept away into the crowd. Turn to <u>235</u>.

238 Yes the time is right! You are coming to the end of your spell and all is working – you hope. Roll the dice:

2 to 11, Turn to <u>251</u>.
12, Your spell fails! Turn to <u>235</u>.

239 <u>Mark off B</u>.

Stepping up to the window you ask the purser for information about any ships departing for the Mystic Isles. As he thumbs through huge stacks of papers you read a sign on a billboard.

<u>Warship to the Mystic Isles</u>
The war gallery, Perfidia, is accepting wizards of ample talent to sail directly to the Mystic Isles.

See Purser

(239 cont'd)

The purser then answers saying, "We have two ships leaving in the morning. One is a round ship sailing with a cargo of sugar. It however is going only as far as Wellsport. You will have to gain further passage there. We also have an elven long boat for hire. And I'm afraid that is it."

"Which one is Perfidia," you inquire?

"Oh neither," replies the purser. "The Perfidia has canceled its' voyage. It seems there wasn't enough interest. She's a fine ship though. I can contact her Captain if you're interested in a fast ship, plenty of protection and a direct route."

You ask for the prices and general speed of the ships. You ascertain that the round ship is slow but cheap. The long-boat is fast and expensive but it offers better protection. The Perfidia is fast, protected, and medium priced due to splitting the cost with other wizards.

Checking your gold tams you decide to:

(A) Take the roundship, Cago, for 500 gold tams? <u>Subtract the gold from your character sheet</u>. Check the roundship's symbol and turn to <u>255</u>.

(B) Hire the elven crew of the Lady Varaë? <u>Subtract 1000 gold tams from your character sheet and check the long boat symbol</u>. Turn to <u>250</u>.

(C) Pay 650 gold tams for passage aboard the warship Perfidia? <u>Subtract the amount and circle the warship symbol on your character sheet</u>. Turn to <u>250</u>.

240 Dropping from the sky comes one of the guards carrying a red staff. The guard's flying tackle sends you both sprawling across the ground.

(Continued next page)

(240 cont'd)

Do you:

(A) Immediately start to fight the guard? Turn to <u>296.</u>

(B) Push him away and run? Turn to <u>283</u>.

(C) Surrender explaining that you panicked? "I'm innocent," you shout! Turn to <u>290</u>.

241　If <u>L</u> or <u>N</u> is marked, turn to <u>459</u>.

You run for the cover of an alleyway between two buildings. Roll the dice:

2 to 5, Turn to <u>283</u>
6 to 12, Read on!

The city guards are in hot pursuit shouting for you to stop. Do you stop long enough to?

(A) Cast a magical stone wall between the two buildings that will hopefully stop the guards from entering the alley? <u>Mark off 3 manna</u> and roll the dice:

2 to 11, Turn to <u>297</u>.
12, Your spell fails and the guards close in. Turn to <u>262</u>.

(B) Magically attack the three closest to you by casting a *sleep* spell? <u>Mark off 3 manna</u> and turn to <u>228</u>.

(C) Cast a *reverse* spell on yourself to turn away any magic they may cast your way? <u>Mark off 3 manna</u> and roll the dice:

2 to 11, Turn to <u>233</u>.
12, Turn to <u>262</u>.

(D) Keep on running? Turn to <u>281</u>.

242   You see the sword disintegrate! A light green mist envelopes your wrist and twists. Pain rips into your arm as you watch the green mist grow and take form.

Go to the Enchantraen table that follows and roll one die. Check off the damage boxes on your score card.

ENCHANTRAEN

Roll		Damage
1	--------	0
2	--------	1
3	--------	1
4	--------	2
5	--------	3
6	--------	4

If you live read on. If you expire turn to <u>200</u>.

The demon takes form. It's the one you saw before, near your tower.

"Now spell caster. Now do you dare fight me," the demon questions?

Looking at your arm you see the creature's thin tail implanted in the veins of your wrist. Do you:

(A) Curse the demon and attack with any weapon you have? Turn to <u>274</u>.

(B) Try and bluff your way out? Turn to <u>266</u>.

(C) Surrender? Turn to <u>246</u>.

243 The soldier prepares to smash you again when he suddenly turns green and heaves his recently drank beer over a tabletop. Disgusted you turn to 235.

244 "You are in luck today Enchantraen! I have two worthy items to look over."

Knowing you only have time to look over two items you can either choose to look at both of them or one and then choose another category.

"Well, Enchantraen, I have an *Incantation of Knot* and a *Glass Vessel of Pitching*. What will it be today?" Do you ask to see:

(A) The *Incantation of Knot*? Turn to 203.

(B) The glass vessel? Turn to 286.

245 The demon's gone but the cackling voice of an old man remains. "This is twice you have alluded my attempts to stop you on your quest Enchantraen. Hear me and be warned. The third time it will be either you or I who walk away alive. One of us will be dead!"

The voice trails off. Apparently a wizard was talking to you through a *communication* spell. Heeding the warning you realize there is little you can do now. Turn to 276 and go back to your room.

246 You have got to be crazy surrendering to a demon! The demon drains your blood until you faint. Luckily you don't feel the power the demon has gained from your life's blood. You don't see the gleaming faces of the Easterners as they hail the demon as a champion.

"The killer of the great war wizard."

(246 cont'd)

Now your power will be used against the people you most loved. They got you this time Enchantraen. The game for now is over, but if you wish to play again you may. After all, this is High Fantasy and anything is possible. Next time, for the sake of your Western allies, don't let them get you first!

247 A scummy looking warrior smashes a bottle on the bar top and tries to slash you with the broken end. These thieves always try this trick. Do you:

(A) Attempt to cast an *aetherial* spell on yourself and get out? Mark off 4 manna. Roll the dice:

2 to 10, Turn to <u>295</u>.
11 or 12, Turn to <u>238</u>.

(B) Fight the man with any weapon you might have on you?

Go to the Enemy table that follows and roll one die. Check off the damage boxes on the Rogue's Gallery score card for "The Slashing Thief".

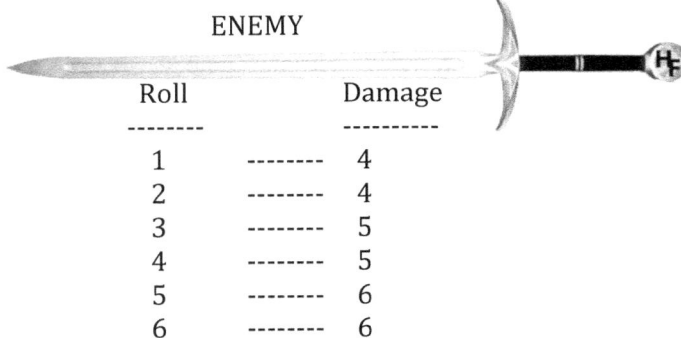

ENEMY

Roll	Damage
1	4
2	4
3	5
4	5
5	6
6	6

Go to the Enchantraen table that follows and roll one die.

(Continued next page)

(247 cont'd)

Check off the damage boxes on your score card.

ENCHANTRAEN

Roll		Damage
1	--------	0
2	--------	1
3	--------	1
4	--------	2
5	--------	2
6	--------	3

If you win, turn to <u>235</u>. If you lose, turn to <u>300</u>.

248   The aether flows and his spell is boosted. The wizard was expecting a 2' x 2' area to burst to flame. You can imagine his surprise when his hand burst into a 10 foot fireball. Since the spell was higher level than he had ever cast before he doesn't even realize what kind of spell he cast. The wizard runs out of line and starts screaming. He tries to put his hand out by throwing sand on it but the magical fire burns on. The crowd is laughing and some of the more knowledgeable wizards are yelling for him to throw it.

In time the man does. Unfortunately it strikes the side of another building setting it on fire. The city patrols are on him in seconds. The man starts pulling vouchers out of his pocket. When the patrol discovers that he doesn't have a voucher for fireballs they haul him off.

As he passes you in handcuffs you snicker, "That was simply an awesome display."

Bewildered-looking the man seems to be happy with the thought that he cast such a high level spell. Turn to <u>423</u>.

249   As the crowd clears, you clear with it. Roll the dice:

2, 3, 5, 6, 7, Turn to 278.
4, 8, 9, 10, 11, 12, Turn to 223.

250   Establishing your bearings do you:

(A) Go to the area of town where the majority of the magical items are for sale? Turn to 275.

(B) Head towards the wharf to book passage for your trip? Turn to 289.

(C) Head for a familiar tavern to find food and lodging? Turn to 363.

251   Your form becomes light and airy. Through the throngs of barroom brawlers you walk completely unmolested. The pain of your wounds causes you to stagger a little while going up the stairs.

"It's still great to get a few rounds of fisticuffs," you think to yourself.

Just then you hear footsteps on the stairs behind you. Turning you see an Eastern soldier running up the stairs with an oddly gleaming blade in his hand.

"Magic" you say out loud.

If R is not marked turn immediately to 222.

If R is marked you can:

(A) Avoid the fight, possibly by walking through the wall. Turn to 288.

(B) Change back and try to fight. Turn to 290.

252   You walk over to the side of the building and carefully inspect the wall. No, there doesn't seem to be any enchantment working upon it now. Reviewing the pages of your magic book you cast the spell. Roll the dice:

2 to 11, Turn to <u>202</u>
12, Your spell failed. <u>Mark off another 4 manna</u> and roll again, or, if you wish you can take a place in line, by turning to <u>423</u>.

253   The tavern is just ahead. Turning, you are in the door. Swoosh! A chair flies past your head. Whirling to your right you see a bloody free-for-all tavern fight. A giant of a man comes screaming towards you with his hands outstretched and his face contorted in a peculiar look of panic. Do you:

(A) Punch out with a spell of strike? <u>Mark off 2 manna</u> and turn to <u>271</u>.

(B) Dive to the side? Turn to <u>215</u>.

254   Snickering lightly to yourself you think back on how many times you pulled the same trick on poor Dreg. Laying your pack on the bed you walk over and splash your face briskly in the washbasin.

Thinking over what's left to be done today you dry your face in the towel.

(A) Have you booked passage for the quickest boat out of here? If you haven't but would like to, leave the tavern through the front door and turn to <u>289</u>.

(B) Have you hit the local wizardly hangouts? If not and you would like to, turn to <u>275</u>.

(C) You will be hungry and you might wish to have a hot meal before retiring. You may head downstairs to the hall by leaving the way you came. Turn to <u>382.</u>

(254 cont'd)

    (D) If you do not wish to go downstairs you can whip up a meal with the simple rations you have on you. Turn to <u>384</u>.

255   The purser hands you a ticket and explains that your ship will be leaving at sunrise. If you miss the boat there is no refund and the next ship won't leave until the following day. <u>Be sure to check the box next to the ship you bought passage for on your character sheet</u>. <u>Also mark the letter B</u> and turn to <u>250</u>.

256   The screaming guards fade behind you. Once in a crowd you feel certain you have lost them. Searching the streets carefully you see no signs of pursuit. Looking around you decide which way to head. Turn to <u>250</u>.

257   If <u>F</u> is marked turn to <u>262</u> regardless of what follows.

If not read on.

"Your papers are in order good wizard. That will sit well with the council if you have to be taken before it," says the head guard.

If <u>I</u> is marked turn immediately to <u>405</u> regardless of what follows.

If <u>P</u> is marked turn to <u>231</u>.

If <u>W</u> is marked turn to <u>357</u>.

If nothing is marked turn to <u>357</u>.

258   The wizard says, "Well I won't rouse them all but let me give you a little demonstration of my power. I'll give that young girl up there a hot foot."

The wizard then begins a spell that you recognize to be a low level *fire* spell. He is probably going to catch the wood floor at her feet on fire.

(Continued next page)

(258 cont'd)

"Hmm, you think. It sure would be interesting to boost the power of his spell." You might even be able to save the girl a little embarrassment. Do you:

(A) Try to boost the spell? Turn to <u>236</u>.

(B) Let him pull his prank? Turn to <u>282</u>.

259   A red light flashes from the guards' staffs and whips towards you. Your defensive *reverse* spell tingles and sparkles with light as it absorbs their spell and hurtles it back towards them. The two guards tumble to the ground with shouts of fury as the magic drains from them.

The three remaining guards turn and run. Do you:

(A) Cast a *sleep* spell on them? <u>Mark off 3 manna</u> and roll the dice:

2 to 11, Turn to <u>226</u>.
12, The guards disappear as your magic fails. <u>Mark off C</u> and get out of here quickly by turning to <u>250</u>.

(B) Leave while you can! <u>Mark off C</u> and leave this area by turning to <u>250</u>.

260   You scratch out the last words of your note when someone taps you on the shoulder. Turning you see a fist powered by an Eastern soldier coming towards your face.

"What's da matter *Spell Spitter*, ain't ya sociable?"

You can:

(A) Take the punch, hoping to strike back.

(260 cont'd)

Go to the Enchantraen table that follows and roll one die.
Check off the damage boxes on your score card.

ENCHANTRAEN

Roll	Damage
1	0
2	0
3	0
4	1
5	2
6	3

Now turn to <u>237</u>.

(B) Try to knock the blow aside with your arm. Roll the dice:

2 to 6, The soldier hits! Go to the Enchantraen table above
and check off your damage boxes. Then turn to <u>237</u>.
7 to 12, The soldier misses! Turn to <u>222</u>.

261 The soldier crumbles at your feet and rolls down the steps.
The sword drops only part way and rests on the third step up.
The glimmer from its blade slowly fades. Do you:

(A) Retire going on up into your room? You can leave the
blade and body to be cleaned up with the rest of the mess.
Turn to <u>287</u>.

(B) Decide you can always use a magic sword and retrieve it?
Turn to <u>272</u>.

262 "You do not obey our laws," the guard snaps. "You shall be
punished for not following the mandates of this land. Seize the
wizard!"

(Continued next page)

(262 cont'd)

Before you can hope to react red slashing lights whip from staffs. The lights wrap you up like one of your own *binding* spells. Wait! You feel it now. The aether is starting to drain. The magical binding is absorbing the aether. Soon no magic will work close around you.

"Bring any witnesses to the crime," shouts the commander.

Down the streets of the great city they take you. Turn to <u>428</u>.

263   One of the many flying bottles smashes against your head.

Go to the Enchantraen table that follows and roll one die. Check off the damage boxes on your score card.

ENCHANTRAEN

Roll		Damage
1	--------	0
2	--------	0
3	--------	1
4	--------	1
5	--------	2
6	--------	3

If you are still up, turn to <u>235</u>. If your damage boxes are all checked off turn to <u>300</u>.

264   Over the top of the wall comes one of the guards holding a red staff.

"He's flying!" you say somewhat amazed.

He is looking down the alleyway. Apparently he didn't expect you to stay.

(264 cont'd)

Do you:

(A) Shout a warning that you will have to slay him if he continues to pursue you? Turn to <u>290</u>.

(B) Cast a *binding* spell on him? <u>Mark off 1 manna</u>, and roll the dice:

2 to 9, Turn to <u>294.</u>
10 to 12, Your spell fails and the guard retaliates. Turn to <u>268.</u>

265 Roll one die:

1, 2, 3, Turn to <u>379</u>.
4, 5, 6, Read on!

You miss kicking the half-wit and find a dagger sticking in your foot.

Go to the Enchantraen table that follows and roll one die.

Check off the damage boxes on your score card.

ENCHANTRAEN

Roll		Damage
1	--------	1
2	--------	2
3	--------	3
4	--------	3
5	--------	4
6	--------	5

If you expire turn to <u>411</u>. If you live read on!

(Continued next page)

(265 cont'd)

Smashing out with your fist you strike back.

Go to the Enemy table that follows and roll one die. Check off the damage boxes on the Rogue's Gallery score card.

ENEMY

Roll		Damage
1	--------	0
2	--------	1
3	--------	1
4	--------	2
5	--------	3
6	--------	4

If you defeat him turn to <u>235</u>. If he is still alive he screams, "You tried to kick me!"

Go back to the Enchantraen before and roll for more damage.

266 Standing as erect as you can under the pain you manage to make a grim smile part your lips.

Staring steadily into the demon's face you say, "Drink my blood foul one and we shall be as one, or should I say your power will be mine. Drink deeply. It will take much of my strength to properly possess such a bulky form as yours."

Roll the dice:

2 to 8, Turn to <u>284</u>.
9 to 12, Turn to <u>291</u>.

267 The bloody job is soon completed. Being careful to clean your dagger blade you turn to leave. Just then you hear an ominous laugh echo through the town streets. Probably just a drunken

(267 cont'd)

rebel. <u>Mark off K</u> and go back into the streets by turning to <u>250</u>.

268   Roll the dice:

2 to 5, Turn to <u>283</u>.
6 to 12, His spell fails. Wait, the fool's closing in for a hand-to-hand fight. Do you:

(A) Try to cast your *binding* spell once more? <u>Mark off 1 manna</u>. Roll the dice:

2 to 9, Turn to <u>294</u>.
10 to 12, Your spell fails again. Turn to <u>296</u>.

(B) Run for it? Turn to <u>240</u>.

(C) Stand and fight? Turn to <u>296.</u>

269   "Someone has told you haven't they Enchantraen? Come on you sly devil, I'll show you the broach."

El takes you back and lifts a small jewel case out. Inside is an exquisite blood-red stone. The color seems to pulse with the very life force of man. You take the stone and attempt to decipher its magic in El's backroom study. Soon you discover that the broach has amazing healing powers. As soon as your life force begins to slip away the broach will automatically restore your health. It works like this. Anytime your defense reaches zero the game instructs you to turn to a scene. With the broach you won't have to. Instead you simply erase all damage on your character sheet and resume fighting! Unfortunately the broach can only do this once.

The broach costs 2000 gold tams El lets you know.

(Continued next page)

(269 cont'd)

"What," you begin to protest, but she quiets you by retorting that your life is worth at least 2000 gold tams.

If you want it you must first have the gold. <u>Mark the 2000 gold tams</u> off the character sheet. Then reread this scene. You must know how to use this magical item. The book won't tell you again. Remember and turn to <u>230</u>.

If you don't want it or don't have the tams tell her no and turn to <u>230</u>.

270   The three guards fall to the ground like tin soldiers. Before you can smile over your triumph the remaining two guards answer with a magic of their own. One of the guards lifts a red staff high into the air and recites the words of a powerful incantation. Roll the dice:
2, 3, 5, 6, 7, Turn to <u>262.</u>
4, 8, 9, 10, 11, 12, Turn to <u>299</u>.

271   Roll the dice:

2 to 10, Turn to <u>225</u>.
11 or 12, Turn to <u>321</u>.

272   You reach down to pick up the blade and feel it tingle in your hand. It's a pity that you are so far from your study. It would be nice to know what properties this sword possesses.

If <u>M</u> is marked, turn immediately to <u>242</u>.

If <u>M</u> is not marked but <u>L</u> or <u>N</u> is marked, turn to <u>293</u>.

If neither is marked turn to <u>301</u>.

273 "Good, very good," says El. "I have two nice treasures to choose from."

You know that you can only look at two magical items so you will just pick one for now.

"Which do you wish to see Enchantraen":

(A) The ivory unicorn?" Turn to <u>207</u>.

(B) The stake of confusion?" Turn to <u>221</u>.

274 With one arm impaled by the demon's tail you are hindered greatly in combat. With your free hand you draw your best weapon and swing.

Go to the Enemy table below and roll one die. Check off the damage boxes on the Rogue's Gallery score card.

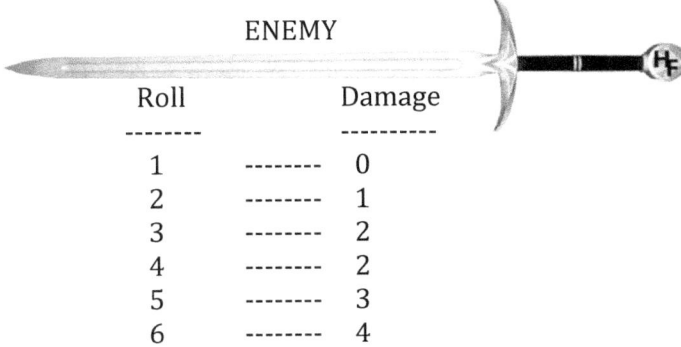

	ENEMY	
Roll		Damage
--------		----------
1	--------	0
2	--------	1
3	--------	2
4	--------	2
5	--------	3
6	--------	4

If the demon dies turn to <u>277</u>. If it lives, it sucks further at your life's blood!

Go to the Enchantraen table that follows and roll one die.

(Continued next page)

(274 cont'd)

Check off the damage boxes on your score card.

ENCHANTRAEN

Roll		Damage
1	--------	0
2	--------	1
3	--------	1
4	--------	2
5	--------	3
6	--------	4

If you expire the demon laughs one last time as you turn to 200. If you live for goodness sakes go to the first enemy table and strike harder!

275   If H is marked off turn to 440.

The streets of the great city are always crowded with merchants and buyers. It isn't until late evening when shops close that the people finally thin out. When walking through this area of town you are always fascinated by the strange mixture of creatures that gather here. There are Easterners, Westerners, Penoi, elves, dwarves and everything else imaginable.

There! Just ahead is your favorite shop. Oh no, the entrance is crowded. To wait in line will cost you at least 2 candles. Mark off H. Do you:

(A) Wait in line? Turn to 232.

(B) Leave and come back later? Turn to 250.

(C) Use a *passage* spell to make a flamboyant but non-violent entrance? Mark off 4 manna and turn to 252.

276 If E is marked turn immediately to <u>403</u> to decide what you want to do once you are in your room. If not, do you:

(A) Leave your room and the tavern to book passage on a ship? Turn to <u>289</u>.

(B) Go down to the bar for a hot meal since the fighting has stopped? Turn to <u>382</u>.

(C) Stay in your room and enjoy a peaceful meal with just you and your ration supply? Afterwards you can go to bed. Turn to <u>384</u>.

277 The demon's look of surprise is one you will never forget. How you managed to defeat it will be written in the annals of High Fantasy history as one of this world's greatest struggles. In other words Enchantraen, you were darn lucky.

If L or N is marked, turn to <u>245</u>.

If neither is marked catch your breath and proceed on up into your room. Turn to <u>276</u>.

278 The city guards come forward. There are five of them. Two remain back with glowing red staffs in their hands, while the other three advance.

"Stand your ground and do not attempt to escape," shouts the leader. "Name yourself and take out your vouchers," he commands. Do you:

(A) Run for it? Turn to <u>241</u>.

(B) Tell him that you are Enchantraen and get out your vouchers? Turn to <u>257</u>.

(C) Lie and tell him you have no vouchers because you just teleported here on urgent business? Turn to <u>262</u>.

(Continued next page)

(278 cont'd)

(D) Magically attack the three closest to you by casting a *sleep* spell on them? Turn to <u>228</u>. <u>Mark off 3 manna</u>.

(E) Cast a *reverse* spell on yourself? Roll the dice and <u>mark off 3 manna</u>.

2 to 11, Turn to <u>233</u>.
12, Turn to <u>262</u>.

279 The Eastern soldier still on the stairs quickly closes with you and swings his sword. In your present state you can neither perform magic nor physically fight. You may attempt to dodge the strike and then run, or return to solid form and fight. Do you:

(A) Choose to dodge allowing the soldier to swing at you?

Roll the dice:

2, 3, 5, 6, 7, The soldier swings and misses. Turn to <u>322</u>.
4, 8, 9, 10, 11, 12, The soldier hits! <u>Mark off 3 damage points</u>. If you expire turn to <u>200</u>. If you live choose again.

(B) Return to your normal state and fight? Turn to <u>298</u>.

280 <u>Mark off E.</u>

"How generous good wizard!" exclaims Dreg. "I hope you enjoy your nights stay."

Dreg enters the room, pulls down the bed sheets and turns to leave. He bows and on his way out he points and says, "Please use the back stairs if you wish to have dinner or a drink."

When Dreg has left you turn towards the door he pointed at. You always thought that was a closet. Oh well.

(280 cont'd)

Stretching out on the bed you think over what still has to be done before you retire for the night.

(A) Have you made passage on a ship? If you want to leave and head towards the dock simply go down the front stairs, hit the street and turn to <u>289</u>.

(B) Have you visited your favorite magical shop? If that sounds good, leave through the front, and turn to <u>275</u>.

(C) If you're done you could probably use a good hot meal about now? You may leave by using the back stairs. Turn to <u>375</u>.

(D) If you desire you could always simply eat your rations in your room to avoid any further trouble. Turn to <u>381</u>.

281   Roll the dice:

2 to 5, Turn to <u>256</u>.
6 to 12, Turn to <u>240</u>.

282   The walkway bursts to flame and the girl screams and jumps out of the way. She turns back and looks down the line to see who cast the spell. When she zeros in on the prankster you start to chuckle. She is an elf. Elves are powerful opponents when they study the craft.

With a wave of her hand the bully's own shadow stretches out and kicks him in the rump. Hard!

Bewildered the bully tries to step out of the way but naturally the shadow follows and strikes again.

Frightened, the bully runs in and out of the shadows of the buildings with his own shadow following, relentlessly kicking

(Continued next page)

(282 cont'd)

him as goes. The comical sight veers around a corner and is gone.

The elf extinguishes the fire and looks directly at you.

With an obviously saucy sprit she says, "You wouldn't happen to be with him would you?"

"Of course not, " you mildly answer. "That was worthy punishment you gave that joker. Who are you anyway?"

"I am Elwë, mate on the Lady Varaë, a longboat docked here. Who might you be?"

"I am Enchantraen from Nautpolis."

"I am sorry for the tough times that have befallen your city," she replies.

She comes back and takes a place in front of you in the line. By the time she takes her turn you have become rather good friends. She leaves after making her purchases. <u>Mark off J</u> and turn to <u>423</u>.

283   Your muscles begin to ache then tighten. A few more steps and you find yourself falling to the ground. The paralysis stops just short of becoming so painful that it causes you damage.

"Blast you guards," you curse through your teeth as they approach. Turn to <u>262</u>.

284   The demon draws back in horror. You try not to grimace too much when his foul tail rips out of your arm.

"You are truly a devil's *devil, War Wizard*," hisses the demon. "I shan't fight a greedy, curse-of-a-human like you."

(284 cont'd)

The demon instantly bursts into green mist and vanishes. Wiping the sweat from your brow you breathe deeply as you begin to walk up to your room.

If <u>L</u> or <u>N</u> is marked turn to <u>245</u>. If not you must turn to <u>276</u>. With a pained smile on your lips you head to your room.

285 It will be a long time before these guards get loose.

Checking the last knot you go back into the streets.

<u>Mark off G</u> and turn to <u>250</u>.

286 El says, "Good choice Enchantraen, I like this one myself, although I'm not sure how it works."

She reaches high behind a dust-covered shelf and pulls out a small wooden box. Inside the velvet lined box is a tiny crystal vessel. It looks like a small boat with a hull so shallow it would surely capsize.

You lift the vessel out and ask El to escort you to her study. She takes you into a large back room and leaves you. There among the books and wizardly tools you discover the true properties of the shallow craft.

By placing the vessel in water it will immediately give the roughest sea a mirror smooth surface. The vessel calms all waters.

El returns and tells you she won't part with the object for less than 1000 gold tams.

"Outrageous" you protest, but she cuts you short by saying you can use it over and over again. If you want the vessel subtract 1000 gold tams from your character sheet and <u>mark off the letter V</u> and turn to <u>230</u>.

(Continued next page)

(286 cont'd)

If you don't want it just tell her so.

Turn to <u>230</u>.

287   You slip quietly into your room and bolt the door. Before you can turn around something heavy thuds against the door.

If <u>L</u> or <u>N</u> is marked you hear an elderly voice say, "Move over foul demon." Turn immediately to <u>245</u>.

If <u>L</u> or <u>N</u> are not marked you hear a voice say, "Don't sleep too comfortably sweet Enchantraen."

A second thud is heard but this time it sounds as if it came from the floor by the door. All is quiet now. Do you:

(A) Prepare for sleep? Turn to <u>276</u>.

(B) Open the door? Turn to <u>350</u>.

288   You turn on the stairs and walk through the wall quite easily in your ghostly form. Once through the wall you enter a small room.

Shuffling under the covers of his bed a mustached man suddenly rises and screams for help, quickly reaching for his sword. Do you:

(A) Spirit back out the wall? Turn to <u>279</u>.

(B) Try to explain your predicament? Turn to <u>325</u>.

289   If <u>B</u> is marked turn immediately to <u>208</u>.

It isn't long before you come to the *Wharf of the Three Rivers.* The wharf is enormous for an inland port. The port is well-guarded by several different units of merchant guard. The port

(289 cont'd)

also includes a very large shipyard where many of the West's finest ships are constructed.

Looking over this mass of turmoil is the Yard Master and his pursers. All ships that dock present the purser with cargo and sailing time tickets. Passengers or merchants then contact the purser for prices and information. You go to the central building where information on sailing times can be obtained. There are two purser's windows dealing with ticket information. Do you:

(A) Wish to go to the sailing information window? Turn to 239.

(B) Go to the ticket exchange window? Turn to 365.

290 "Innocence is not for us to decide," says the guard.

Shortly the other guards catch up. A red light leaps from a staff and heads your way.

The light binds you as neatly as any of your own *binding* spells. Then you realize the subtle difference. This magic also drains the aether around you!

"Take this wizard away," shouts the guards. Turn to 428.

291 The demon draws harder at your blood. Nice try Enchantraen but you must now try something else.

Go to the Enchantraen table that follows and roll one die.

(Continued next page)

(291 cont'd)

Check off the damage boxes on you score card.

ENCHANTRAEN

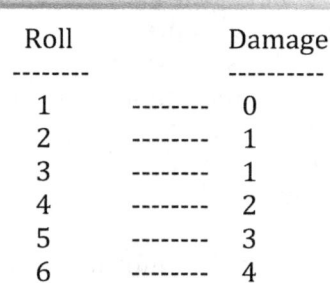

Roll	Damage
1	0
2	1
3	1
4	2
5	3
6	4

If you expire turn to <u>200</u>. If not do you:

(A) Fight the demon with one of you weapons? Turn to <u>274</u>.

(B) Surrender? Turn to <u>246</u>.

292 Turning you see another Eastern soldier swinging a chair at your back! Naturally you try to dive out of the way! Roll one die:

1, 2, You roll into the crowd. Turn to <u>235</u>.
3,4,5,6, You are hit! Read on.

Go to the Enchantraen table that follows and roll one die.

(292 cont'd)

Check off the damage boxes on your score card.

ENCHANTRAEN

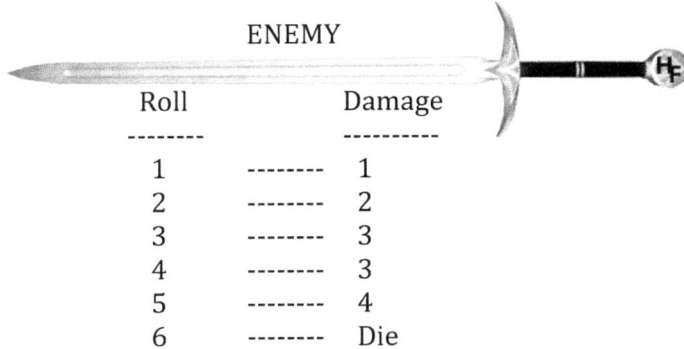

Roll		Damage
1	--------	0
2	--------	0
3	--------	1
4	--------	2
5	--------	3
6	--------	4

If you are knocked out, turn to <u>300</u>. If you are still up you swing back.

Go to the Enemy table and roll one die. Check off the damage boxes on the Rogue's Gallery score card.

ENEMY

Roll		Damage
1	--------	1
2	--------	2
3	--------	3
4	--------	3
5	--------	4
6	--------	Die

If the soldier is unconscious turn to <u>235</u>.

If not, he swings back, return to the Enchantraen table. If he swings back 3 times and you are both standing turn to <u>243</u>.

293 As you reach for the sword you hear an old man's voice say, "We're getting greedy now aren't we dear Enchantraen."

Looking around the stairwell you cannot seem to locate where the voice was coming from. A sizzling pain rips into your arm. The sword disintegrates and spews great clouds of green mist over the staircase. The pain in your arm comes from where the green mist has touched it. The mist begins to twist and take on the form of a hideous demon. Gasping in pain you see the demon's tail solidify in the veins of your wrist.

Go to the Enchantraen table that follows and roll one die. Check off the damage boxes on your score card.

ENCHANTRAEN

Roll		Damage
1	--------	1
2	--------	1
3	--------	1
4	--------	2
5	--------	3
6	--------	4

"Well, well little spell binder. Your blood is better than I anticipated," hisses the demon's voice.

From someplace odd laughter fades away into the air. Do you:

(A) Curse the demon and physically attack the creature with whatever weapon you can grab? Turn to 274.

(B) Try to bluff your way out? Turn to 266.

(C) Surrender? Turn to 246.

294   The light blue light leaps from your hand, flies through the sky, and the guard tumbles to the ground securely bound. As his body thuds on the cold hard earth the guard shouts, "Surrender and I'll go easy on you."

Do you:

(A) Cancel your spell and explain your innocence? Turn to <u>290</u> knowing that the other guards might be working their way through the buildings.

(B) Slit the braggarts throat? Turn to <u>267</u>.

(C) Run for it seeing that your magical wall is holding? Turn to <u>256</u>.

295   You concentrate on the words of your spell. Your fingers intricately trace out the pattern to form the spell. In short, you have left yourself totally vulnerable to the slashing bottle. The bottle gouges and twists into your arm. Cursing yourself for misjudging the time it takes to cast the spell you must now <u>check off 2 damage boxes</u> permanently for the rest of the game. This wound is critical and cannot be healed the normal way. Angered now you swing back.

Go to the Enemy table that follows and roll one die. Check off the damage boxes on the Rogues Gallery score card.

ENEMY

Roll		Damage
1	--------	1
2	--------	2
3	--------	2
4	--------	3
5	--------	5
6	--------	Die

(Continued next page)

(295 cont'd)

If the thief dies turn to <u>235</u>. If he lives he too curses and swings back.

Go to the Enchantraen table that follows and roll one die. Check off the damage boxes on your score card.

ENCHANTRAEN

Roll		Damage
1	--------	1
2	--------	1
3	--------	2
4	--------	2
5	--------	3
6	--------	3

If you expire turn to <u>200</u>. If you live get, mad and strike again. Go to the Enemy before and swing!

296 Picking your best melee weapon you strike out.

Go to the Enemy table that follows and roll one die. Check off the damage boxes on the Rogue's Gallery score card.

ENEMY

Roll		Damage
1	--------	2
2	--------	2
3	--------	3
4	--------	4
5	--------	5
6	--------	Die

(296 cont'd)

If the guard dies turn to <u>281</u>. If he is still alive he strikes back.

Go to the Enchantraen table that follows and roll one die. Check off the damage boxes on your score card.

ENCHANTRAEN

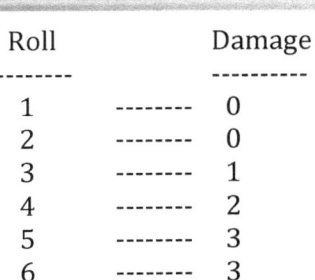

Roll		Damage
1	--------	0
2	--------	0
3	--------	1
4	--------	2
5	--------	3
6	--------	3

If you expire turn to <u>200</u>. If you are still alive return to the Enemy table and strike again!

297 More solid than the real buildings themselves, your stone wall appears blocking the alleyway. You can hear the guards cursing but you cannot see them. Do you:

(A) Run, hoping your wall will hold? Turning to run full tilt down the alley you must also turn to <u>281</u>.

(B) Stand and get ready to cast another spell in case the wall fails? Turn to <u>264</u>.

298 With the gleaming magic blade in his hand the soldier strikes.

Go to the Enchantraen table that follows and roll one die. Check off the damage boxes on your score card.

(Continued next page)

(298 cont'd)

ENCHANTRAEN

Roll		Damage
1	--------	1
2	--------	1
3	--------	2
4	--------	2
5	--------	3
6	--------	3

If you expire turn to <u>200</u>. If you live for goodness sakes strike back.

Go to the Enemy table that follows and roll one die. Check off the damage boxes on the Rogue's Gallery score card.

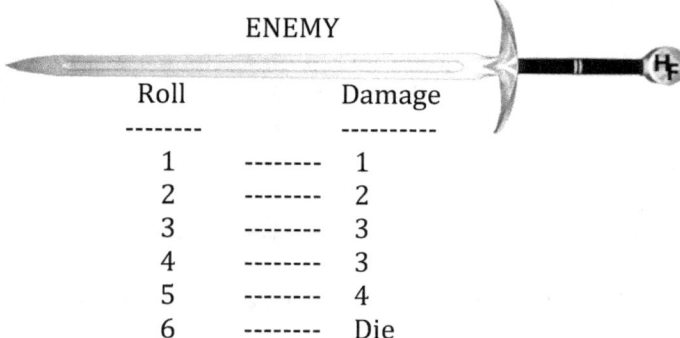

ENEMY

Roll		Damage
1	--------	1
2	--------	2
3	--------	3
4	--------	3
5	--------	4
6	--------	Die

If he dies turn to <u>261</u>. If he lives return to the Enchantraen table and watch out. The soldier strikes back.

299 Suddenly the two remaining guards turn and flee.

"Their sorcery failed," you chuckle.

<u>If I is marked off</u> turn immediately to <u>434</u>.

(299 cont'd)

Otherwise do you:

(A) Stop them in their tracks with a *sleep* spell? <u>Mark off 2 manna</u> and roll the dice. Roll the dice:

2 to 9, Turn to <u>226</u>.
10 to 12, The guards disappear as your magic fails. Quickly you move to lose yourself in the streets. <u>Mark off C</u> and turn to <u>250</u>.

(B) Let them go and continue about your business? Going into the streets once more you turn to <u>250</u> and <u>mark off the letter C</u>.

300 <u>Mark off R</u> if it isn't already.

When your eyes flutter open you find yourself resting in your room. A cold rag lays across your forehead and Dreg, the innkeeper is caring for you.

"Nasty cut there great one," Dreg begins. "I don't think it is anything serious however. Rest up a bit. I have to leave you now to go and tend to my other guests."

As Dreg leaves you pick yourself up off the bed and decide what to do next.

If <u>E</u> is marked turn to <u>406</u>. Do you:

(A) Want to leave the tavern and head towards the wharf to book passage? Turn to <u>250</u>.

(B) Want to go to the local magical shops? Turn to <u>275</u>.

(C) Want to go back down to get a hot meal? Turn to <u>382</u>.

(D) Stay in your room and eat rations? Turn to <u>384</u>.

301   The sword handles nicely. Add +1 to your dice roll when using it against any opponent. The sword has other magical properties but you do not have the time to explore these. Since you are traveling lightly you may only carry one sword. If you like this sword better than any you are carrying at this time make a special note on your character sheet and keep it. If you don't want it, disregard it and leave it by the body.

Turn now and go back to your room, <u>276</u>.

302   The great stallion is swift and gentle to command. You derive a great deal of excitement from its steady flight. The Pegasus seems to float more than fly through the air. Only the racing wind and the spinning ground give you any indication of the creature's great speed. It isn't long before you and the beast learn the ways of each other. You think you would like to have one of these fine creatures for yourself. Perhaps when you become an Elder you will have the power to find one.

What's left of the day passes quickly. You are afraid to ride long into the night. If you were to go to sleep it could be a nasty fall. You guide Constellia to a suitable location for camp up on a high crest. You tie the stallion and eat a quick meal of cold rations. As the night settles in you observe something strange. The landscape is littered with small campfires!

Diving to your belly you search the darkness in disbelief. It must be Eastern horse patrols. There are hundreds of them. Luckily none of them seem to be camped close to you. Apparently the use of Almon's Pegasus is saving you a lot more than just time.

Finally you decide to chance a nights' sleep and you drift off into an uneasy slumber. Turn to <u>317</u>.

303   The spell takes shape and forms around the necklace. With great care you start to lift it and bring it towards you. Turn to <u>337</u>.

---

304   Your spell gently grabs hold of her and you pull. The swamp lets out a loud sucking sound as she is pulled free. You shake her lightly to dislodge some of the muck. Turn to <u>348</u>.

305   Roll the dice:

2, 3, 5, 6, 7, Turn to <u>338</u>.
4, 8, 9, 10, 11, 12, You fail to cast the spell before the soldier closes the gap. Turn to <u>279</u>.

306   "I thought so," Sluss knowingly chuckles. "Well for now I'm headed towards that star," and he points towards the direction you saw the explosion.

"I will have to travel all night though or the locals will have it stripped and sold before I can get there."

Sluss looks at you from the side with cold eyes and asks if you might be interested in the same thing. You quickly dismiss those worries and tell Sluss you have more pressing matters in Jerican. The wizard laughs and the tension between you is gone.

Sluss begins a long narrative of his wizardly travels and you feel content to lay back and listen while supper cooks.

If <u>W</u> is marked turn to <u>346</u> immediately.

If <u>JJ</u> is marked turn to <u>362</u>.

If neither is marked then turn to <u>374</u>.

307   Just then a small dagger flies and strikes the back of the Magi's neck. As the Magi tumbles to the floor a small, ugly looking halfling comes forward to remove the knife.

Grinning up at you through broken teeth like a black rodent says, "Maybe, you next wish to challenge the great Pierl?"

(Continued next page)

(307 cont'd)

Do you:

(A)Kick the little creep away with your foot? Turn to <u>265</u>.

(B)Attempt to bind the halfling? <u>Mark off 1 manna</u> and turn to <u>352</u>.

(C) Tell him you have no wish to waste one half a spell on him? Turn to <u>391</u>.

(D) Say, "Nice little dagger trick Pierl. In fact it is the nicest I've seen," in your most flattering tone? Turn to <u>353</u>.

308   Instinctively your hand reaches out and clasps the arm of the young boy. Your Charmed Warning Stone falls from his grasp.

"Oh please, great one, she made me do it," he says pointing towards the girl.

Standing about 10 feet from you is a very self-assured young woman.

"Let him go," she says in a low voice, "or I will call for the City Guards and explain how you like to molest small children." Do you:

(A) Release the boy and warn them to leave this area and you alone? Turn to <u>311</u>.

(B) Toss the boy towards the girl and hit them with a two manna *binding* spell? In a crowded street though, this could attract attention. Turn to <u>369</u>.

309   Your spell fails and the figure steps back in surprise.

If <u>A</u> is marked turn to <u>354</u>. If not turn to <u>349.</u>

310   Roll the dice:

2 to 5, Turn to <u>332.</u>
6 to 12, You find that party way across the room ... turn to <u>235.</u>

311   "You cursed Western dog," the girl shouts as her belt buckle is loosed.

With a flick of her wrist the buckle becomes a blur of spinning blades. As the blade races your way, you see only the vague image of the girl's changing shape in the background.

"Laytant," you curse!

There is no defense capable of stopping the spinning death.

Go to the Enchantraen table that follows and roll one die. This table is only for the spinning blades. Check off the damage boxes on your score card.

ENCHANTRAEN

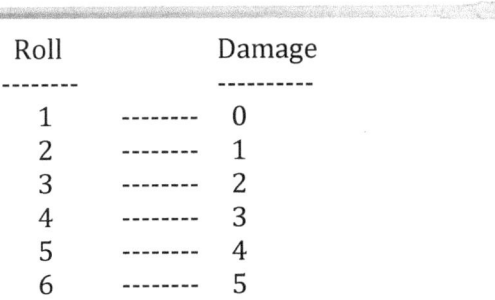

Roll		Damage
1	--------	0
2	--------	1
3	--------	2
4	--------	3
5	--------	4
6	--------	5

If you live draw your best melee weapon and fight! If you expire turn to <u>200</u>.

(Continued next page)

(311 cont'd)

Go to the Enemy table that follows and roll one die. Check off the damage boxes on the Rogue's Gallery score card.

ENEMY

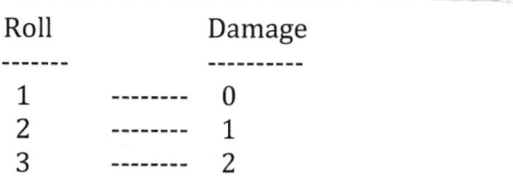

Roll		Damage
1	-------	1
2	-------	2
3	-------	2
4	-------	3
5	-------	4
6	-------	0

If the laytant dies, turn to <u>364</u>. If it lives, it pulls a dagger and fights.

Go to the Enchantraen table below and roll one die. Check off the damage boxes on your score card.

ENCHANTRAEN

Roll		Damage
1	-------	0
2	-------	1
3	-------	2
4	-------	2
5	-------	3
6	-------	3

If you expire turn to <u>200</u>. If you live return to the Enemy table and go through it again!

312 You form the light in your bare hands but table it momentarily before you give your last warning.

"This is your last life ghost! Show yourself to me or I will call forth enough light to make this area as bright as day sending you to the underworld."

About 3 feet away you see the ghost materialize. In a rage he curses how he came to you in friendship and how you hastily killed him.

"Silence fool" you shout! "Haven't you yet learned who you are talking to? I am Enchantraen, spirit! You should be glad it was a merciful death."

The ghost trembles with rage but stays silent.

"You should never approach someone like myself without properly announcing yourself. I am pressed for time and can't deal with you now; but know this. You have my permission to return to my tower. When I come back I will figure out a way to stuff that miserable soul of yours back into that useless carcass!"

The ghost looks at you in disbelief.

"You will be good company for my familiar and besides ghosts don't eat much."

"But," begins the ghost.

"Begone spirit before I change my mind."

The spirit vanishes and you squash the light. Sluss stirs and you sit back down. "What happened?" asks Sluss.

"You were just about to leave and chase down the star," you say in a determined voice.

(Continued next page)

(312 cont'd)

A little puzzled Sluss picks up his things and scrambles off into the night. You lay down, smooth out your robe determined to get a good night's sleep. Turn to 316.

313　Just then the waters bubble. Up and down the marshy stream claws and scaly green hands slowly emerge. With the clicking noise common to their dialect, their leaders order an attack. There are so many of the scaly scum it is hard to count them. In this number trolls can be deadly even to a wizard like yourself.

Do you:

(A) Wish the girl luck and run for it while you can? Turn to 333.

(B) Stay your ground and work on the makings of a powerful *transmute* spell? Mark off 4 manna and turn to 355.

314　Roll the dice:

2 to 7, Turn to 1004.
8 to 12, Turn to 309.

315　The laytant's claws dig sharply into your shredded throat. The laytant pulls back sensing that his kill is complete.

"You should have stayed at home Enchantraen," the laytant chokes. "You were great in your day but you tried the patience of my masters once too often."

The laytant lifts a blood-soaked claw and shouts, "For the Blessed Kingdoms!"

The last thing you see is its descending claw. For you the game is over. Turn no further.

316   If <u>L</u> or <u>N</u> is marked, turn immediately to <u>343</u>.

<u>Mark off the next day and replenish all manna and erase all damage.</u>

The following day, you break camp early and head out once more. Soon you pass travelers on the road and farmhouses can be seen in the distance along the way. Up and over a hill and .... Turn to <u>201</u>.

317

<u>Mark off the next day and replenish all manna and erase all damage.</u>

In the morning you awaken to a strange sight. The early morning sun rays are refracting through the rainbow. The land is covered with dots of blue, green and yellow. It's then that you notice that the only red light is shining on you! Quickly you roll over to find Eastern patrols moving your way. They are still too far off to be an immediate threat. The phenomenon passes but you have no desire to stay. You decide to eat breakfast on the back of the Pegasus so you quickly mount up. Off you race and the sensation of speed envelops you. Looking down you see Eastern horse patrols roaming the countryside.

On you fly steadily until noon.

Then a second phenomenon strikes you. The sun is at its zenith. The light passing through the rainbow seems to cause the earth to dance to unheard music. Everything sways as your body seems to fill with power. The sensation is wonderful. You feel as though there is nothing you can't do. You feel so strong that you have to release the mounting pressure.

(Continued next page)

(317 cont'd)

"Out of my way dogs. It is I, Enchantraen, passing by. I go to take my proper place with the Elders on the Mystic Isles. Bow to my passing."

You then throw your head back laughing. Your voice seems to echo and carry for a long distance. You swear that the horse patrols seem to pull up and listen even though you know it should be impossible for them to hear you.

Away you fly on the safety of the Pegasus. For now you escape the dangers. Soon the feeling of power passes but you feel gladdened from the experience. Turn to 500.

318   As you rocket through the air you feel the Swamp Rogue's magic tearing at your flesh. It takes all your concentration but you manage to break free. Without hesitating you fly on towards the city. You realize it would be a waste of energy to fight a Swamp Rogue here in the wilderness. You have more important things to consider at the moment.

You race ahead exhilarated by the freedom of flight. You continue on until the spell fades and you are forced to land. From there you walk on creating plenty of distance between you and the dangers of the swamp. Turn to 333.

319   Roll the dice:

2, 3, 5, 6, 7, Turn to 334.
4, 8, 9, 10, 11, 12, Turn to 367.

320   You discover too late that there is nothing you can do to escape. A bolt of light rips up your spine. Luckily you pass out before the magic runs its course! Mark off KK and turn to 469.

321   Your spell miserably fails and you find yourself struggling with a giant Mountain Magi who has just run headlong into you. You swing at the giant with your fist.

(321 cont'd)

Go to the Enemy table that follows and roll one die. Check off the damage boxes on the Rogue's Gallery score card.

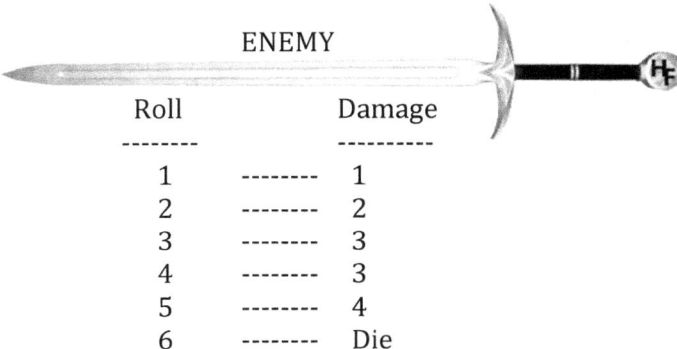

ENEMY

Roll		Damage
1	--------	1
2	--------	2
3	--------	3
4	--------	3
5	--------	4
6	--------	Die

If you have scored 7 points against the Magi, turn to <u>307</u>. If not read on!

Go to the Enchantraen table that follows and roll one die. Check off the damage boxes on your score card.

ENCHANTRAEN

Roll		Damage
1	--------	0
2	--------	1
3	--------	2
4	--------	2
5	--------	3
6	--------	4

If you are knocked out turn to <u>300</u>. If you live go back to the Enemy table and strike again.

322 You have successfully dodged the soldier's blows. You capitalize on this opportunity by stepping back and:

(A) Solidifying while attempting to cast a spell before the soldier can close in once more. Turn to <u>305</u>.

(B) Running through the wall. Turn to <u>288</u>.

(C) Solidifying and fighting hand-to-hand with the soldier. Turn to <u>298</u>.

(D) Turning to run away by continuing on up the stairs. Roll the dice:

2, 3, 5, 6, 7, You hear a smashing sound coming from behind you. Turn to <u>222</u>.

4, 8, 9, 10, 11, 12, The soldier unfortunately catches you before you can escape. Turn to <u>298</u> and add +2 to the soldier's roll when swinging at you.

323 Your mind gently enters the bound woman.

"Honestly girl what's the problem?" you whisper in her thoughts.

"Below me, they're in the swamp! Help me!"

"Calm down woman. Who's down there?"

"Trolls! Scores of them."

"Uch!" you involuntarily shudder. "I hate those nasty things!" Turn to <u>313</u>.

324 "Later Sluss," you shout as you scramble off into the night!

You run through most of the night until a few hours before dawn. You come across a deserted shack and take shelter from

(324 cont'd)

a passing rain shower. You get little sleep but it must suffice. Turn to 316.

325   "I mean you no harm," you begin.

The man jumps from the bed and moves toward you. Just then the door bursts open and the soldier engages him in deadly combat. Since both men obviously wish to do you harm after they finish with each other you decide it would be better to leave. Going back up the stairs you hear more footsteps coming. Turning, you see the innkeeper running up followed by 5 guards. The innkeeper obviously noticed the soldier break into the man's room. Snickering to yourself you solidify and turn to 276.

326   The spell takes effect. Quickly you look around but see nothing new. Confused about what's going on, you turn to 358.

327   The light blue light leaps across at you but you simply knock it away with your hand.

"How dare you," you shout in rage!

Sluss collapses to the ground. Apparently the spirit has left him.

"Stop where you are," you shout unable to see the spirit.

Do you:

(A) Cast a *light* spell to stop the ghost? <u>Mark off 1 manna</u> and turn to 312.

(B) Let it go? Turn to 335.

(C) Pick up what you can and run? Turn to 344.

328   You move over a little closer to the body. It is obviously too late to do anything for the body but you could still get the necklace. You could:

(A) Cast a *telekinesis* spell and pull the necklace towards you. Mark off 2 manna and turn to 303.

(B) Wade in towards the body. You could always turn back if it gets too deep. Turn to 366.

(C) Decide to leave well enough alone and leave. Turn to 337.

329   "My name is Sluss, from Goldchester," the person informs you.

Sluss starts to unravel a tightly sealed pack and slide out choice pieces of meat. They too are wrapped and are quickly tossed into the fire.

After a brief pause Sluss says, "And you must be Enchantraen."

A little surprised to be recognized you:

(A) Attack with a *binding* spell! Mark off 1 manna and turn to 1004.

(B) Answer, "Yes," and ask, "Where are you going and on what business?" Turn to 306.

330   The staff flickers in the wraith's hand but Shefast makes its own reply. The great staff is the undisputed authority here. The staff calls on its minions from the heaven and the sky rips apart in answer. The lightning plummets, pays tribute to the staff and then flashes towards the wand and wraith. Both explode into a million fragments and the only thing left is the roll of the thunder. You place the staff down in awe.

That night before you fall off into deep slumber, you make a mental note to explore all of the staff's powers when you return home. Turn to 316.

331   Something grabs you by the kneecap and spins you around. A nasty looking halfling standing about 3 feet tall brandishes a dagger at you.

"Me cut pretty wizard with nasty blade," hisses the little man.

Do you:

(A) Kick the little creep away with your foot? Turn to <u>265</u>.

(B) Attempt a *binding* spell? <u>Mark off one manna</u> and turn to <u>352</u>.

(C) Tell him you have no wish to waste one half a spell on him? Turn to <u>391</u>.

(D) Say, "That's the finest dagger I've ever seen," in your most flattering tone? Turn to <u>353</u>.

332   Bottles smash and chairs fly as you meticulously make your way to the innkeeper's side. The innkeeper finishes off his adversary with a sharp right-cross.

"I hope this is not what has become of your fine Inn's hospitality," you say.

Smiling, the innkeeper is up and wiping his hands.

"Enchantraen! This is no place for you. Please let me take you to your room."

Heaving bodies out of the way, Dreg, the innkeeper heads back to the lobby. Once out Dreg immediately takes you up the stairs.

"Sorry about the noise but it seems to have become a common occurrence around here," Dreg apologizes.

(Continued next page)

(332 cont'd)

From a side door an Eastern soldier springs out and begins to swing his sword at your exposed side! Turn to <u>222</u>.

333

<u>Mark off the next day and replenish all manna and erase all damage.</u>

<u>Erase any marks over GG.</u>

You make good time for what remains of the day. Before night fully sets in you find a comfortable place to camp and build a liberal fire.

Roll the dice:

2 to 5, Turn to <u>316</u>.
6 to 12, Turn to <u>345</u>.

334   You walk back towards the bridge. Veering off to one side, you bend down to look beneath it. You see a woman submerged to her waist in the swamp. Her hands are tied above her head and her mouth is gagged. Her eyes are wild with warning. Sensing danger you ... Turn to <u>358</u>.

335   The air is still for only a brief moment. Sluss lifts himself up and shakes his head. Putting his hands on his head he slowly looks up. When you see his eyes there is no question that he is once again *possessed*! The light blue light flickers around his hands once more.

Roll the dice:

2 to 4, Turn to <u>1004</u>.
5 to 12, Turn to <u>327.</u>

336   You cross the bridge but all is quiet. You reason that whatever has captured the girl is gone at this time or was frightened off when you came. Turn to 340.

337   Suddenly the swamp explodes. Large chunks of slime and debris cascade down on you knocking you off your feet. Quickly you stand back up only to come face to face with your antagonist. A Swamp Rogue's whirling wild eyes stare down at you. You realize you have but one chance to fend off its attack. Knowing Swamp Rogues are highly magical, you:

    (A) Try to paralyze the creature. Mark off 3 manna and roll the dice:

        2, 3, 5, 6, 7, Turn to 356.
        4, 8, 9, 10, 11, 12, Turn to 341.

    (B) Cast a *fly* spell on yourself and rocket away. Mark off 3 manna and roll the dice:

        2 to 5, Turn to 318.
        6 to 12, Turn to 356.

    (C) Cast a *reverse* spell on yourself for added protection. Mark off 3 manna and roll the dice.

        1 to 5, Turn to 356.
        6 to 12, Turn to 347.

338   A *transmute* spell is all you can think of on the spur of the moment. Mark off 4 manna and roll the dice:

2 to 11, Turn to 388.
12, your spell fails and the soldier closes in. Turn to 279.

If you don't have 4 manna left consider the spell to have failed and turn to 279.

339   You quietly rise and grab a simple stick. You draw the outline of a giant pentangle on the ground, digging where the turf is thick and taking all precaution to make certain the lines are complete and unbroken. Then you seat yourself in the center and begin the chant of *summoning*.

As you say the words you concentrate on the face you saw in the dream. Your mind travels through an endless void in a desperate search. You start to give up, thinking it was only a dream, when the contact is made.

The brief exchange of thought is deadly. You discover he is a puppet of Lord Gaoler. Once you explain your challenge the lich readily accepts. One rarely gets the chance to challenge one of your stature on an equal basis. When your spell is finished the lich appears on the fifth point of the star you drew on the ground. You stand realizing only one of you will leave its parameters alive.

"Since I am the Challenged I choose the contest of fire," hisses the lich.

A silent nod of your head is your only answer.

You both chant the words of the *fire* spell as you circle from point to point on the pentangle. As the fire begins to flicker on your fingertips you both charge like bulls towards each other. Your hands lock in a death grip over the top of your heads. The flames flare and roar into the air as both of your powers feed the flames. The fire grows greater than the size of a bonfire and then greater still to the size of a wheat field set ablaze. The surrounding countryside becomes aware that two great wizards are in battle. Suddenly the flame concentrates around both of you. The country folk know that one of the wizards is now dead.

Roll the dice:

2, 3, 5, 6, 7, Turn to <u>395</u>.
4, 8, 9, 10, 11, 12, Turn to <u>1000</u>.

340   You untie the girl and she starts sobbing.

"Thank you," she cries over and over again.

Once you calm her down she explains that trolls grabbed her from the bridge. She tells you she lives near here and that her husband must be worried sick. It's so unusual to have troll hunting parties this far west of the gouge. Accepting someone's undying gratitude has never been easy for you so you cut her short and tell her to be on her way. She hands you what appears to be a gem. You touch it and find it to be rubbery.

"Take this with my gratitude," she explains. "Shape this into the form of your most precious possession. If you ever lose that item snap it after it hardens and the item will return to you." She smiles and leaves.

Without hesitating you shape the thing to look like your staff Shefast.

Check the yes box on your character sheet next to *Gem to return Shefast*. Remember how the gem works.

If you lose Shefast erase the yes box next to the gem and check the yes box next to Shefast. Shefast will magically reappear and you can use it again. Remember how this gem works. This book won't prompt you again. Turn to <u>333</u>.

341   The creature jerks then quietly stops as you gain control of its nervous system. Unable to stop itself the creature begins to sink back into the swamp. Your spell should hold long enough that the creature will undoubtedly suffocate before it can surface to get the needed air.

You look around but the creature's sudden exodus from the marsh destroyed or at least has hidden both the body and the necklace. Still you feel glad to have defeated the creature when you did.

(Continued next page)

(341 cont'd)
It's hard telling what would have happened if it gained control of you by completing its attack!

Breathing a little easier you turn and walk away. Turn to <u>333</u>.

342 You walk on through the day making good progress. The ground begins to get mushy beneath your feet and you realize that you are getting too close to the marshlands by the Gouge. You alter your course and proceed until you come to an unexpected body of water. This ground is still mushy and the water stretches too far to easily cross it. You look up and down the edge until you find a bridge.

The bridge is of solid construction made up of stout timber and stone. It looks surprisingly well kept. You easily cross it and start on your way. Behind you, you hear a muffled gurgle.

It could be swamp gas or one of the nasty creatures that live there, or nearly anything. Do you:

(A) Continue on? Turn to <u>333</u>.

(B) Go back to investigate? Turn to <u>319</u>.

343 That night you dream about a burning countryside. Your countryside! The surrounding farms around Arcania are turned to ash. A demon force drives the Eastern soldiers through the woods searching for your tower. Every night you see their torches coming closer to your home.

Then it happens. An ancient wizard appears and threatens you from the very top of your tower. The wizard's skin is drawn tightly over the bones of his face. From his contorted features you guess that his life force has been artificially extended. You know this type of a creature to be a *lich*. You stalk each other around the tower top but he always seems to have an unknown advantage.

(343 cont'd)

You wake up in a cold sweat. The night air is chill so you wrap your blanket closer around you and stir the fire's embers. The dream seemed too real and it has left you feeling upset. You wonder how much of it is true. You mentally check with Jenevan and find that the tower is secure. Conversing with your familiar settles your nerves and you relax.

If the lich is real you have the power to challenge it in an outright dual. However, before the lich would accept your summoning, you would have to promise the creature an equal fight meaning you have 50% chance of losing. The thought of putting everything on the line might be a bit risky. Maybe you would be better off to wait until the lich shows himself.

Do you:

(A) Forget the dream and go back to sleep? Turn to <u>218</u>.

(B) Put everything on the line with a challenge even though you can't be positive the creature exists? Turn to <u>339</u>. <u>Mark off 4 manna</u>.

344   The light blue light strikes you and neatly binds you up. You tumble to the ground helpless.

No better off than a beggar, lying on your back, you expect to see Sluss glowering over you at any second. Instead the ghostly image of a man appears.

"Well great wizard, so I have finally got your attention. It only cost me my life. You wrongly killed me at your own doorstep wizard. I could have helped you. Instead look at me."

He stoops and passes a transparent hand through your heart. It sends icy chills down your spine.

Just then the binding dissolves. Sluss cancelled the spell. Sluss

(Continued next page)

(344 cont'd)

staggers and falls again. The ghost vanishes!

Do you:

(A) Try a *light* spell? <u>Mark off 1 manna</u> and turn to <u>312</u>.

(B) Pick up your things and run? Turn to <u>324</u>.

345   The night is full of stars. They stretch from horizon to horizon resting in the sky like fine jewels on black velvet. You feel content for the time just to rest gazing at the glistening rainbow and its surrounding stars. It's as if you were staring into the bottomless treasure chest of the world.

As the night passes your thoughts drift through fleeting moments of your past. At last your mind rests on stories you were told in your childhood by your mother. Those were simpler times before the East had begun their invasion. In those days the loose-knit Western Kingdoms squabbled over grain prices and weather predictions. No one then knew about the turmoil breeding on the other side of the *Asius* wall.

A star falls. You see it strike the ground in the distance and burst into a shower of blue sparks. There should be some good metal for magic weapons over there," you think to yourself.

"Greetings" comes a voice that sends you whirling around.

Standing about 10 feet from you is a robed figure with a backpack in one hand and a book in another.

Do you:

(A) Immediately attack with a *binding* spell? <u>Mark off 1 manna</u> and turn to <u>314</u>.

(B) Return his greeting and offer a seat by the fire? Turn to <u>329</u>.

(345 cont'd)

(C) Tell the figure to leave you in peace? "I do not take kindly to visits in the night". Roll the dice:

2, 3, 5, 6, 7, Turn to <u>376.</u>
4, 8, 9, 10, 11, 12, Turn to <u>354</u>.

346 His tale goes on and on like so many traveling tales do until you are only half listening. His story continues until he comes to his travels past the southwest side of the Gouge.

"There I saw a most peculiar sight. Late at night I heard weeping so I went into the woods to investigate. There I found a man, at least what I thought was a man weeping over the body of a dead panther or jaguar or something."

"What," you say, sitting upright quickly.

"That's not the half of it," he continues. "When I approached the man simply vanished. Needless to say, I high-tailed it out of there."

Sluss reaches in to grab a piece of meat then suddenly jerks back. He begins to choke but suddenly stops and rises. In a deep voice, very unlike his own, he shouts down at you.

"I cry no longer you bloodthirsty murderer."

A light blue light flickers around Sluss's arm. Roll the dice:

2 to 4, Turn to <u>344</u>.
5 to 12, Turn to <u>327</u>.

347 The Swamp Rogue's eyes swirl and your body is barraged by a mass of swirling colors. Your own magic replies with a protective shell that forms around you holding the Swamp Rogue's magic at bay. The lights are funneled up above your head where they hesitate a moment before they are flung back towards the creature.

(Continued next page)

(347 cont'd)

The lights strike the creature who screams, falling back into the swamp. The creature attempts a ghastly transformation, but its' painful thrashing sends it back to the depths of the swamp before the magic is complete.

Finally the swamp stops stirring. You look around but the necklace is gone. It was probably buried deep in the muck stirred up from the creature.

You feel rather lucky that the creature's magic wasn't able to get through to you. You turn and walk away, glad to be away from the marshlands and on your journey once more. Turn to 333.

348   A scaly arm lifts from the swamp and sends a slime-covered shaft whistling your way. The shaft sizzles against the magic of your missile protection gem and veers off missing you completely. Turn to 313.

349   "Hey wizard" replies the figure. "That's a fine greeting. I come in peace!"

Do you:

(A) Apologize and ask the figure to be seated? Turn to 329.

(B) Attack once more with a *binding* spell? Mark off 1 manna and turn to 314.

(C) Tell the figure that you are not looking for company and to leave on fear of its life? Roll the dice:

2, 3, 5, 6, 7, Turn to 354.
4, 8, 9, 10, 11, 12, Turn to 376.

350   The door creaks open. In the hall, crumbled at your feet, are the remains of the dead Eastern soldier. The hall and stairway are empty and quiet. Kicking the remains away you close the

(350 cont'd)

door and make ready for what sleep you can. You are so very tired. Turn to <u>276</u>.

351   Indeed the next few days are restful. Even the nights prove quiet. Thankful for the short rest you approach Jerican late on the second day. Turn to <u>201</u>.

352   Roll the dice:

2 to 6, The halfling is neatly wrapped. His dagger falls from his hand and slides over to your feet. Its blade glimmers and fades. If you leave the dagger alone you will see that the halfling disappears quickly in the throngs of people. Turn to <u>235.</u>

7 to 12, the spell is interrupted by a sturdy chair cracking against your back.

Go to the Enchantraen table that follows and roll one die. Check off the damage boxes on your score card.

ENCHANTRAEN

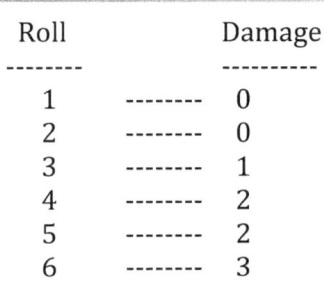

Roll		Damage
1	--------	0
2	--------	0
3	--------	1
4	--------	2
5	--------	2
6	--------	3

Turn to <u>200</u> if you expire. Turn to <u>235</u> if you live.

353   "Oh, Oh! You like pretties do you," says the halfling.

With that he flips the dagger over in his hand. Before you can hope to react he throws the dagger at your head. You see the blade moving towards you as if it were in slow motion. Ducking and closing your eyes you sense that perhaps the blade was misthrown. The air from its swift passing brushes against your face. Before your eyes can fully open again you hear the deep gutted gurgle of death from behind you.

As you rise again, a body bumps you and tumbles to the ground. An Eastern soldier lies dead and a black halfling stands grinning. Before you can thank him a blindsided tackle sends you back into the middle of the brawl. Turn to <u>235</u>.

354   "Curse you foul wizard" comes the hollow voice of a wraith! "This time I have brought a present for you."

A brass wand leaps to his hand and he chants. You recognize the wand. Westerners call the wand the *Curse of Edla*. Seeing death stare you in the face you realize that you have only one chance. You decide to:

(A) Run. Turn to <u>320</u>.

(B) Pick up Shefast knowing his chant works on lightening. Turn to <u>330</u>.

(C) Cast a *transmute* spell on the wraith? <u>Mark off 3 manna</u> and roll the dice.

   2 to 6, Turn to <u>368</u>.
   7 to 12, Turn to <u>320</u>.

355   With a wave of your hand the upper layer of the swamp is turned to stone. Scores of trolls are stuck fast in the solidifying muck. The trolls cluck and chatter, straining at their bonds. You carefully survey the situation until you are certain that none are loose. With your skill and a little luck you see that

(355 cont'd)

you have got them all. Calmly you walk across the hardened marsh towards the largest looking troll you can find. With one well-placed kick to the side of the creature's head the swamp goes silent.

"You worthless toads!" you shout up and down the marsh. "Do you realize who you dare to defy? It is I, Enchantraen."

Your words are followed by soft clucks.

"If I wish to take one of your prey from your hunting clans then you should offer two to me with gratitude."

You suddenly stoop low next to a protruding head. With your boot you push the head to the side. Your dagger flashes in your hand.

"I should leave the whole tribe sightless for this insult".

You stand again and slowly walk so that they all can see you.

"Perhaps it would be better to run a river of fire down this gulley and sear your worthless heads from their shoulders."

After a pause you give them your final decision.

"I choose to let you live this time so that you can tell others of your mistake. Remember *swamp frogs,* you live by the grace of Enchantraen."

You jump across to the other bank and walk towards the girl. Luckily she isn't caught. The trolls will become free later once your spell wears off. <u>Mark off JJ</u> and turn to <u>340</u>.

356

Mark off the next 2 days and replenish all manna and erase all damage.

Your spell takes effect just as you planned. You begin to feel safe when the Swamp Rogue's eyes swirl with an iridescent collage of colors. Sparks shoot down your spine and the worst of all possible things happens to a wizard; you go unconscious!

Unfortunately you don't know how long you were out when you finally come to. You wake up lying face down in the grass.

All your possessions are with you but you realize that you are manna-less. Mark off all your manna! Sitting up you can only guess what the Swamp Rogue used you for. Luckily your memory is wiped completely clean. Your bones ache as you stand to get your bearings. Jerican is someplace to the north of here, you guess. Catching your breath you decide there is little else to do now but to try and make it to the city. Turn to 333.

357   "The wizard is an enemy of this city," shouts the girl.

"Untie them," shouts the guard "let's get your story first wizard."

The guard pulls you to the side and starts to question you. Suddenly the guard who was untying the girl gives a low moan and turns around. Your view of the girl is blocked until the dying soldier falls to his knees. Then all you see is the vague image of a creature as it teleports away.

Another guard comes running to the guard who is questioning you.

"They were laytants, sir" the man gasps.

(357 cont'd)

"Bloodhounds of the East," the head guard whispers as he turns towards you. "You have been marked Enchantraen. Make your stay in our city brief. We do not want other citizens to be harmed while they track you down."

The soldiers then pick up their wounded comrade and move away. The crowd that had gathered clears away. You straighten your robe and collect your thoughts. The East obviously doesn't want you to succeed. It's no surprise that they would send some of their human bloodhounds to track you. Well, they know where you are now. But that doesn't mean they can stop you. Knowing there is nothing to do about it at the moment you turn to 253.

358   Do you:

(A) Cast a *telekinesis* spell and pull her out? Mark off 3 manna and turn to 304.

(B) Cast a *reverse* spell on yourself? Mark off 3 manna and the letters GG. Turn to 359.

(C) Cast a *see invisible objects* spell? Mark off 4 manna and turn to 326.

(D) Run away while you still can? Turn to 333.

(E) Walk over to the other side of the bridge? If there still is no sign of danger you will slide down the bank and pull the girl free. Turn to 336.

(F) Cast a *communications* spell on the girl so she can tell you what's going on? Mark off 4 manna and turn to 323.

359   The spell envelopes you nicely. There is no sign of trouble … yet! Turn to 358.

360   A strange quizzical look comes over the girl's face.

"Good grief, you are a pervert," she exclaims! "Guards! Help, help us from this pervert" she shouts and people start clearing the street.

Do you:

(A) Draw a dagger and threaten her. Turn to <u>278</u>.

(B) Become afraid of the danger, threaten her, and depart leaving her bound in the street? Turn to <u>249</u>.

361   "Boom!!" The spell works, knocking the glass out of the windows. For a moment the crowd is silenced.

Roll the dice:

2, 3, 5, 6, 7, Turn to <u>398</u>.
4, 8, 9, 10, 11, 12, Turn to <u>377</u>.

362   His tale continues until finally it comes near the end.

"You might wonder how I knew your name?" he questions. "I was crossing a rather nicely kept bridge when a rather crude voice called up from beneath it."

Mocking the guttural tones, Sluss says, "Is dat you Enchantraen."

"Well, looking over the edge all I see are trolls from bank to bank. Naturally I say yes!"

"Dat's alright then" replied the largest troll, "You'se can go by, wit me blessings."

"A little shaken by the experience I hurried along until I saw your fire. From the size of your book I guessed you must be the wizard."

(362 cont'd)

> You chuckle and the night goes on in similar fashion. After supper Sluss says goodbye and chases off after the fallen star. You lay out a bed roll and fall asleep. Turn to 316.

363   If R is marked turn immediately to 387.

If R is not marked but D is marked, turn to 253.

If neither R nor D is marked, turn to 211.

364   The bloodhound of the East is dying at your feet. Its claws and fangs are rendered harmless.

"Who sent you?" you ask the dying creature.

"Lord Gaoler" gasps the laytant. "You will die just as surely as you have killed me," says the laytant. "The Dark Lord himself will stop you if he must".

The laytant is quiet.

The Dark Lord would be too much even for you. Looking around you decide to disappear before the authorities arrive. No one can fault you for defending yourself against a laytant, but sitting in a jail for questioning will surely delay you. You realize that the East is out against you in full force. Gathering your thoughts you proceed to 253.

365   Walking up to the window you hear the purser begin to grumble.

"What's the matter? Can't you make up your mind? What do you want to exchange?" is the purser's greeting to you.

(Continued next page)

(365 cont'd)

Do you wish to exchange?

(A) A longship or roundship ticket for another? Turn to 412.

(B) A Perfidia ticket for another? Turn to 409.

366   After your first few steps you feel the marshland move beneath your feet. Well, you thought it was the marshlands until... Turn to 337.

367   Veering off from the bridge you angle back so that you can get a good look underneath the stone structure. The marsh is slowly bubbling just to the other side of the bridge. A badly decomposed body oozes up through the thick slime. You turn away from the ghastly sight when your eye catches a finely crafted gold necklace around its neck.

Do you:

(A) Leave and resume your trek towards the great city? Turn to 333.

(B) Investigate? Turn to 328.

368   The spell takes hold and the wraith screams. Erase the mark on A. The wand glows and the wraith struggles to aim. You dive out of the way! Turn to 320 and mark of KK.

369   Roll the dice:

2 to 7, Turn to 385.
8 to 10, Turn to 373.
11 or 12, Turn to 397.

370   The Eastern soldiers flee in instant panic taking half the inn's clientele with them.

"Who dares disturb Enchantraen of Nautpolis," you shout.

Looking around the room you see turning faces and timid smiles, until a figure steps out of the shadows. It's a Penoi, a fearless Eastern soldier that you have encountered around Fortress Ellendar. This nemesis always fights with magical weapons. You see them now. Strapped to the Penoi's side is a set of daggers. Wait, he's starting to throw one at you! You have just enough time to:

(A) Duck behind the flaming table! Turn to 407.

(B) Cast a *reverse* spell to try and turn the flying dagger back. Roll the dice:

   2 to 7, Turn to 429.
   8 to 12, Turn to 407.

371   Roll the dice:

2, 3, 5, 6, 7, Turn to 380.
4, 8, 9, 10, 11, 12, Turn 399.

372   You hear the shots ricochet around the room. Luckily they missed you but you have exposed yourself by lying on the ground. Roll the dice:

2 to 5, Turn to 235.
6 to 12, Turn to 389.

373   The boy is bound but your spell seems to become absorbed into the small silver belt buckle that the girl is wearing. Turn to 311.

374   Sluss remarks how unusually clear the trail was north of the Gouge.

(Continued next page)

(374 cont'd)

He hardly saw any Eastern soldiers the entire way. He fears they might have all pulled back further to the west for some foul reason. The conversation is good until after supper. Then Sluss excuses himself and chases off after the fallen star. You take out your bed roll and make ready for a good night's sleep. Turn to 316.

375   When you open the back door you see a stairway leading down. At the bottom of the stairs is a door with a tiny amount of light streaming out where it is cracked open. The light disappears when the door quietly shuts. Do you:

    (A) Continue down the stairs being very cautious? Turn to 408.

    (B) Cast a magical *lock* spell on the bottom door and stay in your room to eat rations? The *lock* spell won't last all night but it might allow you enough time to set up a proper defense. Mark off 2 manna and turn to 424.

    (C) Pause a few moments, turn invisible and carefully proceed down the stairs? Mark off 4 manna and turn to 396.

376   The figure turns and runs in a cold fright into the night. You hate nighttime visitors you think to yourself as the figure disappears.

The rest of the night is peaceful and quiet. Unrolling your bed sheet you are soon asleep. Turn to 315.

377   Something thuds against your back and sends you sprawling into the center barroom. Immediately the fighting starts up again. The local townsman that tackled you is getting his face smashed by an Eastern soldier while you ... Turn to 235.

378   The assassin has succumbed to your power and sinks helplessly to the floor. Going over to his body you search and find an important document. It reads:

(378 cont'd)

> *"The Western wizard Enchantraen is to be stopped at all costs. I contract your clan to assist me in this matter of great political consequence. Cost is of no importance. This paper gives you authority to use the laytants, soldiers of the Blessed Kingdom, and other people subject to my authority to accomplish this edict. All who read this paper are to give you any assistance within their power to expedite your mission. All who see this shall obey as if I were giving the orders directly.*
>
> > *Read and obey,*
> > *Lord General Gaoler*

Further searching reveals a pouch of 100 gold tams that you quickly add to your character sheet. You kill the unfortunate creature but leave its body on the steps as a warning for any others who might venture this way during your stay.

Do you:

(A) Continue on down to the door? Turn to <u>394</u>.

(B) Go back to your room for a hearty meal of rations? Turn to <u>381.</u>

379 The solid strike of your foot lifts the halfling off his feet and sends him flying into a crowd of people. Just then … Turn to <u>235</u>.

380 You're out and back into the area where you first entered. As you start to go up the stairs footsteps behind you cause you to turn around. An Eastern soldier is closing in on you. Turn to <u>222</u>.

381 The meal is simple but nourishing. Cleaning up the last of your crumbs you think over, once more, the day's business. It is important to make sure you have booked passage on a ship.

(Continued next page)

(381 cont'd)

If you decide to leave the tavern, go down the stairs and turn to <u>250</u>.

If not then you are ready to take the final precautions before going to bed. Turn to <u>424</u>.

382   Luckily the fighting has stopped and it sounds fairly peaceful at the bar. Going down the stairs you turn at the bottom and pass through the door that leads to the eating tables. When you enter the room you hear chairs scoot across the floor. Since the bar is slightly darker than the stairs you just left it takes your eyes a moment to adjust. In the back corner, by a door, is a table of Eastern soldiers. They are all standing looking at you. Several have their hands on the hilts of their sword.

Do you:

(A) Take a seat in another corner where you can face them? Turn to <u>410</u>.

(B) Go back up to your room where eating will be a little safer? Turn to <u>384</u>.

383   Oh Enchantraen! You didn't fall for that old magic sword trick did you? The blade adds to your offense just long enough to bury itself into your chest. Then dissolves!

Go to the Enchantraen table that follows and roll one die.

(383 cont'd)

Check off the damage boxes on your score card.

ENCHANTRAEN

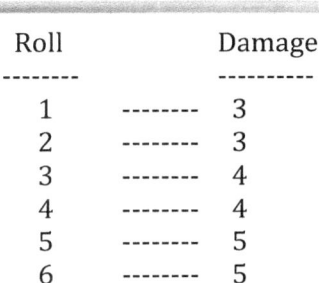

Roll		Damage
1	--------	3
2	--------	3
3	--------	4
4	--------	4
5	--------	5
6	--------	5

If you live you find that the halfling is gone. Turn to <u>235.</u>

If you expire turn to <u>200</u>.

384 In your room you lay out your simple meal. It's a shame to have to eat this way but sometimes a little prudent living can save you time and a mountain of wasted energy. When your meal is complete you must decide whether:

(A) You want to go to the wharf to book passage. You should do this before retiring for the evening. Leave the tavern by turning to <u>250.</u>

(B) If you have already booked passage a good night's sleep is certainly in order. Turn to <u>390</u>.

385 Success! At least temporarily. Both youngsters are bound in the shining light blue color of your magic.

(Continued next page)

(385 cont'd)

Do you:

(A) Slowly walk up to them and tell them that you could easily snuff out their short lives but instead you have chosen to be merciful. Merciful, that is, if they promise not to bother you for the rest of your stay. With that you turn and walk away leaving them sitting in the streets to think about it. Turn to <u>253</u>.

(B) Tell them to speak and spare no details about who they work for and what their intentions are? Turn to <u>360</u>.

386   Mark off O.

It's a shame it had to happen. Sometime later, perhaps when you are settling down to sleep, you will notice that your *Charmed Warning Stone* is gone. By the time you do notice it, it will be too late to try and find it. For now, mark through the magic item and consider it lost. Turn to <u>253</u> and continue play.

387   Doing your best to avoid any trouble you sneak through the front door. Quietly going up the stairs you are stopped dead in your tracks. Footsteps on the stairs behind you turns you around to find an Eastern soldier charging up the stairs after you. He must have been waiting in ambush. In response to the threat one spell comes clearly to mind. You can turn aetherial and walk away if you like. Do you:

(A) Attempt the spell? <u>Mark off 4 manna</u>. Roll the dice:

   2 to 11, Turn to <u>413</u>.
   12, Turn to <u>298</u> because your spell fails.

(B) Fight the soldier head on? Turn to <u>298</u>.

388   The Eastern soldier's scream is drowned in the turmoil from the bar. His body gushes down the stairs and dribbles off the last step. The sword drops partway down and lies there glimmering as though beckoning you. Do you:

(A) Go to retrieve it? Turn to 272.

(B) Retire into your room? Turn to 287.

389   A table leg cracks across your back.

Go to the Enchantraen table that follows and roll one die. Check off the damage boxes on your score card.

ENCHANTRAEN

Roll		Damage
1	--------	0
2	--------	1
3	--------	1
4	--------	2
5	--------	3
6	--------	4

If you are knocked out, turn to 300. If you are still awake stand up and get ready for the next round. Turn to 235.

390   The bed is comfortable enough. Before you close your eyes you make certain the door is locked and that your book is by your side. Your thoughts fade away into dreams about tomorrow's trip aboard the ship.

If Q is marked turn immediately to 448.

If Q is not marked, but E is marked, turn to 436.

If neither is marked, turn to 425.

391 Offended by your short jokes the halfling throws himself into melee against you.

He strikes out with his dagger.

Go to the Enchantraen table that follows and roll one die. Check off the damage boxes on your score card.

ENCHANTRAEN

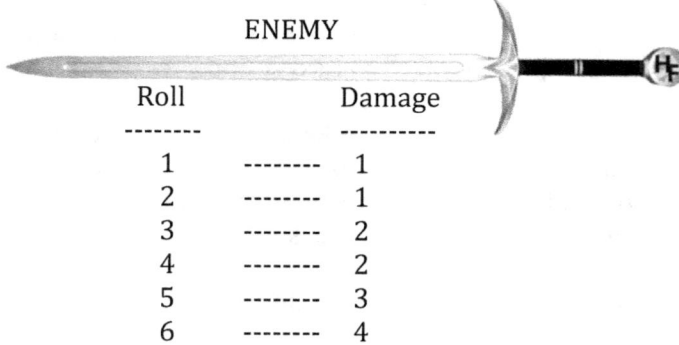

Roll		Damage
1	--------	1
2	--------	2
3	--------	3
4	--------	3
5	--------	4
6	--------	5

If you expire turn to <u>300</u>. If you are still up then swing back with your best weapon!

Go to the Enemy table that follows and roll one die. Check off the damage boxes on the Rogue's Gallery score card.

ENEMY

Roll		Damage
1	--------	1
2	--------	1
3	--------	2
4	--------	2
5	--------	3
6	--------	4

If he dies kick him out of the way and turn to <u>235</u>. If he lives watch out! Go back to the Enchantraen table as he swings again.

---

392   Unfortunately it's very late and the wharf is closed. There are guards lining the port and protecting ships. It is useless to try anything here. It would be better to go back to the tavern and get a good night's sleep. Traveling through town you see that everything has closed down. Soon you come to the tavern. Turn to <u>363</u>.

393   A series of loud bangs sends you spinning. Some drunken alchemist has decided to unload his guns into the crowd. He will have emptied his guns before you can stop him. Do you:

(A) Drop to the ground to try and avoid the shots? Turn to <u>372</u>.

(B) Try to duck out of the tavern? Turn to <u>371</u>.

(C) Cast an *ethereal* spell on yourself hoping the shots will give you enough time to complete your spell? <u>Mark off 4 manna</u>.

Roll the dice:

2 to 7, Turn to <u>251</u>.
8 to 12, Unfortunately your spell is interrupted by a shot.

Go to the Enchantraen table that follows and roll one die. Check off the damage boxes on your score card.

ENCHANTRAEN

Roll		Damage
1	--------	0
2	--------	1
3	--------	1
4	--------	2
5	--------	3
6	--------	4

(Continued next page)

(393 cont'd)

If you have checked off all your damage boxes turn to <u>300</u>. If not turn to <u>235</u>.

394   At the bottom of the stairs you listen. There must be a table near the door. It sounds like a group of Eastern soldiers talking.

"It won't be long now," one of them says. "I hope old lizard lips will remember us when he gives the wizard's head to Gaoler."

The responding laughter indicates that there must be at least 10 men outside the door. Do you:

(A) Go back to your room and set a trap? Turn to <u>424</u>.

(B) Try the old "I'm a demi god, don't mess with me," trick to get these creeps off your back so you can get a good night's sleep? It will cost you <u>4 manna</u> and is very risky. It's been known to backfire. Turn to <u>404.</u>

395   The heat of the flames quickly consumes the dry bones of the lich and the fire dies away. The air is left crisp and clean. You drop to the ground exhausted. It was a terrible chance you took but that will be one less minion of the Dark Lord to chase you. As you fall into helpless slumber you realize that once again in your splendid career you are successful! Turn to <u>218</u>.

396   All light bends around your form making you virtually invisible to the human eye. Quietly you proceed down the stairs. The door at the bottom opens and a figure enters the staircase. The door is quickly shut behind him. The serpentine head of the creature turns your way as its claw grabs the dagger from its mouth.

"It's a Black Assassin," you think.

(396 cont'd)

There can be no mistaking its intent. Calmly you assess your situation. Luckily it's not an Eastern bloodhound so it can't smell you out.

The staircase however is too narrow to allow it to pass by unnoticed. It's moving up the staircase toward you now. Do you:

(A) Attempt to put the creature asleep with a spell? <u>Mark off 2 manna</u> and roll the dice:

2 to 7, Turn to <u>378.</u>
8 to 12, Turn to <u>414</u>.

(B) Give the assassin a quick kick to the midriff before he notices you? Turn to <u>437</u>.

397 Your spell fails! The young boy runs but the girl stands her ground. Turn to <u>311</u>.

398 The crowd is thinning out now. Those who are able, pick themselves up and stagger to the bar. Others pick up what is left of their friends and drag them out. Dreg and the other tavern workers immediately go about setting tables and chairs upright. For now the fight is over. You decide to forget Dreg and go up into your room to clean up.

If <u>R</u> is marked turn to <u>276</u>.

If not read on…

Halfway up the stairs a set of footsteps turns you around. A drunken Eastern soldier is trying to follow you.

When you look at him, he puts his finger to his lips and says, "Shhh, I'm trying to be … to be shhneaky." Turn to <u>222</u>.

399   Before you can get away an Eastern soldier jumps from a table and tackles you.

Go to the Enchantraen table that follows and roll one die. Check off the damage boxes on your score card.

ENCHANTRAEN

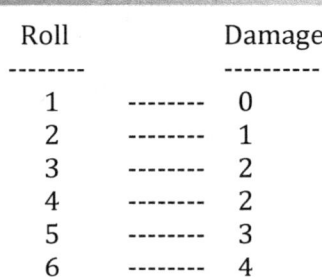

Roll		Damage
1	--------	0
2	--------	1
3	--------	2
4	--------	2
5	--------	3
6	--------	4

If you expire turn to <u>200</u>. If you live you may try to kick the soldier off you by using his own momentum to carry him into the crowd. Roll the dice:

2 to 8, Over the top of you he goes! Turn to <u>235</u>.
9 to 12, He falls on top of you! When he rolls off he takes a lopping swing at you with his sword.

Go to the Enchantraen table that follows and roll one die. Check off the damage boxes on your score card.

ENCHANTRAEN

Roll		Damage
1	--------	0
2	--------	0
3	--------	1
4	--------	1
5	--------	2
6	--------	3

(399 cont'd)

If you expire turn to <u>200.</u> If you live then hit him back in a hurry.

Go to the Enemy table that follows and roll one die. Check off the damage boxes on the Rogue's Gallery score card.

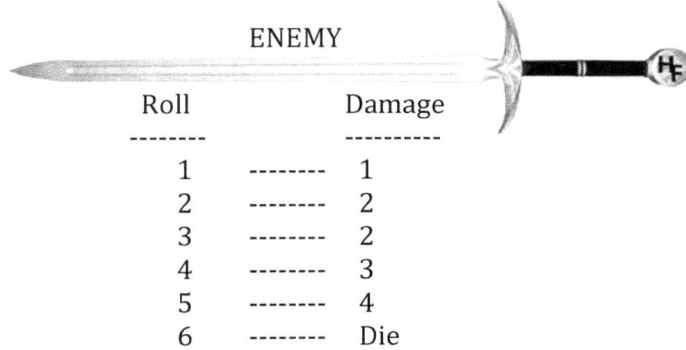

ENEMY

Roll		Damage
1	--------	1
2	--------	2
3	--------	2
4	--------	3
5	--------	4
6	--------	Die

If he expires turn to <u>235</u>. If not go back to the Enchantraen table and lookout! He's swinging at you again!

400 The assassin has ducked out the door. It sounds like there is a group of men moving tables and chairs. You prepare yourself for the worst but it doesn't happen. Whoever or whatever is on the other side of the door is probably prepared and waiting. Do you:

(A) Charge the door, kick it down, and confront the killer head on? Turn to <u>420</u>.

(B) Go back to your room to eat rations? There you might lay traps on the stairs and take the time to prepare a defense. Turn to <u>424</u>.

401   Swinging at the Black Assassin.

Go to the Enemy table that follows and roll one die. Check off the damage boxes on the Rogue's Gallery score card.

ENEMY

Roll		Damage
1	--------	0
2	--------	1
3	--------	1
4	--------	2
5	--------	3
6	--------	4

If he expires, turn to <u>378</u>.

If he lives he naturally swings back!

Go to the Enchantraen table that follows and roll one die. Check off the damage boxes on your score card.

ENCHANTRAEN

Roll		Damage
1	--------	0
2	--------	1
3	--------	1
4	--------	2
5	--------	3
6	--------	4

If you expire turn to <u>200</u>. If you still live return to the Enemy table and strike again.

402   You stand up and walk part way over to the table where the Eastern soldiers are sitting.

You shout, "Little one! I wish to sleep without worrying about the scurrying of rats. Leave this place while I still have patience with you."

The soldiers stand and go for their swords. Quickly you complete your spell and their table bursts into a blazing inferno. Roll the dice:

2 to 5, Turn to <u>370</u>.
6 to 12, Turn to <u>417</u>.

403   Do you:

(A) Leave to make passage on a ship? Go back downstairs and turn to <u>289</u>.

(B) Go to the bar to get a hot meal? You may go the quickest way by using the back stairs. Turn to <u>375</u>.

(C) Decide to stay in your room for the rest of the night and snack on your ration supply? Turn to <u>381</u>.

404   Concentrating on the incantation of your *fire* spell you feel its power grow. With your right hand held high the fire gathers painlessly around it. Brighter and hotter the fire grows. Soon the flames are so hot the walls begin to scorch and threaten to burst into a red hot lava on their own. Grabbing the dead assassin in your left hand you kick down the door. Throwing the assassin across the table of the surprised Eastern soldiers you follow up with the fireball. The table collapses and bursts to flame. Most of the Eastern soldiers scatter, screaming as their clothes burn.

(Continued next page)

(404 cont'd)

"Who would dare to send this street dog to disturb my slumber," you shout. Roll the dice:

2 to 8, Turn to <u>417</u>.
9 to 12, Turn to <u>370</u>.

405   "What seems to be the problem here" demands the guard.

"It's late," says the purser "and this wizard is threatening me. I have explained that I cannot refund the money because the Captain has already got it."

"Look good wizard," the head guard begins. "That is the law. If you want another ticket you're welcome to purchase one. If not, move along."

Do you:

(A) Purchase another ticket?

>   Cargo, the roundship ....   500 gold tams
>   Lady Varaë, the longboat ....   1000 gold tams

>   After purchasing your ticket you leave and go back into the streets. Turn to <u>250.</u>

(B) Magically attack the three closest to you by casting a *sleep* spell on them? Turn to <u>228.</u>

406   It is getting very late now and the shops have unfortunately closed. Disappointed you turn back to <u>250</u> and choose again.

407   Your precautions fail!

The air whines in pain as the dagger races through it. The dagger turns in midair as if it were being directed towards you. When it strikes you, you discover that it was made of thin glass.

(407 cont'd)

It smashes against your coin purse and spreads a thin film of liquid over it. Then the pain begins. The liquid causes the gold tams you carry to become magically charged by the aether.

Go to the Enchantraen table that follows and roll one die. Check off the damage boxes on your score card.

ENCHANTRAEN

Roll		Damage
1	--------	1
2	--------	1
3	--------	3
4	--------	4
5	--------	5
6	--------	Expire

If you live the reaction stops. Turn to 419. If you expire turn to 200.

408   The door swings open and a dagger flies your way. A Black Assassin from the serpentine clan is bounding up the stairs after you. Roll to see if the dagger strikes you.

2 to 6, The dagger misses! Choose A or B that following.
7 to 12, The dagger hits!

Go to the Enchantraen table that follows and roll one die.

(Continued next page)

(408 cont'd)

Check off the damage boxes on your score card

ENCHANTRAEN

Roll		Damage
1	--------	1
2	--------	2
3	--------	3
4	--------	4
5	--------	5
6	--------	Expire

If you expire turn to <u>200</u>. If you live you have just enough time to:

(A) Try to put the assassin to sleep with a spell. <u>Mark off 2 manna</u>. Roll the dice:

    2 to 7, Turn to <u>378</u>.
    8 to 12, Turn to <u>401</u>.

(B) Stand and fight! Turn to <u>401</u>.

409 "Hey, what is your name? It wouldn't happen to be Enchantraen would it? Look, that ship is sailing upon your special request. If you want to change your mind now I'm afraid I can't refund your money. The Captain of the ship already has it." Do you:

(A) Keep your ticket and leave heading back to the street? Turn to <u>250</u>.

(409 cont'd)

(B) Purchase another ticket?

Cargo, ... 500 gold tams
Lady Varaë, ... 1000 gold tams

Check the boat you choose and leave by returning to the street. Turn to <u>250</u>.

(C) Threaten the clerk with violence? Turn to <u>418</u>.

410   Your obviously calm reaction seems to take effect on the soldiers. They too sit down and resume eating. You can tell by the quick glances and low mumbles that they are talking about you. All Easterners are your enemy but here in Jerican those hatreds are supposed to be left behind. If you met these soldiers anywhere else there would be an instant fight. They seem to be going along with the rules so why can't you. Dreg the innkeeper comes with your order. After eating you find that nothing has changed. The Eastern soldiers are still talking and the room is relatively peaceful. There is a soldier arguing with another man at the bar, but for now it seems to be purely a philosophical argument.

Do you:

(A) Leave now and go back to your room? Roll the dice:

2 to 7, Turn to <u>390</u>.
8 to 12, Turn to <u>427</u>.

(B) See a reason why you should break the uneasy truce with the soldiers and attempt to clear them out of the bar? Turn to <u>433</u>.

(C) Leave the bar to go out and book passage for a ship if you haven't already? Turn to <u>289.</u>

411   As the halfling comes in to finish you off he begins to laugh. "You're tough for a Westerner *book-looker*. Here, drink this and remember not to mess with those bigger than you."

You realize that your life is leaving you. With little choice left you drink. The halfling rises and walks out of the bar. Erase all the damage you have taken. You are instantly healed. Unfortunately you pass out. Turn to <u>300</u>.

412   "No problem," says the purser. Do you want:

(A) The Cago, a roundship for 500 gold tams?

(B) The longship, Lady Varaë for 1000 gold tams?

(C) The Perfidia can still be commissioned for 750 gold tams?

After deciding, make the proper correction to your gold and check the correct ship you are taking on your character sheet. Leave now and turn to <u>250</u>.

413   Your form becomes light and airy.

"Stay your ground child of demons," you say to the soldier. "You cannot harm me now."

The soldier smiles and draws a brightly gleaming blade.

"Magic" you whisper to yourself.

Knowing that the blade can hurt you do you:

(A) Avoid the fight possibly by walking through the wall? Turn to <u>288</u>.

(B) Change back and try to fight. Turn <u>298</u>.

414   Your spell fails and the assassin unwittingly walks toward you. He is too close to walk away from. You are now forced to try and kick him away.

Roll the dice:

2 to 7, 11, Turn to 421.
8, 9, 10, 12, You kick but discover that you are too close to the assassin to strike him with sufficient force. The assassin instinctively grabs and catches your leg. Now you must fight the creature hand-to-hand. Turn to 401.

415   Over your shoulder you see a flash of blue light. What! The creep just tried to bind you. Turning around you try and face him straight on. Instead, he averts his eyes upward and whistles as if nothing happened.

Do you:

(A) Turn back around and wait? Turn to 423.

(B) Leave the line after threatening him and decide not to wait any longer? Mark off 4 manna to cast a *passage* spell to gain entry. Turn to 252.

(C) Leave and come back later? Turn to 250.

(D) Attack the wizard with a *paralysis* spell? Mark off 2 manna. Turn to 445.

416   Mark off Q,

You open the door and magically set the symbol. Your fingers trace the pattern over and over until the aether materializes and sticks fast to the door. Closing the door, you slide the dresser in front of it. Turn to 390.

417 The Eastern soldiers who can still stand scatter out of the room in utter panic. Many of the inn's guests do the same. Dreg, the innkeeper comes running in with blankets to put out the fire.

"Really Enchantraen," he says between laboring breaths, "the smell drives away the customers."

Laughing to yourself you take a seat. Dreg brings you a free drink and anything else you want. For the rest of the night you will have a trouble-free sleep. Finishing your business you go over the day's events to make sure you haven't forgotten anything. Most important of all is to make sure you have made arrangements for a boat to give you passage towards what Westerners call the Mystic Isles. Do you:

(A) Leave the tavern and hit the streets? Turn to 250.

(B) Call it a night and go up to your room? Turn to 390.

418 "Help, this creep is trying to rob me," shouts the purser!

Before you can do much else turn to 278 and mark off I.

419 The Penoi leaps across the burning table and you find yourself locked in a death struggle.

Go to the Enemy table that follows and roll one die. Check off the damage boxes on the Rogue's Gallery score card.

ENEMY

Roll		Damage
1	--------	1
2	--------	2
3	--------	2
4	--------	3
5	--------	4
6	--------	Die

(419 cont'd)

If the Penoi expires turn to <u>417</u>. If he lives duck because here it comes.

Go to the Enchantraen table that follows and roll one die. Check off the damage boxes on your score card.

ENCHANTRAEN

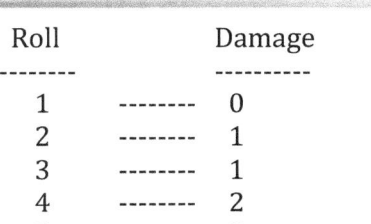

Roll		Damage
1	--------	0
2	--------	1
3	--------	1
4	--------	2
5	--------	3
6	--------	4

If you live get up and hit him by returning to the Enemy table. If you expire turn to <u>200</u>.

420   Good grief Enchantraen! You must be either brave or crazy.

The door flies open and you find the bar has mostly cleared out. What you thought to be adversaries preparing for battle ended up being scared men clearing out.

Dreg, the innkeeper, comes up and says, "Calm down Enchantraen. You cleared all the Eastern scum out. For that, great one, I owe you at least one free meal. Please have a seat."

With that Dreg scurries away to prepare your meal.

<u>Mark off Q.</u> After a wonderful meal you go back to your room. Turn to <u>276</u>.

421   The kick lands solid into the creature's midriff. Down the stairs he tumbles, striking his head solidly against the closed door. The creature starts to stand but ... Turn to <u>378</u>.

422   Determination grips your face as you swing at the leering serpent of death.

Go to the Enemy table that follows and roll one die. Check off the damage boxes on the Rogue's Gallery score card.

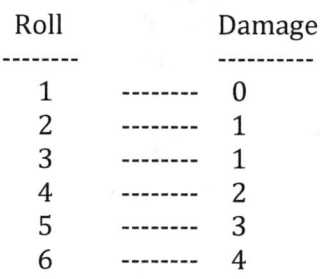

ENEMY

Roll	Damage
1	0
2	1
3	1
4	2
5	3
6	4

If he expires turn to <u>455</u>. If he lives he attacks.

Go to the Enchantraen table that follows and roll one die. Check off the damage boxes on your score card.

ENCHANTRAEN

Roll	Damage
1	0
2	1
3	1
4	2
5	3
6	4

(422 cont'd)

If you expire turn to 430. If you live return to the Enemy table and swing harder!

423   Soon the time passes and it becomes your turn. A little woman comes to wait on you. She is the owner of the shop and you have known her for a long time. You remember when she was begging for magical items from adventurers on the street corners. Her name is Eletrianipolical. For obvious reasons you call her El.

"Today El, I would like to see some of your very best merchandise. I'm taking a rather important voyage and I will need something a little special," you say. "I only have time to inspect two pieces so make them special if you would."

"For you good wizard my shop is an open showcase," she begins.

"What will it be today? Would you like to see something in the realm of:

(A) Nautical magic? Turn to 244.

(B) Healing magic? Turn to 269.

(C) Combat magic? Turn to 273.

424   Mark off E if you haven't already.

Back in your room you find a large dresser that will easily slide in front of the door. Before you do this you must decide whether you want to place a fear symbol on the staircase. This will cost 4 manna points if you are willing to expend it.

If you wish to set the fear symbol mark off 4 manna and turn to 416.

(Continued next page)

(424 cont'd)

If you do not wish to set the fear symbol simply slide the large dresser over. This should give you enough time to react if someone tries to intrude through that door.

You should have booked passage on a ship. If you haven't, leave the inn through the front door and turn to <u>250</u>. If you have finished for the day turn to <u>390</u>.

425   The creaking of a door awakens you. You look at the front door and see that it is still closed. The sound of a padded footfall helps you to zero in on the sound someplace behind you. Up and out of bed you now see a back door that is slightly ajar. Wasn't that a closet door? You start a spell but not before ... Turn to <u>426</u>.

426   A vial smashes against the floor. Suddenly the room is charged with a low-burning blue light. When you prepare for a magical attack you discover that your power is gone. With a fearful realization you discover that the blue light is actually burning aether. The room is being exhausted of the energy from which you draw your magic. Do you...

(A) Dive behind a chair to take cover? Turn to <u>443</u>.

(B) Charge the assassin for a hand-to-hand confrontation? Turn to <u>422</u>.

427   As you start to walk out of the bar the argument you overheard turns into an outright fist fight. Punches are thrown and men go running to assist whatever side they are for.

"Not again," you say as you turn away trying to leave. Turn to <u>399</u>.

428   The guards who capture you take you down several main streets. You feel embarrassed to be tied and paraded through the streets like a common criminal. You are, after all, Enchantraen the War Wizard. The guards take you to another set of guards. They are going to turn you over to the new guards who will then take you to be judged. Quietly you wait calculating your chances. Then the opportunity for escape comes if you wish to take it. The guards unbind you so that the new guards may secure you with their own chains. It's during this brief pause of freedom that you may decide to act.

Do you:

(A) Turn invisible? It will <u>cost 4 manna</u>. Roll the dice:

   2 to 11, Turn to <u>439</u>.
   12, Your spell fails. Turn to <u>442</u>.

(B) Allow yourself to be taken before the judges confident that your reputation will save you? Turn to <u>442</u>.

429   The dagger curves in a dramatic arc. When it strikes the shield of your spell it rebounds back with equal force striking the Penoi. The dagger's effects are minimal if any because … Turn to <u>419</u>.

430   The assassin slays you in the name of Lord Goaler and the Blessed Kingdom. He honestly slays you out of his hatred for all mankind.

"Death to you Round Eyes," screams the assassin as he lays you low with the death stroke.

So ends the bright career of Enchantraen of Nautpolis; destroyed in the dark room of a small tavern, shielded from the eyes of those who would help.

If you wish to play further you must return to the start and begin again.

431   It is short work for five Black Assassins to bring you down.
They bind your hands and toss you on the bed. All doors are
securely locked and all the furniture is piled up in front of
them. The assassins as a group could easily kill you now, but
they are not without their code of ethics.

You lay quietly as one of them explains their gruesome plan for
you. An exhaust aether vile is exploded in the room so that all
magic will be impossible. You are to fight all five assassins one
at a time. At the end of a fight remember to leave all the
damage you have accumulated on your character sheet. If you
beat all five, turn to 453. If you expire, which is very likely,
turn to 430.

You strike the assassin, praying it will be a solid hit.

Go to the Enemy table that follows and roll one die. Check off
the damage boxes on the Rogue's Gallery score card.

ENEMY

Roll		Damage
1	--------	0
2	--------	1
3	--------	1
4	--------	2
5	--------	3
6	--------	Die

If he expires begin again until you have killed five of them.

(431 cont'd)

Go to the Enchantraen table that follows and roll one die. Check off the damage boxes on your score card.

ENCHANTRAEN

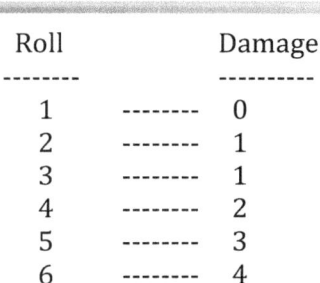

Roll		Damage
1	--------	0
2	--------	1
3	--------	1
4	--------	2
5	--------	3
6	--------	4

If you live return to the Enemy table and roll again. You must beat all five!

432   A searing mind-probe touches you so forcefully that there can be no mistaking its presence.

"It's useless to lie to us Enchantraen. We can tell such simple falsehoods as this." Turn to 473.

433   The quickest way to clear them out is to confront them directly. Pondering your alternatives you come up with an idea that will cost you 4 manna points. The simple illusion of a burning table should do the trick.

(A) If you want to continue mark off 4 manna points turn to 402.

(B) If you decide to go to your room instead turn to 390.

(C) If you decide now to leave the bar altogether turn to 250.

434   The purser and two remaining guards yell for help. The rest of the wharf guards come running to the rescue. Soon you will be too out-numbered to fight. Turning for the safety of the street you disappear into the winding alleyways. Turn to <u>250</u>.

435

<u>Mark off the next day and replenish all manna and erase all damage.</u>

By foot, the lands of Fortress Ellendar will be about 2 days away. In the early years you fought along with Tancred, the Western commander, to regain his fortress from Lord Gaoler. Since then the struggle over that land has been constant. The Dark Lord Gaoler needs it to house his troops and feed them off the rich farmlands surrounding it. Outside of Nautpolis, Tancred seems to be the last Western general capable of an outright confrontation with the Dark Lord. Tancred, he is clever. He always has been. As you walk along you find yourself wishing that you had stayed in touch. He could be a great help to you now if he still holds his homelands.

It's noon now and the sun is at its zenith. The sun's rays burn at the odd rainbow causing it to become brighter. When you sit to prepare your lunch you notice the weird effect the rainbow has on the plants. It seems like the plants are growing right before your eyes. Before you can go to examine them you feel a burning sensation at your side. Your magical items are red hot! You cast them to the side and watch them sparkle with flecks of energy. Then it strikes you. It feels as though your body pulses with power. The stark realization of your incredible abilities floods over you. You can't contain your joy any further.

You turn towards the West and shout, "It is I, Enchantraen who will answer the Challenge. I am coming to take my proper place on the Mystic Isles. Beware all who might stand in my path!"

(435 cont'd)

Your voice seems to echo across the land and carry for a long, long way. Picking up your things you again take off down the road with a new spring in your walk. A small flock of crows leave their resting place in the trees and race on ahead. The world seems to be yours for the taking. Turn to 457.

436 A thud against the back door gets you up and out of bed. A second thud and you see the door and chest slide open. It's dark and you are having trouble focusing. Something obviously is trying to come in. Since you can't see your target you decide to:

(A) Cast a *stone wall* spell to seal off the back stairs. Mark off 3 manna and roll the dice:

2 to 8, Turn to 451.
9 to 12, Turn to 426 and your spell fails.

(B) Wait for a better target. Turn to 426.

437 With a mighty shove the assassin is caught off guard and rolls down the staircase. Striking the bottom closed door the assassin rebounds quickly to his feet. He sniffs the air in a confused manner. Realizing his obvious disadvantage he wildly tosses the dagger up the stairs, opens the door, and runs out into the bar.

Roll to see if the dagger hits!

2 to 4, It hits!
5 to 12, It misses! Turn to 400.

Go to the Enchantraen table that follows and roll one die.

(Continued next page)

(437 cont'd)

Check of the damage boxes.

ENCHANTRAEN

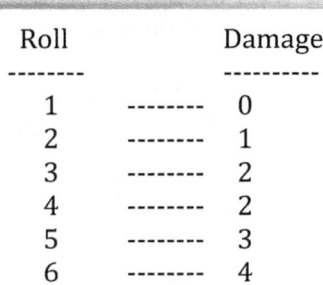

Roll		Damage
1	--------	0
2	--------	1
3	--------	2
4	--------	2
5	--------	3
6	--------	4

If you expire turn to <u>200</u>.

If you live turn to <u>400</u>.

438   If <u>K</u> is marked turn to <u>460</u>.

If <u>C</u> is marked turn to <u>1002</u>.

If <u>G</u> is marked turn to <u>464</u>.

If none of the above are marked turn to <u>478</u>.

439   You sense the light bend around your form as you turn invisible.

"The wizard's gone," shout the guards. Immediately the guards start testing to see if it was an *invisible* spell or a *return* spell that caused you to vanish. Moving out of the way you know you must react while you still have the advantage.

(439 cont'd)

Do you:

(A) Start an *illusion* spell? <u>It will cost another 4 manna</u>. Roll the dice:

   2 to 11, Turn to <u>475</u>.
   12, Run because your spell failed. Turn to <u>458</u>.

(B) Run? Turn to <u>458</u>.

440 If <u>B</u> is marked turn again to <u>406</u>.

Upon revisiting the shop you find no change in the length of the line. It has been some time now. You do notice however that some of the same people are standing in line for a second run through. Do you:

(A) Wait in line? Turn to <u>232</u>.

(B) Leave again? Turn to <u>250</u>.

(C) Use a *passage* spell to make a flamboyant but nonviolent entrance? <u>Mark off 4 manna</u> and turn to <u>252</u>.

441 The lightning leaps to your call and vaporizes the leading rider. Unfortunately there are 39 to go. Granted, some of the horses bolt and run but the majority are too close to stop now. You continue to blast away as best you can.

Many fall but there are always more soldiers to finish. Eastern soldiers can be brave.

The steadily plummeting lightning pinpoints your location and enemy reinforcements soon begin to arrive.

The last thing you remember is being pinned to the ground with a lance at your throat. Slipping away into unconsciousness ... Turn to <u>469</u>.

442   The new guards bind you firmly. Quietly one of them apologizes for having to do this to you but it's just their job. They bring you in front of an ivory colored building and take you to a small waiting room. One of the guards goes in to announce the arrival of a new prisoner. The guard returns with a surprised look on his face. The judges wish to see the prisoner immediately. Apparently the judges realize who you are which accounts for this speedy trial.

You are taken into a room and placed at a table before the judges. The guards come forward to announce your crimes.

If <u>F</u> is marked turn to <u>467</u>.

If not, turn to <u>438</u>.

443   The assassin throws his dagger. It whips towards you with deadly accuracy.

Roll the dice:

Go to the Enchantraen table that follows and roll one die.

2 to 5, Mark damage boxes on your score card. Read the next paragraph if you live, or turn to <u>430</u> if you expire.

ENCHANTRAEN

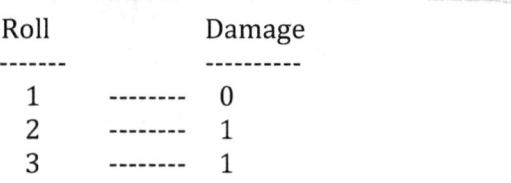

Roll		Damage
1	--------	0
2	--------	1
3	--------	1
4	--------	2
5	--------	2
6	--------	3

(443 cont'd)

7 to 12, It barely misses you!

Now it's your turn to throw a dagger.

Roll the dice:

2 to 7, You hit!

Go to the Enemy table that follows and roll. Check off the damage boxes.

ENEMY

Roll	Damage
1	1
2	1
3	2
4	2
5	3
6	4

If the assassin expires turn to 455. If he lives turn to 422.

8 to 12, You miss! Turn to 422.

444 The air is suddenly sucked out of the cocoon. Your nose and ears burst and bleed. As the cocoon contracts you are no longer able to struggle. You feel the first bone snap as you slip into unconsciousness. Turn to 200.

445 The spell takes effect and the wizard falls to the ground choking. You did the spell so quickly and subtly that few noticed. Those who did notice aren't telling. A cry comes out for the city guards. They pick the man up and take him off to be healed. The guards question but no one gives them any clues to the man's problems. After they leave you smile, turn back around and wait in line. Turn to 423.

446 You have committed yourself now. There is no stopping or the Dendri will surely turn on you. You decide to plummet straight on and sink your claws into the demon's back. With a loud scream you strike.

Since you are a very large eagle striking from the rear there is a chance you can kill instantly.

Roll the dice:

2 to 5, Turn to 465.
6 to 12, Turn to 495.

447 Your hunch was wrong. They are not following you using an invisible scout. How then? You haven't felt a sensitive probing for you. You know of no magic that can seek you out yet it is always possible that something like that exists.

Disappointed you mount up and ride out. Turn to 498.

448 A stumble on the backstairs causes you to sit upright in bed. A hissing scream and another stumble gets you out of your bed with book in hand. Listening, you hear footsteps receding down the stairs. Moving the dresser you carefully open the door. Beginning the first few words of your spell you will be ready if there is any trouble. You swing the door wide just in time to see five black assassins fleeing in utter panic. It's hard to tell what would actually scare those gruesome creatures into a panic, but you are thankful for your magic none the less. Laughing, you close the door and bed down once more.

The rest of the night is quiet and restful. When morning comes you are ready to go and catch your ship. Turn to 450.

449 As the soldiers charge down on you, you calmly assess the situation. They have no bows. That is good. It doesn't look like they have any substantial magic either. Good, a *reverse* spell won't be necessary. First you should stop their orderly charge. A *wall* spell would do it but that would block your view

(449 cont'd)

of them. Ah, just the thing. A tremor to split the earth. <u>Mark off 4 manna</u> and roll the dice:

2 to 11, Turn to <u>479</u>.
12, Turn to <u>470</u>.

450

<u>Mark off the next day and replenish all manna and erase all damage.</u>

In the morning you catch an early breakfast in the dining hall. Thanking Dreg you leave to make sure you have plenty of time to catch your ship. When you open the door you catch a glimpse of dazzling lights. In a blink they are gone. The whole city looked spotted with bright colors of green, blue and yellow. You ask Dreg if he saw it but he says no.

There is little time to contemplate so you rush on down the streets until you get to the wharf. You check your ticket and board your ship. With all your equipment on board you check the ship over as the last minute preparations are made.

The ship slips out of its dock and into a large lake. The lake is lined with storefronts and houses built on long poles driven into the ground. In front of the buildings are small levees built to hold back the occasional flood waters. The early morning lights from lanterns and torches reflect off the waters producing quiet romantic effects. This is the side of the city you have never really experienced. It seems that your quest for the betterment of your people has left you very little time for some of the simpler pleasures in life. There was someone once but that was so long ago.

(Continued next page)

(450 cont'd)

The ship heads out of the harbor and you watch the giant protective chain lower at the harbor gate. From the mouth of two great stone dragons the chain lowers and you ease on out into the mighty river Tress.

The ship slowly passes the city's outer walls.

Wait! You can't believe it. There is an army encamped outside the city. The camp is surrounded by blazing torches but there can be no mistaking the insignia on the banners. It's the Dark Lord Moribund's troops.

You duck below the ships railing as if the troops might see you. What is Moribund doing this far north? He is usually stationed down around Moorguard. Peering over the railing, you finally take in the whole picture. The Eastern army is surrounded by a larger force. It looks like the free standing army of Jerican is holding Moribund's troops in check.

What is going on? You decide to spend the rest of the day in cover out of the sight of men. Going to your berth you spend the rest of the day reading. You don't need that kind of trouble yet. The fewer people who know who you are, even among the ship's crew, the better.

Except for when your meals are served you have no contact with the crew.

If you are aboard the:

(A) Cargo, Turn to <u>703</u>.

(B) Perfidia, Turn to <u>706</u>.

(C) Lady Varaë, Turn to <u>709</u>.

451   The wall solidifies and a creature screams, trapped inside.
Thumps and bangs resound against the wall but it holds firm.
A hiss of disgust can be heard followed by a set of descending
footsteps. The assailants have failed. They won't dare make
another attempt on your life tonight.

Breathing a sigh of relief you uneasily sit down. You can take
care of any unwanted bodies in the morning when it will be
safer. All is quiet and soon you fall back into an easy slumber.
Turn to 450.

452

Mark off the next day and replenish all manna and erase all
damage.

In the early morning you are awakened by a strange panorama
of lights. The early sun striking the rainbow causes the light to
become refracted. The world is covered in dancing sparkles of
greens, blues, and yellows.

"It's beautiful," you whisper.

Then you notice that the only red light that you can see is
shining… on you!

The panorama fades and turns back into sunlight. Quietly you
prepare your breakfast. Soon the morning phenomenon is lost
to more pressing matters. Do you continue on heedless of the
death threats, or turn and go another way? If you go on
perhaps you can hide so that they cannot follow you. Maybe
you could disguise yourself? Turning back would mean less
bloodshed for sure but the lost time could easily doom your
chances of success.

(Continued next page)

(452 cont'd)

Running out of time you decide to:

(A) Head on towards Fortress Ellendar? Turn to <u>471</u>.

(B) Turn back towards Jerican. Turn to <u>494</u>.

453   Impossible! You truly are great! Collect 1000 gold tams from the bodies. Praise be to Enchantraen the greatest of all wizards. Take my undying admiration and rest now. You return to bed knowing that you can get rid of the bodies in the morning when it will be safer. After what you just went through though there is not much left to be afraid of. Turn to <u>450</u>.

454   "You dare to disturb me while I rest," you shout. "Begone from here before you anger me."

Some troops turn to leave but one brave soldier comes forward.

"There is death behind you fools if you turn back. We have all seen the wizard. We must stop the wizard's progress at all costs," shouts the soldier.

He then blows on his horn, and charges around the end of the chasm. Five men rally around him. Another horn blasts and you realize that more troops are on their way. Turning you see another unit closing in. Do you:

(A) Use what little time you have left to change shape and fly out of here? <u>Mark off 4 manna</u> and roll the dice:

    2 to 11, Turn to <u>466</u>.
    12, Turn to <u>470</u>.

(452 cont'd)

(B) Pull your dagger and fight? Turn to <u>492</u>.

(C) Start blasting with Shefast? Turn to <u>496</u>.

455   The assassin dies at your feet but not before it lets out one loud death cry. A set of pounding footsteps can be heard coming up the now obvious back stairs. It's a group of assassins to take over where their comrade failed. Wait, the burning aether has stopped. Your magic returns! Do you:

(A) Close the back entrance with a stone *wall* spell? <u>This will cost 3 manna</u>. Turn to <u>451</u>.

(B) Stand and fight the impossible odds because you are out of manna, or just plain daring. Turn to <u>431</u>.

456   The Dendri turns and shouts across the void of blackness, "Enchantraen did you think to escape us up here. You were warned and you disobeyed."

A whip lashes out and strikes you.

Roll the dice:

2 to 5, Turn to <u>476</u>.
6 to 12, Turn to <u>502.</u>

457   By the end of the day you find a suitable place to make camp. Being only one full day's walk from Arcania you doubt that there will be much trouble. Still, you take some precautions for safety. Sitting in front of a low burning fire you think over what happened at noon today. The surge of uncontrollable power seemed to last for only a short time. If you could only retain that feeling all day long.

A low drumming sound cuts your thoughts short. Placing your ear to the ground you recognize the sound of horsemen riding

(Continued next page)

(457 cont'd)

full speed towards you. You are on your feet with book in hand. Peering through the night shadows you can trace a black figure on a jet black horse. The rider pulls his horse up just short and you are unable to get a good look at him.

"Are you Enchantraen?" comes a hollow voice.

All you can see is a large horse with a man in black riding it. It looks as though the man has a large sword and pouch strapped to his side.

"Who asks?" is your only reply.

"I am a messenger from the High Lord General's army."

"Which Dark Lord," you reply.

The man hisses at your degrading reference to his master.

"The Lord Gaoler, General to the Master, Keeper of the Blessed Kingdom and conqueror of the lands you now stand upon."

"Who?" you ask,

"You are Enchantraen" hisses the messenger. "I have traveled a long way to find you."

"At your service," you say bowing, knowing that you can no longer disguise your identity.

"The High Lord General wishes me to tell you this. He watches your every move. The roads from here to Wellsport are guarded by the full army of Lord Gaoler. All Western wizards, especially you, will be stopped. The Master himself has issued these orders."

He then unwraps a small parchment.

(457 cont'd)

> "*Be it known to all that Lord Gaoler has fallen into disfavor with the Blessed Kingdom. To redeem himself he must stop the trek of Western wizards to the Mystic Isles. The one named Enchantraen is to be stopped above all others. All who hear this proclamation are bound to assist in any way. Hear and obey.* So says my Master."

"Lord Gaoler says this. If you continue this way you will mar the country you love best. All who pass you by will be slain unless they stop you. He bid me to tell you that he will stop you himself if that is what it takes to regain favor with my Master. As proof of his word he sends this."

The messenger unbinds the sack at his side, reaches in and tosses an object your way. It is the bloody hat of Almon, your neighbor.

"The words of my Master even apply to me. You see Enchantraen now that I have met you I must stop you or I will die just like your friend."

In the flash of an eye the man readies a long spear and kicks his horse into a charge, but not before you react. Do you:

(A) Cast a *transmute* spell that will turn him into solid stone? <u>Mark off 2 manna</u> and roll the dice:

2 to 7, Turn to <u>483</u>.
8 to 12, Turn to <u>461</u> because your spell failed.

(B) Dive to the side and attempt to strike with a weapon? Turn to <u>477</u>.

458   After your first few steps your invisibility fades away. The guards must have negated it somehow. Five guards are in hot pursuit. Turn to <u>241</u>.

459   A light blue light leaps from the crowd binding you tightly. You hear an old man's voice laughing.

The Captain of the guards comes forward and says, "Thank you but we don't need any help."

You catch a glimpse of a lich (ancient wizard) disappearing into the crowd. Turn to <u>262</u>.

460   "The wizard has *killed* in his attempt to escape us," says the guard.

The judges all look shocked. They converse among each other until the third judge speaks.

"It is customary in our land to bind you in servitude to the survivors of the man you killed. In that way you can best help those you have affected. Yours is a different case. As long as you remain in our city more lives are in danger. We have received reports that yet another Eastern army has mobilized and is heading this way. We want you out of Jerican. Give your word Enchantraen that if you live through this quest you will return to make proper payment."

You of course agree.

As you turn to leave one of the judges says, "Have a fair journey Great One. For the sake of your Western allies hurry. I fear the *Challengings* will be over soon."

Out the door and back in the streets you check the sky for the rainbow's presence and turn to <u>250</u>.

461   The man in black rides on past you and turns his steed with amazing agility.

Standing up in his stirrups he screams, "You or I wizard" and tosses his spear.

(461 cont'd)

You move to fend off the strike. Instinctively your hand rises to knock away the spear. Surprisingly the spear strikes but does no damage. Instead the shaft begins to bend and elongate as it wraps around you. Before you can scream you find yourself suffocating in a cocoon. You are losing consciousness. Mechanically you start to recite the words to the *fire* spell. You discover that you can move your hands just enough to complete the spell. It will cost you one manna to complete it. Do you:

(A) Continue the spell? <u>Mark off one manna</u> and roll the dice:

    2 to 10, Turn to <u>497</u>.
    11 or 12, Turn to <u>444</u> and your spell fails.

(B) Struggle physically with your constricting cell? Turn to <u>485</u>.

462   The spell works! Back into the air you leap. Perhaps you can make it all the way to the fortress with this spell. The fog is thick but you climb until it begins to thin out.

No! It's still here. The fear starts to come over you once more. Turn to <u>474</u>.

463   The man goes down and the impact leaves him senseless.

"More," you yell lifting your bloody dagger.

The rest back off until they feel safe enough to turn and run.

Watching them run you quickly mount up. There will be others you guess but at least they will approach you now with respect. Turn to <u>480</u>.

464   A guard steps forward and says, "At one time during an attempt to capture the wizard the Great One held our men powerless. It was in the wizard's best interest to kill the guards to cover the trail. Instead the wizard drug the guards out of harm's way."

"This is the Enchantraen we all know," begins the judge. "For this we will give you a valuable piece of information. Do not take the Perfidia out of here. We have reason to believe it is an Eastern ship rigged to gather unsuspecting Western wizards and carry them to their doom." Now turn to <u>478</u>.

465   <u>Erase the mark on S.</u>

The Dendri screams. Suddenly you are surrounded by a burst of flames. You pass through but your feathers are smoldering. The fog wets them down but they seem to burn from an unnatural flame. Your spell will soon end!

You would have preferred to set down in a better location but down you go through the fog. The closer to the ground the thicker it becomes. It soon becomes evident that you cannot continue in this form. You land and transform back.

Your arms feel like lead weights as you care for your burned skin. Turn to <u>482</u>.

466   <u>Mark off S.</u>

First you adjust the straps on your pack. Next you slip quickly from your robe. Holding your hand upright you finish your spell. There is a pause while you watch the charging Eastern soldiers begin to lower their lances.

The transformation begins. Your skin tingles as the feathers first appear. Spreading your wings you know that you were successful. Picking up the remaining gear in your claw you leap into the air. The air is accelerating as it rushes past your gigantic wings. You have become a Roc, the great eagle-like birds the size of horses. Gaining safety through altitude is no

(466 cont'd)

problem. You circle once before flying off. Below the soldiers are cursing and throwing whatever they have.

You are much too high to worry about their efforts. Gaining a little more altitude you fly off. You can maintain this shape for one hour. By then you should have made plenty of distance between you and the soldiers. Looking down you see the land covered with groups of Eastern horse patrols.

They are everywhere! Just then a peculiar sight catches your sharp eyes. A small flock of crows are trying to keep pace with you. Crows would normally chase a giant eagle from their territory. These crows are trying to follow. That's it! These are the eyes of the Dark Lord. The crows have been giving your position away.

You slacken your pace allowing the crows to catch up. Then you act. Banking to the right you plummet down on the flock. Your claws rip and tear. You circle again and dip. With your brains in the body of the great bird it becomes short work. The crows are slain or wounded to the point where they will not be able to follow you any longer. Banking away you race off once more. Turn to 500.

467   "The accused has improper vouchers your Honor," says the guard.

"What have you to say to this Enchantraen?" asks the middle judge.

Do you:

(A) Lie and tell them that it is mistake? Turn to 432.

(B) Tell them that you respect the city mandates but that you are on a mission that fully warrants such conduct? Turn to 473.

468   You overcome the momentary fear. Calm yourself, you think. Panicking will only worsen your prospects. If you feel it, it might feel you. You will need a clear head to react.

There's a flicker of fire coming from your left!

Do you:

(A) Dive to quickly avoid it? Turn to <u>488</u>.

(B) Turn left and go after it while you still hopefully have the advantage? Turn to <u>491</u>.

(C) Hover to see what happens? Turn to <u>474</u>.

469

<u>Mark off the next day and replenish all manna and erase all damage.</u>

When you finally come to, you find yourself lying in hay. You try to sit up and discover that your hands are bound. You push yourself up with your elbows and look around.

You have been captured! You are inside an enclosed wagon. Looking through the bars you see an escort of Eastern soldiers riding on all sides of the cart. Your throat is parched and your wounds are aching. Someone has apparently gone to a great deal of trouble to bandage you. You adjust several of the bandages and check to make sure all of them are reasonably clean.

"Where are we going soldier?" you ask.

"There is someone special who wishes to see you dog! Now lay down in your kennel and stop your yapping."

(469 cont'd)

It is hard to estimate how long you have been out. The soldiers are heading back towards Jerican. Your book is gone. Your hands are bound and you are surrounded by at least 40 soldiers.

It is getting late but it looks as if the soldiers are making plans to continue on through the night. At this pace you will be too far out of the way to ever hope to make it to the Mystic Isles. You are certain that whatever they have in mind for you isn't good. No, if you're going to escape it's going to have to be soon. There is more than your life at stake now.

You could make mental contact with Jenevan, your familiar, and ask her to come to the rescue. Although you're not sure exactly where you are you still can guess that her arrival will take several days at least. No, that is too long. If you could get your hands free you have memorized enough spells to give this crew a good fight.

Do you:

(A) Lie down and pretend you're asleep? Then you could rub your bonds against a nail or the bars in hopes of freeing your hands. Turn to 614.

(B) Wait a little while then fake an illness caused by your wounds? Apparently they want you alive and healthy or they wouldn't have gone to such a great extent to heal you in the first place? Turn to 643.

(C) Wait for a less dangerous attempt? They will have to take you out of the cage sometime. Turn to 685.

470   The spell has failed! The horses are coming at a dead charge. The first lancer is less than ten feet from you. There is no time for a spell. Do you:

(A) Pull your dagger and fight? Turn to 492.

(B) Fire Shefast if you still have it? Turn to 441.

471   Before you leave on your new-found steed a thought occurs to you. Somehow they are following you. You have been careful to watch for riders on the outskirts. Maybe they are invisible? To cast a spell to see will cost you 4 manna.

Do you:

(A) Cast a spell that will allow you to see invisible objects? Roll the dice and mark off 4 manna:

2 to 11, Turn to 447.
12, Roll again if you wish to cast the spell. It will cost you another 4 manna. You may also change your mind and choose (B).

(B) Mount and ride out determined to see this thing to the end? Turn to 498.

472   Again and again the demon attempts to set your feathers aflame. The wet fog hinders his efforts. Your claws dig into the flaming body. The pain is real but desperation fills the place of the pain. With a final effort you snap the substance that holds the flame together. The demon's sword and whip fall through the fog. Turn to 465.

473   "We are all too aware of your mission Enchantraen. Do you not know about the Eastern army stationed at our city's walls? Some Dark Lord has dispatched a large number of soldiers who attempted to infiltrate our city. They planned to march in and slay you wizard. Apparently the Dark Lord underestimated our determination to maintain the neutrality of our city. His

(473 cont'd)

army has been captured and stripped of their weapons. You too have made a similar mistake. For disobeying our mandates you will be fined 1000 gold tams or the forfeiture of your famous staff Shefast. If you have neither of these you will forfeit all other magical items and money you possess. Our city will remain neutral in this dispute."

Erase the proper items from your character sheet. If you give up the godstone erase the mark on <u>P</u>.

"What else has this wizard done," says the second judge. Turn to <u>438</u>.

474 No, there has got to be a way to escape it. You can feel it searching for you. It's here in the fog. You stop and hover unsure about which way to go. Just then the fog turns black. You've been found! There! It shows itself. A light is burning in the distance. It's... it's a Dendri, a denizen of flame. If <u>S</u> is marked turn to <u>456</u>.

If not, do you:

(A) Turn the stallion to flee? Turn to <u>488</u>.

(B) Yell at the foul beast to hold up? Turn to <u>484</u>.

(C) Go in for the attack head-on? Turn to <u>513</u>.

475 "I am Enchantraen you fools," you shout as your illusion takes shape. "I am not a common criminal to be judged by the likes of you. Come to my aid sweet pets and rid me of these pests."

The air around the guards is suddenly filled with gruesome beings. A tangle of the most fearsome creatures you can image threaten the guards until they turn and flee in panic. You could kill a few of them if you like but you choose not to.

(Continued next page)

(475 cont'd)

"Remember that it was Enchantraen who spared your lives," you shout as they leave.

You drop the *illusion* and *invisible* spell when you are sure they are far enough away and cannot see you. Mark off C if it isn't already and turn to 250.

476   Not only does it strike but it wraps around you! Before you can struggle the demon pulls you close to its side. The heat from its body burns. A thud on the back of the head causes you to crumble into unconsciousness. Turn to 469.

477   You strike with all of your strength.

Go to the Enemy table that follows and roll one die. Check off the damage boxes on the Rogue's Gallery score card.

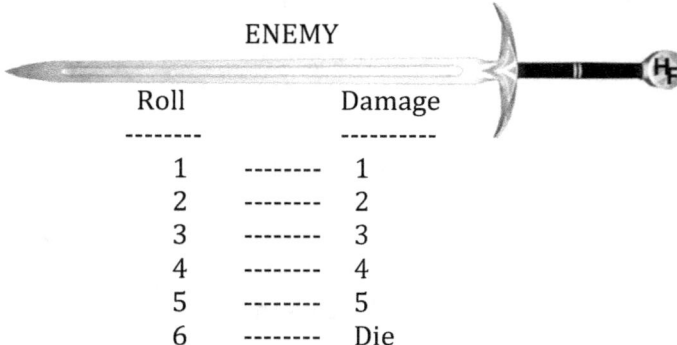

ENEMY

Roll		Damage
1	--------	1
2	--------	2
3	--------	3
4	--------	4
5	--------	5
6	--------	Die

If it expires turn to 489. If it lives it tightens around you.

Go to the Enchantraen table that follows and roll one die.

(477 cont'd)

Check off the damage boxes on your score card.

ENCHANTRAEN

Roll		Damage
1	--------	0
2	--------	1
3	--------	2
4	--------	2
5	--------	3
6	--------	4

If you expire turn to <u>469</u>. If you live turn to <u>461.</u>

478 "Your crimes have been judged and accounted for. All other charges are dropped. The Merchant Council bids that we give you this message. Leave our city as soon as possible. Your presence here puts our city in jeopardy. One Eastern army has been stopped at our gates already. A second army is advancing. The Eastern Dark Lords threaten to break our truce of neutrality. All this trouble has been caused over a simple wizard from Nautpolis. Hear me Enchantraen. As long as you are here you are protected from their threats, that is until they tear our walls down stone by stone. History shows, however, the *Challengings* cannot last much longer. Be swift to leave our city Enchantraen for both our sakes."

Bowing, you turn and leave for the street once more. <u>Erase any marks on K, C, or G.</u> Turn to <u>250</u>.

479 As your mouth utters the words your fingers begin to feel like they are moving through gravel. The earth starts to tremble. With a heave of your arms the earth splits open right before the charging horsemen. The rip in the earth is 10' x 20' and the horses at a dead charge cannot stop. The first 10 go down

(Continued next page)

(479 cont'd)

before they realize what happened. The next ten try to slow but the momentum of the horses behind them push them into the chasm. The remaining troops are in a panic with their horses twisting and bucking beneath them! Do you:

(A) Start blasting with Shefast? Turn to <u>496</u>.

(B) Yell at the troops not to bother you while you are resting? Turn to <u>454</u>.

(C) Summon a whirlwind? <u>It will cost you 3 manna</u> points. Roll the dice:

  2 to 11, Turn to <u>487</u>.
  12, Turn to <u>490</u>.

480   Onward you goad your mount. It is essential that you make good time. The fortress shouldn't be more than a day or a day and a half away.

You hear the horns blowing in the distance. You continually change directions but still the Eastern horse patrols seem to follow.

What is it! How can they follow you like this?

Over the crest of a hill comes another Eastern horse patrol. It starts to parallel you about 600 feet away. That's 500 feet out of spell range. These soldiers are in much heavier armor than you. That means it will be harder for them to carry their riders. Again you see no bowmen or magicians among them. Turn to <u>506.</u>

481   The cocoon begins to shudder as you tighten your grip on the band. The cocoon begins to spin and unravel. You increase the pressure until you hear a loud crack.

(481 cont'd)

In your hand the cocoon transforms until you find yourself clutching the neck of the rider in black. Tossing him down you stagger away. Apparently the rider and cocoon were one and the same. Breaking the cocoon also killed the rider. Turn to 489.

482   You are walking through the farmlands of Fortress Ellendar. The fog is lightening up but the night is coming in to replace it. You walk out of a plowed field to find a small dirt road. Knocking the clods from your boots you continue up the road. It has been a while since you have seen or heard any Eastern patrols and their blasted horns.

Thunder rips through the sky and echoes off. It is distant. Perhaps you can find shelter before the rain hits. You continue up the road when you notice how continuous the thunder rumbles. It isn't quite natural but you can't seem to put your finger on it.

Steadily you make your way through the fog. First the dogs start barking. Then you see a light in the night. It is a farmhouse. The fog is so thick now you were less than 50 feet from it before you saw it. There are people peering out the windows looking for what is disturbing the dogs. These farmers should be friendly enough to your cause. The thunder continues and you go to the house to ask for shelter. Turn to 521.

483   Your fingers trace the pattern while you utter the secret words. The man on the horse groans in agony and falls from the side of his horse. When he hits the ground his arm shatters. The horse runs harmlessly past you. Turn to 489.

484   No! You can't let it get you. You unconsciously scream and turn in midair.

"NO!" comes out as a screech as you attempt to fly.

(Continued next page)

(484 cont'd)

Through the fog flashes a searing fireball.

"No!" you screech again and attempt to fly out of its path. That's when the second fireball strikes you dead center.

Go to the Enchantraen table that follows and roll one die. Check off the damage boxes on your score card

ENCHANTRAEN

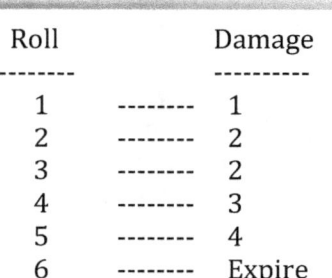

Roll		Damage
1	--------	1
2	--------	2
3	--------	2
4	--------	3
5	--------	4
6	--------	Expire

If you expire turn to <u>469</u>. If you live turn to <u>501</u> and roll again.

485   Struggling against the ever-constricting bonds you feel yourself weakening. Your hand slips into a band of rubbery cocoon. With all your strength you pull trying to snap the band. You know this could be your last chance to escape.

Roll the dice:

2 to 5, turn to <u>481</u>.
6 to 12, Turn to <u>444</u>.

486   In the end the flames are too much. Your feathers begin to smolder and catch fire. Diving, you try to escape but the wind only makes the fire worse. You feel the demon's whip strike and wrap around you. Turn to <u>476</u>.

---

487 The wind brushes your cheek. Around and around it goes, building momentum. When it reaches its height you send it over the chasm into the midst of the Eastern soldiers.

Screaming horses plummet down the chasm and race off in horror. The few remaining soldiers fall into utter panic. As they run you send the whirlwind after them; relentlessly on their trail.

There will be others coming soon, you think as you mount up. Maybe next time they will be a little more cautious. Turn to <u>480</u>.

488 If <u>S</u> is marked turn immediately to <u>499</u>.

Down you and your Pegasus fly. The Pegasus quickly pulls up. The fear has obviously affected the stallion. When you coaxed it to flee, the stallion must have lost confidence in you. The creature begins to buck in utter panic. Meanwhile the fear within yourself begins to multiply. Whatever is out there is closing in on you. Do you:

(A) Try to calm Constallia with soft words and gentle tones? Turn to <u>515</u>.

(B) Drop from the beast and attempt to change shape during free fall? It's dangerous but possible from this height. <u>Mark off 4 manna</u> and roll the dice:

2 to 9, turn to <u>505</u>.
10 to 12, Turn to <u>510</u>.

489 The Dark Lord and his Master must be desperate to subject his people to this kind of situation. The rider in black didn't have a chance and yet he charged you anyway.

The Dark Lord has presented you with a formidable problem. If you go this way you will leave a wake of death. However,

(Continued next page)

(489 cont'd)

turning back will certainly cost you a great deal of time. As you ponder the situation you finish the grisly duty of burying the poor farmer's remains.

You make certain that the rider in black will not harm you or anyone else again. Then you coax his horse to you. It seems to be a fine mount. It could save you a little time if you use it. Putting out your fire you leave your camp.

Going a little further into the night you find another suitable place for sleep. Tying the horse to a tree you make yourself as comfortable as possible. Tonight you will sleep on the problem and decide in the morning about which way to go. Turn to 452.

490 Your spell fails! Your only hope is to unhorse and slay the leader of the charging men! Pulling a dagger, you prepare to attack the man as he rides towards you. You attempt to knock the lance aside and leap. Roll the dice:

2, 3, 5, 6, 7, Turn to 463.
4, 8, 9, 10, 11, 12, You fail. The man rides past you and turns his mount. Soon you are surrounded by first five, then the rest of the troops. Realizing your limits turn to 678.

491 To the left you race to hopefully catch your adversary off-guard. The white fog turns black! A little further and you see it. The demon commander! The Dendri, a fire demon cloaked in fear and darkness. It is searching for you but luckily it is turned and looking the other way.

If S is marked, turn immediately to 446.

There is just enough time to cast a spell as you sweep past it. There is virtually no chance to cast a spell directly at it. Its magic resistance is too great. Thinking fast you weigh your options.

(491 cont'd)

(A) A blast of cold could really disrupt the fiery nature of this demon. <u>Mark off 4 manna</u>.

Roll the dice:

2 to 11, Turn to <u>549</u>.
12, Your spell fails!

The fire demon then lashes out with its whip as you go by. Turn to <u>507</u>.

(B) You can try to fly by it if you don't have the manna to cast a spell. Turn to <u>507</u>.

(C) You may also blast it with Shefast if you have it. Roll the dice:

2 to 10, Turn to <u>532</u>.
11 or 12 Turn to <u>507</u>.

492   You and your dagger against all those charging Eastern soldiers! You're a good wizard Enchantraen, not an army. The soldiers make quick work of you. Soon you are beaten into unconsciousness. The last thing you remember is the arrival of more troops as if the first 40 weren't enough. Turn to <u>469</u>.

493   You lie quietly in the hay when a shocking noise comes from behind you. The door to your cage opens! Turning you stand to see a man.

"You kill me at your own doorstep and yet I come back to help you," says the man.

He vanishes with a grim smile leaving you standing in an open cage.

The commander yells, "Kill the wizard." Turn to <u>673</u>.

494

<u>Mark off the next day and replenish all manna and erase all damage.</u>

You regain your bearings and take the most direct route possible towards the great city. You aren't giving up but needless killing is not in your nature.

You attempt to mount your new horse but are soon bucked off. You pick yourself up but the horse has already galloped out of spell range. You walk off disgusted.

Going as swiftly as you can you feel the Dark Lord's eyes staring at your back? You know he is laughing now but you will be smarter next time.

The day passes and you make camp. The night also passes uneventfully. Apparently cooperating with the Dark Lord has some advantages. At least you had one full day of peace.

The next morning you awake and are off once more. Turn to <u>176</u>.

495   You dive at the creature, claws extended. On the first pass you miss, but not on the second. You have little choice but to fight. In your bird-like form you cannot cast spells.

If only the people could see the two titans battle in the air. The demon of flame matched against a monstrous eagle. It is the stuff legends are made of, but when you are fighting for your life it doesn't seem so glamorous.

Go to the Enchantraen table that follows and roll one die.

(495 cont'd)

Check off the damage boxes on your score card.

ENCHANTRAEN

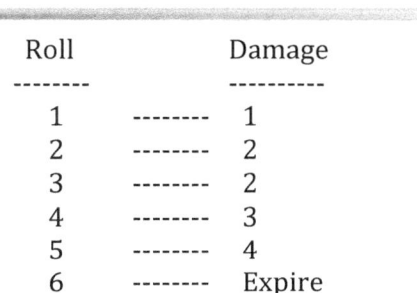

Roll		Damage
1	--------	1
2	--------	2
3	--------	2
4	--------	3
5	--------	4
6	--------	Expire

If you expire turn to <u>486</u>. If not read on!

Go to the Enemy table that follows and roll one die. Check off the damage boxes on the Rogue's Gallery score card.

ENEMY

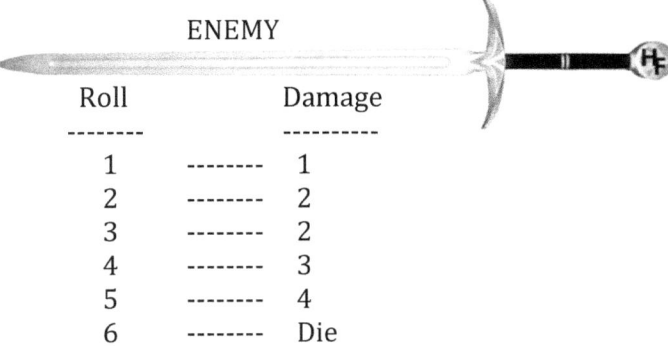

Roll		Damage
1	--------	1
2	--------	2
3	--------	2
4	--------	3
5	--------	4
6	--------	Die

If the Dendri expires turn to <u>472</u>. If not return to the Enchantraen table and fight on.

496   The lightening plummets from the heavens in answer to your call. The horses rear and buck in panic. Many soldiers fall into the abyss. Then you hear more horns blowing around you. Away in the distance you spot a second unit charging towards

(Continued next page)

(496 cont'd)

you. Then you see a third and a fourth. The lightning must have pinpointed your location! You have only moments before you will be overwhelmed. You better think clearly Enchantraen or this could be the end! Do you:

(A) Turn Shefast on the second unit of charging horsemen? Turn to <u>441</u>.

(B) Pull your dagger and make ready to fight? Turn to <u>492</u>.

(C) Cast a *change shape* spell on yourself? If you could fly out of here you could easily make it to safety. You of course would have to leave the horse behind. <u>Mark off 4 manna</u> and roll the dice:

2 to 11, Turn to <u>466</u>.
12, Turn to <u>492</u> because your spell has failed. You have only time to pull your dagger.

497 Your body aches and then bursts into flames. Luckily the magical fire doesn't burn up the oxygen. The cocoon tightens but quickly expands in an attempt to escape the searing flames. The heat becomes too much and the cocoon begins to smolder. A surprising thing happens. The cocoon brings to scream and tear itself apart.

The cool night air rushes in. The cocoon falls to your feet smoldering as you stumble away from it. You search the area quickly looking for the rider in black's next attempt.

"You cannot harm me," you shout into the night. "I tire of your silly game."

"Do not mock me," comes a weak voice from behind you.

(497 cont'd)

Turning around you see that the smoldering cocoon has transformed and lying on the cold ground is the rider in black. His body is torn and burned.

"Taunting a dying man will not save you Enchantraen. I and your farmer friend are only the first in the wake of death you will leave if you continue this way."

The man gasps and rolls over face down. Turn to <u>489.</u>

498   You kick your mount into a steady trot. The rainbow glistens overhead and in the distance cawing crows can be heard. You continually search the countryside for any signs of being followed.

By noon the surge of power from the rainbow strikes you again. It leaves you with a new hope and a feeling of confidence.

Stopping sometime later you water your horse from a small stream. A horn blows and echoes through the land! Over the edge of a hill comes a unit of Eastern horsemen. The banner of Lord Gaoler is being held high by the first rider. There must be at least 40 men in the unit. Eastern soldiers don't blow their horn as a chivalrous acknowledgement of their coming. They only blow horns to signal others of their kind. Your heart is pounding but your head is cool. You never liked being the prey of lesser creatures.

Do you:

(A) Prepare a magical attack to teach the troops the proper manner to approach a war wizard? The attack you have in mind will use a lot of manna but if it's successful it will insure you that future attacks like this won't happen. Turn to <u>449</u>.

(Continued next page)

(498 cont'd)

(B) Change shape to try and fly from this area? You will have to leave the horse behind. <u>It will cost you 4 manna</u>. Roll the dice:

2 to 11, Turn to <u>466</u>.
12, Turn to <u>470</u>.

499 There is practically nothing faster than a plummeting eagle! Down you go with the air racing around you. The tension you feel begins to slacken. You must be pulling away from it.

Soldiers, demons, and creatures of all kinds have been sent out to stop you. It has lost your trail for now. You shudder one last time, shaken by the fleeting encounter. Your spell is almost over. It would be safest to transform back to normal now and continue on by foot. Then again, the fog seems awfully thick down here. Do you:

(A) Transform back and cast another spell so that you can continue on in your giant eagle form? <u>Mark off 4 manna</u> and roll the dice:

2 to 11, Turn to <u>462</u>.
12, Your spell has failed. You may cast it again but it will cost you <u>4 more manna</u>. If not, choose (B).

(B) Continue on foot? Turn to <u>482.</u>

500 From this altitude the world passes quickly by. You see the patchwork of farms below. You must have entered the territory of Fortress Ellendar. The fortress itself is probably a day away. Flying in and out of the clouds you occasionally catch a glimpse of the Eastern horse patrols below. They must be all over the place in a desperate search for you and other wizards.

(500 cont'd)

There is a thick fog laying around the land of the fortress. You enter it and find that you are soon soaking wet. On you fly as the fog becomes thicker.

Your body shudders. There is an extremely evil being nearby! You feel it. It is hidden in the fog somewhere. Turn to 501.

501 Roll the dice:

2 to 5, Turn to 468.
6 to 7, Turn to 474.
8 to 12, Turn to 484.

502 The whip strikes but it fails to wrap around you. Do you:

(A) Dive to avoid the Dendri? Turn to 488.

(B) Turn to attack it head on? Turn to 495.

503 The whip lashes and the Pegasus jumps to miss it. The demon attempts to use this to its advantage and move in closer to you. It's now a contest of tactics between your great mount and the demon. Constellia attempts to dodge again to allow you a chance to fight.

Roll the dice:

2 to 5, Turn to 520.
6 to 12, Turn to 544.

504 Back down through the fog you and Constellia go. Soon you find a suitable place to land. When you dismount you notice the great stallion's labored breathing. Without warning the beast tumbles over, an arrow sticking from its belly.

Stooping down to the Pegasus' side you remove the arrow and administer to the wound. The great stallion would have given

(Continued next page)

(504 cont'd)

its life to obey your commands. It didn't even buck when it was hit. The horse kicks and stands back up. It is stronger now but still unable to carry you.

The constant tread of soldiers comes closer. You thank the beast and shoo it. It turns and flies away. Running into the fog you try to disappear. Turn to <u>482</u>.

505 <u>Mark off S</u>.

Down you plummet reciting the words to your spell as if they were your last prayer. The transformation takes form and you spread your arms to discover you can fly! You turned yourself into a giant eagle.

The creature hunting you seems close. Fear grips you once more. Somewhere above poor Constellia gives out a death cry.

Do you:

(A) Continue to plummet in a controlled fall? Turn to <u>499</u>.

(B) Stop to hover and look around? Turn to <u>474</u>.

(C) Turn, soar up and look to fight now that you know the general location of the creature? Turn to <u>491</u>.

506 Do you:

(A) Charge the unit? Turn to <u>517</u>.

(B) Spur your horse on to try and outrun them? Turn to <u>543</u>.

(C) Continue forward at a brisk pace? Turn to <u>524</u>.

507   Flying towards the creature you sweep past it arcing upward. With your back to the Dendri you only hear the whip lash out. Roll the dice:

      2 to 5, Turn to <u>476</u>.
      6 to 12. Turn to <u>539</u>.

508   The arrows miss you. The great beast kicks once and spreads its great wings. In a valiant effort the Pegasus attempts to land. Too late. The stallion begins to roll out of control. You attempt a spell. <u>It will cost you 4 manna</u> and the roll of the dice. Roll the dice:

      2 to 7, Turn to <u>505</u>.
      8 to 12, Turn to <u>530</u>.

509   On you go content to allow them to follow. Again and again they sound their horn to signal other troops. Finally their horn is answered by first one, then another, and another, and another.

      You realize your mistake when you see a full unit of Eastern bowmen sitting directly in your path. From each side you see several new horse units charging your way. Your slow pace allowed them to set their trap. In all there are at least 600 men charging at you. Quickly looking around you see no way to ride out so you dismount and prepare yourself. Turn to <u>535</u>.

510   What a time for your spell to fail! All you can think of is your mother's face right before you hit the ground.

      Splat!!

      Well at least from this height the remains won't be recognizable. Your legend will live on even if you don't. Sorry Enchantraen but if you wish to play anymore you will have to pick yourself up (put the pieces together) and start all over.

511   As you pass over the demon its cries of anguish are followed by an explosion. The unnatural fire of the dismembered demon flares into a wall. The Pegasus tries to veer away but it is too late. When you pass through the wall you begin to smolder. The fog quickly dampens it but fails to put it out.

The great stallion whinnies in pain. You are forced to go down immediately. In a steady downward motion Constellia carries you regardless of its pain. You land in a thick fog. Quickly jumping from the back you find that you are not hurt nearly as bad as the Pegasus. You immediately start to administer to the noble beast. It is obvious however that it will be some time before it can carry you again.

In the distance you hear the steady tread of Eastern soldiers. You will have to move quickly to avoid being caught. Unfortunately Constellia can't go with you. Thanking the noble steed you send it off into the safety of the fog while you walk in a different direction and try to disappear. Turn to <u>482</u>.

512   Your spell fails and the soldiers are on you. Another attempt would be insane. There is only one thing left to do and that is … turning to <u>568</u>.

513   The creature sees you coming and attacks with a:

Roll the dice:

2, 3, 5, 6, 7, Turn to <u>537</u>.
4, 8, 9, 10, 11, 12, Turn to <u>525</u>.

514   <u>Erase the mark on Z.</u>

You kick your laboring mount and it reluctantly begins to gallop. The soldiers seem to keep pace so you kick the flanks of your mount harder until the soldiers start to drop back. There, up ahead is a thick fog. If you could make it to that perhaps you could lose them.

(514 cont'd)

Horns start to sound from all around you. A unit of Eastern foot soldiers comes charging out of the fog in front of you. On each side new horse patrols appear at a distance moving towards you.

There are at least 600 soldiers converging on you. To call it a trap would be an understatement. Worst of all, some of the soldiers have bows. There is a slight opening to your right if you can get there before the Easterners close it. Maybe you can still lose them in the fog. Do you:

(A) Kick the great black beast for a final run? Turn to <u>564</u>.

(B) Stop and dismount to prepare yourself for the worst? Turn to <u>535</u>.

515 Quieting the beast seems impossible and your own fears begin to grow!

Roll the dice:

2 to 8, Turn to <u>534</u>.
9, Turn to <u>550</u>.
10 to 12, Turn to <u>484</u>.

516 The air turns black around you. The pain is piercing but brief. As the arrows pass by the sky returns to normal – briefly. The sky bursts into bloody hues of crimson and you fall into unconsciousness. Turn to <u>469</u>.

517 You swiftly turn your black mount and charge. The 40 Eastern soldiers must have heard about your previous encounters with their kind. They turn and run blowing twice on their horn.

"What are they signaling?" you wonder.

(Continued next page)

(517 cont'd)

Do you:

(A) Continue to charge after them? It will take a little time to catch them but you are sure you can. They are however headed the opposite direction. Turn to <u>177</u>.

(B) Stop your charge and turn back towards the fortress? Turn to <u>528.</u>

518   Around you go in the fog until the fear suddenly presses against you once more. Even the stallion shivers between your legs. Turn to <u>501</u>.

519   No! Your horse stumbles and throws you. You roll away unharmed but when you turn to go back to your horse you find its neck is broken. You often wondered what you would do with 600 screaming soldiers converging on you. There is only time for one action before they strike. Your head is still aching from the fall but you think you see wizards mixed in with the charging horsemen. Do you:

(A)   Try to turn invisible and sneak out? <u>Mark off 4 manna.</u> Roll the dice:

2 to 10, Turn to <u>557</u>.
11 or 12, Turn to <u>512</u>.

(B)   Change shape to fly off? <u>Mark off 4</u> manna and roll the dice:

2 to 10, Turn to <u>540</u>.
11 or 12, Turn to <u>512</u>.

(C)   Stand your ground and surrender? Turn to <u>568</u>.

520   The sword crashes down. The stallion realizes its mistake and rears to strike with its fore hooves. The sword cuts the unfortunate creature deeply.

(520 cont'd)

Down you plummet through the fog. You need <u>4 manna</u> to save yourself. You recite the first few words of your *change shape* spell.

<u>Mark off the 4 manna</u> and roll the dice:

2 to 9, Turn to <u>505</u>.
10 to 12, Turn to <u>510</u>.

If you don't have the manna, turn to <u>510</u>.

521 You walk up to the front door and knock. The door swings wide and you find the end of an arquebus shoved over your nose.

"Oh I'm sorry," says a lean farmer as he lowers the gun. "I thought you were more of those soldiers."

"As you can see kind sir, I am not. I am a simple traveler looking for shelter. If I could only stay in your barn to avoid the coming rain I would be glad to pay you."
You hold out several gold tams. The farmer shoves a lantern out the door and looks you over.

"Well, you look like you could use a little rest. Come inside."

You enter into a small one-room farm home. A woman is crying in the corner.

"Get us some food woman," the farmer says.

The woman rises to obey. You can now see the bruises around her face.

"She's a little upset," apologizes the farmer. "Some Easterners came by this way and beat her."

(Continued next page)

(521 cont'd)

"Didn't Tancred's men come to protect her?" you ask in a leading manner.

"No, I'm afraid not. That thunder you hear isn't thunder at all. Lord Gaoler is attacking the Fortress. The thunder is the alchemist's cannons firing from the fortress."

The woman lays out two bowls of soup as you sit down.

"I guess Lord Gaoler's attacking the fortress is a common occurrence," you say between spoonfuls of the light broth.

"No, actually it's not. The Dark Lord's looking for a special wizard. They were going to kill my wife here because they thought we were helping the wizard. I was in the fields but I guess they almost killed her when a messenger rode in. My wife tells me the messenger was a knurled old man who was as agile as a young buck. He broke in the door, just as they were taking the blade to her, and ordered the soldiers to follow him immediately. He said that Tancred is screaming from the battlements that the wizard is safe within his walls. Lord Gaoler has ordered his troops to surround it."

A mug of splashing ale is set down on the table and a grin crosses your face. The old fox Tancred has given you the best protection he could afford. With the troops surrounding the fortress your travels should be easier.

"Well it's over now," you say trying to be as reassuring as possible.

"That's what I told the missus," retorts the farmer, "but she keeps babbling about a curse the old man shouted at her when they rode off. She won't tell me what he said but I told her not to worry about it. Words are words and she should be glad she escaped the sword."

(521 cont'd)

After the meal you and the farmer sit and warm yourselves by the fireplace. His wife climbs into a loft to go to bed. You talk a while but the fire makes you drowsy. The farmer hands you a lantern and you head towards the barn. Inside you find the most accommodating haystack and fall into exhausted slumber. Turn to <u>548</u>.

522   Down you go racing through the fog. The pressive fear begins to leave you. You realize that you are pulling away from your nemesis.

Wait! You hear the clatter of metal from below. The fog begins to thin. What? You command the great stallion to rise. As it obeys, you and your Pegasus soar in a sweeping arc over a full unit of Eastern bowmen. Below is an army on the march! The great stallion begins its upward climb when the first wave of arrows are loosed.

Roll the dice:

2 to 8, Turn to <u>546</u>.
9 to 12, Turn to <u>508</u>.

523   The magic that is killing the lich is gone, otherwise healing would be impossible. Teetering on the edge of death you grab the old one and bring him back. When he is able to stand once more you order him to fulfill his promise.

"Go now to Lord Gaoler and destroy him. Tell him that it is I who have sent you."

<u>Mark off U</u> and turn to <u>533</u>.

524   The soldiers seem content to follow from a safe distance. Occasionally they blow a horn. You feel like the fox in this chase.

(Continued next page)

(524 cont'd)

Do you:

(A) Continue on at the same pace? Turn to 509.

(B) Turn and charge the unit? Turn to 517.

(C) Spur your horse onward to try and outrun them? Turn to 543.

525   Whip and flaming sword! The whip lashes out first.

Roll the dice:

2 to 5, Turn to 476.
6 to 12, Turn to 503.

526   Mark off S.

The feathers prickle through your skin as you jump into the air before the transformation is complete. Speed is everything to a giant eagle. You are an eagle the size of a horse. Your arms are powerful instruments of flight and you soar upward into the heavens.

Below, the soldiers are screaming orders. They fan out looking for you suspecting that you are trying to run away. Once high enough you start to pass in and out of clouds. A flock of crows comes out of the clouds and practically collides with you. Your *invisible* spell is unnecessary so you drop it and continue to fly. Turn to 500.

527   A cooling sensation envelopes your body. For the rest of this encounter you are shielded from the full damage caused by fire. If you are struck by fire subtract 2 from any damage done to you. This only lasts for this encounter and you

(527 cont'd)

must remember to subtract the 2 points. The book won't prompt you again.

If this is the second time you cast a fire *resistance* spell then you are impervious to all natural fire. Turn to 501.

528   When you stop, so do the soldiers. They quickly regroup but keep their distance. They begin to pace you once more. Cursing the cowards you turn to 506 and decide what to do.

529   The doors fly open. You start to run but the image of the farmer stops you. He is standing at the door with his gun in his arms.

The woman hesitates. The demonic expression on her face softens and she says, "Kill him! Quickly, before the wizard can escape."

The farmer lifts his gun.

Do you:

(A) Cast a *binding* spell on the farmer? <u>Mark off 1 manna</u> and roll the dice:

    2 to 11, Turn to 559.
    12, Turn to 571 because your spell fails.

(B) Cast a *control* spell on the woman to try and stop her? <u>Mark off 3 manna</u> and roll the dice:

    2 to 6, Turn to 566.
    7 to 12, Turn to 547.

(C) Shout at the farmer to stop? Turn to 571.

530   No! Your spell has failed. Over the head of the beast you tumble uncontrollably downward. Branches start snapping and cracking breaking your fall. A sharp crack sends you into unconsciousness. Turn to <u>469</u>.

531   The light blue light leaps from your hands and binds her arms tightly together. She loses her balance and drops the anvil. A deep guttural cry emits from her lips. With a mighty heave she rips the binding lights and breaks your spell. The force of her struggle tears deeply into the flesh on her arms but she moves with no pain. She waves her hands and ... Turn to <u>570</u>.

532   Once again the mighty staff commands the heavens to obey. All around you lightning races to strike the staff and then hurl itself off towards the demon. It strikes and the creature screams.

    You have just scored one point against the demon. It takes 4 points to destroy it. Make a mental note of the total number of points you have scored against it.

    If you haven't scored 4 points turn to <u>539</u>.

    If you have scored 4 points turn to <u>511</u>.

533   You are standing in the barn drenched in sweat. The woman is alive and the farmer is kneeling by her.

    "She was cursed," he sobs. "She didn't know what she was doing."

    "I know," you say as your senses slowly come back.

    You turn quickly when you hear the sounds of approaching horses.

    "It's an Eastern patrol" the farmer whispers. "Run while you can. If they find you here we are all doomed."

    Gathering your gear you steal away into the night. Turn to <u>580</u>.

534   The calm in your voice works. The great stallion is intelligent enough to feel the power in you even under these circumstances.

Fear presses against you both but you fight it. Then you see a flicker of fire in the fog. Do you:

(A) Cast a fire *resistance* spell on yourself? <u>Mark off 4 manna</u> and roll the dice:

2 to 11, Turn to <u>527</u>
12, Turn to <u>484</u> because your spell failed.

(B) Dive once again to try and escape? Turn to <u>522</u>.

(C) Turn to the stallion in a sweeping arc and close in on your adversary? Turn to <u>491</u>.

535   Do you:

(A) Stand your ground and surrender? Turn to <u>568</u>.

(B) Turn invisible and try to walk out? <u>It costs you 4 manna</u>. Roll the dice:

2 to 11, Turn to <u>575</u>.
12, Turn to <u>512</u>.

(C) Change shape and fly out? <u>That costs 4 manna</u>. Roll the dice:

2 to 11, Turn to <u>540</u>.
12, Turn to <u>512</u>.

(D) Turn invisible and then change shape? The 2 spells will cost 8 manna. There is also the chance that you do not have the time to cast 2 spells before you are run down.

(Continued next page)

(535 cont'd)

Mark off 4 manna for the first spell and roll the dice:

2 to 6, Turn to 557.
7 to 12, Turn to 561.

536 Steel fingers tighten around your neck. You strike out but the woman feels no pain and does not react. You strike again and again but it is useless. Your windpipe collapses and you sink away from this world. If L or N is marked turn to 541. If not turn to 200.

537 A fireball! On you race as the demon releases its flaming fury your way.

Go to the Enchantraen table that follows and roll one die. Check off the damage boxes on your score card.

ENCHANTRAEN

Roll	Damage
1	1
2	2
3	3
4	4
5	5
6	6

If you go unconscious turn to 469. If you survive turn to 542.

538 Your robe is flecked with foam as you race towards the fog. The bowmen on your left dare not fire for fear of hitting the horsemen closing in on your right. Your mount stumbles but regains its balance and continues the race.

You've got the edge! Into the fog you race until it becomes thick enough to conceal you. Then you sharply change your

(538 cont'd)

direction. Riding on the soft soil of the farmland you slow your pace and listen. The Eastern soldiers are racing away from you going in the wrong direction!

When you feel it is safe you dismount and listen for any sound coming from the dense fog.

The great black horse's knees buckle and it falls. Coaxing it to its feet you try to get the horse to walk in circles. It doesn't work. The poor creature will probably never carry a rider again. Wiping down its coat you gently pat the animal and send it away to fend for itself. Then you turn and quietly walk into the farmlands of Fortress Ellendar. Turn to 482.

539 The whip snaps but fails to wrap around you. Up you soar into the fog and out of sight once more. You become a little disoriented in the dense fog and lose track of where the creature was located. Do you:

(A) Hover to get your hearings? Turn to 474.

(B) Dive to avoid it? Turn to 522.

(C) Circle to find it? Turn to 518.

540 The feathers prickle through your skin. Your arms suddenly feel immensely strong. Up into the air you leap even before you have totally transformed into the giant eagle the size of a horse. Up you soar, your speed increasing as the transformation completes. There is a full unit of Eastern archers you must escape. Speed is everything. Hopefully you have caught them off guard. Two hundred and forty arrows could easily put an end to your escape. Bravely roll the dice:

2 to 5, Turn to 516.
6 to 12, Turn to 554.

---

541   The lich (a wizard with an unnaturally extended life) appears before your fogging vision.

"I have tracked you for some time wizard. My master Lord Gaoler will be most pleased when I present him with your head."

The swinging arc of a blade is all you see. Turn to <u>200</u>.

542   Do you:

(A) Cast a *cold* spell at the fiery demon? Roll the dice and <u>mark off 4 manna</u>:

2 to 11, Turn to <u>549</u>.
12, Turn to <u>507</u>.

(B) Attack with Shefast if you still have it? Roll the dice:

2 to 10, Turn to <u>532</u>.
11 or 12, Turn to <u>507</u>.

(C) Fly by it unwilling to attack just yet? Turn to <u>507</u>.

543   If <u>Z</u> is marked turn immediately to <u>514</u>.

Your horse races forward. Immediately the soldiers attempt to follow. Soon it becomes evident that your conclusions were correct. Their heavy armor slows their mounts down and you pull away from them. Their commander sounds his horn and attempts to follow. This continues until finally the distance becomes too great. Looking back you watch their commander blow his horn for the last time as his unit canters to a stop.

Just then a horn sounds in front of you. A second unit enters the scene and moves to pace you. Their horses are fresh and yours is breathing heavily. You slow to a trot and look the situation over. <u>Mark off Z</u> and turn to <u>506</u>.

544   The Dendri swings and the stallion dances in the air. The blow swings wild! Turn to 542.

545   You have made it past the rank of soldiers. The units are spreading out to search the area. Their magicians are casting *negate* spells in all directions. For the moment you are out of their range.

Away you race in a frantic game of hide-and-go-seek. You continually dodge and they constantly pursue. Just as you feel your spell wearing off you see a dense fog rolling in. You run for what seems like hours to reach it.

At last the fog wraps you in its protection. Resting on one knee, you watch your spell completely wear away. You hear the soldiers passing but none come near enough to find you. At last you stand and walk off. Turn to 482.

546   Arrows whirl past you and disappear into the fog. You apparently surprised them as much as yourself. As you and Constellia disappear into a fog bank you smile.

Gods they must think you're gusty to fly past a full unit of soldiers. Do you:

(A) Climb back into the air? Turn to 474.

(B) Land in a safe area out of the direction that you suspect the army is marching? Turn to 504.

547   Your mind races towards the woman's. You enter her thoughts and quickly search for control. An old man's face looms deeply in the darkness of her thoughts.

"Possessed," you cry.

Heedless of any danger to your physical body you struggle for

(Continued next page)

(547 cont'd)

control of the woman. The force you oppose is infinitely strong and it starts to break your will.

"No," you shout, "I am Enchantraen."

You dig into the depths of your past. You recall the trials you suffered when retrieving the Temples of Nautpolis. You recall the struggle you had wrestling the great sword *Sun Child* from its captors only to give it away to a friend.

"I am Enchantraen," you shout again. The old one's will snaps like a dry bone.

If <u>L</u> or <u>N</u> is marked, turn to <u>560</u> and <u>erase any marks</u> over the letters. If not turn to <u>533</u>.

548 You're sitting high upon a throne. From this height you can see clearly across the Western Kingdoms. Below you are servants and throngs of worshippers.

They pile gifts at your feet and bring you food and wine aplenty. Across the land you can see the dark armies marching. With a wave of your hand storms sweep them away. The crowds cheer. A young woman comes forward and places a beautiful necklace of pure *electrum* around your neck. Without warning the necklace constricts, choking you. You wake from your dream.

The old farmer's wife is squeezing the life out of you with her bare hands. You strike with your fist and attempt to pry her off.

She is uncommonly strong. Your groping hands grab something and pull. A small cast iron anvil falls from a shelf and strikes the woman full in the back. You feel the impact even though her body is shielding yours. Ribs snap and yet the woman tightens her grip. You strike again and manage to roll away.

(548 cont'd)

On your feet you turn facing the woman. She didn't even cry out when the anvil struck her. She grabs the anvil and raises it above her head like it was a toy, but not before you ...

(A) Turn and run for the barn door? Turn to <u>556</u>.

(B) Throw a dagger at her? Turn to <u>578</u>.

(C) Cast a *binding* spell on her? Mark off 1 manna and roll the dice:

2 to 11, Turn to <u>531</u>.
12, Your spell fails! Turn to <u>556</u>.

549   The cold forms in front of your hands then races ahead. The fog crystallizes as the cold passes through it. It strikes the demon directly. Flames leap like shredded skin and fly off the screaming creature. Your Pegasus arcs upward as you pass over the Dendri.

Go to the Rogue's Gallery and mark off two damage boxes from the Dendri.

If you haven't scored 4 points yet turn to <u>539</u>.

If you have scored 4 points turn to <u>511</u>.

550

You are sure you could have quieted the beast if only you weren't hit by the fireball.

Go to the Enchantraen table that follows and roll one die.

(Continued next page)

(550 cont'd)

Check off the damage boxes on your score card.

ENCHANTRAEN

Roll		Damage
1	--------	1
2	--------	2
3	--------	3
4	--------	4
5	--------	4
6	--------	5

If you go unconscious turn to <u>469</u>.

If you live you find yourself plummeting through the fog, thrown off the beast. You have only one chance to save yourself and that takes 4 manna points.

If you don't have the manna turn to <u>510</u>. If you do, try to calmly roll the dice and be sure to subtract the <u>4 manna points</u>. Roll the dice:

2 to 9, Turn to <u>505</u>.
10 to 12, Turn to <u>510</u>.

551   The spell dances and flares on your fingertips. Quickly it bursts into flame.

The woman charges you heedless of the danger. You toss the fireball and it strikes her dead center. The flames engulf her but she charges through it. With the strength of a giantess her steely fingers close around your neck.

With her dress flaming she starts choking the life from you. You strike her but it does no good. You strike her again and again. She feels nothing. Through the throbbing in your ears you hear boards cracking.

(551 cont'd)

Her hands release you and she drops you to the ground. Stars float in your vision but clear quickly.

The woman is beating the farmer off her back. Finally she smashes the farmer against the wall and he drops off her. The woman turns towards you once more. The world is still spinning when you rise. How can you stop her?

Do you:

(A) Decide you can't stop her through traditional spells and decide to levitate her in to the air and out of the way? <u>Mark off 3 manna</u> and roll the dice:

2 to 11, Turn to <u>573</u>
12, Turn to <u>536</u>.

(B) Try to reason with her telling her to please stop? Turn to <u>536</u>.

552

<u>Mark off the next day and replenish all manna and erase all damage.</u>

It is late in the morning when you finally rise. The fog is thinning and the sun reflects against it in wild reds and oranges. Getting such a late start you decide to snack on dried meats as you walk. You establish your bearings and head off on a course that will hopefully lead you around the fortress.

By noon you feel better but the fog seems to negate any effect the rainbow might have on you. Topping a crest you see

(Continued next page)

(552 cont'd)

Fortress Ellendar, its central tower of dark granite silhouetted against the exploding hues of the orange and blood red sky. The long sweeping road that rises gently past the side towers is choked with Eastern soldiers!

Puffs of smoke from the cannons drift around its mountain walls like a fine pearl necklace. The soldiers aren't trying to storm the fortress. They seem content to surround it, supposedly keeping you bottled up inside.

You are closer to the fortress than you wished to be. You must be more tired than you thought to have misjudged the direction. Now you will have to be careful and try to avoid running into an outer patrol. You wish you could personally thank the old fox Tancred for his help, but that will have to wait. You start off on a careful route around and away from the fortress.

The terrain is rocky but the further you travel past the fortress the smoother it becomes. You walk on finding a small wooded area and then back out onto farmland.

The trek across the farmland will be the most dangerous because there is so little to conceal you. Your cloak is covered with dirt from traveling on the road. At least you will blend in from a distance. If indeed the Eastern troops are behind you then it should be short work to travel to Wellsport. There you can catch a ship and be on your way.

The day passes uneventfully. Not a soldier in sight. You look for a place to make camp. In this area one place seems as good as another. As you prepare your meal you smell storm clouds rolling in. This time it really looks like rain. You find sticks and attempt to build a small shelter. The rain sets in and after a time you fall into a damp sleep.

In the middle of the night you are awakened by a series of loud booms. Thunder you think.

(552 cont'd)

Looking up you think you see a giant man falling from the sky. The giant hits the earth and a great splash of water follows. On the ground there is nothing but a small body of water. The man is gone. The thunder rips the sky once more. It must be a passing storm giant warring with the clouds. You often wanted to experiment with Shefast (providing you still have it). Do you:

(A) Pick the staff up and go out into the rain? Turn to 584.

(B) Decide you have enough trouble without going out to start some more? Turn to 583.

(C) Your staff is missing or you just want to sleep? Turn to 583.

553 Shefast answers your commands and plucks the lightning from the sky. Down the lightning falls to strike the staff and then races back up into the clouds. The lightning strikes the largest form dead center. The air rips apart with raging thunder. Searing shafts tear at the clouds sending them fleeing in all directions. Do you:

(A) Strike again with the staff? Turn to 598.

(B) Call out to the sky? Turn to 563.

(C) Start striking at the smaller forms? Turn to 572.

554 Mark off S.

The air clatters with sporadic air shots. By the time the soldiers organize to fire an effective volley it is too late. The arrows race towards you but fall short of reaching you.

The sky is yours as you race away from the infuriated soldiers. Turn to 500.

555   <u>Mark off Y</u>.

"By the elements of air, water, and fire I swear to be loyal to you and your cause."

The staff acts on its own once more. The power within it breaks free and surrounds the storm giant.

The giant screams, "I will obey Shefast. I will obey!"

The earth trembles from his cries. Shefast's power totally envelopes him. The staff then calls it back. The light races towards the staff. In a flash all is quiet and dark once more. The staff trembles and glows faintly. Deep within the wood of ash rests the storm giant. A silent companion ready to do your bidding when you call.

Exhausted you return to the shelter and drop into dreams of being the master of lightning and thunder. In the morning you turn to <u>600.</u>

556   She casts the anvil as if it were a toy.

Go to the Enchantraen table that follows and roll one die. Check off the damage boxes on your score card.

ENCHANTRAEN

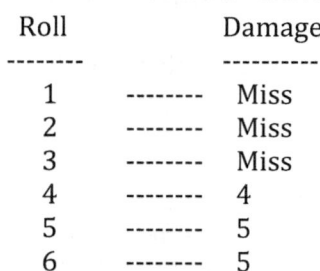

Roll		Damage
1	--------	Miss
2	--------	Miss
3	--------	Miss
4	--------	4
5	--------	5
6	--------	5

If you are dying she closes in and ... Turn to <u>536</u>. If you live turn to <u>570</u>.

557   You see the light bend around. You are sure that you are invisible to the human eye. The Eastern soldiers are in a panic.

Then the spell stops! The nearest unit of horses charges you down. The last thing you remember seeing is an Eastern wizard finishing a *negate* spell.

Unconsciousness overcomes you all too quickly. Turn to <u>469</u>.

558   "I am Enchantraen, giant," you shout trying to make yourself heard above the noise.

"Enchantraen," the giant echoes? "Normally that would mean nothing. Lord Gaoler mentioned you to me however. Why would the Dark Lord want you dead so badly?"

Waiting for the thunderous voice to echo away you reply, "He fears what I might do once I have gained a seat among the Elders."

"He bids me to slay you or he will seek vengeance against me. I have no need of such trouble but tell me quickly before I burn out your life. Is there any reason why you should live?"

Do you:

(A) Drop to your knees and tell him that the good of the Western Kingdoms rests on your shoulders. Turn to <u>587</u>.

(B) Put the staff away to start a spell to change shape? <u>Mark off 4 manna</u> and turn to <u>586</u>.

(C) Hold the staff in front of your and tell the giant that you are Enchantraen. The real question is whether you should allow him to live! Turn to <u>579</u>.

559   The light blue light leaps from your hand and wraps around the farmer.

"No you fool," he shouts as he falls to the ground. Turn to <u>536</u>.

560   It feels as if you are spinning in a great black void. The old man is lying at your feet. He is a lich (an ancient wizard). The lich raises a gnarled hand.

"I have tracked you down and laid traps all along the way. Here you catch me and I must die. Know this Enchantraen. You defeated me but it was my master's own decree that kills me. You see," the lich goes on with a weak laugh. "Lord Gaoler made me swear to destroy you if I saw you. To let you pass would destroy me. What a stupid thing to swear. Now I must die simply because you broke my control over an old woman."

The lich coughs and chokes unable to speak further.

Do you:

(A) Tell the lich that you are a healer and that you will save him if he swears to take vengeance against his old master? Turn to <u>523</u>.

(B) Tell him to choose his sides a little more wisely in his next life and break your control over him? Turn to <u>533</u>.

561   Roll first for invisibility.

2 to 11, Read the next paragraph.
12, Turn to <u>512</u>.

The light bends around you and you are certain that you are hidden from the human eye. The charging soldiers start to panic but the Eastern magicians come forward. The troops are uncomfortably close now as you chant the second spell.

(561 cont'd)

Mark off 4 manna and roll the dice:

2 to 10, Turn to 526.
11 or 12, Turn to 557.

562   You could:

(A) Cast the *reverse* spell on yourself and hope that your magic is powerful enough to ward off the magic of the fence. You could simply cast it on yourself and charge the fence. Mark off 4 manna and turn to 593.

(B) Try to fly over the fence. Perhaps its magic doesn't extend to great heights. Mark off 3 manna and turn to 621.

(C) Attempt a *negate paralysis* spell. If it works you might free these people as well as help yourself. Mark off 1 manna and turn to 616.

(D) Turn back to 574 to experiment further.

563   "Master of Storm, come down and talk with me. I ..." your voice is soon lost among the thunder.

The giant figure herds the others along in front of it. Soon they will be well out of range. Do you:

(A) Strike out at the largest creature with Shefast? Turn to 598.

(B) Call out again? Turn to 588.

(C) Strike out at a smaller figure? Turn to 572.

564   Onward your mount charges as the troops close in around you. It's going to be close. Roll the dice:

2, 3, 5, 6, 7, turn to 519.
4, 8, 9, 10, 11, 12, Turn to 538.

565   Shefast is sheltering the Storm Giant. Dare you release the giant against the Dark Lord? Can the Dark Lord turn the creature against you? Do you:

(A) Command the staff to release the Storm Giant? Turn to 611.

(B) Decide against it! You will save the giant for some other purpose. Turn to 603.

566   Your mind races to gain control. You enter the woman's head and start searching for an area to settle in and control. Then you see it. An old man's face smiles.

"Possessed" you shout!

Your spell is broken and the old man's face laughs. Turn to 571.

567   You carefully proceed to the nearest victim. As you approach you see the workings of a *paralysis* spell. The woman is still breathing and seems unharmed. She probably sees and feels your approach but she simply cannot move. She is a wizard. The whole group appears to be Westerners. Up ahead is a man who has fallen over. You think you recognize him but you cannot be sure.

Do you:

(A) Go up to the man for a closer look? Turn to 589.

(B) Retreat back to a place of safety to think things over? Turn to 574.

568   You place both hands on top of your head. The charging men stop and the horses back away to give the bowmen a clear shot if they need it. It seems like an eternity before a spokesman comes forward. Gently easing his horse through the throngs comes a high ranking soldier. He timidly comes forward aware that a cornered lion is not defenseless.

"You are smarter than they told me wizard," he says in false bravado as he dismounts.

Walking over to you he attempts to put on the air of courage in front of his troops. Grabbing the officer as a hostage crosses your mind but you quickly discount it. The bowmen would gladly kill him for the prize of a great wizard like yourself.

"There is someone who wishes to see you" the Commander says.

Then with a quick move he bangs you on the head with the butt of the dagger.

"Ouch," you call out. "Come Commander, you must try and make it a clean hit."

Red-faced the Commander strikes you again and you tumble into unconsciousness. Turn to <u>469</u>.

569   "No, no, no," a voice shouts in your mind. "He is returning. Help us. We will be devoured. Help ..." and the spell is broken.

Obviously the man is delirious with fear and unable to answer questions. Turn back to <u>574</u> and choose again.

570   The doors slam shut and a chilling wind races through the barn. The main door rattles and bangs. Turning, you see the woman coming at you once more.

(Continued next page)

(570 cont'd)

Do you:

(A) Try to cast a *portal* spell to magically unlock the barn door? <u>Mark off 2 manna</u> and roll the dice:

2 to 7, Turn to <u>529.</u>
8 to 12, Your spell fails. Turn to <u>592</u>.

(B) Conjure a fireball to throw against her? <u>Mark off 4 manna</u> and roll the dice:

2 to 11, turn to <u>551</u>.
12, Your spell fails. Turn to <u>592</u>.

(C) Pull your dagger and fight? Turn to <u>592</u>.

571 The farmer raises his gun and fires. The shot strikes his wife who crumbles to the ground. The barn is filled with a stunned silence.

"You are Enchantraen, aren't you wizard," the farmer says in hushed tones.

"Yes".

"I know now that the old man's curse was real. She was forced to kill you if she ever saw you."
The farmer goes over to his wife.
"Only the silver shot can stop one so possessed" the farmer whispers.

You see the glimmering round ball that the farmer loaded his gun with.

"I'm sorry," is all you can think to say.

(571 cont'd)

"It's not you, it's the East. They are the killers," whispers the farmer.

You hear horses coming down the road.

"That would be more Eastern patrols" the farmer whispers. "Escape while you can. Maybe someday you can change things."

Lost for words you turn and disappear into the night. Turn to 580.

572   Shefast is quick to obey. Lightning races down and strikes the staff, then returns to the sky. One of the smaller giants is hit dead center and falls. By the time the giant hits the ground there is nothing left but a puddle of water.

The larger storm giant turns his cloud as if it were a chariot. Closer now to the ground the giant thunders, "Brother, I can't see you. Are you nearby?"

The cloud sweeps overhead completely ignoring you. Do you:

(A) Call out that there is no brother nearby, just you. "It is I who commands the lightning." Turn to 594.

(B) Strike out with the staff? Turn to 598.

(C) Allow the giant to sweep out of sight of you? Once it is far away maybe it will be out of range to hurt you. Then call out to it. Turn to 588.

573   The woman is nearly on you when the spell takes hold. You lift her into the air. Holding her there with your mind you look her over.

Her eyes glow red and she foams like a mad dog.

(Continued next page)

(573 cont'd)

The farmer says, "This is the curse. She must destroy you to remove it. Can't you help her?"

You could try a *control* spell on her but that could also be dangerous. Do you:

(A) Attempt the *control* spell? Mark off 3 manna and roll the dice:

2 to 11, Turn to 547.
12, Turn to 566.

(B) Tell the farmer that there is nothing you can do? Turn to 571.

574 The back of the posts look plain enough but the sides away from you have odd carvings of misshapen men on them. Trying to go around the fence looks impossible. The fence is lined with people all the way. This is obviously a trap but how can you beat it?

Do you:

(A) Cast a rock? Turn to 585.

(B) Detect magic by moving up closer to the fence? Turn to 589.

(C) Try a *communication* spell to ask one of the people what happened? Mark off 3 manna and turn to 597.

(D) Run head long at the fence and hope for the best? Turn to 589.

(E) Delve deeply into your magic book and try to beat this thing? You think you have enough information to try something. Turn to 599.

575   The light bends around your form. In a flash you are invisible to the naked eye. You quickly turn and run for the nearest opening. The soldiers panic and immediately fan out. Magicians come racing forward waving their arms. You have no choice now. You must try and squeeze through the lines.

A group of horsemen! There's a small gap. You carefully run to squeeze through. If they find you now it's all over. Roll the dice:

2, 3, 5, 6, 7, Turn to <u>557</u>.
4, 8, 9, 10, 11, 12, Turn to <u>545</u>.

576   The staff again obeys. This time lightning rips from the body of the giant, strikes the staff and races back again. Infuriated the giant retaliates and casts his lightning your way. The bolts race your way but the staff intervenes, catches them and hurls them back with even greater force. The air screams and the surrounding shrubs catch aflame. The giant is unhurt.

"Who are you," the giant booms?

"I am Enchantraen," you bellow back as loud as you can.

"It can't be that a mere wizard can have such power!"

Turn to <u>579</u>.

577   Go to the Enchantraen table that follows and roll one die.
Check off the damage boxes on your score card.

ENCHANTRAEN

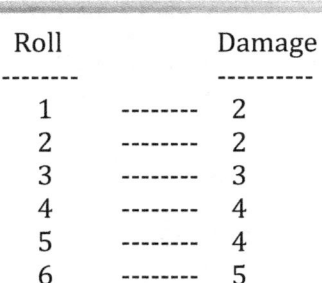

Roll		Damage
1	--------	2
2	--------	2
3	--------	3
4	--------	4
5	--------	4
6	--------	5

If you live turn to <u>596</u>. If you expire turn to <u>200</u>.

578   The dagger strikes deeply into her belly. Again the woman
shows no pain even as the blood trickles from the wound's
edges. Turn to <u>556</u>.

579   It is then that the staff chooses to make itself known. Lightning
races from all corners of the sky striking the staff. The staff
glows more brightly than the giant. The area seems to glow as
if it were broad daylight.

"It is Shefast," the giant booms falling to its knees. "I see you
now master and I obey."

You feel nearly uncontrollable power ripple up your arms from
the staff. The master of lightning, controller of thunder
authority, above even the storm giants. You knew the staff had
hidden powers but you never guessed this.

(579 cont'd)

Even now you don't know how to completely control the staff but you can:

(A) Release the energy and slay the giant? Turn to <u>590</u>.

(B) Command the giant to vow allegiance to you and your cause or you will smite him for his insolence. Turn to <u>555</u>.

580 You stumble through the fields until you simply can go no further. You spread out your bedroll and fall face down exhausted. There you sleep while the cannons thunder and the magnificent rainbow arches across the sky. Turn to <u>552</u>.

581 ... gently touches a young woman's mind.

"Who are you?" you ask.

"I am a wizard named Ella. I was on my way to Wellsport when I came across this. I was going to help these poor people. I tried to detect the magic when I was overcome and paralyzed."

"Who did it?" you ask.

"I don't know. I have only been here a short time. The magic is too powerful. You should flee while you can."

Your spell is broken and you turn back to <u>574</u> to reconsider.

582 Away into the night you run. Any moment you expect the end to come. Instead you hear a thunderous roar of laughter.

"Shefast!" Turning around you see the storm giant rising into the sky clutching the staff in its hands. <u>Mark the staff off your character sheet.</u> The giant races off leaving everything else in your camp behind.

(Continued next page)

(582 cont'd)

When it is safe you return to your camp and crawl back into your makeshift shelter. Exhausted, you fall asleep and the rest of the night passes with quiet rainfall. In the morning you turn to <u>600</u>.

583　The lightning quickly passes but the rain remains behind. Settling into your shelter you quickly fall back into slumber. Your dreams are filled with wild thoughts of lightning mastery and lands of thunderous servants. In reality however the night passes quietly. In the morning you turn to <u>600</u>.

584　Looking skyward you see odd shapes of giant men silhouetted against the moons and rainbows. There is one shape larger than most. Do you:

(A) Try to strike the large form with lightning? Turn to <u>553</u>.

(B) Call out to the sky? Turn to <u>563</u>.

(C) Strike a smaller form with lightning? Turn to <u>572</u>.

585　The rock arches high into the air striking some invisible force, pauses then falls on through. Turn to <u>574</u>.

586　Before you can complete your spell lightning strikes.

Go to the Enchantraen table that follows and roll one die.

(586 cont'd)

Check off the damage boxes on your score card.

ENCHANTRAEN

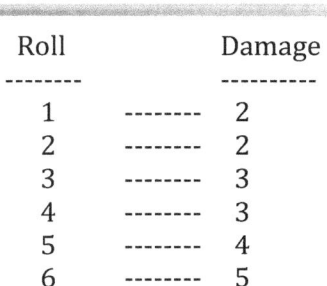

Roll		Damage
1	--------	2
2	--------	2
3	--------	3
4	--------	3
5	--------	4
6	--------	5

If you expire turn to <u>200</u>. If you live turn to <u>596</u>.

587 "What do I care for kingdoms. Lord Gaoler promises not to bother me if I slay you." The giant calls and the lightning races your way. Turn to <u>577</u>.

588 "I bid thee to come down from your cloud," but it is too late.

The storm giant forces the cloud giants on and soon all are out of range. Left standing in the rain you turn back to your shelter. There you seek sleep and safety, even if you are little more wet than usual. In your dreams you see storms, lightning, and masters of thunder. In the morning you turn to <u>600</u>.

589 It starts in an odd but effective manner. When you moved within range of the fence its magic takes effect. First your feet become solidly riveted to the ground. You begin to swoon but find that you are unable to fall. The sky goes black and the paralysis sets in.

There you stand motionless for a short while. Unexpectedly you can move again!

Then it happens. Turn to <u>620</u>.

590   The staff obeys once more. A mighty bolt 10 times the size of what you are used to seeing shoots across and strikes the storm giant. The poor creature shatters and breaks apart sending bolts racing amongst the foliage. The light dies out followed by one last thunderous clap. Several places on the ground are smoldering. You quickly start putting out the fire, helped by the rain.

      Exhausted you return to your shelter and tumble into dreams of storms, lightning, and kings. In the morning you turn to <u>600</u>.

591   The spell takes effect. The sense of weightlessness overcomes you and you lift into the air. Up and up you go until you feel safe enough to attempt it. With all your speed you fly due west over the fence in the direction of Wellsport.

      It's like trying to follow an arrow fired directly at you. The fence posts move as the little carved men come to life. With incredible speed they leap and fly towards you. You prepare a spell but you are not fast enough. Tiny hands grab you and you knock them off. Then another set and another grab you, dragging you downward. You again attempt a spell but fail. When your feet touch the ground you push and throw the creatures off you. Then it happens! Turn to <u>620</u>.

592   The woman is on you like a panther. Her steel fingers choke you with the strength of a giantess. You strike her and nothing happens. You strike again and again but she feels nothing. The world starts to blur.

      You hear wood splinter. The farmer has broken into the barn. He races across and jumps on his wife's back. She drops you to try and pry him off. Stars fill your eyes as the blood rushes back. She throws the farmer, her husband against the wall like a rag doll. Then she turns back towards you.

(592 cont'd)

You rise on one knee and:

(A) Decide you can't stop her through the traditional use of spells and decide to detain her with a *levitate* spell? <u>Mark off 3 manna</u> and roll the dice:

2 to 11, Turn to <u>573</u>.
12, Turn to <u>536</u>.

(B) Try to reason with her? Turn to <u>536</u>.

(C) Fire Shefast? Roll the dice:

2 to 7, Turn to <u>1005</u>.
8 to 12, Turn to <u>536</u>. The staff fails!

593   The spell settles firmly around. Gathering courage you step towards the fence. Another step and suddenly it feels as if your body is being torn apart. The power infused within the fence is enormous. It tears at your spell like a mountain lion. Your knees feel as though they are going to buckle. Roll the dice:

2 to 8, Turn to <u>605</u>.
9 to 12, Turn to <u>628</u>.

594   The storm giant pulls its cloud to a halt. Striking the cloud with his fist it shatters and he plummets to the ground.

The giant is brilliant white, wearing clothes tattered and wet with his rage. He moves towards you.

"Who dares to tamper with the fire that is rightfully mine?" Do you:

(A) Drop the staff and run? Turn to <u>582</u>.

(Continued next page)

(594 cont'd)

      (B) Strike out with the staff? Turn to <u>576</u>.

      (C) Tell him your name? Turn to <u>558</u>.

      (D) Put the staff away and attempt a *control* spell on the creature? <u>Mark off 4 manna</u> and turn to <u>586</u>.

595   You could:

      (A) Cast a *reverse* spell on yourself and hope that your magic is powerful enough to ward off the magic of the fence. You could simply cast it on yourself and charge the fence. <u>Mark off 4 manna</u> and turn to <u>593</u>.

      (B) Try to fly over the fence. Perhaps its magic doesn't extend to great heights. <u>Mark off 3 manna</u> and turn to <u>591</u>.

      (C) Attempt a *negate* spell. If it works you might free these people as well as help yourself, but you must move closer to get within range. <u>Mark off 4 manna</u> and turn to <u>616</u>.

      (D) Turn back to <u>574</u> to experiment further.

596   With your robes still smoldering do you:

      (A) Attempt a *control* spell? <u>Mark off 4 manna</u> and turn to <u>586</u>.

      (B) Drop to your knees and tell him that the good of the Western kingdoms rests with you? Turn to <u>587</u>.

      (C) Drop the staff and run? Turn to <u>582</u>.

      (D) Strike with Shefast, uncertain about what lightning could possibly do against a creature who seems to be composed of the stuff? Turn to <u>576</u>.

597   Your mind reaches across and ... Roll the dice:

2, 3, 5, 6, 7, Turn to 569.
4, 8, 9, 10, 11, 12, Turn to 581.

598   The great staff harnesses the wild lightning and summons it to you. Up the bolt races striking the form once more. A cloud crumbles and a giant white form plummets to earth. When it strikes it sounds as if the earth splits. The form rises. Before you stands a giant of brilliant white light. The giant's clothes are jagged and wet with the fury of his temper.

Like booming thunder a voice shouts out, "Who dares tamper with my fire."

It is a storm giant! This creature is many more times powerful than even you. Do you:

(A) Drop the staff and run? Turn to 582.

(B) Strike again? Turn to 576.

(C) Tell the giant your name? Turn to 558.

(D) Put the staff away to attempt a *control* spell in the creature? Mark off 4 manna and turn to 586.

599   Roll the dice:

2, 3, 5, 6, 7, Turn to 595.
4, 8, 9, 10, 11, 12, Turn to 562.

600

<u>Mark off the next day and replenish all manna and erase all damage.</u>

The morning is bright. The night is damp and you are happy to rise early. Breaking camp you begin the last leg of your trek across the land. You should be able to reach Wellsport by nightfall. Tomorrow you will book passage and set sail. Perhaps the sea will be a little more welcoming than the land.

Somewhat stiff and sore you set out at a good pace. Soon the terrain turns from farmland to gently rolling hills. There are no Eastern patrols to bother you.

Several candles before noon, you stop on top of one of the larger hills and search the surrounding lands for pursuit. From the hilltop you look northeast and find that nothing is following. When you look towards the west you see that the land is also clear. There seems to be a set of fence posts stretched across the land but that should be no problem to cross. It looks like some people are crossing over the fence.

Wait! They aren't moving. Perhaps they are waiting or making camp. You descend the hill relatively sure that you are safe. Down and over another hill you finally see the fence once more.

The people haven't moved! You immediately duck, aware of danger. The fence posts are up but there is no wire or fencing strung between them. The people aren't moving!

The fence seems to stretch on forever.

The people aren't moving!

(600 cont'd)

Do you:

(A) Toss a rock by the fence? Turn to <u>585</u>.

(B) Detect magic? You will have to move much closer to get within spell range. <u>Mark off 1 manna</u> and turn to <u>589</u>.

(C) Try to approach the nearest victim? Turn to <u>567</u>.

601   The earth opens and swallows the wolves. They snarl and leap at the edges unable to get out.

"Forget your pets Dark One. The contest is between you and me," you shout!

The Dark Lord angers and the sky flames brighter.

"Agreed" he replies flatly. Turn to <u>603</u>.

602   Incredibly your spell works. The Dark Lord freezes! The wolves transform into men. They were captured Western soldiers all along.

Gasping, you walk closer to the Dark Lord. On the Dark Lord's chest his godstones flare and he begins to move. Your spell cannot hold him. Turn to <u>603</u>.

603   Do you:

(A) Strike out with Shefast providing you still have it? Roll the dice:

2 to 10, Turn to <u>615</u>.
11 or 12, Turn to <u>636.</u>

(B) Try to change shape to either escape or physically fight? <u>Mark off 4 manna</u> and turn to <u>627</u>.

(C) Cast a tremor at his feet? <u>Mark off 3 manna</u> and roll the dice:

2 to 11, Turn to <u>629</u>.
12, Turn to <u>636</u>.

(D) Attempt to turn him to stone with a *transmute* spell? <u>Mark off 4 manna</u> and roll the dice:

2 to 11, Turn to <u>636</u>.
12, Turn to <u>602</u>.

(E) Move towards the shaft of light breaking through the cloud. Turn to <u>635</u>.

(F) Cast a *reverse* spell on yourself for protection? <u>Mark off 4 manna</u> and roll the dice:

2 to 11, Turn to <u>647</u>.
12, Turn to <u>636</u>.

(G) Spit in your hand, draw your best weapon and charge? If <u>Z</u> is marked, turn to <u>618</u>. If not turn to <u>619</u>.

604   The light is somewhat refreshing but for now you have more important matters that concern you. The Dark Lord is ... Turn to <u>641</u> if <u>Z</u> is marked. If not turn to <u>640</u>.

605   The power increases with each step forward. So does the pain but you brave it and continue forward. Then the power becomes so strong that it feels as if you walked directly into a brick wall. There is a loud crack. The fence's power is broken and so is your spell. Your body aches and you start to move but then it happens! Turn to 620.

606   A piece of a flaming cloud strikes you and sets your feathers aflame. The Dark Lord laughs. When you hit the ground you change back and the flame goes out.

Go to the Enchantraen table that follows and roll one die. Check off the damage boxes on your score card.

ENCHANTRAEN

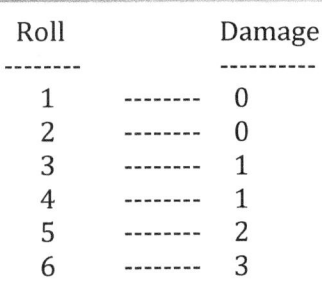

Roll		Damage
1	--------	0
2	--------	0
3	--------	1
4	--------	1
5	--------	2
6	--------	3

If you expire turn to 622. If you live turn to 619 if Z is not marked.

If Z is marked you see the Dark Lord ... Turn to 641.

607   Erase any marks on Z and AA.

"You insolent pig," the Dark Lord spurts bloodily at you. "You will pay! You will pay!" he repeats over and over again as he fades away.

All begins to quiet as the burning stops. The Dark Lord has teleported back to the East.

(Continued next page)

(607 cont'd)

"Flee before your better," you shout and raise your arm in triumph.

The spell on the fence is broken. The captured people have witnessed the whole thing. They rush towards you and a cheer breaks out. Turn to 609.

608   The last of the spell is spoken when you hear the crackling power of the fence. Your hands are suddenly frozen. You struggle to no avail.

"I am Enchantraen," you shout. "You cannot bind me as you would a common servant."

You pull with the power of your rage. The air seems to tear and you pull even harder. One after the other the fence posts explode. As you move your hands farther apart more posts explode and burst to flame. As far as you can see in either direction there is smoke rising skyward.

The people move again, released from the trance. They all witnessed your deed and as soon as their voices return the shouting begins. The voices grow in power as even the people you can't see begin to chant it. Turn to 609.

609   "Enchantraen, Enchantraen, Enchantraen!"

Soon you are overwhelmed with well-wishers.

When they lift you, you shout, "To Wellsport!"

As they carry you, you finally grasp how many people were actually caught in the trap. There is an army escorting you to Wellsport.

Onward they march until an Eastern patrol is unfortunate enough to cross their path. You catch a slight glimpse of men

(609 cont'd)

being pulled from their horses. Your army marches on shouting the entire way.

At dusk you reach the small fishing village and the army has broken into song.

Finally you get them to put you down. You walk out to the city's small port seeking a ship to take you towards the Mystic Isles. You are disappointed when you only find a small fishing boat.

You approach one of the fishermen and ask him if any ship is expected to dock soon. He tells you he wouldn't know. You ask him if there are any ships at all going to the Mystic Isles. Eyeing the crowd behind you he says that his ship is leaving in a couple of days.

"No I have to go sooner than that," you say disappointed.

Then the crowd takes over. Fearing for his life, the crowd throws you and the crew aboard and the Captain quickly follows. The Captain has a sudden change of heart. He decides he can leave tonight. The crowd pushes the ship from its dock. The sails unfurl as you say your final farewell.

There are no other wizards to go with you. The Dark Lord did manage to murder many of your capable colleagues as they stood frozen by the fence. He probably traveled the fence daily destroying all the notable wizards he could find. There is nothing you can do about that now. Ahead is the promise of the Mystic Isles and perhaps revenge. Turn to <u>730</u>.

610 It doesn't take you long to walk through the town to get to the dock. You search up and down the wharf looking for a suitable ship. There is none. You spot a fisherman getting out of his boat. His crew is unloading a large catch. Turn to <u>712</u>.

611   "To me servant! I have your first task." The staff obeys and with a clap of thunder the storm giant appears.

"You fool," the Dark Lord shouts at the storm giant. Do you so openly defy me?"

The Dark Lord waves his hand and the giant straightens and turns your way.

"Kill the wizard," the Dark Lord commands. The giant steps your way but then Shefast intervenes. A shot of lightning bursts from the staff and strikes the giant. The giant is thrown back but rises unhurt.

The Dark Lord is stunned to see the giant turn and cast a bolt of lightning his way.

Go to the Dark Lord's table that follows and roll one die. Check off the damage boxes on the Rogue's Gallery score card.

DARK LORD

Roll		Damage
1	--------	1
2	--------	2
3	--------	2
4	--------	3
5	--------	4
6	--------	Die

If the Dark Lord dies turn to <u>622</u>. If not he draws his sword and strikes back at the Giant!

Go to the Giant's table that follows and roll one die.

(611 cont'd)

Check off the damage boxes on the Rogue's Gallery score card.

GIANT

Roll		Damage
1	--------	2
2	--------	3
3	--------	3
4	--------	4
5	--------	4
6	--------	Expire

If the storm giant expires turn to 638. If he lives go back to the Dark Lord's table and hit him again!

612   Pulling a dagger, the Dark Lord throws it. The dagger immediately breaks in midair and transforms into a liquid the color of congealed blood.

If <u>AA</u> is marked turn to <u>637</u>.

If not, the liquid strikes and burns through you. <u>Mark off 5 boxes of damage</u> from your character sheet. If you live turn to <u>603</u>. If you expire turn to <u>622</u>.

613   The light strikes you and it happens again. It must be noon! The power surges and stirs deeply within you. Erase 2 damage points if you have any. With renewed strength you face the Dark Lord. Just before the light moves away you ....

(A)   Draw a weapon and charge? Turn to <u>632</u>.

(B)   Cast a *fire* spell at him? <u>Mark off 4 manna</u> and turn to <u>623</u>.

(C)   Fire Shefast? Turn to <u>631</u>.

614   If <u>W</u> is marked turn to <u>493</u>.

You quietly nestle down into the hay. After a short while you move your hands back and forth across a nail in minute strokes. Working consistently for many candles the leather straps fray and start to give way.

Roll the dice:

2 to 5, Turn to <u>656</u>.
6 to 12, Turn to <u>630</u>.

615   The lightning descends from the sky, strikes the staff and hits dead center into the Dark Lord's chest. The staff's charge dissipates slightly as you watch blue flames race across the Dark Lord's breast plate.

"Lightning protection," you gasp, "but not complete protection."

Go to the Enemy table that follows and roll one die. Check off the damage boxes on the Rogue's Gallery score card.

Dark Lord

Roll		Damage
1	--------	0
2	--------	1
3	--------	2
4	--------	2
5	--------	3
6	--------	4

If the Dark Lord dies turn to <u>642</u>. If he lives turn to <u>641</u>, if <u>Z</u> is marked. If not turn to <u>640</u>.

616   You start the first few words of your spell and move forward. You are trying to time the *negate* spell to take effect just as you reach the power of the fence.

Roll the dice:

2 to 8, Turn to <u>589</u>.
9 to 12, Turn to <u>608</u>.

617   <u>Mark off Z.</u>

The last of the wolves dies. Somehow you managed to live. Badly bloodied you turn to find the Dark Lord smiling down at you and ... Turn to <u>641</u>.

618   The Dark Lord steps back and draws a flaming sword. Smiling he beckons you to him. He knows that he is the master of sword and that you are not. You realize now that unless he is already badly hurt you are in trouble.

Go to the Enchantraen table that follows and roll one die. Check off the damage boxes on your score card.

ENCHANTRAEN

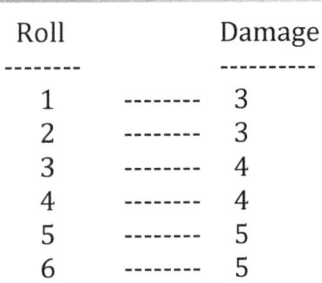

Roll		Damage
1	--------	3
2	--------	3
3	--------	4
4	--------	4
5	--------	5
6	--------	5

If you expire turn to <u>622</u>. If you live you are lucky and you may try to strike him.

(Continued next page)

(618 cont'd)

Go to the Enemy table that follows and roll one die. Check off the damage boxes on the Rogue's Gallery score card.

DARK LORD

Roll		Damage
1	--------	0
2	--------	0
3	--------	0
4	--------	1
5	--------	2
6	--------	3

If he dies, which I can't believe, turn to <u>642</u> and count your blessings. If not go back to the Enchantraen table and take your lumps.

619 You draw your weapon just as the wolves are on you. It is then that you realize they are magical. Six jaws snap around you.

Go to the Enchantraen table that follows and roll <u>six</u> dice (one for each wolf).

(619 cont'd)

Check off the damage boxes on your score card.

ENCHANTRAEN

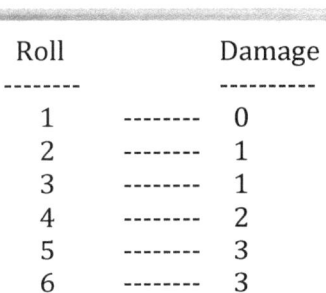

Roll		Damage
1	--------	0
2	--------	1
3	--------	1
4	--------	2
5	--------	3
6	--------	3

If you expire turn to 622. If you live you discover you must kill a wolf to get rid of it! It will not be hurt otherwise.

ENEMY

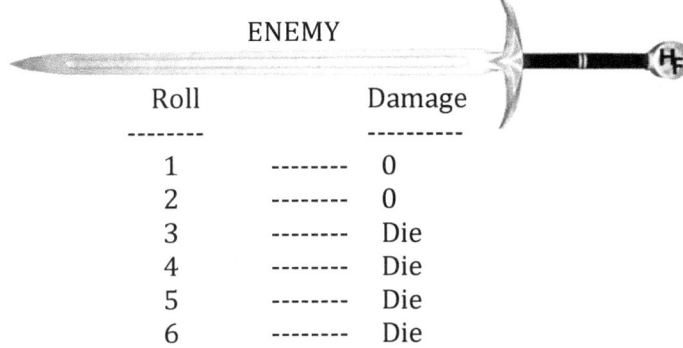

Roll		Damage
1	--------	0
2	--------	0
3	--------	Die
4	--------	Die
5	--------	Die
6	--------	Die

If this was the last wolf killed turn to 617. If more wolves remain go back to the Enchantraen table and let each remaining wolf strike you!

620 It started with a distant rumbling in the ground. At first you thought some powerful wizard had cast an enchantment to wake the earth elemental. You were wrong. The ground does not shake from a mighty force. It shakes in revolt from being walked on by some malign creature. Yes, the trembling is consistent with the footsteps of a man. Something awesome is

(Continued next page)

(620 cont'd)

walking towards you from the other side of the hill. Your mind races through the possible protective spells you might cast around you. When the black storm clouds burst to flames sending harmless ash cascading to the ground you decide it would be useless.

You are right.

The first to top the hill are six black wolves. They form a crescent-like protective half-ring around the top of the hill, but none of them sit. They each assume a crouched position ready to spring. The trembling earth stops for two heartbeats. All you see is the burning clouds reflecting in the wolves' coal black eyes.

The trembling begins and light perspiration breaks out on your forehead. The black fog rolls to the top of the hill. Again you see the fire reflect in the swirling mass. The fog settles and the creature is slowly revealed.

His hands are upraised and his head is tilted back towards the sky. His armor is a finely woven black chainmail. Set carefully into his chest plate are the pearl godstones that both reflect and emit their own light. The tilted chin begins to lower and you can see the lips beginning to shape a word. All you can do is close your eyes and pray that the Dark Lord is not going to utter your name ...

If Z is marked turn immediately to 652.

If U is marked turn to 625.

If Z or U are not marked but Y is marked turn to 565.

If none of these are marked turn to 603.

621   The feeling of weightlessness overcomes you as you rise. Up
and up you fly. Higher, and higher, attempting to put as much
distance between you and the fence as possible. To fall from
this distance will mean instant death. With all your strength
you fly due west towards Wellsport and over the fence. When
you fly directly over the fence a crackling sound and rumble
starts.

You are over! Below it appears as though the fence has come
to life. The posts themselves seem to move. That was easy.
Just then you see a black cloud forming ahead of you.

You pull up short and prepare a *defensive* spell. The cloud
takes shape and you see a huge head of the Dark Lord staring
at you. Your hands unconsciously begin to motion. The head
speaks. "It is not over wizard. You have not won yet! I will
curse you and your race before this is over." The head fades
and you stop the spell.

Off you fly until the sensation of the noon sun overtakes you.
Once again you are flushed with the sense of power and you
laugh to yourself. You recognized a certain amount of
frustration in the Dark Lord's voice. Although the war isn't
over the battle is yours!

Away you fly until the spell ends. Then you set down and walk
the rest of the way to Wellsport. Turn to 610.

622   Erase any marks on Z and AA.

The Dark Lord rushes to your side. He bends down and
splashes a vile in your face. You suddenly feel revived but
unable to move.

"Don't die on me sweet Enchantraen. I can't make it that easy
on you. Let me cut away the parts I don't like. The rest of you
will follow me around for a long time.

(Continued next page)

(622 cont'd)

The Dark Lord rises and draws a flaming sword. Exactly what he does with you is superfluous at this point. Let's just say that he is not kind enough to let you die.

Your loud and lingering scream echoes across the land and the game is over. Please don't let him get you next time.

623 You complete the spell as you have many times before. You wait for the familiar fire to spring into your hand but it doesn't happen. Instead a fountain of flame shoots up at your feet. With the force of a volcano, lava steams towards the Dark Lord.

He waves spells of protection but you discover you can feed even more power into your spell. Flames leap up around him. He is temporarily lost from your sight but you can hear the cries of anguish.

A flaming column leaps into the air. As the trailing flames fall away you see the Dark Lord fly up into the air.

Beating out his burning body with his hands he shouts... Turn to <u>607</u>.

624 The arrows come but you are too high for them to do much damage. Many crackle and fall away stopped by the protection from your gem.

Go to the Enchantraen table that follows and roll one die.

(624 cont'd)

Check off the damage boxes on your score card.

ENCHANTRAEN

Roll		Damage
1	--------	0
2	--------	0
3	--------	1
4	--------	1
5	--------	1
6	--------	2

If you expire turn to <u>200</u>. If you live turn to <u>659</u>.

625 The Dark Lord speaks. In a deep bass voice he says, "Come forward my plaything."

From out of the black mist crawls the lich you sent to kill him.

The once great magic-user has been badly mutilated. Both legs and one arm are missing. The lich moves by dragging along on its stomach, pulling with its one good hand. The lich lifts its head and you see that its face is torn and swollen from where its eyes used to be. The lich lifts a hand and there on its palm is an eye.

The lich waves it around looking and cries, "Death now Master, please."

The Dark Lord shouts "Look and behold your fate Enchantraen. My pet needs a playmate. I shall take you two wherever I go! You will become the best of playmates."

If <u>Y</u> is marked turn to <u>565</u>.

If not, trembling you should turn to <u>603</u>.

626

Mark off the next day and replenish all manna and erase all damage.

Death seems imminent. You search your cell and discover that they have taken your things. Slapping the side of your robe in disgust you wonder why they even bothered to heal you. That's when you find the godstone. How is it possible that they overlooked it?

The stone tingles and your cell door vanishes. Cautiously you peer out. Outside your cell you realize that you must be on one of the lower decks. There are other doors that you guess to be cells like yours. You feel a familiar tug in one direction. That must be where your book is hidden. Slowly you move to what you think is the back of the ship. You find a porthole and crates. Looking out the porthole you see nothing but open sea. You feel the tug again. You are very close to your book. You grab a crowbar and start prying. The cracking timber is loud but necessary. You find it! There in the bottom of the crate are all of your belongings nicely bundled in your backpack.

As you reach for your things you hear men coming. You jump to the portal. Dangling half in and half out of the ship is how they find you. The deck of the ship is filling with Eastern sailors carrying green tipped arrows. You decide to:

(A) Continue to squeeze through? Turn to <u>1006</u>.

(B) Stop and throw your godstone saying, "Save me now!" <u>Erase the mark on P</u> and turn to <u>770</u>.

627   You start the spell and feel the aether flow in rhythm with your fingers. In your mind you visualize a giant eagle. This bird has always been one of your favorites.

(627 cont'd)

In this form you may:

(A) Fly off into the sky. Turn to <u>606</u>.

(B) Attack! Subtract any damage you have already taken and turn to <u>618</u>. Use the damage boxes for the eagle on the Rogue's Gallery.

628   The power floods towards you but your spell throws it back. Forward you go and with each step the power increases. So does the pain. Your body threatens to shake apart and you find that you can only inch forward.

"I am Enchantraen," you repeat over and over to yourself forcing yourself to move.

Just as it feels as if you can go no further the power snaps. You fall to your knees and roll violently to your stomach. Your body is drenched in sweat. Rising you see that you have crossed the fence. It would take a Dark Lord to infuse the fence with such power.

Just then the noon day sun strikes you and fills you with power. You might not have won the war but you certainly have won this battle. Laughing, you stand and race off towards Wellsport.

The rest of the day passes and you can't help but smile when the tiny fishing port comes within sight. Turn to <u>610</u>.

629   The Dark Lord starts to stumble as the earth splits. Then the pearl godstone flares and the earth stops and obeys. Regaining his balance the Dark Lord laughs and ... Turn to <u>641</u> if <u>Z</u> is marked. If not, turn to <u>640.</u>

630   You think a soldier has seen your trick. You hear a horse riding up behind you. Holding your breath you are relieved to see the horsemen ride past you to take a position at the point. You carefully snap the leather but leave it dangling loosely around your wrists. This way your hands are free enough to cast a spell but it still looks as if you are bound. Your cage is locked.

You could:

(A) Magically unlock it so that no one notices. Then you could kick it open and transform into a giant eagle and fly away. Maybe that will surprise them enough for you to escape before they can use their bows. This plan will cost you six manna to cast the full series of spells if everything works. Turn to 644 and mark off 2 manna if you want to start.

(B) Kick the door open and jump. Turn to 687.

631   You command the great staff to blast. This time however something is different. For a moment you are aware of the great power that rests within the staff. You tap into that power and call it forth.

The sky rips and tears overhead. From all corners lightning races to the staff. Gathering momentarily the lightning leaps forth towards the Dark Lord. When it strikes, huge chunks of earth are blown apart by the impact.

If it were not for the Dark Lord's godstones and protections you are certain there would be nothing left of him.

Go to the Enemy table that follows and roll one die.

(631 cont'd)

Check off the damage boxes on the Rogue's Gallery score card

DARK LORD

Roll		Damage
1	--------	3
2	--------	3
3	--------	5
4	--------	6
5	--------	Die
6	--------	Die

If the Dark Lord lives turn to <u>641</u> if <u>Z</u> is marked.
If <u>Z</u> is not marked turn to <u>640</u>.

If the Dark Lord dies turn to <u>642</u>.

632 Charge Lord Gaoler and do combat. Turn to <u>618</u>.

<u>Also add 2 to your roll</u> when attacking the Dark Lord.

633 Your spell sputters and fails. The Dark Lord has incredible magic resistance. A costly lesson to learn. The wolves are on you. Turn to <u>619</u>.

634 Lord Gaoler rushes towards you in an attempt to lock you in combat.

(Continued next page)

(634 cont'd)

As he advances do you:

(A) Cast a *tremor* spell at his feet to split the earth and swallow him up? <u>Mark off 3 manna</u> and roll the dice:

2 to 11, Turn to <u>629</u>.
12, Your spell fails! He is one you now and you must draw your weapon. Turn to <u>618</u>.

(B) Blast with Shefast and then prepare to fight? Roll the dice:

2 to 10, Turn to <u>649</u>.
11 or 12, It fails, draw a weapon and turn to <u>618</u>.

(C) Pull your weapon and fight? Turn to <u>618</u>.

(D) Cast a stone wall into his path? <u>Mark off 4 manna</u> and roll the dice:

2 to 11, Turn to <u>653</u>.
12, The spell fails. Draw your weapon and turn to <u>618</u>.

(E) If <u>Y</u> is marked you may release the storm giant. Turn to <u>611</u>.

635   Roll the dice:

2 to 7, 10, Turn to <u>613</u>.
8, 9, 11, 12, Turn to <u>604</u>.

636   The pearl godstones on the Dark Lord's chest flare and tamper with your magic. They change *fate* and your magic fails! The Dark Lord laughs at your petty efforts and ... Turn to <u>641</u> if <u>Z</u> is marked. If not turn to <u>640</u>.

637   The death threat turns in midair and races back towards the Dark Lord. With a wave of his hand and a scream the liquid is brushed aside and your *reverse* spell is negated. Erase any marks on <u>AA</u> and turn to <u>603</u>.

638   <u>Erase the mark on Y</u>.

The Dark Lord staggers away from a burning column of fire. That is all that is left of the giant.

If the Dark Lord's defense is below 7 turn to <u>607</u> immediately.
         If not turn to <u>603</u>.

639   Only the faintest click can be heard as a smile crosses your lips. The door unlocks. All is well so far.

Now comes the most dangerous part. <u>Mark off 4 manna</u>. The change shape spell is difficult to cast without using a lot of arm movement. You bury your arms under the straw to help hide their movement. Slowly you begin the words to your spell.

"Silence wizard," a soldier shouts!

Do you:

(A) Stop your spell? Turn to <u>656.</u>

(B) Continue on acting as if you are in a dream? Turn to <u>666</u>.

640   <u>Mark off Z</u>.

"Attack," the Dark Lord commands.

The six great wolves' spring even before the Dark Lord finishes his command. Bounding at you like a pack of death.

(Continued next page)

(640 cont'd)

Do you:

(A) Split the earth to try and swallow the wolves up? <u>Mark off 3 manna</u> and roll the dice:

2 to 11, Turn to <u>601</u>.
12, Your spell fails! Turn to <u>619</u>.

(B) Ignore the wolves and try to attack the Dark Lord directly with a transmute sell? <u>Mark off 4 manna</u> and roll the dice:

2 to 11, Turn to <u>633</u>.
12, Turn to <u>602</u>.

(C) Fight! Turn to <u>619</u>.

641 Roll the dice:

2 to 4, Turn to <u>612</u>.
5 to 9, Turn to <u>634</u>.
10 to 12, Turn to <u>645</u>.

642 <u>Erase any marks on Z or AA.</u>

The Dark Lord Gaoler staggers back and falls to his knees. His mouth drops open in astonishment as blood erupts from his ears and nose.

"You devil," Gaoler gasps. "You puny little fluff. The Master has cloned me you know. Someday my other selves will return to the West."

The Dark Lord falls forward on his hands.

In sobbing anguish Gaoler screams, "Help me Master," and falls forward on his face, dead.

(642 cont'd)

A black bolt of thunder launches into the sky and the body is gone.

You have killed a Dark Lord. The astonishment of it begins to sink in when the cheering erupts. The spell on the fence is broken. The freed people rush towards you. Turn to 609.

643   You start by coughing. Slowly you work up to gasps of pain rolling back and forth. You keep it up until ...

Roll the dice:

2 to 8, Turn to 672.
9 to 12, Turn to 658.

644   Your fingers move and you mumble the words that will unlock your cage. You attempt to disguise your enchantment as a disturbing dream in case a soldier overhears you.

Roll the dice:

2 to 5, Turn to 650.
6 to 12, Turn to 639.

645   The Dark Lord waves his own spell of death and hurls it your way. It seems like Death itself is calling for you as you fight off the horror of his enchantment.

If AA is marked turn to 637.

If not, you find yourself capable of dispelling it partly before it strikes.

Go to the Enchantraen table that follows and roll one die.

(Continued next page)

(645 cont'd)

Check off the damage boxes on your score card.

ENCHANTRAEN

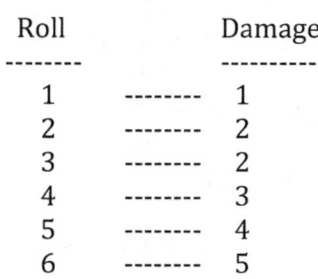

Roll		Damage
1	--------	1
2	--------	2
3	--------	2
4	--------	3
5	--------	4
6	--------	4

If you expire turn to <u>622</u>. If you live turn to <u>603</u>.

646 The arrows race towards you. They were better prepared than you hoped.

Go to the Enchantraen table that follows and roll one die. Check off the damage boxes on your score card.

ENCHANTRAEN

Roll		Damage
1	--------	1
2	--------	2
3	--------	2
4	--------	3
5	--------	4
6	--------	5

If you live turn to <u>659</u>. If you expire turn to <u>200</u>.

647   <u>Mark off AA</u>.

The spell takes hold and you feel its strength. It is a good cast you smile to yourself. Just then the Dark Lord ... Turn to <u>641</u> if <u>Z</u> is marked. If not turn to <u>640</u>.

648   A soldier charges towards you. Without stopping your chant you step back into the cage. The soldier slams the door but it doesn't lock. The momentum of his charging mount carries him past the wagon and forward. Turn to <u>666</u>.

649   The lightning strikes but the Dark Lord has protection!

Go to the Enemy table that follows and roll one die. Check off the damage boxes on the Rogue's Gallery score card.

ENEMY

Roll	Damage
1	0
2	1
3	2
4	3
5	3
6	4

If the Dark Lord dies from the blast turn to <u>642</u>.

If he lives you have just enough time to draw a weapon before he engages. Turn to <u>618</u>.

650   "The wizard's loose," shouts the commander.

You stop your spell realizing the danger. You begin a spell of protection when the butt of a lance strikes your head. While unconscious the soldiers bind you once more. It is a long time before you regain consciousness. Turn to <u>685</u>.

---

651   In the middle of your spell a soldier charges forward on your blind side. He strikes you with the blunt end of his sword and you fall. Turn to <u>687</u>.

652   "Enchantraen," comes the voice that reaches through the air. "I can't let these savages have you."

    The Dark Lord pulls a gleaming blade. "I have waited too long for this. I shall cut away those parts I don't like and save the rest for myself. You shall be my pet and stay with me always."

    The blade lowers and your scream echoes across the land.

    Ouch! The End.

653   The Dark Lord strikes the wall. In screams of rage he tears at the wall with his bare hands, but not before you turn to <u>603</u>.

654

    <u>Mark off the next day and replenish all manna and erase all damage.</u>

    The next morning you are up and out before noon suffering slightly from cabin fever. The ship's progress is steady. This part of the river runs slowly. There are over 100 tributaries that feed the Tress and the further down you travel the faster the water flows. The river is deep enough to allow plenty of draft for even the largest seagoing vessel.

    The river Tress is a good and steady river. There are few oxbow lakes and levees along the way. Later downstream you can expect to pass through large cliffs where the river has cut through rock for ages. Looking deep into the muddy water you seem to feel a part of the good fertile soil that the river will deposit downstream.

(654 cont'd)

The water stirs and a school of fish leap. Surprised, you step back and then it happens to you again. It is noon and the sun is filtering through the magical rainbow. It stirs deep within you and grows. A feeling of power sweeps through you, trembling over your body. The feeling builds until the pressure becomes too great to contain your joy any longer. You are on your way to the Mystic Isles to challenge an Elder and then become one yourself. What could be better?

"Out of my way foolish ones," you shout, "I have a purpose! I have a destiny to fulfill."

Your voice seems to echo across the lands. The crew turns astonished to see their quiet passenger making such an outburst. The power dwindles but it leaves you feeling positive and even more determined. You walk towards the bow of the vessel willing to face the coming challenges head on. The first of these challenges is not far away.

Your ship is heading due west toward Wellsport. It is here in one of the bends that you witness the East's second flagrant violation of the treaty they signed with the city of Jerican. The East has lined the river with barges to force ships to stop so the soldiers can search them. There are several ships pulled to the side even now. You duck when you see an Eastern horse patrol passing your boat on the northern bank. The commander of the patrol is shouting orders for your Captain to drag anchor and make preparation for a boarding party.

If you are aboard the Cago turn to <u>671.</u>

If you are aboard the Perfidia turn to <u>681</u>.

If you are aboard the Lady Varaë turn to <u>691</u>.

655   A shout from over the next hill catches the attention of many soldiers. The illusion is of 50 well-armed Western knights coming to the rescue. The majority of the Eastern soldiers flee in panic, knowing they are no match against such an elite group.

The Eastern commander is also affected by the illusion. He, however, has a duty. He spurs his mount towards you in an effort to capture you and throw you over this horse. You will be forced to drop the illusion to properly meet the charge of the soldier. Wait! He has your equipment. You hold the illusion until the soldier is right up on you. This makes him think that you are being submissive. He attempts to pull you up. When he reaches down you swing up, plant both feet on the side of the horse and push. The soldier is pulled from the saddle. As the Commander drops to the ground your *illusion* spell dissipates. Turn to 657.

656   The blunt end of a lance jabs you in your side and rolls you over. You attempt to hold your hands together but the jolt forces them apart.

"The wizard's untied," shouts the soldier! Turn to 673

657   You scramble up and ride! You hear soldiers rallying in pursuit. You lie close to the mount's neck to make as small a target as possible for the archers. Arrows whiz past! You hear a horn which is quickly answered by another up ahead. Spurring your mount you turn and head west. The soldiers dare not pursue a fully armed wizard too closely.

On and on you go listening to the horns blowing around you.

If BB is mark turn to 674. If KK is marked turn to 1001. If not turn to 480.

658   A lance pokes through the bars and the Commander says, "I have just the thing for your cough if you keep it up."

A sharp jab stresses his point. The Commander is smarter than you thought. The soldiers are very alert now to any possible attempts you might make to escape. With nothing else to do you sit and wait for a more opportune time. Turn to <u>685</u>.

659   You shake your bundle of belongings from the saddle. You circle to get your bearings and then race off towards the west. Traveling in this form should help you make up for some of the time you lost by being captured.

Determined to make the Mystic Isles you turn to <u>697</u> if <u>BB</u> is marked. If <u>KK</u> is marked turn to <u>1001</u>, otherwise turn to <u>500</u>.

660

<u>Mark off the next day and replenish all manna and erase all damage.</u>

In the morning all signs of pursuit are gone. You do your best to shake off last night's nightmare but the cloudy skies don't help. You gather your things and walk on. The day remains cloudy until late afternoon.

You start to sit down and rest at the top of a hill when you see it. Turn to <u>688</u> if <u>BB</u> is marked, otherwise turn to <u>201</u>.

661   You complete the spell and the soldier says, "Thank you," and moves away.

"Wizard," shouts a second soldier to your far left. Blades are drawn and soldiers charge for the attack.

(Continued next page)

(661 cont'd)

Thinking quickly you:

(A) Prepare a magical attack? Turn to <u>665</u>.

(B) Jump for the river? Turn to <u>690</u>.

662   Do you:

(A) Go ahead and wait for the search? Maybe they are after gold and treasure. Turn to <u>683</u>.

(B) Change shape into a large turtle and climb over the side? There is a chance you could lose some of your belongings doing it this way. Turn to <u>698.</u>

663   <u>Mark off S.</u>

The archers, who are ready, fire! Many of the arrows simply crackle against your missile protection gem but some get through.

Go to the Enchantraen table that follows and roll one die. Check off the damage boxes on your score card.

ENCHANTRAEN

Roll	Damage
1	0
2	1
3	1
4	2
5	2
6	3

If you expire turn to <u>200</u>.

(663 cont'd)

If you live you find that you are still able to complete the words to your spell. The transformation begins and you feel the feathers prickle through your skin.

Up you race, climbing for altitude. Suddenly you realize that you need your book! You bank and dive in your giant eagle form ... Turn to 667.

664   The blade slashes deeply into your arm and the bindings are cut.

Go to the Enchantraen table that follows and roll one die. Check off the damage boxes on your score card.

ENCHANTRAEN

Roll		Damage
1	--------	0
2	--------	1
3	--------	2
4	--------	2
5	--------	3
6	--------	4

If your defense falls to zero turn to 700, immediately. If not read on.

As the bindings fall away you see the soldiers beginning to flood in.

"To me Sebastobol!" you shout and lift your arms.

The soldiers pause and step back expecting to see the ancient serpent rising from the ground at any moment. That brief

(Continued next page)

(664 cont'd)

pause is all you need. It will take <u>3 manna</u> to complete this spell. If you have it <u>mark it off</u> and roll the dice:

2 to 11, Turn to <u>680</u>.
12, Your spell fails. Turn to <u>700</u>.

If you haven't got the manna, turn to <u>700</u>.

665 <u>Mark off BB</u>.

You lift your hands to start a spell when stars flash before your eyes. As you fall you twist to see the ship's Captain standing behind you with a club in his hands.

"Not on my ship" he bellows as you fall into unconsciousness. Turn to <u>469</u>.

666 <u>Mark off S</u>.

You finish your spell!

A soldier gallops up to the back of the cage and shouts, "What have you done!"

The change begins.

"This," you retort as you kick the door open in his face.

The swinging door knocks the soldier off his horse. You leap into the air even before the transformation is complete. In midair you get your wings and turn to <u>667</u>.

667 You dive at the soldier that you sense has your belongings. The soldier screams and falls from the horse. Your powerful claws dig into the saddle.

(667 cont'd)

Up you climb, the horse screaming beneath you. The saddle breaks and the horse falls. You hear the words you feared most.

"Ready, aim, - Fire!"

You can only hope that the soldiers were slow to prepare.

Roll the dice:

2 to 5, Turn to 646.
6 to 12, Turn to 624.

668 The search party's commander orders the soldiers off the ship. They obey and you see two barges being pulled to the side to allow the Cago to pass. As the ship eases by the blockade you return to your berth and breathe a sigh of relief.

"Those idiots," you think. "Soon they will discover my identity and regret it." Turn to 694.

669 When you unbundle your pack you are relieved to find that everything is there. The cover of your book is wet and so are the edges of your pages. You lay it out to dry and stretch across the deck yourself. The sun dries your clothes. When you rise to go to the evening meal you see something that causes you to stop cold.

You see the last of an Eastern horse patrol disappear into the light woods.

How long have they been following you? Do they recognize you? These and other questions will be answered in the following days.

Turn to 694.

670   The Eastern soldier moves through your defenses and places the dagger at your throat.

"Would you like to repeat that wizard," the Easterner sneers.

Do you:

(A) Say, "I am a healer and no more"? Turn to <u>689</u>.

(B) Try to kick the rogue away since he obviously knows you? Turn to <u>692</u>.

671   You run to the Captain's side and say, "Don't do it Captain."

"Look wizard you must be crazy. This is a cargo ship with a hold full of merchandise. Check the freeboard wizard. We're riding low. Those barges will tear us apart. Besides, these devils won't be interested in a cargo of sugar. We've got nothing to hide."

The Captain then goes to the bridge and orders the mate to comply. You dare not tell him your name. They might turn you over just to protect their own hides. There is still time to react. If <u>K</u> is marked turn to <u>677</u>.

If not, turn to <u>662</u> and decide.

672   "Healer! The wizard's sick," shouts the commander. "You were told to keep the Westerner healthy until we reach camp."

The healer rides forward and jumps up on the back of the cage. The wagon never stops as the healer opens the door and climbs in. As he approaches you rub a bandage on your arm. The healer bends down with a knife to cut away the bandage to check the supposedly infected wound. It is now or never!

You throw your arms up and the knife slices you bindings. With a swift kick you knock the healer back. He hits the door

(672 cont'd)

which swings open and he falls out the back. With lightning speed you are up and at the door. Turn to 673.

673   Do you:

(A) Cast a change shape on yourself to become a giant eagle and fly away? There will be a slight delay before the spell completely takes effect. It will cost you 4 manna. Roll the dice:

2 to 7, 10, Turn to 648.
8, 9, 11, 12, Turn to 651.

(B) Jump for the Commander on his horse? You believe he has your belongings. Turn to 693.

(C) Dive off of the back? Turn to 687.

674   It takes some doing to lose the soldiers. You turn and change direction and then turn again. Each way you turn you can still hear the horn. Then you see it. Turn to 688.

675   The Commander is up and pulls you out of the stirrups. You both tumble to the ground. You find the soldier's dagger and pull it. You throw your arm back giving you enough room to swing the blade. Three lances poke your back. Looking up you see three riders. You drop the blade, roll off, and stand up. Turn to 678.

676   Several of the soldiers turn to ride off in fear! You attempt to make the illusion of charging western knights more real. The Commander doesn't believe it and orders his men to surround you. An arrow crackles against the gem's protection, and the illusion fades.

Go to the Enchantraen table that follows and roll one die.

(Continued next page)

(676 cont'd)

Check off the damage boxes on your score card.

ENCHANTRAEN

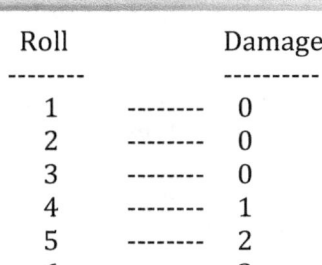

Roll		Damage
1	--------	0
2	--------	0
3	--------	0
4	--------	1
5	--------	2
6	--------	3

If you expire turn to <u>200</u>. If you live you find that you are soon wrestled to the ground and imprisoned once more.

Back in your cage you attempt to heal yourself but that proves impossible with your hands bound so tightly. Angered and humiliated you can do nothing now but wait. Turn to <u>685</u>.

677 You have the *Incantation of Knot*. You could use it to give the boat a burst of speed that will hopefully break through the barricade.

If you are determined to try it turn to <u>695</u> and proceed.

If it sounds too risky turn to <u>662</u>.

678 You lift your hands to surrender. An arrow thumps into your back.

Go to the Enchantraen table that follows and roll one die.

(678 cont'd)

Check off the damage boxes on your score card.

ENCHANTRAEN

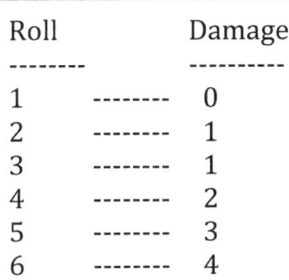

Roll		Damage
1	--------	0
2	--------	0
3	--------	0
4	--------	1
5	--------	2
6	--------	3

If you expire turn to <u>200</u>.

A soldier tackles you from behind and you are soon tied up once more. Thrown into the cage you feel humiliated and angry. There is little to do now. You can't even heal your wound. It is a long, long ride with the soldiers watching you all the way. Turn to <u>685</u>.

679   The soldier slashes and the blade bites deeply.

Go to the Enchantraen table that follows and roll one die. Check off the damage boxes on your score card.

ENCHANTRAEN

Roll		Damage
1	--------	0
2	--------	1
3	--------	1
4	--------	2
5	--------	3
6	--------	4

(Continued next page)

(679 cont'd)

If your defense falls to zero turn to 700. If not, you kick the soldier away and run back into the middle of the circle. Snarling you charge yet another soldier. The soldier's blade lifts and so does your battered arms. Turn to 686.

680 The spell takes effect. Staring at the ground you watch your body becoming absorbed into your own shadow!

Having become the shadow you quickly move to mix in with the soldier's own shadow. Confusion runs through the crowd. Magicians start casting *negate invisibility* spells. Archers fill the air with arrows but no one can find you. The bonfire provides you with excellent cover. Quietly and swiftly you pass from shadow to shadow totally unseen by the panicking soldiers.

You stop cold in your tracks. You have stumbled across the area of camp where the horses are staked. You feel the presence of your book nearby. You pass from horse to horse until you find attendants caring for the horses of the men who captured you. They are taking their saddles off and rubbing the horses down. You approach slowly until you are sure you know where your book and equipment are bound. They are in a saddle that is still strapped to a horse.

The confusion in the camp is becoming louder. Without even thinking you drop the *shadow* spell. The boy caring for the horses watches you rise up from the shadows. In stark terror he screams and runs. Hoping to take advantage of the confusion you grab the reins jump up and ride!

Kicking the flanks of the horse you race into the night. You bend over the neck of the horse to give the archers as small a target as possible. On you race, the soldiers in hot pursuit.

Your mount is tired to begin with and you realize it cannot keep up this pace. You are heading west which is the direction

(680 cont'd)

they expect you to go. In a snap decision you turn and head east towards Jerican.

On through the night you rush until the sounds of pursuit fade behind you. Finally your mount gives out and you are forced to stop for what is left of the night.

The horse is run into the ground. You chase it off in case you are still being followed. If any are still following, hopefully they will see the horse's tracks and trail it instead of looking for you.

Finding what little shelter there is you sleep restlessly until the next morning. Turn to <u>660</u>.

681   You turn to the Captain and ask him not to allow it.

The Captain smiles and says, "Don't worry wizard. This is a full-sized war galley. They won't stop us. We will cooperate enough to allow a small boarding party. After that, well, my crew can handle it."

You conceal yourself and watch a party of Eastern soldiers board the ship. The Captain greets them with a group of 50 of his best men. They exchange a few words but you are too far away to hear them. Do you:

(A) Cast an *ESP* spell that will allow you to hear? <u>Mark off 3 manna</u> and turn to <u>711</u>.

(B) Stay hidden and wait? Turn to <u>725</u>.

682 When you unbundle your pack you lay out and look through your belongings. Your book is intact. The cover is wet and the edges of several of the pages are also.

The staff! The staff Shefast is gone! You look over the railing into the dark waters. It could be anywhere by now.

Your eyes shoot quickly up from the water to the bank. There you see an Eastern horse patrol trailing the boat. Immediately you duck and the patrol disappears into the light forest. Did they see you? You ease back to a place of concealment. Only the following days will tell.

Check the gone box for your staff Shefast and be sure to ignore any options to use it from here on. Turn to 694.

683 You gather your things from your berth and come back up to the deck. By the time you get there, soldiers are already boarding and questioning the crew. A few have gone down to rummage through the hold. One of the crew members points your way and a soldier starts towards you.

"They tell me that you are adept at the art of magic," begins the soldier. "Is that true?"

Do you:

(A) Cast a *suggestion* spell on the soldier that he is mistaken? Mark off 2 manna and turn to 661.

(B) Tell him that you are flattered but you are actually a healer hoping to establish a practice in Wellsport? Turn to 699.

(C) Tell him that you are a wizard and the crewman was correct? Turn to 705.

---

684   The light blue binding leaps from your hands and securely ties him up. Looking across the deck you see soldiers rushing your way with drawn swords. Do you:

> (A) Jump off the side of the ship and swim for it. Turn to 690.

> (B) Prepare to meet them with your best magic? Turn to 665.

685   The wagon rolls on into the night until you fall asleep.

A horn awakens you from your disquieting slumber. The Commander blows the horn again and you hear another horn reply up ahead. In the distance you see fires burning. You sink down into the hay with the sudden realization that you are being taken into an Eastern army camp; a full-sized army.

Judging by the fires there are at least 3000 men! A new set of riders come forward to assist in escorting you. Soon the word goes through the camp that Enchantraen has been captured. Men line the way with torches just to peer into your cage. The entire camp stirs as soldiers rush to see the great war-wizard trapped.

Over the head of the soldiers you see a giant bonfire. In the fire you see large stakes sticking upright. You guess that the remains of the humans strapped to the stakes were once Western wizards.

The wagon pulls up to the side of the fire. The bright light casts deep shadows around the pack of men who surround it. A ghoul's feast, you think to yourself.

"Animals," you scream at the haunting crowd.

A cheer breaks out among them when they see your fear. Fighting down the panic you realize there is little hope for you.

(Continued next page)

(685 cont'd)

They unlock the back of the cage and a hundred hands grab for you. They lift you high and carry you towards the fire. The crowd's cheering deafens you and you withdraw within yourself. There deep within your bosom comes the voice.

"I am the great war wizard. I am the hope of the West. I am Enchantraen and I cannot die by hands such as these. I will fight!"

With wild eyes you look down at the men and see their shadows dancing around their feet. You develop a plan and resolve yourself to complete it regardless of how hopeless it now seems.

With strength born from desperation you twist and kick until the men carrying you are forced to drop you. When you hit the ground the men move back clearing a small circle around you. They half expect you to shatter the earth when you fall. Looking up you see your reputation weighs heavily on their faces. You jump to your feet but your hands are still bound making you powerless.

A hundred swords are pulled in answer to your challenge. You dash at the nearest blade risking everything on the hope that you can slash your bindings before they finish you off. The soldier panics and swings. You raise your hands. Turn to 686.

686   Roll the dice:

2 to 6, Turn to 679.
7, 8, Turn to 664.
9 to 12, Turn to 700.

687   You hit the ground and roll. Soldiers are drawing swords and readying bows.

(687 cont'd)

Do you:

(A) Change shape to escape? There is a large delay before this spell can take effect. That could prove fatal. <u>Mark off 4 manna</u> and roll the dice:

2 to 6, Turn to <u>663.</u>
7 to 12, Turn to <u>696.</u>

(B) Cast an illusion of Western soldiers charging over a hill to your rescue? Even if you get the spell off they might not believe it. <u>Mark off 4 manna</u> and roll the dice:

2 to 9, Turn to <u>655.</u>
10 to 12, Turn to <u>676.</u>

(C) Surrender realizing that you cannot run. Turn to <u>678.</u>

688　It is the river Tress. A large war galley passes by. A ship headed west! You spur your mount forward and attempt to keep pace with the ship. You call to the ship's crew that you wish to come aboard. You explain you are in bad need of passage and you are willing to pay.

It seems like a miracle when the ship stops and sends out a rowboat to pick you up. You gather your things, make a short trip back to the ship. There you climb up the rigging to the main deck. You are greeted by the Captain and twenty archers. You raise your hands in a sign of peace and say that you are willing to pay for passage. Turn to <u>707.</u>

689　"I am a healer," you insist. The soldier lowers his blade.

"A real wizard of any consequence wouldn't allow me to put him so close to death's door without a struggle. Even if you are a wizard you can't be much."

(Continued next page)

(689 cont'd)

The soldier spits on you and turns to walk away. Do you:

(A) Let him go? Turn to <u>668</u>.

(B) Prepare a spell to teach this soldier some manners. Turn to <u>665</u>.

690 A volley of arrows plummets and crackles against the protection given off by your shield.

Go to the Enchantraen table that follows and roll one die. Check off the damage boxes on your score card.

ENCHANTRAEN

Roll		Damage
1	--------	0
2	--------	1
3	--------	1
4	--------	2
5	--------	3
6	--------	4

Turn to <u>698</u> if you live.

Turn to <u>469</u> if you expire and <u>mark off BB</u>.

691 A young elf named Elwë quickly comes to your side.

"The Captain wishes to hear your instructions. He says the barricade cannot stop us but he awaits your decision."

(691 cont'd)

Do you:

(A) Say, "We stop for no one"? Turn to <u>719</u>.

(B) Order the ship to stop and allow the soldiers to come aboard? Turn to <u>708</u>.

692   You kick and strike the soldier in the midriff. He buckles over as you slam your hands down on his exposed back. Soldiers shout warnings and start to charge you.

Do you:

(A) Attack with magic? Turn to <u>665</u>.

(B) Change shape and jump? Turn to <u>690</u>.

693   You jump for the Commander and roll him from the saddle. You both hit the ground at the same time. A swift kick sends him sprawling. You turn to attempt to mount his jittery horse. That's when you see your equipment in his bags. Roll the dice:

2 to 7, Turn to <u>657</u>.
8 to 12, Turn to <u>675</u>.

694

<u>Mark off the next 2 days and replenish all manna and erase all damage.</u>

The Cago can only go a ways further before it once again becomes too dark. As the ship lumbers to a halt you begin to pace the deck. This ship is too slow! You will be glad when it docks at Wellsport. Maybe then you can get something a little more suitable to your mission. As you turn to go to your cabin

(Continued next page)

(694 cont'd)

you think you catch a glimpse of soldiers on a distant hill. You stare but see nothing further. Going to your berth you fall asleep and into dreams of the coming greatness you hope to achieve.

So goes the next two days aboard the lumbering ship. At the end of the fourth day exasperated by the lost time, you finally near Wellsport. Turn to <u>745.</u>

695   Turning from the Captain you go below and head straight to the chain locker where the anchor is stored. The anchor is lowered so you snap the chain. The Cago begins to drift.

Rushing to the bridge you see the crew start to panic. There are several boats rowing towards your ship filled with Eastern troops. The lead boat begins shouting warnings to the others about a trap.

The Captain runs to your side and says, "What have you done. They are going to fire on us."

You have already begun an incantation. You hardly hear his curses. <u>Mark off 3 manna.</u>

The ship leaps forward just as the first set of arrows rain across the deck. Crew members go down while others jump ship. Unfortunately the steersman is one of the crew who jumped.

You grab the wheel and steer the ship between the two barges that open to allow the ships that have been searched to pass. You hope that this will be the weakest part of the blockade.

The second rain of arrows strikes. By the third the keel of the ship hits the tip of one of the barges. Ropes snap and wood splinters as the ship is carried forward by the force of your spell. Water flies and the barges give way. You look back to see the Eastern boats becoming swamped by your wake.

(695 cont'd)

There is shouting and confusion from both the ship and the shore as the Cago crashes through and sails downstream.

The shipmen on the Cago are streaming into lifeboats and deserting the ship. The Captain's commands go by unheeded.

Roll the dice:

2 to 5, Turn to 714.
6 to 12, Turn to 702.

696   The soldiers are quick to react. A flurry of arrows are sent your way.

Go to the Enchantraen table that follows and roll one die. Check off the damage boxes on your score card.

ENCHANTRAEN

Roll		Damage
1	--------	1
2	--------	2
3	--------	3
4	--------	4
5	--------	4
6	--------	5

Other soldiers are charging with lances. The spell is impossible to complete. Turn to 678 if you live. Turn to 200 if you expire.

697   Around and around you fly searching up and down the river for a ship. Traveling as a giant eagle is quick but it will cost you too much manna to sustain this shape for long. You need a ship and night is coming quickly.

(Continued next page)

(697 cont'd)

Your sharp eyes finally pick one out. It is the Perfidia. Your spell is almost gone so you decide to take the ship. Down you plummet. Crewmen start to run in panic at your arrival. You gently come down and land on the bulwark to the stern of the ship. There you change back and readjust your equipment. When you finish you see the Captain coming forward with bowmen at his side.

You raise your hand in a sign of peace and explain to the Captain that you only wish passage to the Mystic Isles. Turn to 707.

698 Time is of the essence. You wrap your book in leather and try to make it as watertight as possible. You quickly adjust the straps on your back and slip over the side of the ship. You recite the words to the spell and jump into the muddy waters where you feel the change coming on. As the water goes up around your body you feel your back becoming strong and firm. You are content to sink a while feeling safe in the brown murky depths. Your mind has slowed somewhat in your new body but it still functions. Slowly you swim far downstream. With the barges well behind you, you head towards the shore. There you find a rock to climb up on and sun yourself. If BB is marked turn to 729. If not, turn to 701.

699 "A healer you say. Very interesting!" The soldier suddenly turns on you and lashes with a dagger.

Do you:

(A) Bind him? Mark off 1 manna and turn to 684.

(B) Try to knock the knife away? This means you risk a slash to the throat. Turn to 670.

700   <u>Mark off Z.</u>

The soldiers overcome their fear and jump for you. First one, then another. You struggle but to no avail. They tie you securely and lift you up for the fire once more. Then it happens. Turn to <u>620.</u>

701   From the rock you watch the soldiers search the ship.

You feel as though you have all the time in the world. The search goes quickly. Two barges are pulled aside and the Cago is allowed to pass. You ease into the water and swim in a path to intercept the ship. When you reach the side of the ship you turn back and climb up the rigging.

You reach the deck dripping wet. The Captain runs to your side.

"Where have you been? They threatened to seize the ship if I didn't tell them where you were. They brought in a sensitive to search our minds. What have you done to them?"

Your reply to the Captain's questions is simple. "I have booked passage aboard your ship Captain. If you would be so kind as to sail it I think we can both fulfill our duties."

Angered, the Captain leaves and you pull your equipment up over the edge.

Roll the dice:

2 to 5, Turn to <u>682.</u>
6 to 12, Turn to <u>669.</u>

702   Horse patrols gallop after you but the terrain along the shore soon becomes rough and wooded. The patrols start making wide detours that slow them down. Unable to keep up with the speed of your ship they start to fall behind and eventually out of sight.

(Continued next page)

(702 cont'd)

The Captain finally gains control of what is left of his crew and comes to your side.

"Look wizard," he bellows, "do you mind if I have my ship back."

"Do you plan on turning back?" you question.

"Hardly," shouts the angry Captain. "They will skew us for sure now if they can catch us."

Smiling you release the wheel and say, "Carry on Captain. I'll be in my bunk if you need me."

You turn away with a laugh as you disappear below deck. Turn to 694.

703   The Cago is a merchant ship meant for shallow waters or at best hopping along the ocean shore. Even with its hold full of sugar there isn't enough ballast to keep the ship from violently rocking. You are sure that you are going to suffer from mal de mer by the time you reach the delta.

The ship drops anchor and slowly drags to a halt. It will be too dangerous to try and navigate the river at night. The ship rocks on through the night and you sleep peacefully and undisturbed. Turn to 654.

704   "The devils will sink us for sure. You are a bad risk," shouts the Captain at you.

He curses all wizards as the second shot rings out.

Roll the dice:

2 to 5, Turn to 718.
6 to 12, Turn to 747.

705   The soldier draws his blade and you immediately prepare your magic. He shouts a warning to the others and then charges. You raise your hands to begin a short incantation. Turn to <u>665.</u>

706   The Perfidia is a strong sturdy ship. Her crew consists of 150 well-trained and disciplined sailors. She has two decks and is powered by both sail and oar.

On the river the Captain relies on the oars for speed.

The Captain orders that the anchor be dropped. The river is too difficult to navigate in the dark.

It is clear that there are other wizards aboard besides yourself but you are not interested in talking with them. At least not yet. This night passes quietly. Turn to <u>654</u>.

707   "This ship is headed towards the Mystic Isles. We are not making any stops along the way," barks the Captain.

"That is fine with me," you smile. "I was going there anyway."

The Captain glances at your book and says, "Wizard."

The bows are lowered and the Captain says that passage is 200 gold tams. If you have it you find that you are welcome and in good company. <u>Mark off 200 gold tams</u> and turn to <u>722</u>. If you don't have it turn to <u>752</u>.

708   The Captain obeys and the Lady Varaë glides to a halt. An Eastern rowboat pulls up to the side and only one man boards. A few words are exchanged and the man heads your way escorted by a dozen elves.

 As the man approaches you see he has a glazed look over his eyes.

Only a wizard of your caliber could detect a *control* spell so easily.

(Continued next page)

(708 cont'd)

Do you:

(A) Allow the man to approach? Turn to <u>734</u>.

(B) Yell to the elf that the man is controlled and is not acting of his own free will? Turn to <u>727</u>.

709   The Lady Varaë is a sleek and fast ship. It has only one deck and no hold. The elves prefer to sleep in the open air. There is a poop deck towards the stern where a berth is provided for passengers. The crew consists of 50 well-armed elves that are as sleek looking as their craft. The ship's power comes from the elves themselves. They sit in the back of the vessel and sing. As they sing the craft glides smoothly through the water. When one elf tires another replaces him and the ship continues on. Even at night the ship does not stop. To an elf there is no difference in navigating at night or day. As you sleep the ship floats on making excellent time. Turn to <u>654</u>.

710   Your ship glides easily out to sea. The ocean spray is refreshing. Even though night is coming the ship sails on. The ship and Captain are as comfortable in the sea as they were on the river. You guess that the Isles must be one or two days away now. With excitement swelling in your chest you turn smiling towards your sleeping bunk.

"The sea! It won't be long now!"

Roll the dice:

2 to 9, Turn to <u>750</u>.
10 to 12, Turn to <u>787</u>.

711   Your spell takes effect in the middle of the Eastern Commander's conversation.

"... the seal is real! What is going to happen to them?"

(711 cont'd)

"That is my job," says the Captain. "Have no fear we will dispose of them the way we have been instructed. Your cooperation will be passed along."

The Captain puts away a piece of paper and the soldiers turn to leave.

Turn to 743.

712   "Is there any ship sailing towards the Mystic Isles?" you ask.

"Most every boat has sailed by now," he answers. "We will be going back that way in a day. Now that they dropped the *protective* spells the fishing is too great for us to pass up."

"I need to leave before that," you answer back. "Look, how much do you make on a good day?" you ask.

The fisherman says he makes about 100 tams.

"It's more like 50," you retort. Checking your gold you;

(A) Bribe him to leave tonight? That will cost you 100 gold tams. Turn to 720 and mark them off.

(B) Find you don't have the tams and must wait? Turn to 741.

713   Several of the crew make it to the bank before you. They are greeted by Eastern soldiers waiting in ambush. The water suddenly splashes around you, but your gem of protection wards off most of the arrows.

If you expire turn to 469 and mark off BB.

If you live you find arrows floating downstream. Searching the bank you see the dim outline of soldiers perched on a cliff. It seems that all of the bowmen are focusing their fire on you!

(Continued next page)

(713 cont'd)

You dive under the water hoping that the muddy color and darkening sky will protect you. With lungs bursting you are forced to surface and you come up next to Elwë.

"Flee Enchantraen," she pants. "It is our duty to save you."

A few more arrows fly your way.

Go to the Enchantraen table that follows and roll one die. Check off the damage boxes on your score card.

ENCHANTRAEN

Roll		Damage
1	--------	0
2	--------	1
3	--------	1
4	--------	2
5	--------	2
6	--------	3

If you expire <u>mark off BB</u> and turn to <u>469</u>.

If you live you follow after the young girl. The sound of the fierce fighting is soon fading behind you. After a ways Elwë turns toward the bank. You both climb out soaking wet. The chill of the air whips around you.

"That way to Wellsport," Elwë points.

"But I can help," you protest.

"Not as much as if you make it to the Mystic Isles. Go quickly. Your arguments will cost more lives."

You steal off into the night.

(713 cont'd)

There is no sound of pursuit. After several hours you find yourself stumbling in need if rest. You feel sick. No place feels comfortable while your equipment is soaked.

Finally you stop and rest. Here. Here you can rest. You surrender and sleep at last. Turn to <u>600</u>.

714 <u>Mark off BB.</u>

You notice that the ship begins to list badly towards the port. You release the wheel and run over to the side. There you see the damage. The timbers are shattered and even the keel is cracked. In short, the ship is going down. On deck you see that most of the lifeboats are gone. Those in the water have become target practice for Eastern archers. Even the men who are swimming are being shot. You have to get off. You decide to change shape and jump. Turn to <u>698</u>.

715 The arrows come once more with deadly accuracy as your special protection struggles to ward off the danger.

Go to the Enchantraen table that follows and roll one die. Check off the damage boxes on your score card.

ENCHANTRAEN

Roll		Damage
1	--------	1
2	--------	2
3	--------	2
4	--------	3
5	--------	4
6	--------	5

If you expire <u>mark off BB</u> and turn to <u>469</u>.

If you live turn to <u>728.</u>

716 The Captain is yelling for the crew to calm down. You look back towards him and see how uncommonly calm he is behaving. Behind him on the poop deck blinks a small light. The catapult draws back and fires but the missile shoots wide, missing you by several hundred feet. Turn to <u>732</u>.

717 Docking is short work. You are more than happy when you step off the gangway. It is now very late but you still might catch a seaman on duty. You scramble across the dock just as anxious to find a new ship as you are to leave this old tub behind. Turn to <u>712</u>.

718 As the rock descends you realize its magical properties. Its descent is so fast that it actually bursts into flame. Miraculously it misses. It lands so close to that steam wisps over the deck. Turn to <u>732</u>.

719 "In that case the Captain asks that you take shelter. We need the space to properly react."

A little surprised you step under the wooden poop deck but remain in a position to observe. The elves begin to string their bows but they always hold them below the railing out of sight of the soldiers.

Elwë and another elf take a position at the bow of the ship. They begin a chant and you recognize the spell to be one of *passage*.

Half of two barges disappear. The remaining halves immediately take on water and sink.

"They have made an opening!" You smile.

The moment the opening appears the elves stand up firing their bows. With deadly accuracy a row of soldiers collapse before they realize they are being attacked.

(719 cont'd)

Other soldiers attempt to rally with a volley of their own. The elves strike again and the soldiers' attempted volley is cut short.

The soldiers panic and hide behind barricades. Any soldier brave enough to show his face is brought down with the inhuman accuracy of the elves.

The elves stand erect on the deck with arrows drawn back to their ears. They never shout and no orders are given. Each one knows his duty. On the bank a captain's cry for attack is cut off by a single deadly shot. Then the bank is quiet.

No soldier makes a noise for fear of giving away his hiding place. In silence the Lady Varaë eases forward and past the barricade.

It isn't until the ship is well down the river that the elves finally relax their guard. Even then there is no shouting on the shore.

The Lady Varaë sails on with the only noise coming from the quiet voice of the river Tress. Turn to 740.

720   You throw the tams across his deck and say, "Let's sail."

The fisherman grabs a few of his crew and makes ready. You are smiling almost as big as he is when you finally drift out to the open sea. Turn to 730.

721   "Wait," says the Captain looking through a spy glass.

"They carry the colors of Eastern war galleys."

The Captain immediately orders the ship hard to port.

"Maybe they haven't spotted us yet."

(Continued next page)

(721 cont'd)

Several candles pass and a second sighting is made. Three more ships approach from the port side.
"It has to be a blockade," stammers the Captain. "The dogs must have blockaded the islands!"

He again orders the ship to turn. This time leeward in an attempt to run the blockade. You can see that running the blockade is going to be awfully close. Do you:

(A) Tell him to run the blockade? If <u>K</u> is marked turn to <u>748</u>. If not, turn to <u>769</u>.

(B) Tell the Captain to wait while you think out a plan? Turn to <u>746</u>.

722

<u>Mark off the next day and replenish all manna and erase all damage.</u>

The great warship can only go a little ways further before it must stop for the night. With a crew of 150 there are always at least 50 sailors on duty. The ship is regimented and military in its procedures. You are cared for with the cold indifference expected in all military life. As guards are posted you go below to the second deck where your cabin is located.

You refuse the company of other wizards and prepare for a night's sleep. You noticed at least five wizards aboard of obvious Western origin. You are reluctant to converse with them. You are all obviously headed towards the same place. You are concerned that you might have to fight one of them at the *Challengings*.

So passes another day aboard the ship.

(722 cont'd)

At the beginning of the 3ʳᵈ day you catch an unusual sight. You think you see a catapult perched on a cliff. It can't be! The ship passes by the cliff unharmed. If that was a catapult it would have fired on you. No, it must have been something else. By the end of the 3ʳᵈ day you are drawing near Wellsport. Turn to 745.

723   You pause momentarily to watch the sails of the three approaching ships. When you turn around you see the Captain shutting the door to his cabin. You shout at the Captain but he doesn't hear you. You go towards the stern of the boat and walk up to the Captain's door. You start to knock but notice that the door isn't latched.

You kick the door aside and say, "Look Captain you've got an important cargo here and I think you should show a little more caution."

The Captain turns around with a surprised look on his face. You see him slip a black vile into his belt.

"Well perhaps you're right Enchantraen. Let's go and have another look." The Captain smiles and starts to go out the door.

Do you:

(A) Follow him out? Turn to 737.

(B) Stop and question him? Turn to 749.

724   A volley of arrows strikes the water around you.

Go to the Enchantraen table that follows and roll one die.
Check off the damage boxes on your score card.

ENCHANTRAEN

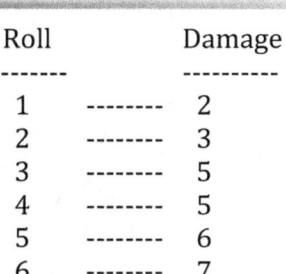

Roll		Damage
1	--------	2
2	--------	3
3	--------	5
4	--------	5
5	--------	6
6	--------	7

If you expire, <u>mark off BB</u> and turn to <u>469</u>. If you live read on.

The crew that makes it to shore is being systematically
butchered. Somewhere amongst the wreckage you hear the
Captain's voice.

"Don't fire! If you want the wizard we will help. We have no
quarrel with you."

You don't wait for the answer. You dive in the muddy water
and swim until your lungs feel like bursting. When you surface
you are next to a large bobbing crate. The sailors are searching
the water and the soldiers are running up and down both
banks. You see your pack with your book being hauled up on
the bank. Turn to <u>728</u>.

725   The Captain pulls out a piece of paper and the soldiers examine
it. A few words are exchanged and the soldiers depart. Turn to
<u>743.</u>

726   The elf, Elwë joins hands with several of her crew members.
They chant and again even though the language is different you

(726 cont'd)

recognize the spell. They are invoking a powerful *interference* spell over the ship. Their chant increases in volume as the second shot is fired.

Roll the dice:

2 to 5, Turn to 747.
6 to 12, Turn to 718.

727   The elves are quick to respond. They grab the man and push him to the deck.

"Death to the West," he screams!

A loud explosion rocks the ship. The man is blown apart and so are the elves holding him down. The hull of the ship is splintered and the Lady Varaë begins to list. A rain of arrows descends from the bank and more elves go down.

Those remaining take up positions and return the fire.

The cause is hopeless. Soon the ship will go down and the elves will no longer be able to fire. In the water they will be sitting ducks. Do you:

(A) Prepare to leave by using a *change shape* spell? Mark off 3 manna and BB. Turn to 690.

(B) Stay to help as best you can? Turn to 736.

728   Do you:

(A) Cast a *water* spell? Mark off 3 manna and roll the dice:

2 to 11, Turn to 738.
12, Your spell fails! Turn to 715.

(B) Swim downstream trying to escape? Turn to 715.

729   The ship goes down until only its masts stand above the water. The water of the Tress turns bloody red as the archers slowly locate their targets. Some who are taken ashore are given quarters, probably just long enough to be questioned.

Slapping his horse on the flanks the horse jumps and runs ... your way! The man, obviously a wizard, dives into the river and swims. A patrol of Eastern archers bursts through the woods and turn heading after the horse.

The horse pulls up short and stops near you. The horse looks back towards its master seemingly too loyal to desert him. That loyalty was his master's undoing. The soldiers seeing the riderless horse stop and dismount. They search the river until the wizard is forced to break the surface of the water for air. It is little contest from this point and the archers make short work of it.

Your spell stops! You shift back to human. Suddenly exposed you take a chance on the only escape possible and jump on the horse. The surprised soldiers react quickly and send arrows flying past your head.

"Wizard tricks," comes the shout from behind you.

The soldiers mount up and ready to track their new game.

You use your short head start to your advantage. You first head away from the river and attempt to lose them in the forest. Horns blow behind you. On you race temporarily lost from their sight. Then you hear horns starting to blow from other directions around you. They must be everywhere. You turn your mount back towards the river. The horns blare and for the moment you believe you have lost them. Then you see it! Turn to <u>688</u>.

730   The little craft rolls and rocks with the waves, skipping along at a fine pace. The Captain tells you that you will probably spot the islands sometime tomorrow. The air is crisp and the open expanse of the sea seems inviting. You return to your bunk

(730 cont'd)

and sleep knowing that you can finally sleep as long as you want without fear of being attacked in the night. At least that is what you hope. Turn to 750.

731   The Captain says, "Certainly," and pulls out the vile.

He says that there is plenty more in the cabin chest. As he starts to hand it to you he tries to uncork it.

"NO!" you shout and grab for the vile.

Roll the dice:

2, 3, 5, 6, 7, Turn to 775.
4, 8, 9, 10, 11, 12, Turn to 757.

732   The ship rounds a sharp bend and you drift out of sight of the catapult. This crew rallies with shouts of triumph. Looking back you see that they cannot turn the catapult in time to try again. You join in the celebration until a crewman shouts that Wellsport is sighted.

If you are aboard the Cago, turn to 717.

If you are aboard the Lady Varaë, turn to 710.

If you are aboard the Perfidia, or don't know, turn to 756.

733   "Don't worry wizard. The crew's alert to any danger. We will be at the islands before dark."

The Captain laughs, pats you on the back and goes to his cabin. Do you:

(A) Follow the Captain to protest? Turn to 723.

(B) Move to the stern? Turn to 772.

734   In a low, monotone voice the man says, "My Eastern Masters wish me to give Enchantraen their heart-filled good wishes."

With that the man mechanically slaps his chest.

The explosion that follows rips a hole in the hull and sends you tumbling to the back of the ship.

Go to the Enchantraen table that follows and roll one die. Check off the damage boxes on your score card.

ENCHANTRAEN

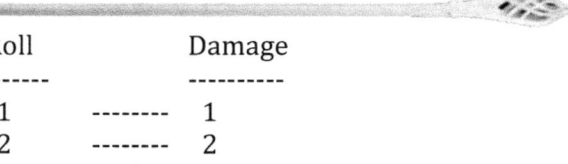

Roll		Damage
1	--------	1
2	--------	2
3	--------	2
4	--------	3
5	--------	4
6	--------	5

If you expire <u>mark off BB</u> and turn to <u>469</u>. If you survive the blast you may read on.

You stagger to your feet to find that the ship is already listing badly. The surviving elves attack the rowboat. The other elves see their fate and start jumping overboard. The Eastern soldiers begin a bloody rain of arrows that no one can survive. There is no hope to save the crew. Do you:

(A) Prepare to escape by using a *change shape* spell? <u>Mark off 3 manna and the letters BB</u>. Turn to <u>690</u>.

(B) Stay to help as best you can? Turn to <u>736.</u>

735   A smash with your fist sends the Captain flying. Out the door you run to find ten men running your way. You also feel your power coming back.

Do you:

(A) Attempt to slow them down with a barricade? <u>Mark off 3 manna</u> and turn to <u>744</u>.

(B) Run to the side and jump with a plan of escape in mind? Turn to <u>762</u>.

736   You run to the Eastern lifeboat and kick away the few men left trying to board. The rain of death descends and you are hurt badly. You strike out magically and many Easterners go down. At last the rain of arrows wounds you too badly to carry on. You attempt to escape but it is too late. The final wave of arrows hit and all goes black. Mark off <u>BB</u> and turn to <u>469</u>.

737   You walk out the door with the Captain. He stops short.

Gazing out towards the ships the Captain says, "I can't be sure but I think you have a right to be afraid. Go to the bow. I'll have the men unlock the cutlasses."

You run to the front of the ship concerned about the approaching ships. You strain your eyes across the ocean. Turn to <u>772</u>.

738   Balancing as best you can on the side of a crate you begin your enchantment. Your hands slow their motion and it feels as though they are moving through the muddy bottom of the river. You make the simple motion of a child splashing playfully at the men on the bank. The difference is that most of the river responds!

As you move your hand forward the river follows.

(Continued next page)

(738 cont'd)

From the depths of the Tress the water rises, forms and rushes towards the bank. Your tiny splash turns a wave of destruction.

Crashing down from twenty feet it washes many of the soldiers into the river. You allow yourself to be pulled along by the slower aftertow. When you wash ashore you turn back to see the water receding with enough force to whiplash against the far bank.

In the confusion you luckily find your equipment and run. The soldiers left standing are afraid to intervene. They hid their cowardice by assisting others from the drowning waters. You run changing your course hoping to throw off any pursuit. When they reorganize they will gather enough courage to follow. There is some truth to old sayings about safety in numbers.

On you plunge through the rolling hills. When night finally settles firmly around you find the sounds of pursuit are long behind you. Fatigue is your worst enemy now. You search for a good place to rest but fine none.

Finally you collapse. You can go no further. You try to rest for a short time and plan to move out again when you can. It never happens. Once you succumb to sleep you remain in a very deep one until the morning. Turn to <u>600</u>.

739   Slipping quietly over the side of the ship you swim with steady strokes towards the boat. You angle your approach so that there is no way for the fishermen to miss you. Looking back at the Perfidia you see that they haven't missed you. As the boat approaches you yell for help.

A few of the crew jump off the ship and help you aboard. The small vessel smells like fish and cheap ale. They bring you a blanket and you tell them you fell overboard. They bring you ale and you act grateful. The fishermen have been celebrating their best catch of the year.

(739 cont'd)

"Ever since they dropped the *protective* spells around the islands fishing has been great."

They drink in joy and you feel as though you have done the right thing. Looking back at the disappearing warship you can't help but feel safer now. There were too many unanswered questions aboard that ship. How did it so easily pass through all the Eastern traps?

The small boat docks and you head ashore with the hopes of finding a faster ship. Partway up the dock you stop.

Wait! Maybe the fishing boat can take you. Turning around you head back. Turn to <u>712</u>.

740   (Special: <u>Heal yourself and renew all manna</u>)

Since the sleek longship never rests you should make it past Wellsport by tomorrow evening. Tonight you rest thinking that tomorrow you will be out to sea.

The next day passes with gentle winds and fair skies. Towards nightfall you approach Wellsport. Turn to <u>745</u>.

741

<u>Mark off the next day and replenish all manna and erase all damage.</u>
You think over the possibility of forcing him to go. You dismiss the prospect. Sailing with an unwilling crew into this kind of danger would be suicidal.

As each hour passes you search the port for a capable ship. None come. After one day you return and the Captain is true to his word.

(Continued next page)

(741 cont'd)

The little vessel eases out of port and at last you are on your way. The day passes quickly and you spend it reviving your manna. The night comes before you realize it. Turn to <u>730</u>.

742   The minute the door shuts you know you made a mistake. You have just locked yourself in a room where you are powerless. Tiny splinters fly from the door from the gunfire. Men start beating down the door.

"Stop or I will kill your Captain."

A second volley of gunfire quickly destroys the plan. A stray bullet catches your shoulder crackling against the missile protection on your gem.

Kicking the Captain's body aside do you:

(A) Surrender? Turn to <u>754</u>.

(B) Throw your things out the porthole and jump? At least in the sea you will have your powers back. Turn to <u>768</u>.

743   When the Captain walks back your way you ask him what he said.

"I told them that they were violating a treaty and that if they didn't want a bloody war on their hands they would let me pass."

He pats you on the shoulder and says, "Don't worry wizard, we will take care of you."

He walks by and resumes his position at the bridge.

You walk to the stern of the ship. Off into the river you see two barges being pulled to the side. The Perfidia glides forward and passes through them. Soon the barricade is behind you and you are making good progress once more. Turn to <u>722</u>.

744   You wave your hand and a wall separates you from your adversary. This gives you time to think. Three large Eastern warships are closing in! Turn to 766.

745   You stand at the bow of the ship looking forward to seeing and feeling the ocean spray. The river cuts deeply through the land now and cliffs occasionally rise to either side of the ship. The land is hilly but it makes no difference to the river. It has long since cut through these obstacles.

Your mind drifts and you think about the past days. It seems that at noon you are always overcome with feelings of hope and pride. The rainbow shines above even now as a promise of opportunity.

Splash!

A cascade of water soaks you. You look up at a cliff and see another giant catapult resting there. A cry of confusion passes through the crew as they watch the gigantic catapult reload.

If you sail on:

(A) The Cago, turn to 704.

(B) The Perfidia, or don't know what ship you're on turn to 716.

(C) The Lady Varaë, turn to 726.

746   Neither you nor the Captain are sure of how far it is to the islands. You both know they are close. You could sneak overboard. Change shape to a porpoise and attempt to swim the rest of the way. It will be dangerous because you can't be sure you have enough manna. Then again you could save the ship and crew and yourself from possible capture.

(Continued next page)

(746 cont'd)

Do you:

(A) Continue on with the plan and go? Saying your farewells you jump and turn to <u>785</u>.

(B) Decide against it and try to run the blockade? If <u>K</u> is marked turn to <u>748</u>. Turn to <u>761</u> if you are aboard the Lady Varaë. Turn to <u>769</u> if you are aboard the fishing boat.

747   The giant rock flies into the air. When it reaches the top of its arc it suddenly changes. On its descent it gains unnatural speed. Its velocity increases too quickly and the rock actually bursts into flames.

"No," you scream as the rock strikes dead center in the ship.

Timbers split and crack as the rock passes through and sizzles at the river's bottom. The ship goes down almost immediately.

Crewmen grab anything that floats and swim for shore. Somehow you manage to avoid being sucked down by the ship and swim towards the north bank. If it is the Lady Varaë going down behind you, turn to <u>713</u>. If it is the Cago, turn to <u>724</u>.

748   The *Incantation of Knot* that you picked up at Jerican will definitely add speed to your ship. You calmly say the spell and feel the ship lurch forward. <u>Subtract 4 from your roll on the next scene</u>. If this makes your roll fall below 2 simply turn to the scene indicated for 2.

Turn to <u>761</u> if you are aboard the Lady Varaë.

Turn to <u>769</u> if you are aboard the fishing boat.

<u>Remember to subtract 4 on the next roll!</u>

749   "What was that?" you question.

"Oh this! Just medicine I have to take. You see I was cursed by a wizard once and the healers tell me this is the only thing that will hold off the curse. Disgusting I know, but I have to keep going somehow."

The Captain continues towards the door.

Do you:

(A) Follow, but keep it in mind to discuss it with him at a later time? Turn to <u>737</u>.

(B) Grab him by the shoulder and turn him around? You want a better answer. Turn to <u>759.</u>

750

<u>Mark off the next day and replenish all manna and erase all damage.</u>

You dream about your arrival. The cliffs of the islands are crowded with palaces decorated in gold and silver. The islands' populous hang from the balconies waving scarves and cheering as the ships from all over the world arrive.

A coach pulls up to the dock and you climb inside. The ten white horses prance up the polished cobblestone street towards the True One's castle. The ten Elders are there to embrace you and congratulate you on your journey.

Inside the castle are long corridors of magical items lining the walls each displayed within glass cases. They sit you on a throne and servants come to pick up the poles fastened beneath it.

(Continued next page)

(750 cont'd)

They hoist you on their shoulders and with renewed cheers from the crowds you move towards a door.

Behind that door is where the *Challengings* take place.

Just before the door opens a violent shake wakes you.

"Ships have been sighted" comes the husky voice of the sailor.

Clearing the sleep from your eyes you realize that you have already slept past noon. You scramble out of your bunk, gather your things and hurry to the bow of the ship.

There you scan the horizon until you see the billowing of three sails.

"What is it?" you ask the Captain.

"I don't know. Maybe its ships leaving the islands after dropping off their passengers."

If you are aboard the fishing boat, turn to <u>721</u>.

If you sail with the Perfidia, turn to <u>733</u>.

If you sail with the Lady Varaë, turn to <u>764</u>.

751   The hull of your ship suddenly explodes as the water rushes in. The crew of the war galley shouts in triumph as your vessel begins to sink.

It now becomes every man for himself. You jump into the water but the pull of the sinking ship threatens to suck you under. You grab a piece of floating wood. Then arrows crackle against your missile protection.

(751 cont'd)

Go to the Enchantraen table that follows and roll one die. Check off the damage boxes on your score card.

ENCHANTRAEN

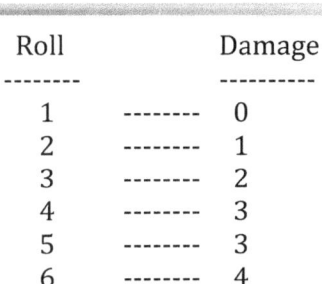

Roll		Damage
1	--------	0
2	--------	1
3	--------	2
4	--------	3
5	--------	3
6	--------	4

If you expire turn to <u>770</u>. If you live read on.

Changing shape is your only hope. The ship is pulling you down and the archers are preparing to fire once more.

If you have <u>4 manna mark it off</u> and turn to <u>785</u>.

If not, you feel yourself going down. Turn to <u>790</u>.

752 The Captain agrees to allow you passage anyway for whatever is left of your gold. He does ask that you perform some duties to work off the rest. Several of his crew are sick and he asks you to look at them. Once that is accomplished you find your company quite welcome. Turn to <u>722</u>.

753 You know now that they have found you. You guess a sensitive is aboard one of the ships and guiding them towards you.

As the little ship races onward you judge it is going to be close. The Captain turns trying to keep as much distance between his craft and the war galley.

(Continued next page)

(753 cont'd)

"We aren't going to make it," screams the Captain.

With surprising agility a war galley maneuvers toward you. There are bowmen aboard. They test fire twice to gauge the range. Do you:

(A) Cast a *reverse* spell around you and the craft? <u>Mark off 4 manna</u> and turn to <u>779</u>.

(B) Save your magic for a strike directly against the war galley? Turn to <u>763</u>.

754 The door swings open and you are escorted out at gunpoint. Before you reach the main deck a gun butt sends you sprawling and into unconsciousness. Turn to <u>770</u>.

755 You hold on to some passing debris and work your spell. Arrows rain down a certain death, except your missile protection gem turns most of them aside.

Go to the Enchantraen table that follows and roll one die. Check off the damage boxes on your score card.

ENCHANTRAEN

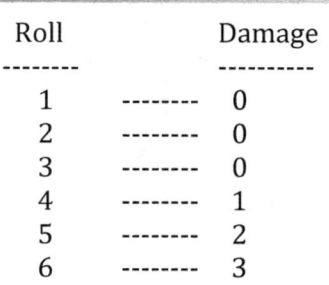

Roll		Damage
1	--------	0
2	--------	0
3	--------	0
4	--------	1
5	--------	2
6	--------	3

If you expire turn to <u>770</u>.

If you live you quickly adjust your straps on your pack and turn to <u>785</u>.

756 The Captain and crew are busy hoisting the sails. The sails unfurl and a course is set directly towards the Mystic Isles. You lean over the railing smelling the fresh crisp air. Then you see a small fishing boat off the starboard side. It sounds like the crew is celebrating. Lanterns are shining and men are laughing. The ship is headed towards the port at Wellsport. A strange idea crosses your mind. Their fun looks so inviting. Do you:

(A) Slip quietly over the side of the ship and swim towards the fishing boat to board? Turn to <u>739</u>.

(B) Stay where you are since such a side adventure might slow you down and hamper your chances? Turn to <u>710</u>.

757 You grab the vile and shove the Captain helplessly to the side. When you touch the vile you immediately know what it is. It's an exhaust aether potion. Such a potion would leave you powerless if used.

You grab the Captain by the neck.

"Tell me what's going on Captain or I swear I'll feed you to the sharks."

In frightened tones the Captain spills his guts.

"We are running Western wizards to the East. Those ships you see are Eastern. They have a blockade up and down the coast. We pick up the Western wizards and turn them over. It's as simple as that."

"Simple! Simple, you idiot! You're destroying the balance. You are nothing but a traitor."

The Captain yells for help. You put your hand over his mouth and knock him out. As calmly as possible you walk out the door. No one seems to have heard his cry. Turn to <u>766</u>.

758 When the galley finally fires the arrows are so thick that they darken the sky. Elwë's spell is somewhat effective but not absolute. Some of the crew members are hit and collapse.

Go to the Enchantraen table that follows and roll one die. Check off the damage boxes on your score card.

ENCHANTRAEN

Roll	Damage
1	0
2	1
3	1
4	2
5	3
6	3

If you expire turn to <u>770</u>.

If you live you see the Lady Varaë suddenly veer and pull alongside the ship. Then you see the strange markings along the hull. On the main deck is a catapult ready to fire. Do you:

(A) Aid Elwë with a *reverse* spell of your own? <u>Mark off 4 manna</u> and turn to <u>767</u>.

(B) Cast a *passage* spell on the side of their ship? The sudden hole should sink them. Turn to <u>773</u>.

(C) Cast a *fireball* spell at the catapult to hopefully disrupt the men firing it? <u>Mark off 4 manna</u> and roll the dice:

2 to 11, Turn to <u>778</u>.
12, Your spell fails! Turn to <u>795</u>.

(D) Stop and watch hoping for a more opportune time? Turn to <u>795</u>.

759 You spin him around and the Captain shouts for you to keep your hands off him. Do you:

(A) Ask him to hand you the vile? Turn to 731.

(B) Smash the vile with your fist by hitting him in the belt? Turn to 775.

(C) Bind him with a spell and take the vile yourself? Mark off 1 manna and turn to 757.

(D) Warn him not to try anything? You tell him that he will be the first to go if there is trouble. Turn to 737.

760 The catapult fires sending a fiery ball in a perfect arc down through any *protective* spells and then straight through the hull of the ship!

Turn to 751.

761 The elves feed power into the vessel and it lurches forward. The ship is sleek and fast as it glides through the water. There are so many war galleys.

Roll the dice:

2 to 5, Turn to 789.
6 to 12, Turn to 792.

762 You hit the water closely followed by a barrage of arrows.

Go to the Enchantraen table that follows and roll one die.

(Continued next page)

(762 cont'd)

Check off the damage boxes on your score card.

ENCHANTRAEN

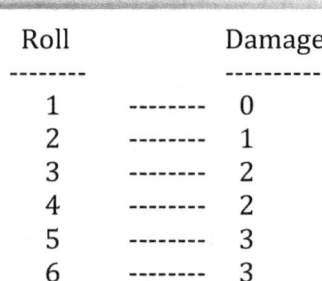

Roll		Damage
1	--------	0
2	--------	1
3	--------	2
4	--------	2
5	--------	3
6	--------	3

If you expire turn to <u>200.</u> If not read on!

When you hit the river you swim toward a crate from the wreckage. There you see the Eastern war galleys closing in. You must change shape and flee. You adjust the straps on your pack and begin the spell. <u>Mark off 4 manna</u> and turn to <u>785.</u>

763   The sky darkens as the arrows fly. Many of the crew die instantly. If not for your gem so would you.

Go to the Enchantraen table that follows and roll one die. Check off the damage boxes on your score card.

ENCHANTRAEN

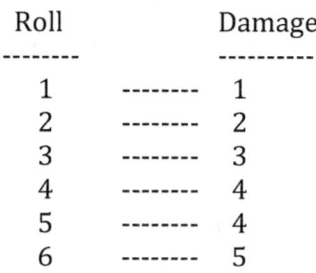

Roll		Damage
1	--------	1
2	--------	2
3	--------	3
4	--------	4
5	--------	4
6	--------	5

(763 cont'd)

If you expire turn to <u>770</u>.

If you live you see that the fishing boat has passed to the side of the ship. There you see the bowmen readying to shoot once more. There is also a large catapult in the center of the ship aiming your way. You also notice strange symbols carved on the side of the galley.

Turn to <u>794</u>.

764 With eyes sharper than your own the Captain finally says that the approaching ships are Eastern war galleys. He points off the port and starboard sides saying that he sees other warships out there also. He tells you it must be a blockade. Although you can't see them you believe him. You ask him if he can get through and he tells you he doesn't know. He awaits your orders. Do you:

(A) Tell the Captain to wait while you think of a plan? Turn to <u>748</u>.

(B) Tell him full speed ahead. Run the blockade? If <u>K</u> is marked turn to <u>748</u>. If not turn to <u>761</u>.

765 At last the elves shoot. The arrows hiss forward from point-blank range. They explode against the hull and timber splinters. Confusion passes through the Eastern crew as their ship starts to take on water.

The Lady Varaë glides past turning sharply to escape the other galleys. Turn to <u>789</u>.

766 Your mind calculates the situation. There is no way to fight the Easterners even with the five powerful wizards as allies. The Easterners wouldn't go wizard hunting without the proper equipment to handle them. Besides the islands are so close now.

(Continued next page)

(766 cont'd)

You could change shape and fly. No, they will see you and pursue. You could still change shape into a porpoise and swim. They could never follow you traveling mostly under the water.

You take immediate action. You climb on the railing and yell. "It's a trap! Flee for your lives."

The other wizards immediately swing into action but you don't wait to see what they do. Instead, you jump. Turn to 755.

767   You join forces with Elwë. The sky again darkens but no missiles strike.

Before you can rejoice the catapult fires. Roll the dice:

2, 3, 5, 6, 7, Turn to 760.
4, 8, 9, 10, 11, 12, Turn to 783.

768   You see your possessions hit first. You squeeze slowly out the small hole. From above you hear sailors shouting. Turn to 762.

769   The tiny vessel skips along the top of the waves. The ship is definitely too slow but maybe they won't spot it in time because of its size.

You hold your breath and roll the dice:

2 to 3, Turn to 781.
4 to 12, Turn to 777.

770   When you come to you are stuck in a small 3 foot by 3 foot room. You have been stripped and there is an *exhaust aether* spell working in the area which makes you powerless. Although you don't remember much you guess you lost the fight. Your cage rocks steadily until you realize that you are aboard a ship.

(770 cont'd)

The East has captured you and they are taking you to their homeland. The situation is desperate.

If <u>P</u> is marked turn to <u>626</u>, otherwise read on.

It isn't known whether you ever escaped. One thing is for sure however, you didn't make it to the Mystic Isles this game! The *Challengings* are over!

THE END

771   You swim until your spell fails. With a final leap you look for the isles but can't find them. You are treading water once more in your human form.

If you have <u>4 manna left mark them off</u> and turn to <u>784</u>.

If you have run out of manna turn to <u>793</u>.

772   The ships move slowly towards you. They look large. You never really cared for sailing much but they do look impressive. You stare for a long time trying to make out their colors. Your eye catches some passing debris. It looks like the wreckage of a ship. You look back towards the ships. Finally, when the ships come closer you see the flags, Eastern! They are Eastern war galleys! You shout for the Captain and he comes forward.

"It is too late to run," he says. "We will have to fight."

He orders his crew to arms. He gathers up the wizards and explains that he will need help to win this. He asks you to save your magic however until he gives the orders. His voice is calm and assuring. You and the other wizards take your places as instructed and wait.

The three ships come towards you like hungry wolves.

(Continued next page)

(772 cont'd)

The Captain gathers his crews around him one last time. The fighting will start in moments. You can see the enemy sailors hanging from the rigging ready for battle. The Captain approaches you with fifty of his men to give his final orders.

He grabs a vile from his belt and breaks it on the deck. You feel the effects immediately. When the aether is exhausted there is no mistaking the effects. Your magic has become useless.

"Get them," shouts the Captain and a hundred hands grab for you.

In an instant it all adds up. Passing by the catapults was just too easy. The ship must have been signaling the artillery men when you saw the blinking lights.

Three wizards go down immediately. You jump up on the bulwark temporarily out of reach. The fourth wizard jumps overboard but dies before he hits the water. The archers are waiting for the next one to leap. You look over the crewmen's head to see an Eastern war galley closing in. Death in the water would have to be better than on the ship!

You jump! Luck is with you. Most of the archers must have fired the first time. At least you are alive when you hit the water. Turn to <u>755.</u>

773   You begin your spell when Elwë yells for you to stop.

"Can't you see the markings on the hull? It might come back!"

Do you:

(A) Continue anyway? <u>Mark off 4 manna</u> and turn to <u>751</u>.

(B) Stop? Turn to <u>795.</u>

774   The second wave of arrows hit and more of the crew go down.

Go to the Enchantraen table that follows and roll one die. Check off the damage boxes on your score card.

ENCHANTRAEN

Roll		Damage
1	--------	0
2	--------	1
3	--------	1
4	--------	2
5	--------	3
6	--------	4

If you expire turn to <u>770</u>. If you live you see the catapult fire.

Roll the dice:

2 to 9, Turn to <u>760</u>.
10 to 12, Turn to <u>796</u>.

775   The vile breaks and you feel the effects immediately. It is an exhaust aether potion. Without aether you cannot work your magic. The sudden loss of power causes you to swoon. The Captain runs to the door and shouts for help. You hear crewmen running. Do you:

(A) Shove the Captain aside and run? Turn to <u>735</u>.

(B) Pull the Captain back and shut the door? Turn to <u>742</u>.

776   Your little ship skips past the large war galley. Your crew shouts with glee but it is cut short. From behind the first ship comes the second, unseen before. The Captain swerves to avoid a collision. That's when the alchemy guns on the second ship fire!

(Continued next page)

(776 cont'd)

Roll the dice:

2, 3, 5, 6, 7, Turn to <u>751</u>.
4, 8, 9, 10, 11, 12, Turn to <u>788</u>.

777 The Captain of the small vessel says, "We must turn back wizard. With you on board, they will sink us for sure."

You hardly hear the Captain's words. You have just felt the contact of a sensitive on the fringes of your mind. Do you:

(A) Accept a communication with whomever is trying to get through? Turn to <u>786</u>.

(B) Ignore the sensitive? Turn to <u>753</u>.

778 The fireball forms on your fingertips and you immediately launch it towards the catapult. When it strikes, fire spreads and men scream. The catapult fires wildly missing your ship. Turn to <u>798</u>.

779 The sky turns black as the arrows scream your way. Many are returned, yet some fall through and some of the crew go down. Your gem of missile protection guards you well.

The tiny ship passes to the side of the galley. The bowmen are ready to fire once more. You now see the strange markings on the side of the ship. There is also a catapult aimed your way!

Turn to <u>794</u>.

780 The arrows fly once more. A few break through but luckily they miss you and most of the crew. Before you rejoice there is still the catapult.

(780 cont'd)

Roll the dice:

2 to 7, 10, Turn to <u>760</u>.
8, 9, 11, 12, Turn to <u>797</u>.

781   The tiny vessel speeds along but the war galleys don't respond. They obviously believe you to be simple fishermen. You sink to the deck in utter disbelief at your good fortune.

The moment is heightened even further when a sailor yells, "Land ho!"

Racing forwards you come to the Mystic Isles. You made it! Turn to <u>800</u>.

782   The catapult fires and arcs through the sky. It bounces against the *protective* spells and flies back towards the war galley. Turn to <u>765</u>.

783   The two of you weave your protection around the ship. The first volley is fired from the war galley. The sky turns dark from the descending arrows.

Several arrows make it through and some of the elves drop. Still, no elf returns the fire.

The Lady Varaë veers to pull alongside. There you see a large catapult loaded and ready to fire. You also notice strange markings on the ship's hull.

(Continued next page)

(783 cont'd)

Do you:

(A) Continue to aid Elwë with another *reverse* spell? Mark off 4 manna and turn to 767.

(B) Cast a *passage* spell on the side of their ship? The sudden hole should sink it. Turn to 773.

(C) Cast a *fireball* spell at the catapult to hopefully disrupt the men ready to fire it? Mark off 4 manna and roll the dice:

2 to 11, Turn to 778.
12, Your spell fails! Turn to 795.

(D) Stop and wait for a more opportune time? Turn to 795.

784   You change back and swim off in what you believe to be the right direction. You cover another great distance in a desperate search for the islands.

Roll the dice:

2, 3, 5, 6, 7, Turn to 798.
4, 8 to 12, Turn to 771.

785   You feel a short muzzle sprout from your face. Your skin becomes slick and your belly white. With powerful strokes you swim off into the great expanse of the sea.

You stay under water as long as you can to hide the fact that you have a pack strapped to you. Occasionally you break the surface to breathe. Away you go with all your speed towards the Mystic Isles.

(785 cont'd)

Roll the dice:

2 to 6, Turn to <u>798</u>.
7 to 12, Turn to <u>771</u>.

786   You catch the glimpse of a smiling Eastern sensitive. He sends a mind blast that ripples through your brain. You try to cut off the connection but it is too late.

Go to the Enchantraen table that follows and roll one die. Check off the damage boxes on your score card.

ENCHANTRAEN

Roll		Damage
1	--------	0
2	--------	1
3	--------	2
4	--------	3
5	--------	4
6	--------	5

If you expire turn to <u>770</u>. If you live turn to <u>753</u>.

787

<u>Mark off the next day and replenish all manna and erase all damage.</u>

You are awakened before dawn the next day. While lying in your bunk you feel the ship rock violently to and fro. Coming to the main deck you are splashed by the wind and water.

"How bad's the storm Captain," you shout about the gale?

(Continued next page)

(787 cont'd)

"Very," comes the distant reply. "She's strong but short. If we can ride her out it will be over soon. It's hard telling how far off course she might blow us though."

The storm increases steadily and the crew ties things down including themselves to wait it out.

You start to return to your cabin when the lookout yells, "Reef off the starboard."

The Captain runs to the side of the ship. He turns with a pale wet face and starts barking orders to the steersman.

"Heave to man or we will be dashed to bits!"

You see the waves swell and ripple across the jagged shoals.

If <u>V</u> is marked turn to <u>801</u>. If not you must trust your fate to the worthy hands of the crew!

Roll the dice:

2 to 5, Turn to <u>809.</u>
6 to 12, Turn to <u>820</u>.

788　The shots splash harmlessly around you. You sail on. The lumbering war galleys turn for chase but it is too late.

A crewman shouts, "Land ho!"

The Mystic Isles loom before you. You have made it! Turn to <u>800</u>.

789　The Eastern warships turn in great sweeping motions to cut you off. It is going to be close.

The crew continues to feed the ship their power. The ship splits the waves and washes them to the side. As you near the

(789 cont'd)

Eastern Galleys it looks as though you are going to make it. In desperation one warship turns broadside and opens fire with their alchemy guns. The shells splash harmlessly around you.

You're through! You shout with joy as you see the islands rising in the distance. Behind you the galleys turn but their big lumbering hulks are no match for Lady Varaë's sleek speed. You're going to make it! Turn to <u>800.</u>

790 You look around and there is nothing. No land. Nothing to hold on to. You start to panic. You've got to rest your legs. You stop kicking and sink down below the surface.

You never come up.

Sorry Enchantraen but this happens in games and life.

Take courage however. This was a good effort. Return to the start of the adventure if you wish to play again.

791 It's the islands! You can't believe it. With the last of your strength you swim and swim. They cannot stop you. You have got to make it. On and on you swim.

First the seaweed tickles your legs then you feel sand beneath your feet. Struggling up on hands and knees you stumble to the shore entirely exhausted. You feel sick and faint but you made it! Turn to <u>800</u>.

792 The race is on. The lumbering warships turn in the water to try and bottle you up. Suddenly the crew breaks their concentrated effort and moves to different positions aboard the ship.

"What is it?" you ask.

"We are preparing to fight. We aren't going to make it," comes the level reply.

(Continued next page)

(792 cont'd)

The ship continues forward but at a much slower pace. This time the steersman is trying to single out a galley.

The Captain opens a leather box and distributes the sleek red arrows within.

You can hear your heart beating as you watch the war galley draw near. The Lady Varaë looks to be on a collision course with one of the ships.

The war galley fires testing arrow shots to determine range. Once in range they will open up with a volley from several hundred men.

Elwë is preparing a *reverse* spell to send back as many of the arrows as possible.

Do you:

(A) Join her and add the strength of your spell to hers? <u>Mark off 4 manna</u> and turn to <u>783</u>.

(B) Wait hoping to use your magic in a more decisive manner? Turn to <u>758</u>.

793   You are out of manna. You still haven't found the islands. You are tired. Very tired! Your legs cramp as you try to swim. In final desperation you use the very last of your energy to search.

Roll the dice:

2 to 10, Turn to <u>791</u>.
11 to 12, Turn to <u>790</u>.

794   Do you:

(A) Cast a *fireball* spell at the catapult to disrupt their aim? Mark off 4 manna and turn to <u>796</u>.

(B) Cast a *passage* spell at the hull of the ship? The sudden opening should sink it. <u>Mark off 4 manna</u> and turn to <u>751</u>.

(C) Cast a *reverse* spell around you and the crew? If you have done this once the second spell will increase the first. Turn to <u>780</u> and <u>mark off 3 manna</u>.

(D) Ride by saving your manna? Turn to <u>774</u>.

795   The sky turns dark when the arrows fire. Elwë's spell stops many but some fall through striking you and the crew.

Go to the Enchantraen table that follows and roll one die. Check off the damage boxes on your score card.

ENCHANTRAEN

Roll	Damage
1	0
2	1
3	2
4	2
5	3
6	3

If you expire turn to <u>770</u>. If you live you still must face the catapult!

Roll the dice:

2 to 7, 10, Turn to <u>760</u>.
8, 9, 11, 12, Turn to <u>782</u>.

796   The catapult misfires and goes wide. Turn to <u>776</u>.

797   The catapult fires, hits your *protective* spell, and bounces back across the deck of the war galley. Turn to <u>776.</u>

798   You swim until you feel your spell fading. You leap high into the air and try to spot the islands. When you come down you have turned back to normal.

    It doesn't matter. You spotted them! Turn to <u>791</u>.

799   The spell takes flame and dances on your fingertips. You toss the ball and the catapult crew scatters. The flame causes the ropes to burn and the catapult fires wildly.

    The archers shoot a second time. The wave hits and more sailors fall over. Some arrows make it through your protection.

    Go to the Enchantraen table that follows and roll one die. Check off the damage boxes on your score card.

ENCHANTRAEN

Roll		Damage
1	--------	0
2	--------	1
3	--------	1
4	--------	2
5	--------	3
6	--------	3

    If you expire turn to <u>770</u>. If you live turn to <u>776</u>.

800   Through the sky races a chariot. The chariot is the color of the golden sun. It is drawn by winged horses of so many colors that there appears to be one for each color in the spectrum.

(800 cont'd)

It is a welcomed sight, for it is Rainolic, messenger of the Elders. Without stopping the chariot dives and sweeps you up. Away you ride with the gentle speed of the wind.

"Hail good wizard," says the bronze muscular man named Rainolic.

"There is refreshment in the small box at my feet."

You stoop to open it because Rainolic must use all of his concentration to guide the chariot. <u>You drink and all your wounds are healed. Your manna is also replenished</u> and fatigue slips away in the wide expanse of the sky. <u>Make sure you change it on your character sheet.</u>

You pass by the main central island heading east. All you see are enormous mountains jutting out of the sea.

"Where are the glittering cities," you question?

Rainolic laughs like falling water and says there are none. He explains that he is taking you to a small villa where you can rest. There you will be cared for and you will receive proper answers to your questions. The chariot dips down and you approach a tiny island.

"Is this how all wizards arrive?" you ask.

"No," comes the sparkling reply. "It seems that some wizards have a harder time than others. I am sent out to retrieve those less fortunate".

As you fly closer you see ships unloading below. There are three full-sized Eastern ships docked there.

"There must be 300 wizards getting off down there," you blurt out.

(Continued next page)

(800 cont'd)

"No there is only one," answers Rainolic.

"It's those blasted Easterners. They force the Western wizards to crawl to the islands while they spend vast wealth to insure that their own wizards arrive safely."

Rainolic glares your way with eyes like shooting stars.

"I advise you to forget your political differences on this island good wizard. That kind of thinking can force you to forfeit."

The chariot dives and slows down. You jump and gently roll to a stop. Your arrival is quite a contrast to an Eastern wizard's but at least you are here. Dusting yourself off you look up to see Rainolic already disappearing. As you straighten your road-weary robes small children in black tunics with gold threads run to help you.

The children ask if they can carry your things but you politely decline. You grab the arm of the oldest child.

"What happens next?" you question.

"Well Enchantraen, you are to rest in your quarters for one night. In the morning you will be summoned before the Elders and the tests begin."

"How did you know my name?" you blurt.

"You must have told me."

"I didn't! What tests are you talking about?"

"Please good wizard. I am just a student sent from Tuatha. I come to learn. I don't have the answers."

"Tuatha?" you again question. "Where is Tuatha and why are they privileged to send children here."

(800 cont'd)

"Please no more questions? You make my head hurt. Tuatha is in the lands west of here."

The children escort you down a small line of buildings that look to be more like summerhouses. They are stone on the first floor with plaster and wood upper stories. You see wizards mingling in the street. They are wearing simple white robes. There are also soldiers and mercenaries in common dress but they don't seem to be carrying weapons.

You duck to enter your house and the children follow.

"You are to wear this," a child says handing you a white robe. "Here the markings of country and state are to be laid aside."

You start to ask a question but decide against it.

You can pick out the Eastern wizards easy enough. They're the ones with fifty or more soldiers following them around. The children giggle as if they heard you thinking out loud.

"If it's not too much trouble can you tell me if I'm safe here?" you ask sharply.

"Perfectly," says a child. "No one has ever died here. But if you decide to leave suddenly please tell us. Some of the wizards change their minds and take off without so much as a good-bye. It really disrupts the schedule."

Shaking your head you ask if there is anything else you should know.

"Oh yes! Trouble or bickering will not be tolerated. The Elders, by law, can force you to forfeit if you break those rules. They are very strict. Remember that; no trouble!"

(Continued next page)

(800 cont'd)

Food is placed on a table and the children leave. You sit down to eat. Cracking the shutters by the windows you watch the passersby. Actually there are few wizards that you can see. Most of the people are Eastern soldiers or dignitaries mingled with a few Westerners.

Everyone steps to the side and the street clears. A man passes followed by ten Eastern soldiers.

"Was that Caaron?" you choke.

Caaron is the right-hand man of another Dark Lord named Lord Obloquy. He passes by but you can't be sure.

If X is marked turn immediately to 810.

After you eat do you:

(A) Walk outside to try and gather information that might help you prepare yourself for the coming day? Turn to 830.

(B) Search your quarters and retire? Turn to 825.

801   You remove the small shallow vessel you purchased in Jerican. You toss it over the side of the ship.

The waves immediately swell and threaten to swamp the tiny craft. It doesn't happen. In fact the deck never gets wet. The sea instead calms and the tiny craft bobs like a fine treasure. The wind slows its speed also as though it wants to caress the craft before blowing on by.

Soon the sea is as level as glass. The tiny vessel sails away and so do you on a direct course to the Mystic Isles. The crew cheers you as you turn back for your bunk.

(801 cont'd)

"If there is anything else that I can do for you Captain, please don't hesitate to wake me."

Back in bed you go with an ear to ear smile. Turn to <u>750</u>.

802   Grabbing an oil lamp off a shelf you light it. Walking quickly to the chest you open it and toss the lamp inside. The lantern breaks and flares! Immediately the chest transforms into a screaming lich. Rolling over and over the lich attempts to put out the blaze.

The door swings open and children come running in with water and blankets. They quickly extinguish the blaze and tie the hands of the lich. That is when you notice the light shining in the doorway.

"Who is outside?" you demand from one of the children.

"It's the Elder Filo," gasps one of the children through the smoke.

You start walking carefully to the door. They lift the lich to his feet and a stream of curses flies at you but you hardly hear them. At the door you look out and see an older man leaning on a brightly shining staff. Wherever the light from the staff illuminates seems to change the appearance of the surroundings.

The man is standing on a polished marble floor instead of the cobble stones you see everywhere else. Above him is a high vaulted ceiling of flickering gold and paintings instead of the open sky. Filo the Elder moves closer until you are within his light. Now you can see that he is blind.

"The Circle of Truth has talked much about you since your arrival Enchantraen. Many of the Elders say that as a war wizard you are unfit to compete. Several have proposed

(Continued next page)

(802 cont'd)

already that you be forced to forfeit. Now I must go and tell them that there has already been trouble."

You start to protest but he raises his hand.

"Know Enchantraen that everything you do here is of major importance. This will not go well with the other Elders."

The children walk past him with the struggling lich in tow.

He looks at you as if he can see right through you even though he is clearly blind. Then he turns and walks away. You lie down worriedly on your bed and try to sleep. Turn to <u>832</u> and <u>mark off DD</u>.

803   The Penoi named LaCrosse stands and points an accusing finger.

"This wizard is unfit. Enchantraen is prone to unnecessary acts of violence. The wizard loves nothing else but the wizard's own homelands. We cannot let this mockery of our system continue. I move that we disallow this wizard's rights and call for a forfeiture."

"You are once again denied LaCrosse," comes the even voice of a young female.

If <u>O</u> is marked turn to <u>817</u>.

If not turn to <u>829.</u>

804   <u>Mark off FF</u>.

Suddenly the area around you darkens. You feel the air condense into a cold chill. You try to move but find that to be impossible.

"How dare you defile our homeland with these crude acts of

(804 cont'd)

magic," comes a voice from behind you. "Turn and face your master."

Your body jumps involuntarily around until you see your assailant. It is a humanoid creature with rubbery brown skin. Its chest and waist are thick and its face is offset by a wide powerful jaw. Even though it is not dressed in its usual blue, green, and yellow war gear you recognize it. It is a Penoi. These are creatures spawned by the East from vats. They are prized fighting troops for the East. They are usually soldiers. You have never seen a Penoi magic-user like the one that has you now.

"Which part of the island did you crawl up from? Where is your belt of scalps that your kind so proudly displays," you shout.

The Penoi's hand clamps tighter and you feel as though your bones are about to break. Inside his hand you can see a small statue of... yourself.

"How dare you talk to an Elder in such a manner." The Penoi looks upward and says, "What further proof do you need. I say that Enchantraen must forfeit".

Unseen mouths voice a reply.

Yes, No, No, Yes, No, Yes, No, Yes, No.

"The vote is deadlocked LaCrossa. Release the wizard. Enchantraen's fate will be decided tomorrow."

LaCrossa spits and tosses the statue to the ground. Your knees collapse as you hit the ground hard.

"Listen to me wizard," the Penoi says standing over you. "The Circle of Truth wants to see you in the morning.

(Continued next page)

(804 cont'd)

Don't let me catch you causing more trouble or on this night I personally will decide your fate."

The Penoi turns and walks away. You pick yourself up and walk over to the statue. You crush it beneath your feet.

You walk by the two Eastern soldiers and head towards your apartment.

A Penoi Elder? What is going on?

Maybe you have made this trek before you are ready. No, you came at the right time! Turn to <u>827</u>.

805   When you come to, you feel hands lifting you from the water. You have been picked up by a fishing boat.

You ask the Captain but he tells you that you are the only one he has seen floating in the water. You are strong enough to rise and you immediately check your possessions.

Miraculously everything survived. Even battered as you are you manage to smile when the Captain tells you they are headed on a fishing expedition near the Mystic Isles.

With help from the crew you are carried to a bunk and laid down. You smile and humbly thank them. The Captain slaps you on the shoulder and laughs.

"Perhaps a wizard like you can help us find good fishing."

You laugh and fall into a dazed sleep. Turn to <u>750</u> and <u>mark that you are now on the fishing boat</u>.

806   The oldest looking Elder stands.

"I, Elder Wornadvor, agree with the thoughts expressed earlier by LaCrosse," he says pointing to the Penoi. "This wizard is subject to the whims of a violent temper. We have all seen how

(806 cont'd)

Enchantraen decided to burn the lich rather than bind it. I move that the wizard be forced to forfeit."

Valoria searches the eyes of the other Elders before she speaks.

"The council recognizes your protest but has chosen a more suitable punishment. The wizard will face the trial twice."

Check the next box on the character sheet under trial.

This will be explained later. Turn now to 813.

807   The spell begins to work and the room shifts to a finer focus. Your eyes move around and pass through walls as you thoroughly look over the place.

If N or L is marked turn to 818.

If not, you discover that the room is safe including the new mattress. Feeling a little better you lay down and attempt to rest up for the coming day. Turn to 832.

808   You turn to go back when the two soldiers on the street step out into your path.

"Look Jeal, it's the licker of dog's feet come to bark at the moon and wish upon a star."

They both put their hands to the hilt of their swords.

Do you:

(A) Attack with a *binding* spell? Mark off 2 manna and turn to 804.

(B) Push them aside and walk by? Turn to 838.

809   The ship edges its way towards the reef. The jagged bottom grins up like the bottom jaw of giant. Through skilled seamanship the ship edges forward and the reef passes to the stern of the ship. The bottom drags but no serious damage is done to the hull.

The storm passes as quickly as it came. The Captain reports that little time will be lost and you still seem to be on course. You return to your bunk for a much needed rest. Turn to <u>750</u>.

810   Someone knocks on the door. Cautiously you open it. It's Benolic, the man you sent away at Arcania. His panther rushes by and jumps up on your bed.

"Greetings Master. Can we now talk about my service to you?"

You can only stand there with your mouth wide open as Benolic enters and sits down.

"I've been waiting for you," he says as he pours himself a glass of wine. With the *Challengings* going on it seems to be very easy for anyone to get here except wizards."

With a smile he toasts to your future success.

If <u>O</u> is marked turn to <u>834</u>.

If not, turn to <u>815</u>.

811   When you come to, you find yourself floating alone. You're tired but alive. You check and find that all of your things are still with you. There is little to do at this point except swim. But why not swim with style.

You decide to change shape into a porpoise and head in the direction you believe to be towards the Mystic Isles. If only you knew how far away they were. If only you could be certain of the direction!

(811 cont'd)

You adjust the straps on your pack. You start the spell. <u>Mark off 4 manna</u>. At its completion you push away from the timber and ... turn to <u>785</u>.

812   <u>Mark off DD</u>.

"Stop this blasphemy" comes a shout from behind the front door.

When the door blasts open ... Turn to <u>849</u>.

813   "Do you subject yourself to our laws."

"Yes of course," you answer and your voice seems distant and weak even to yourself.

"Very well," says Valoria. "The questions are short and simple. You may choose two Elders to present the questions. Choose the first Elder now. Turn to <u>855</u>.

814   You lay your head upon your pillow and find the bed to be to your liking. In time you start to drift off.

If <u>N</u> or <u>L</u> is marked turn to <u>841</u>.

If not, turn to <u>832.</u>

815   "I suggest you stay inside for the night. I've seen the soldiers cause a lot of trouble with Western wizards. The only point of interest in this villa anyway seems to be that tall building over there."

You look out the window to see the building Benolic is talking about.

"Stay away from it now though. It is packed with Eastern soldiers."

(Continued next page)

(815 cont'd)

"Well Enchantraen. Do you keep your promise and make me your second or do I move along?"

Do you say:

(A) "Yes, you can be my second." Turn to <u>833</u>.

(B) "No, you cannot." <u>Erase the mark on X</u> and turn to <u>833</u>.

816   You start to thank the Elder when he turns on you like a panther. His light engulfs you and its then that you see that he is blind. He stands there for a few moments and you feel like you have been stripped naked before him.

"The word around the Circle is that you are unfit to serve. There are Elders who are quick to point out that you are a war wizard full of rage and hatred. I see before me a victim of circumstances."

You start to speak but you are silenced by a wave of his hand.

"I must tell them about this. They won't be happy."

He turns to walk away. The marble floor proceeds with him and the door turns to a bright polished oak and gold. He turns there and gives you a warning.

"Everything you do here wizard is of great importance. Remember that!" He turns and is gone.

You move and sit heavily on the edge of your bed. Tired and mentally exhausted you fight back a swelling urge to cry. Overcome by drowsiness you try to sleep. Turn to <u>832</u>.

817   The Penoi shakes his fist at you and says, "As is my right as an Elder I can bring forth any reason why I think this wizard should be forced to forfeit. Last night, as you all know, a

(817 cont'd)

challenger was killed. In the hand of the corpse was this trinket."

The Elder LaCrosse slams down the charmed warning stone you lost during your travels. A gasp goes through the Elders. Elder Ingwë, the male elf rises and looks down at you.

"Upon the penalty of forfeiture Enchantraen answer this question truthfully. Is that piece of jewelry yours?" Do you:

(A) Lie and say no? Turn to <u>840.</u>

(B) Tell the truth? Turn to <u>852</u>.

818 Your eyes stop on a chest. Something's not right. You refocus and search the insides of the chest once more. Nothing's there? Still something is not right. You focus and refocus until the glimpse of an old man's face comes into your mind. You quickly turn away.

The face you saw was a lich, a powerful wizard whose life is unnaturally extended.

Was he in the chest? No! It suddenly becomes clear. He is the chest! He is hiding under a *change shape* spell. You calmly assess the situation. As long as he is in that inanimate form the advantage is yours.

Do you:

(A) Grab an oil lantern and toss it on the chest? Turn to <u>802</u>.

(B) Take the rope that supports your bed mattress and bind the chest shut? Turn to <u>846</u>.

819 The pearl godstone heats then flashes. When the blinding light vanishes so do the soldiers inside the building.

You hear voices from above you.

"There, you all saw it. The wizard must forfeit. I am going to remove the menace."

"Hold," comes a second voice. "It was the godstone not the wizard. Remember Enchantraen does not know how to operate it."

The voices go silent. You look around but see nothing. The street has cleared except for two soldiers who obviously didn't see what happened.

You walk back towards your apartment. Turn to <u>808.</u>

820 The ship eases towards the reef and the tension mounts among the crew. The ship edges forward in a desperate attempt to pass by the jagged teeth of the sea. A huge wave lifts the boat causing it to list badly to starboard. Men are yanked viciously from the deck and tossed into the sea. When the ship comes down it crashes against the reef.

The hull buckles and water rushes in. A second wave washes across the deck and throws you into the icy water. Your body is bashed against the reef twice before you find a scrap of timber to cling to.

Go to the Enchantraen table that follows and roll one die.

(820 cont'd)

Check off the damage boxes on your score card.

ENCHANTRAEN

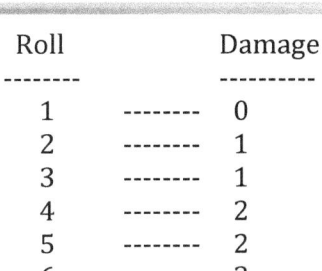

Roll		Damage
1	--------	0
2	--------	1
3	--------	1
4	--------	2
5	--------	2
6	--------	3

If you expire turn to <u>290</u>. You attempt to cast a spell but find that it is hopeless in this disaster.

The water tosses you around like so much driftwood. You continually slip in and out of consciousness but you always cling to your one hope for life – the wrecked timber of the ship. Finally it is too much and you start to slip away.

Roll the dice:

2 to 5, Turn to <u>811</u>.
6 to 12, Turn to <u>805</u>.

821   Your spell takes hold of the package and it lifts from the rail.

"To me," you shout and the package glides over to you.

"No," shouts Kilia as you unwrap it. "That wasn't the purpose of the test."

A laugh passes through the Circle as they see how easily you circumvented Kilia's trap.

"The wizard passes the test," says Valoria.

(Continued next page)

(821 cont'd)

In the package is a child's glass ball. You toss it up to Kilia and turn to <u>813</u>.

822   <u>Mark off EE</u>.

The world grows large around you. An invisible wall has been placed between you and the outside. You scratch wildly with your paws.

Your paws! You must have lost!

Ten faces dance around your eyes. Before you can focus you feel your mind drifting away once more. Turn to <u>828</u>.

823   "No," says Xoeria, "You are misguided."

Check the next trial box on your character sheet and turn to <u>835</u>.

824   The door swings wide and a hundred eyes turn your way. That doesn't concern you. The ceiling does.

It appears as though the roof passes through the sky! Where clouds should be there is a painted ceiling and murals. There is also a balcony. A woman appears on the balcony and waves her hand and the ceiling reappears.

That was an Elder. It suddenly occurs to you what is going on. The surroundings are nothing more than some type of illusion. The Elders are sitting above you and watching!

That explains why the Easterners are so well-behaved. Looking down you see the soldier start to move towards you.

One of them mouths the words, "Death to Enchantraen."

You smile and say, "You don't scare me. I have seen!"

(824 cont'd)

You turn and head down the street.

If <u>P</u> is marked turn to <u>819</u>.

If not, turn to <u>808</u>.

825   You look around and find your apartment has three spacious rooms. Besides the things you brought with you and some furniture there is little else. You test the bed and find it to be too soft. Instead, you unroll your traveling covers and lay down on the floor.

Someone knocks on the door. You crack it open and find three children carrying a new mattress roll.

"Sorry good wizard but it's time to change the beds. I hope we aren't disturbing you."

"What a pleasant coincidence," you smile as they walk in.

They are quickly done and leave once more. As you lay down on the new firm bed you get an uneasy feeling. Perhaps you should check this place over once more. An *ESP* spell would do a thorough job but that would use up 4 manna that you will probably need for tomorrow. Then again, tomorrow may never come. Do you:

(A) Go on to sleep? Turn to <u>814</u>.

(B) Cast the spell? <u>Mark off 4 manna</u> and turn to <u>807</u>.

826   You are correct. You have answered the first question. Turn to <u>844.</u>

827   When you pass by them you see something even worse.

Two wizards drenched in salt water come staggering down the street. You pull your cloak tighter around your head but it's too late. They have seen you. How could those wizards make it to the isles? They can't be experienced enough. The twin wizards from Irliss greet you with slaps on the back. You jump away as one tries to embrace you.

"Please Hector you're going to ruin my robe," you say. "How did you get here?"

Jector stands straight and slaps his hand over his wet shirt. "We have come to claim our right among the Elders."

"Yes," says Hector. "We parted the waters and walked from the mainland."

"A little seems to have spilled back over," you interject.

"Point the way to our new robes Enchantraen. Announce that we have arrived. Let it be known that we have braved all the Eastern tricks and have come forth to claim our prize."

You grab them by the arms and pull them to the side.

"Listen you dolts. You don't win just by showing up. It's dangerous around here. Why don't you get smart for once and get out of here before you get hurt. You aren't ready for the *Challengings* yet. Now quit embarrassing our homelands and leave."

"Nonsense," says Jector, "It was a long swim, I mean walk. We want to see what's around."

"You clowns are hopeless," you say pushing them away. "Just don't look to me for help if you get in trouble."

You open and slam the door to your apartment.

(827 cont'd)

Outside you hear Hector whisper, "I told you no one would believe the one about parting the waters."

As their footsteps become softer you turn and look around your apartment. Turn to <u>825</u>.

828   "I am Enchantraen," are the first words you shout when you regain your body.

Pushing the glass over the rodent scurries away.

"You have followed me across the land haven't you lich?"

You curse as you regain your breath.

"You will die Enchantraen! I have sworn it. The Elders won't let my kind reign on the Circle of Truth. I cannot compete without your body. The Dark Lord has marked you for death. I have an even better purpose in mind."

The lich hisses and prepares a spell that will mean instant death for you if it is completed. You however are faster than he.

Do you:

(A) Attempt a *communication* spell to warn the Elders and then jump for the lich? Hopefully you can do this in time before the lich can finish his spell. If not you could easily die here and now. <u>Mark off DD</u> and turn to <u>849</u>.

(B) Split the earth to swallow him up? <u>Mark off 3 manna</u> and turn to <u>812.</u>

829   The youngest elf stands.

"My name is Elder Valoria," she says. "You have come to claim your place among us, as is your right. There are things we must know about you before the contest can begin. The questions we ask cannot cause you to forfeit but they can make the conditions of your challenging more difficult."

If <u>DD</u> is marked turn to <u>806.</u>

If <u>EE</u> is marked turn to <u>845</u>.

If neither is marked turn to <u>813</u>.

830   You leave dressed in your new white robe and lock the door behind you with the key you found on the dresser. You pull the white hood over your head and attempt to look like all the other wizards in the streets.

Walking along the cobblestone street you see more powerful wizards than you have ever seen in your lifetime. The knowledge and things they could teach you is too much for you to think about. The power contained on this island is enough to topple kingdoms and establish a new order throughout both kingdoms. Yet it sits here passive, content to float on the edge of the world and observe.

You are bumped, interrupting your thoughts. Turning to the side you see another wizard who apologizes.

"I was just looking," he begins and points off into the southwest. "There is the main island. They say all the testing goes on there."

Looking to where he is pointing you see a set of mountains that extend from coast to coast on the island.

(830 cont'd)

"What are the testings?" you ask.

"I don't know," comes a dreamy reply. "All who go there never come back."

The wizard turns and walks off. You turn around quickly and see two Eastern soldiers looking at you. When you notice them they quickly look away.

Down the street you see a building taller than the rest. It looks like a temple or chapel of some sort. Do you:

(A) Go back to your house since it is now nightfall? Turn to 808.

(B) Continue on to the building? Turn to 843.

831   Chinit is an intoxicatingly beautiful woman. The tips of her eyes are slanted slightly and her accent is one you do not recognize.

"Enchantraen, our fellowship is called the True Ones Guild. Is it called that because we, the Elders, believe that ours is the only magic that exists in this world?"

Do you answer simply:

(A) Yes? Turn to 837.

(B) No? Turn to 826.

832   Sleep is slow in coming but it comes none the less.

You stumble along hiding beneath rocks. Always you turn your face trying to hide and not be seen. Soon your back becomes hunched and your feet blistered. You crawl along until you can

(Continued next page)

(832 cont'd)

go no further. Lying there helpless a foot kicks you over to your back. It's Gaoler standing over you.

You wake up early morning in a cold sweat. You sit trying to clear your head. A cool breeze drifts through the window. You rise slowly and dress. Sitting in a chair you stare vacantly at the door waiting for them to come for you.

It doesn't happen that way. Instead the ceiling vanishes. Looking up you see the ten Elders staring down at you. You feel like a hamster in a small box. They don't look so different from you, you think. There are three females. Most of the Elders are human.

There are two elves, a creature you cannot recognize and...

If <u>FF</u> is marked turn to <u>803</u>, if not read on.

Penoi! What is a Penoi doing sitting on the Circle of Truth? You didn't even know their kind could use magic.

These rubbery-skinned creatures are pulled from vats by an alchemist named Denoir, an Eastern dignitary.

If <u>O</u> is marked turn to <u>817</u>.

If not turn to <u>829.</u>

833 "Very well good wizard. Your wishes are mine. I must leave you now so that you can rest."

With that Benolic gets up and he and his panther leave.

(833 cont'd)

Staring out the window at the building Benolic pointed out, do you:

(A) Leave? Turn to <u>830.</u>

(B) Take his advice and retire? Turn to <u>825</u>.

834   "You are in bad need of a second here on the isles," Benolic points out a window. "Those soldiers aren't here for their own good fortune. The talk in the villa is that some of the Elders are proposing that you be forced to forfeit."

"What?" you shout grasping the implications of what he said.

"They found your charmed warning stone on the dead body of a wizard just a few hours ago."

"What!" You slap your arm and find that the charm is gone. "I've been set up," you say sitting down flabbergasted in a chair.

"Yes," he says, "but it isn't over yet. They will challenge you in the morning about it." Turn to <u>815.</u>

835   "The East is a barren land where Western criminals and political prisoners were sentenced. The crimes of these people ranged from stolen bread to the more savage crimes of murder. The land east of Vox was patrolled and any prisoners who attempted to return to their families were slain.

In token acts of defiance the ancestors of the criminals rose up and attacked the borderline kingdoms. When the dwarfs built the great wall the West thought themselves forever rid of the exiles. They never again sent prisoners to the East.

Ages passed and the Eastern population grew. The barren land was no longer able to support the people there.

(Continued next page)

(835 cont'd)

They rallied around a single monarch and attacked. The ancestors of the punished seeking revenge against the ancestors of their jailers. In reality, both sides are guilty, both sides suffer from the wrongs of the past," Elder Xoeria Aoela sites. Turn to <u>855</u>.

836   "I thank you Elder for your help," you say politely.

The Elder moves closer until you stand just within the fringes of his light. He is blind!

"They say that because you are a war wizard that you are unfit. I see great things within you. Tonight you chose non-violence over violence."

Fillo then turns to leave. You try to talk but when he turns back you are silenced.

"We'll tell them and they will be pleased. Rest now Enchantraen. Tomorrow is an important day."

He then turns and disappears into the street. You stumble back into bed very tired and try to sleep. Thoughts of the coming day flutter in and out of your consciousness.

Turn to <u>832</u>.

837   You are wrong. <u>Mark off the next trial box</u> on your character sheet and turn to <u>844</u>.

838   As you push them to the side they continue their taunts but dare not draw sword on you. Turn to <u>827</u>.

839   Elder Xoeria Aoela is rather plain despite his name. He looks like he could have easily been raised in Vox, The Shattered Rose Kingdoms, or any other of the Western cities.

(839 cont'd)

"Enchantraen, many of your kind who come here view the conquering East as black-hearted villains in the history of time. How did the East originate?

Were they:

(A) Subjected people striking back for revenge? Turn to <u>848.</u>

(B) A powerful nation prying on the weakness of the West? Turn to <u>823</u>.

840   When you come to, you are back in the marble hallways of the palace. There is only one Elder standing over you. It is the Elder Valoria, the youngest elf.

Your attempt was a valiant one Enchantraen I knew when I saw you that you hadn't reached your full potential. I hoped you would still win. That is behind you now. Ahead of you is your greatest test of faith. You must lose the bitterness of defeat and wait again for the next *Challengings.*

She lifts you and hands you your things. As you walk she explains that proper passage has been prepared for your return to the Western Kingdoms. You are too tired and hurt to understand much of what she is saying but you take it that she is trying to comfort you.

Soon you are at the dock and on a ship. As the ship heads for the open seas you see her waving farewell, wishing you a safe return. You simply sit at the bow of the ship contemplating your mistake.

Hours pass until a sailor shouts "Ship ahoy!"
You raise to spot the war galleys of the East closing in on you. The anger of seeing them lifts you out of your

(Continued next page)

(840 cont'd)

stupor. You raise an angry fist and shake it at the bobbing sails.

"Not this time Dark Lord but maybe next. I will return to these Isles a thousand times if I have to until I become the victor. There is nothing you can do to stop me. Did you hear me! Nothing! Next time I shall be victorious!"

You chant the words to your *return* spell and vanish back to your tower. There you plot your strategy for your return, and return you shall!

THE END

841   In the middle of a dream about becoming an Elder your mind is suddenly seized. Your eyes open to see a frail old man standing over you. The man is a lich – a powerful wizard whose life has been unnaturally extended. He is drawing your soul from your body.

Out of the side of your eyes you see a small rodent scratching at the side of a glass jar. His magic is powerful. You are unable to use your magic because his spell is too far along and he has you paralyzed. You have only your natural strength to fight him.

Beads of perspiration pop and run down your forehead. You struggle to regain control of your body. At times it feels as though your hands scratch endlessly at an invisible wall. The lich begins to show signs of strain. He increases his concentration. In one last heave of will you try to snap his spell.

(841 cont'd)

Roll the dice:

2 to 5, Turn to <u>822</u>.
6 to 12, Turn to <u>828</u>.

842   Elder Astoria stands. She is of average beauty on the surface, but from inside she radiates the beauty of knowledge and understanding. Her gentle smile slightly veils the enormous power within her.

"Good wizard" she begins. "There is a temple within our walls that harbors a great power that can be tapped by the True One's magic. The name of that power is Sebastobol. It is important that you are acquainted with this power if you are to become an Elder. Is the power a:

(A) God of the past who treads the kingdoms like a giant titan? Turn to <u>865</u>.

(B) Serpent of enormous size with wings? Turn to <u>878</u>.

843   When you walk up to the door of the building you see that it has been left open. You peek inside and see a room full of Eastern soldiers. They are all looking up at the ceiling. Do you:

(A) Open the door wider and look in? Turn <u>824</u>.

(B) Leave well enough alone and go back to your room? Turn to <u>808</u>.

(C) Toss a fireball in and close the door behind you? You can probably hide before any of them get out. <u>Mark off 4 manna</u> and roll the dice. Turn to <u>804</u>.

844   "We do not believe that our magic is the only one. There is planar magic, namonic magic, the magic given through gods, mind magic, and others. I hope that if you become an Elder

(Continued next page)

(844 cont'd)

you will be willing to study these. We are the True One's Guild because we accept the existence of these other forms. We believe however that our way is the truest, untainted by demons and evil. In that way we are truthful to ourselves and to those who know us.

Turn to <u>855</u> if this was your first question or <u>856</u> if this is your second.

845   A black human rises.

"I am Elder Kilia and I say that Enchantraen is not yet ready for the *Challengings*. Last night we all saw how easily the wizard lost to the lich. It is my right as an Elder to call for a test. Enchantraen is to be subjected to a test of wizardly power before the questions begin."

Valoria searches the eyes of the other Elders before speaking. "

Your right is granted Kilia. What is the test you wish this wizard to perform?"

Kilia stands by the edge of the balcony and places a wrapped package on it.

"If the wizard would be so kind as to unwrap it. That will be sufficient, provided the wizard stays there."

Kilia sits down and the room is quiet.

Everyone understands the implication of what he is asking. Since you obviously can't reach the package, he expects you to cast a *hand* spell that will allow you to unwrap it where you stand. That spell is one you have not mastered yet. It is for fifth plane wizards and you are still a fourth.

If you don't pass the test it is all over.

(845 cont'd)

"Now!" shouts LaCrosse the Penoi.

With everything on the line, you decide to cast another spell rather than forfeit. Do you cast:

(A) A *whirlwind* spell to try and blow it towards you? Mark off 3 manna and turn to 850.

(B) A *telekinesis* spell? Mark off 4 manna and turn to 821.

846 You grab a knife and bend to cut the rope away. The door bursts open and children run in towards you. Behind them, just outside the door, shines a bright light.

"Don't cut the bed" shouts one of the children. You rise and turn surprised by their sudden entrance.

"The Elder, Fillo wishes to gain audience with you. May he come in?"

"Well I'm kind of busy," you begin, "but I don't see why not."

An older man swings the door further open. He is carrying a staff that emits a bright golden light. The man is old but obviously unhampered by his age. You notice that as he comes forward the things within the light change.

The dirt floor he stands upon is actually marble. The walls are not plaster, but dark timbers laced with gold.

"Excellent Enchantraen!" Fillo begins. "We were warned of trouble and came here immediately. It gladdens me to see that you have chosen a non-violent way to handle it."

The Elder waves his hand and the children run forward and bind the chest with strong ropes. Then the Elder himself steps

(Continued next page)

(846 cont'd)

into the room. When the light strikes the chest the true form of the lich becomes apparent.

"Take him away," commands Fillo and the children are quick to obey.

The Elder turns and you can see now that he is blind.

"The Circle of Truth has talked much about you since you arrived. Many of the Elders believe you will be unfit because you are a war wizard. This will go well in your favor. I see strength in you Enchantraen. I will tell the others what I have witnessed."

Fillo turns to leave. He stops by the door and its plain wood frame turns to glistening oak and gold.

"Rest now wizard. You shan't be bothered anymore."

With a smile he turns and walks out. <u>Mark off CC</u>. Tired, you lay down and sleep. Turn to <u>832</u>.

847 "Sebastobol is the second oldest living of all creatures known in the West. Although he has many manifestations we see him as a giant winged serpent. Sabastobol the old one, Sabastobol the dragon slayer. In the early days before our history began the dragons crept into his lair and ate the great one's eggs. Although we can't be sure it is said that this is how the dragons gained their great powers. Sabastobol's wrath never subsides as he seeks out the dragons to destroy them for their evil deed. That is why dragons are so seldom seen by humans. They hide in fear of the old one." Turn to <u>855</u>.

848 "You are right Enchantraen. It is nice to see that one who has suffered so much by their hand can still see the truth." Turn to <u>835</u>.

849   Both of your spells are interrupted by a bright light that enters the room.

"We hear you already Enchantraen," comes a mild and even voice.

By the door stands an old man leaning on a white hot staff. The staff emits a weird light that seems to transform the surroundings wherever it touches. The dirt floor around the man looks to be polished marble. The door now looks like solid oak with gold trimming. The ceiling of your apartment is intricately carved wood studded with gold and silver.

"Fillo," the lich spits out. "So they have let even you become an Elder."

Caught between two powerful wizards the lich immediately realizes his plight and starts a *return* spell. If the lich completes it he can return to a safe place where no one can follow. You start a *negate* spell to stop the lich when the Elder stops you.

"You will need your manna for the morning Enchantraen."

The Elder moves forward followed by a group of children. The light from his staff just touches the lich as the Elder finishes his spell.

Commonly the lich would just disappear. This time however you see the lich transformed into a spirit falling through a black and void world. The lich falls down the staff becoming smaller as if he were falling a long way from you. When he reaches the bottom the lich tumbles out the end and into the toppled glass jar that the staff was held over.

You see the lich lying there unconscious before the children pick the jar up and carry it out of the room.

(Continued next page)

(849 cont'd)

If <u>DD</u> is marked turn to <u>816</u>.

If <u>CC</u> is marked turn to <u>836</u>.

850   The wind gathers and forces the package from the ledge. It falls too far away to catch it. When it hits the ground you hear a loud crack. The Elders are stunned and silent.

Valoria stands and says, "I am sorry Enchantraen but you have traveled all this way for nothing. I'm afraid you are not quite ready."

The world around you spins until you faint. Turn to <u>840</u>.

851   "No, this is the theory of the alchemy guild. We believe much different. There has been too many reports of people falling off the end."

<u>Mark off the next Trial box</u> and turn to <u>875</u>.

852   "In truth dear Elders it is mine but I am guilty of no crime."

If <u>CC</u> is marked turn to <u>886</u>.

"Silence," shouts LaCrossa. "Guilt and innocence is not for you to decide.

Another Elder interjects, "LaCrossa did you actually see Enchantraen commit the crime."

"Of course not! I would have stopped it if I had. The children brought it to me and it was given to them by an Eastern soldier named Caaron."

"Caaron is an enemy of mine. I have not committed the crime. I was framed."

A child comes forward from behind the Elder Ingwë. Then Ingwë stands.

(852 cont'd)

"Enchantraen is telling the truth."

"But what about the jewelry," interjects LaCrossa. "If I cannot force this foul wizard to forfeit then I invoke my right to make the challenging more difficult."

"Your right is accepted and Enchantraen's challenge will be made more difficult," say Elder Ingwë.

<u>Mark off the next Trial box</u> on your character sheet. This will be explained later.

Ingwë looks around the Circle and his eyes look momentarily into each one of the Elders.

"We cannot find you guilty of this cruel act Enchantraen. We will search out the person responsible and they will be brought before the council. Let us continue, and Ingwë sits down. Turn to <u>829</u>.

853   Ingwë a brilliant elf stands and states his questions with the fluency of his kindred.

"My people are old beyond the years of your recognizing. We have seen the passing of time. The third age, the Age of Challenge, is the age we now live in. It started when two major events took place. The first is when the East first broke through *Asius* (the dwarven) wall."

"The second was the first sighting of the rainbow that marks the beginning of the *Challengings* in which you now participate. There are two more ages in recorded history. They are The Age of Man, and The Age of the Gods. Which of these was the first recorded period.

(Continued next page)

(853 cont'd)

Was it ...

(A) The Age of Man? Turn to <u>883</u>.

(B) The Age of the Gods? Turn to <u>871</u>.

854   Through the arched entry you see a large natural cavern. The ceiling extends nearly fifty feet above you. The floor extends twenty feet and then drops off into a large ravine. Spanning the ravine is a great stone bridge that leads to another archway. The bridge is very old and crumbling. Lining the edge of the bridge are eternal torches. The torches faintly illuminate the bridge and the rest of the cavern is dark. You can see no other passage or exit from the cavern.

Roll the dice:

2, Turn to <u>868</u>.
3 to 9, Turn to <u>884</u>.
10 to 12, Turn to <u>872</u>.

855   Make sure you only choose two total. If you have already made your second choice turn to <u>856</u>.

Do you choose:

(A) Elder Astoria? Turn to <u>842</u>.

(B) Elder Xoeria Aoela? Turn to <u>839</u>.

(C) Elder Chinit? Turn to <u>831</u>.

(D) Elder Fillo? Turn to <u>860</u>.

(E) Elder Ingwë? Turn to <u>853</u>.

856   Elder Valoria stands after the last question has been asked.

"That is enough," she says. "The degree of difficulty has been established. The *Challengings* will begin Enchantraen if you are willing to compete the next part of the law."

"I do so submit," you answer.

"Good! You are to place all your worldly goods there on the floor. No staffs, charms, jewelry, magical items or weapons can be taken with you. You may keep only your book.

You immediately start disarming yourself. As you stack up your treasures you ask, "Will my things be safe?"

"Actually we cannot guarantee that they will be. Usually there is a second to take care of such things. Our full attentions will be on preparing the next wizard."

If X is marked turn to 888.

"That however will be the least of your worries. The trial ahead should concern you now." Turn to 877.

857   You start to walk on the bridge when LaCrossa suddenly enters! You both see each other at the same time. He stands on the edge of the bridge and begins his spell.
Do you:

(A) Run back the way you came? If GG is marked turn to 873. If not, roll the dice.

   2 to 9, Turn to 885.
   10 to 12, Turn to 950

(Continued next page)

(857 cont'd)

(B) Cast a *transmute* spell on the bridge at his feet? <u>Mark off 2 manna</u> and roll the dice:

2 to 11, Turn to <u>874</u>.
12, Your spell fails! LaCrossa finishes his spell. If <u>GG</u> is marked turn to <u>873</u>. If not, turn to <u>885</u>.

858 Your spell weaves about you until your senses becomes highly aware. At first you catch a glimmer of magic.

Wait! There, halfway across the bridge on the right hand side. LaCrossa must be hiding in the shadows. He must have camouflaged himself with a spell. The advantage is yours. You must react quickly. You sense that he is starting to rise up! Do you:

(A) Attack with a *transmute* spell on the bridge? <u>Mark off 2 manna</u> and roll the dice:

2 to 11, Turn to <u>874</u>.
12, Your spell fails! The Elder rises finishing his own spell. If <u>GG</u> is marked turn to <u>873</u>. If not turn to <u>885</u>.

(B) Leave the way you came? Duck through the archway and turn to <u>950</u>.

859 Halfway across the room the archway on the left blinks and LaCrossa enters. He is as equally surprised to see you as you are to see him. Immediately he starts his chant. Remaining calm you:

(A) Run back the way you came? If <u>GG</u> is marked turn to <u>918</u>. If not, roll the dice:

2 to 5, 10, Turn to <u>950</u>.
6 to 9, 11, 12, Turn to <u>885</u>.

(859 cont'd)

(B) Cast a *transmute* spell above his head? <u>Mark off 3 manna</u> and turn to <u>974</u>.

860   If <u>CC</u> is marked turn immediately to <u>867</u>. If not read on.

The Elder stands and stares blankly at the wall. He is blind.

"Many people have their own theory about our world. Some say it is flat, others round and yet others see us as one branch to a mighty tree. From your area of the world things such as this are seldom discussed. As an Elder however these kinds of questions are of major importance. Even though we cannot be completely sure, which theory do you think the Circle of Truth adheres to?"

Is it the theory that the world is:

(A) Flat? Turn to <u>869</u>.

(B) Round? Turn to <u>851</u>.

(C) Like a tree? Turn to <u>875</u>.

861   As you duck through an archway your feet suddenly become wet. You are standing in an enormous cavern. In the center of the cavern room is a large stagnate pool. It is impossible to tell how deep the water might be. The labyrinth seems crowded with these stagnant pools, tunnels and bridges. There is a ledge running to the right of the pool that is very narrow and crumbly. It leads to the only exit out of the cavern.

Roll the dice:

2 to 8, Turn to <u>898</u>.
9 to 12, Turn to <u>894</u>.

862 The spell sharpens your senses. Even before it takes full effect you see him. LaCrossa is crouching in ambush in the shadows of the next archway. You have little time to react. You decide to:

(A) Cast an *animate* spell on the carving above the doorway? Mark off 4 manna and roll the dice. Instinctively you crouch low as you finish your spell.

2 to 9, Turn to 893.
10 to 12, Your spell fails! LaCrossa sees you and retaliates. If GG is marked turn to 895. If not, turn to 885.

(B) Dive for the archway you just entered hoping to escape? Turn to 950.

863 "The Age of Gods was the first of all recorded history. It is the time when the ancient gods freely walked the world and men cowered at their feet. The skeletal remains of the gods Moorguard and Set Te Mu stand as a reminder of this period. This was the age Sebastobol was born. But before even these, the "old woman" existed." Ingwë sits down and you must turn to 855.

864 Your mind becomes keenly aware of what is around you. You concentrate and sense that there is no life here. Wait! There is magic. You move towards the area and find a small bundle there. Unwrapping it you discover a small vial. You uncork it and drink deeply. Immediately you are aware of new power. On your character sheet return up to 6 manna but never more than you originally had. Grateful to Elder Edla you wrap the sack up and:

(A) Walk across? Turn to 891.

(B) Hide? Turn to 896.

(C) Cast a *reverse* spell? Mark off 3 manna and the letters GG. Now choose again.

---

865   "No Enchantraen! You are wrong. Have you never been to Irliss or seen the great black dragon armor that Sebastobol has given as a gift to the Western kingdoms."

<u>Mark off the next Trial box</u> and turn to <u>847</u>.

866   There is life here! Your mind has become keenly aware of your surroundings. Down your thoughts race through the murky depths. You sense something large and ominous.

You pull back suddenly aware of the danger. The cavern refocuses around you. Whatever it is it is not LaCrossa. You must be wary of it. Do you decide to:

(A) Hide and wait? Turn to <u>932</u>.

(B) Walk around the ledge? Turn to <u>928</u>.

(C) Fly across? <u>Mark off 3 manna</u> and turn to <u>876</u>.

(D) Cast a *reverse* spell? <u>Mark off 3 manna and the letters GG</u>. Now choose again.

(E) Leave the way you came in? Turn to <u>950</u>.

867   Elder Fillo stands. Without the light from his staff he looks quite different from last night. He stares blankly ahead and seems to be truly blind this time.

"As an Elder it is my right to waive your question."

A low murmer spreads around the circle.

"Last night I saw all the proof I needed to convince me that this wizard is ready".

Fillo then sits down. Count this as a choice and turn to <u>855</u>.

868   If <u>HH</u> is marked turn to <u>949</u>.

Your heart starts pounding when you finally see him. LaCrossa rises from the middle of the bridge where he was disguised as a stone. He finishes the last of his spell!

Roll the dice:

2 to 11, If <u>GG</u> is marked turn to <u>873</u>. If not turn to <u>885</u>.
12, His spell fails! Read on!

Even a master like LaCrossa can become befuddled and lose his concentration in the midst of a spell. Do you:

(A) Duck through the archway to escape? Turn to <u>950</u>.

(B) Make him pay for his blunder and melt the stones at his feet? <u>Mark off 2 manna</u> and roll the dice:

> 2 to 11, Turn to <u>874</u>.
> 12, Your spell fails! LaCrossa retaliates. If <u>GG</u> is marked turn to <u>873</u>. If not, turn to <u>885</u>.

869   "No Enchantraen that is not our feeling. It is true that we continually receive reports of people falling off the ends of the earth but being flat is not the total reason."

<u>Mark off the next Trial box</u> and turn to <u>875</u>.

870   If <u>HH is marked</u>, turn to <u>949</u>.

Your heart stops when you see LaCrossa step out of the shadows in the archway finishing the last of his spell! You don't even have time to spit into his face.

Roll the dice:

2 to 11, If <u>GG</u> is marked turn to <u>895</u>. If not turn to <u>885</u>.
12, His spell fails. Read on.

(870 cont'd)

You now have a split second advantage over the Elder. Do you:

(A) Dive for the archway hoping to escape? Turn to <u>950</u>.

(B) Desperately attempt an odd use of your magic and try to animate the carving above the archway? <u>Mark off 4 manna</u> and roll the dice:

2 to 11, Turn to <u>893</u>.
12, Your spell fails! LaCrossa retaliates with his own spell. If <u>GG</u> is marked turn to <u>895</u>. If not, turn to <u>885</u>.

871 Yes this is correct. The age of Man began when mankind wrestled the power from the gods and began to dominate the world. It is the time when man threw off the old superstitions and legends and began thinking on his own." Turn to <u>863</u>.

872 Suddenly LaCrossa enters from the archway on the other side of the bridge. Quickly you duck further into the shadows. He doesn't see you. He starts across the bridge.

Do you:

(A) *Transmute* the bridge at his feet? <u>Mark off 2 manna</u> and roll the dice:

2 to 11, Turn to <u>874</u>.
12, Your spell fails! LaCrossa finishes his spell. If <u>GG</u> is marked turn to <u>873</u>. If not turn to <u>885</u>.

(B) Leave the way you came? Turn to <u>950</u>.

873 You feel the Penoi's spell resound against your *reverse* spell. Winning or failing relies on the strength of your spell and its ability to cast LaCrossa's back.

(Continued next page)

(873 cont'd)

Roll the dice and pray:

2 to 8, Turn to <u>889</u>.
9 to 12, Turn to <u>885</u>.

874   The bridge crumbles at the Elder's feet.

"Nooooo," screams LaCrossa as he falls. "I will be avenged," he screams right before a loud thud echoes back up the canyon.

All is quiet ... Turn to <u>935</u>.

875   "I will admit that this is a most difficult question to put before one who has seldom had the leisure to ponder such matters. None-the-less it is important."

"We believe that the world we know is but a branch of a great ash called Igdresil. With its roots deeply implanted in old worlds we, and the things we call planes are but branches. Each plane is a different world yet we are all a part of the great tree. All the universe is supported by this tree. That is why those who wander too far fall from the edge of the branch, fall and land upon the next branch. This, Enchantraen, we believe to be true!"

Fillo sits and you turn to <u>855</u>.

876   You once again feel the freedom of weightlessness envelope you. You leap into the air and rocket across the cavern towards the second archway. Just past the narrow walkway is a platform that stands before the archway.

(876 cont'd)

Do you:

(A) Fly through the archway at full speed? Turn to <u>951</u>.

(B) Land and walk through? Turn to <u>949</u> if <u>HH</u> is marked.
Otherwise roll the dice:

2 to 6, Turn to <u>944</u>.
7 to 12, Turn to <u>949</u>.

877 "Very well Enchantraen, you must choose which Elder you wish to challenge and replace on the Circle of Truth."

You start to look the Elders over when Elder LaCrossa, the Penoi, jumps up and speaks.

"I cannot serve on the same Circle as this wizard. You must decide whether it is Enchantraen or I you want on your side."

Elder Ingwë, the male elf stands up and slams his fist on the railing.

"Enough LaCrossa! We cannot have this petty jealousy in our ranks." Ingwë looks down at you. "Will you choose this Elder to contest," he says pointing to LaCrossa.

"I have defeated three already Enchantraen. Give me the pleasure," shouts LaCrossa with his wide mouth gaping.

"I see no one better," you reply.

"Done," says Valoria. "Elder Sha Shue will escort you to the grounds.

LaCrossa slams the side of the railing so hard that a piece of it breaks away. He then turns to walk off. The Elders also stand and walk away.

(Continued next page)

(877 cont'd)

Sha Shue waves his hand and a stairway appears. You proceed up it. Elder Sha Shue is the creature you didn't recognize but there is little time now to talk about his heritage.

You follow the Elder through golden halls lined with murals and paintings.

In short panting sentences Sha Shue explains, "Elder Edla is the founder of our guild. He and his craftsmen raised these islands from the seas and lined the interiors of the mountains with great halls and rooms that only the Elders may see. Just before the Age of Man the Elders were in mortal combat with a race of serpent folk. The details of the fighting are unimportant at this time. However let me say that the serpents nearly gained access to the islands through an underground labyrinth. Elder Edla and his craftsmen charmed and trapped the labyrinth. This is where you will fight LaCrossa for the right to sit on the Circle of Truth.

Listen carefully. The rooms and halls of the labyrinth change constantly so that they are never the same. If you turn in your own footsteps and retrace them exactly the way you came you will be lost. Everything behind you will have changed. No one who enters the labyrinth can leave unless they are wearing this."

The Elder pulls out a yellow jewel on a chain and places it around your neck.

"This is called the *amula*. When you are ready to leave, crush it and you will return. Do not lose it or you will be lost forever."

"As you stalk each other through the labyrinth beware of the natural danger also. Elder LaCrossa was truthful when he said he defeated three other challengers. The first one fell to his death when a rock gave way underfoot. The second was defeated magically and the third never returned. His *amula* was probably lost in the struggle."

(877 cont'd)

"To aid the True One's, Elder Edla hid caches of a liquid capable of giving a wizard extra manna in case he or she should run out. These caches are also magically protected and they move from room to room. The rooms will drain you of your manna if you stay inside them too long. These caches could prove very valuable."

The hallway stops and appears to turn into a cave entrance.

"The labyrinth consists of caves and halls. This is one entrance. Elder LaCrossa is being let in by another. He could be waiting for you just inside here or it could take days before you find each other. Remember, if at any time you surrender or wish to leave, break the *amula*. I suggest you clear your mind and begin."

You shake your hands at your side as you meditate. Your opponent is a Penoi. Turning invisible will be useless against him because he can see you anyway. His magic resistance should be extraordinarily high. You must remember to avoid throwing spells directly on him. You fill your mind with spells that effect the area around a person so his superior magic resistance will be to no avail.

Taking a deep breath you step inside. Elder Sha Shue starts to roll a large boulder over the entrance to seal you in. Already your body tingles as the *protective* spells of the labyrinth are activated around you. Just as the stone is nearly in place the Elder gives you his last instructions.

"*Reverse* spells only last while you are in the room you cast it. Beware friend, Penoi's only live ten years. LaCrossa is nine and three quarters. He has little to lose."

The door is closed. Turn to <u>950</u>.

878 "Yes Enchantraen! I thought that one with your abilities couldn't have gotten this far without having at least witnessed the old one's power."

Turn to 847.

879 Your thoughts immediately locate the cache like a divining rod finds water. You find the little bundle hidden under a turned over table. You unwrap the package and remove a vile. Without hesitating you drink deeply. Power flows into your veins. Add back up to the 6 manna and your character sheet but not more than you originally had. Grateful to the first elder you wrap the vile up and lay the package down. Then you decide to:

(A) Walk to the far archway? Turn to 948.

(B) Hide in ambush? Turn to 925.

(C) Cast a *reverse* spell? Mark off 3 manna and the letters GG. Now choose again.

880 The archway leads into a menacing hallway. The two walls and ceiling are lined with two foot spikes. The floor is littered with skeletons and ancient bloodstains. There are stones in the floor next to each skeleton cut like a triangle. Obviously it is those stones that activate the trap. The hallway goes for about 80 feet and stops at the next archway. The hallway is lined with torches. Wait! There is an alcove on the left-hand side. You crane your neck to look but you cannot see the back of it.

Roll the dice:

2 to 9, Turn to 890.
10 to 12, Turn to 942.

881 Halfway across the bridge the room suddenly begins to shake. You are thrown down as pieces of the ceiling collapse and strike the bridge.

If <u>GG</u> is marked you edge along the bridge until ... Turn to <u>949</u>.

If not, roll the dice:

2 or 3, Turn to <u>892</u>.
4 to 12, Turn to <u>906</u>.

882 You find nothing! There is no magic or life in the area. Do you:

(A) Hide and wait in ambush? Turn to <u>925</u>.

(B) Walk across to leave? Turn to <u>948</u>.

(C) Cast a *reverse* spell on yourself? <u>Mark off 3 manna and the letters GG</u>. Then choose gain.

883 "No, this is not the first one. The Age of Man began when mankind wrestled the power from the gods and began to dominate the world. It is the time where man threw off the suppressions of misguided legends and began to develop thoughts of his own."

<u>Mark off the next Trial box</u> on your character sheet and turn to <u>863.</u>

884 The Elder cannot be seen and the cavern is quiet. Do you:

(A) Cast a *detect* spell to search the area for him or any caches? <u>Mark off 2 manna, the letters HH</u> and roll the dice:

2 to 5, Turn to <u>858</u>.
6 to 10, Turn to <u>903</u>.
11 or 12, Turn to <u>864</u>.

(Continued next page)

(884 cont'd)

> (B) Hide and wait for him to come hoping you can ambush him here? Turn to <u>896</u>.

> (C) Walk across the bridge? Turn to <u>891</u>.

> (D) Cast a *reverse* spell on yourself? <u>Mark off 3 manna and the letters GG</u>. Now choose again.

885 "No! No, no, no," you scream as the binding lashes around you. Helplessly you fall to the ground defeated. You struggle against the blue snakes of light that bind you but it is too late. LaCrossa swaggers over to you and stares down. His huge jaw grins as he bends down. You can smell his foul breath when he speaks.

"You sickening upstart. How dare you come to this island! Your cursed race is soon to be extinct. We will see to that. I think I will kill you here after I have toyed with you a bit."

He opens his powerful jaws as if he is going to tear into your soft neck. You spit in his face.

"You whelp," he screams in rage.

His claw of a hand smashes into your chest bruising to the bone. The air wheezes from your lungs but the *amula* is broken. You feel dizzy as you teleport back to the Elders defeated in the end, but alive. Turn to <u>840</u>.

886 Elder Fillo stands and stares blindly at the walls.

"Stop these proceedings immediately. Enchantraen could not have committed this crime. I was with the wizard last night. It is impossible for the wizard to have committed this crime."

LaCrossa yells, "No," but quickly falls silent.

(886 cont'd)

The Penoi's eyes meet the others in the Circle and he sits down.

Elder Ingwë says, "It has been decided Enchantraen to stop this proceeding and to continue on with the *Challengings*. The children will seek out the villain who attempted to frame you and bring him or her before us. Forgive us for doubting you."

The Elder then sits and motions to the Elder directly to his right. Turn to <u>829</u>.

887   There! It's a plant floating along the top of the water by the edge. The plant has eyes!

It must be Lacrossa transformed and waiting in ambush for you. Slowly you become aware of a much larger life force lying dormant deep below the water.

Do you:

(A) Cast a *control* spell on the creature in the depths? You are relatively sure you can control it. <u>Mark off 3 manna</u> and roll the dice:

2 to 9, Turn to <u>916</u>.
10 to 12, Your spell fails! LaCrossa attacks! If <u>GG</u> is marked turn to <u>905</u>.

(B) Leave the way you came? Ducking through the archway turn to <u>950</u>.

888   The door to your apartment bursts open and a panther charges in. Somewhat embarrassed Benolic follows.

"I can watch those," he says too loudly. Then in a whisper he says "Sorry Enchantraen I didn't mean to be eavesdropping."

(Continued next page)

(888 cont'd)

Even in this tension-filled moment you can't help but laugh at your new sidekick. Turn to 877.

889   LaCrossa's spell rebounds against your defense and hurtles back towards him. There his own spell is dissipates against his natural resistance to magic. The shock of seeing his own spell thrown back causes him to panic and he turns to leave.

Do you:

(A) Cast a *transmute* spell on the bridge at his feet? Mark off 2 manna and roll the dice:

2 to 11, Turn to 874.
12, Your spell fails! As he disappears, so do you. Walk through the archway and turn to 950.

(B) Allow him to leave? You also leave by ducking through an archway. Turn to 950.

890   The Elder LaCrossa cannot be seen and the hallway is quiet.
Do you:

(A) Cast a *detect* spell to search the area for him or any caches? Mark off 2 manna and the letters HH. Roll the dice:

2 to 5, Turn to 915.
6 to 10, Turn to 901.
11 or 12, Turn to 938.

(B) Try to hide and wait for him in the shadows of your archway? Turn to 934.

Walk down the hallway being careful to avoid the triangle stones? Turn to 967.

(890 cont'd)

    (C) Cast a *reverse* spell on yourself? <u>Mark off 3 manna and the letters GG.</u> Now choose again.

    (D) Search the hallway? Turn to <u>919</u>.

891   You edge across the bridge feeling very vulnerable. Below you the air rushes through a crevice so deep that you cannot see the bottom. The area in the cavern is dark and the light from the torches makes it hard for you to see past them. The bridge is very old. A stone breaks and falls away into the depths!

    Roll the dice:

    2 to 5, Turn to <u>857</u>.
    6, Turn to <u>868.</u>
    7, 8, 9, Turn to <u>949</u>.
    10 to 12, Turn to <u>881</u>.

892   A large boulder strikes the bridge and down you plummet as the bridge gives way. The six faces of luck were certainly against you. As you fall you realize that it wasn't LaCrossa that defeated you but the labyrinth herself.

    With little else to do you crush the *amula* before you hit, marking the end of the challenge. Turn to <u>840</u>.

893   The carving stirs to your eldritch call. The torches flare to life and the archway becomes a demon's mouth. You rise with a smile on your lips. LaCrossa startles and begins a spell of his own.

    Calmly you say the simple command. "Chew your food wisely my pet."

    The archway collapses around LaCrossa as the stones turn to jagged teeth. The Elder doesn't even scream as his body is torn. The last thing you see on his face is a grim expression of

(Continued next page)

(893 cont'd)

hate and the burning desire to make his pain yours! Turn to 935 as the Penoi falls defeated.

894   LaCrossa enters the cavern from the opposite archway. You both spot each other at the same time. Your heart races as your mind contemplates your options. Do you:

(A) Decide to attack magically? You attempt to *transmute* the ground at his feet to slide him into the pool. Mark off 2 manna and roll the dice:

2 to 11, The ground gives way and the Elder tumbles into the water. Turn to 917.
12, Your spell fails! LaCrossa finishes his spell. If GG is marked turn to 905. If not, turn to 885.

(B) Run the way you came? Roll the dice:

2 to 5, Turn to 951 unless GG is marked, then turn to 949.
6 to 12, If GG is marked turn to 905, if not, turn to 885.

895   The Elder's spell cracks against your defenses. You grimace knowing that all relies on the power of your spell.

Roll the dice:

2 to 8, turn to 909.
9 to 12, Turn to 885.

896   You crouch behind a rock waiting for the Penoi to step into your trap. You wait and you wait, formulating your plan.

Roll the dice:

2 to 5, Turn to 872.
6 to 12, Turn to 908.

897   It holds and his spell is repulsed! His own spell is hurled back towards him but is eaten up by the power of his own magic resistance. More determined than ever LaCrossa begins his next enchantment. Do you:

   (A)   Cast a whirlwind at him? <u>Mark off 3 manna</u> and roll the dice:

   2 to 11, Turn to <u>907</u>.
   12, Your spell also fails! Curses to the six sides of fate. LaCrossa strikes! If <u>GG</u> is marked turn to <u>959</u>. If not turn to <u>885</u>.

898   LaCrossa is nowhere to be seen. Do you:

   (A) Cast a *detect* spell to search the area for him or any caches? <u>Mark off 2 manna</u>, <u>the letters HH</u> and roll the dice:

   2 to 5, Turn to <u>887</u>.
   6 to 9, Turn to <u>866</u>.
   10 to 12, Turn to <u>924</u>.

   (B) Hide and wait for him to come hoping you can ambush him here? Turn to <u>932</u>.

   (C) Walk around the ledge? Turn to <u>928</u>.

   (D) Physically search your side? Turn to <u>988</u>.

   (E) Cast a *fly* spell and fly across to the other side? <u>Mark off 3 manna</u> and turn to <u>876</u>.

   (F) Cast a *reverse* spell on yourself? <u>Mark off 3 manna and the letters GG</u>. Now choose again.

899   Too late to stop, the trap is sprung. Sensing impending death you leap and roll.

(Continued next page)

(899 cont'd)

This daring maneuver saved you from the majority of the crisscrossing spikes that spear out of the walls and ceiling in that area of the hallway.

Still, no one could have been quick enough to avoid them all.

Go to the Entrantraen table that follows and roll one die. Check off the damage boxes on your score card.

ENCHANTRAEN

Roll		Damage
1	--------	0
2	--------	1
3	--------	2
4	--------	2
5	--------	3
6	--------	4

If you expire the last thing you remember is your *amula* breaking.

Turn to <u>840</u>.

If you live, tumble on through the archway while you can still breathe. Turn to <u>950</u>.

900   Your *amula* disintegrates on your chest sending you plummeting through an endless void. The pressing cold and nothingness remains stationery around you yet your senses tell you that you are falling. You recognize the sensation at once. You are being teleported somewhere.

It is impossible to determine the time it takes before the falling sensation stops and the world starts to refocus around you.

(900 cont'd)

At first you hear the cheering voices of the children of Thuatha. The deep red and gold flecked marble floor presses beneath your feet. A large marble room suddenly snaps into view. Nine Elders move as one to embrace you.

You begin to wonder where the tenth Elder is when it suddenly occurs to you. You are the tenth!

Valoria places a simple white gold ring on your hand, the symbol of the Elders. The children carry in a litter with a canopied chair and place you in it. As the children carry you the Elders walk beside you explaining.

"Elder Enchantraen, you will need to examine our storehouse of magics and treasures. It will become your responsibility to bestow quests on good-hearted adventurers and you will need to know which weapon will best suit their cause. The library here is truly marvelous. There are complete texts on new forms of magic. Magic that you never dreamed of. There are explanations of power symbols and the teachings of Elder Edla and ..."

You stop listening. Before you is a large natural staircase that leaves the palace and winds up the side of a mountain.

"Where does that go?" you inquire.

"That goes to the highest point on the islands where ..."

You interrupt, "Where Edla's throne rests".

Jumping from the litter you race up the stairway. Cool air whips around you. You stumble once but quickly rise, continuing your mad rush up the stairs. Around a corner and there it sits before you.

(Continued next page)

(900 cont'd)

You run your hands over the intricate workmanship of the throne. It seems to be cut from a single pearl godstone. The patterns carved into it must act as a guiding force for its wild magic. Without hesitating you seat yourself. The Western

Kingdoms come into view one by one. You glance one way and you see your tower in Arcania clearly as though no magic hides it. Taking a deep breath you do what you have always wanted to do. You gaze eastward. Your eyes race past the city of Vox, past the *Asius* wall and deep into the Eastern Empire.

Gazing this way and that you are determined to find him. You want to be the first to do what no Western adversary has done before. You search for the Dark Lord's Master. The one true ruler of the East. You want to look him in the eyes. Now... now you will not be so helpless before him because you have become a full Elder that sits on the Circle of Truth.

THE END

901 Be sure HH is marked off.

You find nothing. There is no cache or Elder in this hallway. Do you:

(A) Decide to wait and hide in ambush? Turn to 934.

(B) Walk down the hall to the other archway? Turn to 967.

(C) Cast a *reverse* spell on yourself? Mark off 3 manna and the letters GG. Now choose again.

(D) Leave through the archway you just entered? Turn to 951.

902   The creature fans its wings and says, "What is it that you wish of me."

Somewhat befuddled you stammer for an answer. Do you say:

(A) I need my manna points returned so that I may continue through this labyrinth. As the door closes turn to 969.

(B) Bring the one named LaCrossa before me. As the door closes roll the dice:

2 to 5, Turn to 859.
6, 7, Turn to 931.
8 to 12, Turn to 976.

903   The spell blends with the air. You become keenly aware of what is around you. There are no signs of life or magic.

Do you:

(A) Hide and wait? Turn to 896.

(B) Walk across? Turn to 891.

(C) Cast a *reverse* spell? Mark off 3 manna and the letters GG. Now choose again.

904   You carefully move across the room. You glance around expecting to see LaCrossa at any moment. You decide to move to the archway. A breeze suddenly sweeps through the room. You involuntarily inhale and roll the dice:

2 to 5, Turn to 859.
6, Turn to 945.
7 to 9, Turn to 949.
10 to 12, Turn to 972.

905 The Penoi's spell resounds against the protection of the *reverse* spell. In less than a heartbeat you realize that winning or failing relies on the strength of your spell to throw his back.

Roll the dice:

2 to 8, Turn to 926.
9 to 12, Turn to 885.

906 As the rocks crash around you,

Go to the Enchantraen table that follows and roll one die. Check off the damage boxes on your score card.

ENCHANTRAEN

Roll	Damage
1	0
2	1
3	2
4	3
5	5
6	6

If you expire the cave-in eventually smashes the *amula* and you should turn to 840. If you live mark the damage boxes from your character sheet. You crawl across the bridge until ... Turn to 949.

907 Your spell stirs the stagnant air. Quickly your magic gathers strength and the wind howls at your command. LaCrossa smiles, thinking you will try to batter him to death with the force of your whirlwind. That is not your plan.

Harder and harder you send the wind against him until the hallway becomes a screaming wind tunnel. LaCrossa leans forward to brace himself. The Elder attempts a *counter* spell.

(907 cont'd)

That is when you pull the wind back. LaCrossa lurches forward off-balance. As he staggers you send it at him again. He loses his balance and screams when he recognizes your strategy. The next blast tumbles him over the stones and across a triangle.

The spikes race from the walls and ceiling. In a blink of an eye the Penoi is crisscrossed with spikes protruding from all sides of his body. His face is frozen in terror. You are forced to turn away from the ghastly spectacle. Turn to 935.

908   You continue to wait but he doesn't come. Finally the effects of the room wear upon you. The room absorbs 2 of your manna as it shifts through the labyrinth. Mark off 2 manna. You know you must leave before it drains you completely.

Do you:

(A) Leave the way you came? Turn to 950.

(B) Walk across the bridge? Turn to 891.

(C) Cast a *reverse* spell? Mark off 3 manna and the letters GG. Now choose again.

909   LaCrossa's spell is thrown back against him. He becomes bound in his own magic and falls to the ground with curses. He seems capable of ripping away the light blue bindings that enfold him by his sheer rage.

Quickly you cross over and smash his *amula* signaling the Elder's defeat. Smiling, you turn to 935.

910   There he is! Concealed behind a stack of chests he smiles and starts his chant. In a split second you time his rhythm and believe that you might yet beat him. Do you:

(A) Dive back through the archway you came from? Turn to 951.

(B) Dive for the closest archway across the room? Turn to 950.

(C) Attack with a *transmute* spell? Mark off 3 manna and turn to 974.

911   The Penoi is nowhere to be seen and the room is quiet. Do you:

(A) Cast a *detect* spell to search the area for a cache or the Elder? Mark off 2 manna and the letters HH and roll the dice:

2 to 5, Turn to 969.
6 to 9, Turn to 936.
10 to 12, Turn to 931.

(B) Hide and wait hoping to catch LaCrossa off-guard? Turn to 920.

(C) Walk across to the door on the left? Turn to 904.

(D) Walk across to the door on the right? Turn to 939.

(E) Cast a *reverse* spell on yourself? Mark off 3 manna and the letters GG. Now choose again.

(F) Physically search the room? Turn to 965.

912   The steed is magnificent as it races through the air. The speed is breathtaking as the ground rushes by. The creature is gentle and soon you feel as though you belong together.

(912 cont'd)

You race through the night and part of the next day. You wish you could ride this beast all the way to the Mystic Isles but already you sense that Constellia misses his real master.

At last the horse sets you down on firm ground where you both can rest. In time you consent to let the beast go and you walk the rest of the way into town. Turn to <u>333</u>.

913   If <u>HH</u> is marked turn to <u>949</u>.

A light blue light flickers from the alcove. You see the light race towards you. You gasp when you see the ugly Penoi's face peering out of the shadows.

Roll the dice:

2 to 11, If <u>GG</u> is marked turn to <u>959</u>. If not, turn to <u>885</u>.
12, His spell fails! Read on.

As LaCrossa panics you laugh.

"You can't even defeat me with a coward's advantage, evil one!"

Do you:

(A) Duck back through the archway you came in? Turn to <u>950.</u>

(B) Attack with a *whirlwind* spell? LaCrossa is dangerously close to a triangle stone. <u>Mark off 3 manna</u> and roll the dice:

2 to 11, Turn to <u>907</u>.
12, Your spell also fails! LaCrossa strikes back. If <u>GG</u> is marked turn to <u>959</u>. If not turn to <u>885.</u>

---

914   Staying in the best position possible you wait, formulating your plan. Time passes and your eyes grow tired from shifting back and forth between the two archways. Roll the dice:

2 to 8, Turn to 927.
9 to 12, Turn to 894.

915   The hallway focuses and refocuses as you search up and down its walls looking for the Penoi. Sweat suddenly beads on your forehead.

LaCrossa is hiding in the alcove at the far end. Sensing that he has been discovered the Elder begins to rise. With little time to contemplate you try an unusual but deadly way to use your magic against him. Do you:

(A) Cast a *whirlwind* spell? <u>Mark off 3 manna</u> and roll the dice:

   2 to 11, Turn to 907.
   12, Your spell fails! LaCrossa has just finished a *counter* spell. If <u>GG</u> is marked turn to 959. If not turn to 885.

(B) Dive for the archway you just entered hoping to escape?
   Turn to 951.

916   The creature stirs and reacts to your command. You quickly become acquainted with the massive size and strength of the creature you so totally control. You see the plant which is LaCrossa begin to move, apparently disturbed by the undercurrent.

You must act fast. With a total concentration of effort you command the creature to rise and attack with every fiber in its body. Turn to 917.

917   Dormant for untold ages the creature is slow to respond, but once it moves its power is enormous. The water sucks down around it as it rises. The pool is a fountain of stench and

(917 cont'd)

cascading splashes of death. Water floods around you threatening to wash you into the middle of the sickening pool.

You fight for a handhold when it suddenly stops. The cavern is quiet except for the dripping of water from the rocks as it makes its way back into the pool. LaCrossa is gone. Turn to 935.

918   As the Penoi's spell resounds against your *reverse* spell you momentarily stop breathing. Winning or failing now relies on the power of your spell to hold his off.

Roll the dice:

2 to 9, Turn to 961.
10 to 12, Turn to 885.

919   You physically search the walls and floor always trying to watch your step, but still being alert to any danger. Your hand touches a loose stone and mortar crumbles on the floor echoing down the hallway.

Roll the dice:

2 to 5, Turn to 938.
6, Turn to 915.
7, Turn to 942.
8 to 10, Turn to 901.
11 or 12, Turn to 899.

920   Going into the room you grab a large chest and turn it around so that you can conceal yourself behind it. Time passes when ...

Roll the dice:

2 to 6, Turn to 972.
7 to 10, Turn to 931.
11 or 12, Turn to 940.

921   If <u>HH</u> is marked turn to <u>949</u>.

From the small alcove LaCrossa steps with the light blue light playing around his hands. He smiles and sends the binding racing towards you. If <u>GG</u> is marked turn to <u>959</u>. If not, turn to <u>885</u>.

922   You thoroughly search but find nothing.

Suddenly the room shifts through the labyrinth and <u>drains you of 4 manna.</u> Cursing you realize that you must leave now before it drains you completely. Do you:

(A) Leave the way you came? Turn to <u>951</u>.

(B) Walk to the far archway? Turn to <u>949</u>.

(C) Cast a *reverse* spell on yourself. <u>Mark off another 3 manna and the letters GG</u>. Now quickly choose again.

923   Just then LaCrossa enters the room! The six sided fates must be with you because he doesn't see you... yet.

Do you:

(A) *Transmute* the ground at his feet and tumble him into the pool? <u>Mark off 2 manna</u> and roll the dice:

   2 to 11, and the ground gives way and the Elder tumbles into the pool! Turn to <u>917</u>.
   12, Your spell fails! You dive through the archway to escape before he has time to retaliate. Turn to <u>950</u>.

(B) Dive through the archway now to escape? Turn to <u>950</u>.

---

924   Your mind travels through the cavern keenly aware of the surroundings. Magic!

Your mind races to a small area near the pool's edge. There you find a package with a small vile. Carefully you unwrap it and drink it down. <u>Return 6 manna points to your character sheet</u>. Praising Elder Elda you put back the cache when suddenly ... turn to <u>866</u>.

925   You move over to the wrecked chairs and tables and wait. There you formulate a plan of attack if he shows.

Roll the dice:

2 to 7, Turn to <u>943</u>.
8 to 12, Turn to <u>946</u>.

926   LaCrossa's spell rebounds against your defense and hurtles back towards him. The shock of seeing his own spell repelled causes him to go into a rage. You struggle through the archway hoping for a greater advantage the next time you meet. Turn to <u>950</u>.

927   You stay longer than you thought. Finally the effects of the ever-shifting room begins to wear on you. <u>Mark off 3 manna</u>. You realize you must now leave before it drains you completely. Do you:

(A) Leave the way you came? Turn to <u>951</u>.

(B) Walk the narrow ledge to the other exit? Turn to <u>928</u>.

(C) Cast a *reverse* spell? <u>Mark off 3 manna and the letters GG</u>. Now choose again.

928   You slide against the wall easing your way around the ledge. At your feet chunks of the ancient pathway give way and slide into the pool. You realize how vulnerable you would be if you were caught exposed like this. Still, you dare not move too quickly. The stink of the pool offends your nostrils. The dark archway looms just ahead.

Roll the dice:

2 to 5, Turn to 894.
6, Turn to 944.
7 or 8, Turn to 949.
9 to 12, Turn to 954.

929   "Noooooo it can't end like this," you curse. "This can't be real."

The spikes vanish! By disbelieving in an illusion it cannot harm you. You chuckle as you feel yourself magically plummeting through a hidden archway. Turn to 950.

930   You start across the room when LaCrossa enters through the other archway. You both see each other at the same time. With all the calmness you can muster you:

(A) Run back the way you came? If GG is marked turn to 895. If not, roll the dice:

2 to 5, turn to 950.
6 to 12, Turn to 885.

(B) Cast an *animate* spell on the archway's carving just above his head? You can only hope that this odd use of your magic will stop the deadly Elder. Instinctively you crouch when you say the words. Mark off 4 manna and roll the dice:

2 to 11, Turn to 893.
12, Your spell fails! LaCrossa finishes his. If GG is marked turn to 895. If not, turn to 885.

931   The light pad of a footfall and you duck below the top of a chest. LaCrossa enters through the same archway you came from. He enters panting and covered with dust. He leans against the wall to catch his breath and to brush himself off. You have the advantage if you act before he notices you. Do you:

(A) Jump out the far archway before he can strike at you? Turn to 950.

(B) *Transmute* the ceiling above his head into mud? Mark off 3 manna and roll the dice:

2 to 11, Turn to 976.
12, Your spell fails! If GG is marked turn to 918. If not, turn to 885.

932   Sliding along the edge of the cavern you seek the best shelter you can. There is no easy place to hide. Looking around once more you formulate a plan. You could change shape and ease into the water. There you could hide and wait to catch the Elder off-guard. Weighing the possibilities you decide to:

(A) Change shape. Mark off 4 manna and turn to 947.

(B) Stay where you are and hope for the best? Turn to 914.

(C) Change your mind and decide to leave the way you came in. Turn to 951.

(D) Walk across the narrow passageway towards the next archway. Turn to 928.

933   You go quickly through the archway. The light in this room is so bright that it takes your eyes a moment to focus. A sputtering white gem emits a white-hot light that gleams and bounces off the crimson colored room and its gold trimmings.

(Continued next page)

(933 cont'd)

The walls are inlaid with the gold, as well as the fixtures and plush furniture. The room appears to be perfectly kept.

It seems to be a waiting room of some type. There are two archways with closed gold doors beneath them.

Roll the dice:

2 to 8, Turn to 911.
9 to 12, Turn to 931.

934   To the left of the archway is a dark corner. You carefully hide yourself in the shadows. When he enters the hallway his concentration will probably be on the spikes. It is then that you hope to catch him by surprise with an unusual spell. You wait and hope he will show.

Roll the dice:

2 to 7, Turn to 964.
8 to 12, Turn to 942.

935   <u>Erase the checkmark furthest to the right on your character sheet in the Trial area.</u> If it is the last checkmark then turn to 900.

If there are still more boxes checked you know that LaCrossa was saved by his *amula*. He will have been teleported to another area in the labyrinth. You take a deep breath feeling good that so far the game is yours. You are capable of defeating him. The only question is how many times you can win with the odds stacked in his favor. Your *amula* rewards you by <u>replenishing all your manna points.</u>

You turn and walk through the archway. Turn to 950.

936   There is no sign of the Penoi and the cache cannot be found.
Do you:

(A) Hide and wait? Turn to 896.

(B) Walk across to the archway on the left? Turn to 939.

(C) Walk across to the archway on the right? Turn to 949.

(D) Cast a *reverse* spell? <u>Mark off 3 manna and the letters GG</u>.
Now choose again.

937   This archway leads into a large room. The room has walls of
smooth stone obviously crafted by men as opposed to many of
the labyrinth's rooms that are left in their natural state. The
floor is littered with overturned chairs and tables from a battle
long ago.

The next archway is to your right. Above the doorway is the
sculpture of a demon skull or some other unknown creature.
The room is lit by sputtering torches placed in the sculpture's
eyes.

Roll the dice:

2 to 9, Turn to <u>966</u>.
10 to 12, Turn to <u>946</u>.

938   Immediately you detect a magical item hidden behind a loose
stone. The stone is near you so you simply reach out and slide
it from the wall. There you find a small bundle. Unwrapping it
you discover a vile. Drinking it down you feel power flow
through your veins.

<u>Add back up to 6 manna on your character sheet</u>, but not more
than your original total. Grateful to Elder Elda you wrap up the
vile and place it back.

(Continued next page)

(938 cont'd)

Then you decide to:

(A) Walk across to the far archway? Turn to 967.

(B) Hide in ambush? Turn to 934.

(C) Cast a *reverse* spell on yourself? Mark off 3 manna and the letters GG. Choose again.

939   Roll the dice:

2, 3, 5, 6, 7, Turn to 904.
4, 8 to 12, Turn to 972.

940   Continually glancing to the left, then right, and back the way you came, you survey the room. Always on guard you wait patiently. You wait and wait but he doesn't show. The room shifts through the labyrinth and absorbs 2 manna from you. You realize you must leave before it drains you further.

Do you:

(A) Leave the way you came? Turn to 950.

(B) Walk to the archway on the left? Turn to 904.

(C) Walk to the archway on the right? Turn to 972.

(D) Cast a *reverse* spell on yourself? Mark off another 3 manna and the letters GG. Now choose again.

941   Gliding into the water you ease yourself down and quietly wait. Suddenly you feel the water swirling beneath you. Even in reptilian form you become aware of a large creature beneath you. With slow steady strokes you ease out of the water and quickly transform back. Mark off HH.

(941 cont'd)

Roll the dice:

2 to 7, Turn to 927.
8 to 12, Turn to 923.

942 Something moves in the far archway. LaCrossa enters. You both see each other at the same time. The only words the Elder speaks is the beginning of his spell. Do you:

(A) Dive back through your archway? Turn to 951.

(B) Start a spell of your own? The *whirlwind* spell you have in mind will <u>cost you 3 manna.</u> Roll the dice:

2 to 11, Turn to 907.
12, Your spell fails! LaCrossa retaliates. If <u>GG</u> is marked turn to 959. If not turn to 885.

943 You continue to wait but he doesn't show. The room shifting through the labyrinth takes its toll on you. <u>Mark off 3 manna</u> as the room absorbs your magic. You now realize that you must leave before you are drained. Do you:

(A) Leave the way you came in? Turn to 950.

(B) Walk to the far archway? Turn to 948.

(C) Cast a *reverse* spell on yourself? <u>Mark off 3 manna and the letters GG</u>. Now choose again.

944 If <u>HH</u> is marked turn to 949 immediately.

Your heart starts pounding when you finally see him. LaCrossa was hiding as a plant by the edge of the pool nearest the ledge. The plant spews out a deadly gas. The gas is so thick it immediately starts to choke your life away. You start to fall forward into the pool. Somehow you manage to catch yourself

(Continued next page)

(944 cont'd)

and instead fall on the small platform at the end of the ledge just before the archway.

You struggle on your belly towards the archway. You sense LaCrossa transforming back and you hear his footsteps coming behind you. The gas still burns at your lungs.

Go to the Enchantraen table that follows and roll one die. Check off the damage boxes on your score card.

ENCHANTRAEN

Roll		Damage
1	--------	2
2	--------	3
3	--------	3
4	--------	4
5	--------	5
6	--------	5

If you expire, the last thing you will remember is your *amula* breaking. Turn to 840.

If you live you find the gas dissipating, allowing you to move and breathe. You start to stand but LaCrossa casts his next spell. If GG is marked turn to 905. If not, turn to 885.

945   If HH is marked turn to 949.

You gasp when you see the hell-spawned Penoi rise from behind a stack of chests. The dog has got you and there is little to do but pray his spell fails!

(945 cont'd)

Roll the dice:

2 to 9, If <u>GG</u> is marked turn to <u>918</u>. If not, turn to <u>885</u>.
12, His spell fails! Read on!

Knowing that everything hinges on a split second decision, you:

(A) Run for an archway while you can? Turn to <u>950</u>.

(B) Cast a *transmute* spell above his head? <u>Mark off 3 manna</u> and turn to <u>974</u>.

946 Something moves in the shadow of the opposite archway. You dive behind a table. LaCrossa enters in a crouched fighting position.

"I know you're here pale one," he shouts from the archway. His eyes search the room letting you know that he is bluffing. Before he can walk out of the archway you:

(A) Cast an *animate* spell on the carving around the archway he is standing under. <u>Mark off 4 manna</u> and roll the dice:

2 to 11, Turn to <u>893</u>.
12, Your spell fails! LaCrossa sees you and retaliates. If <u>GG</u> is marked turn to <u>895</u>. If not, turn to <u>885</u>.

(B) Dive for the archway you entered? Turn to <u>950</u>.

947 Since the color of the pool is green you decide to transform into a crocodile. That way you will blend in and you can keep your eyes just above the water to watch for LaCrossa.

The spell starts to take effect and you enter the water even before the transformation is complete.

(Continued next page)

(947 cont'd)

Roll the dice:

2 to 8, Turn to <u>941</u>.
9 to 12, Turn to <u>952</u>.

948   You slowly walk across the room glancing in the shadows around you. The room is eerie and makes you feel uneasy.

Wait! Was that a footstep or the pounding of your heart?

Roll the dice:

2 to 5, Turn to <u>930</u>.
6, Turn to <u>870</u>.
7 to 9, Turn to <u>949</u>.
10 to 12, Turn to <u>958</u>.

949   You make it across and still there is no sign of LaCrossa. Taking a deep breath you proceed through the archway. Turn to <u>950</u>.

950   <u>Erase any marks on GG or HH.</u>

Roll the dice:
2 to 5, Go to Table I and roll again.
6 to 8, Go to Table II and roll again.
9 to 12, Go to Table III and roll again.

Table I	Table II	Table III
2 to 5, Turn to <u>854</u>.	2 to 5, Turn to <u>861</u>.	2 to 5, Turn to <u>937</u>.
6 to 8, Turn to <u>933</u>.	6 to 8, Turn to <u>880</u>.	6 to 8, Turn to <u>953</u>.
9 to 12, Turn to <u>980</u>.	9 to 12, Turn to <u>990</u>.	9 to 12, Turn to <u>977</u>.

951   If <u>GG</u> is marked turn to <u>949</u>.

As you duck through the archway a piercing pain shoots through your back. You realize that the attack came from the labyrinth itself. Somehow you must have violated the magical laws that guard this place.

Go to the Enchantraen table that follows and roll one die. Check off the damage boxes on your score card.

ENCHANTRAEN

Roll		Damage
1	--------	0
2	--------	1
3	--------	2
4	--------	2
5	--------	3
6	--------	4

If you live turn to <u>950</u>. If you expire turn to <u>840</u>.

952   The second your foot touches you feel the water move. Quickly you lurch back and the transformation stops. Turn to <u>955</u>.

953   Through the archway you feel an odd sensation pass through your body. When your eyes focus you find yourself standing in a large natural cavern. You are standing on a ledge that leads to a rope bridge that spans across a chasm.

You see a strange sight at the bottom. A group of serpent folk are steadily chiseling away at the side of a rock wall. You sense the magic below and realize that they are working against an *illusion* spell of some type. It's hard to believe that the scaly ones could still be trying to break in!

(Continued next page)

(953 cont'd)

If they only looked up they could see that they could easily climb out. The spell holding them must be very powerful.

Roll the dice:

2 to 7, Turn to <u>987</u>.
8 to 12, Turn to <u>984.</u>

954   At the end of the ledge you turn and step on a platform that rests just before the archway. A large part of the ledge gives way! You leap and one hand catches on a stone. As large pieces of rock slide into the pool you pull yourself up onto the platform. Turn to <u>955</u>.

955   You regain your footing just as the pool erupts filling the room with the stench of its cascading waters. Caught off balance by the floods you are knocked off your feet and sent sprawling towards the archway.

Through the falling water you first see the coal black eyes followed by a gaping mouth. Realizing your best defense depends on getting through the archway you push ahead with all your might. The mouth snaps shut.

Go to the Enchantraen table that follows and roll one die. Check off the damage boxes on your score card.

ENCHANTRAEN

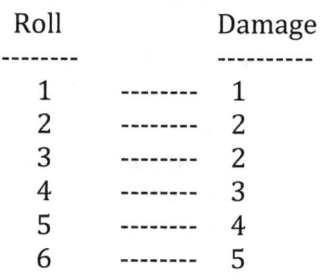

Roll		Damage
1	--------	1
2	--------	2
3	--------	2
4	--------	3
5	--------	4
6	--------	5

(955 cont'd)

If you expire the last thing you remember is your *amula* breaking. Turn to 840.

If you live you find yourself rushing through the archway leaving the water behind. Turn to 950.

956   You find an ideal place to conceal yourself near the bridge. From here you can see both archways and feel relatively safe from discovery. You wait and wait.

Roll the dice:

2 to 5, 11, Turn to 968.
6 to 10, 12, Turn to 960.

957   "Nooooo," you scream as the spikes pierce your body.

Go to the Enchantraen table that follows and roll one die. Check off the damage boxes on your score card.

ENCHANTRAEN

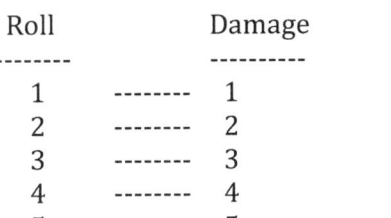

Roll		Damage
1	--------	1
2	--------	2
3	--------	3
4	--------	4
5	--------	5
6	--------	5

If you are unfortunate enough to expire, the last you remember is feeling your *amula* crush. Turn to 840. If you live you realize too late that the trap was just an illusion. The damage done to your body however is real. After subtracting the damage you find yourself plummeting once more but this time through a hidden archway. Turn to 950.

958   Suddenly a trap door springs open at your feet. Another labyrinth trap you curse as you fall towards the jagged spikes!

Roll the dice:

2 to 8, Turn to <u>929</u>.
9 to 12, Turn to <u>957</u>.

959   You tense when the Penoi's spell collides with your *defensive* spell. You swallow hard as your own spell crackles loudly seeming to fail.

Roll the dice:

2 to 8, Turn to <u>897</u>.
9 to 12, Turn to <u>885</u>.

960   LaCrossa enters at the far archway. You stifle the reflex to inhale deeply for fear of giving your position away.

The Elder walks over to gaze down at the chasm. The blood is roaring through your ears. Do you:

(A) Lose your courage and dive to exit the way you came? Turn to <u>950</u>.

(B) Attack with an *illusion* spell cast on the serpent folk with the hope they will do your bidding? <u>Mark off 4 manna</u> and turn to <u>985</u>.

961   The spell is thrown off! There it crackles against his own innate magic resistance.

A look of shock crosses his face as his own *binding* spell wraps him up! You got him with his own magic. He falls to the ground screaming. In his rage he seems capable of tearing the binding apart. You quickly cross over to him and with a laugh you smash his *amula*. In a flare of curses he vanishes. Turn to <u>935</u>.

962   Across the bridge by the far archway you see him. LaCrossa is unwrapping a small bundle, huddling against the far cliff. He obviously doesn't see you. He is too far away to strike him directly with a spell. Yet there are other ways. Do you:

(A) Exit out your archway to avoid the Elder? Turn to <u>951</u>.

(B) Cast an *illusion* spell on the serpent folk below with the hope they will do your bidding? <u>Mark off 4 manna</u> and turn to <u>985.</u>

(C) Cast a *reverse* spell on yourself? <u>Mark off 3 manna and the letters GG.</u> Now choose again.

963   You start to move your way through the chairs and tables looking for anything that is unusual.

Roll the dice:

2, 3, Turn to <u>946.</u>
4, 5, 6, Turn to <u>922.</u>
7, Turn to <u>870.</u>
8, 9, Turn to <u>879.</u>
10 to 12, Turn to <u>882.</u>

964   You continue to wait but he doesn't show. You feel the hallway shift through the labyrinth. <u>It drains you 1 manna.</u> You realize you must move or you will be further drained. <u>Mark off HH.</u> Do you:

(A) Leave the way you came in? Turn to <u>951</u>.

(B) Walk the hallway to the other end? Turn to <u>967</u>.

(C) Cast a *reverse* spell on yourself? <u>Mark off 3 manna and letters GG.</u> Now choose again.

965   <u>Mark off the letters HH.</u>

There are boxes and chests full of worthless trinkets. There are clothes and ornaments but nothing that will help you with your present cause. But then ...

Roll the dice:

2, 3, Turn to <u>940</u>.
4, 5, 6, Turn to <u>972</u>.
7, Turn to <u>910</u>.
8, Turn to <u>936</u>.
9, 10, Turn to <u>969</u>.
11, 12, Turn to <u>859</u>.

966   LaCrossa is not here. At least you don't see him. You glance around the room once more. Everything is quiet. Maybe too quiet. Do you:

(A) Cast a *detect* spell to search the area for him or any caches? <u>Mark off 2 manna and the letters HH</u> and roll the dice:

2, 3, Turn to <u>879</u>.
4 to 9, Turn to <u>882</u>.
10, 11, 12, Turn to <u>862</u>.

(B) Hide and wait for him to come hoping you can ambush him? Turn to <u>934.</u>

(C) Carefully walk across the room? Turn to <u>948</u>.

(D) Cast a *reverse* spell on yourself? <u>Mark off 3 manna and the letters GG</u>. Now choose again.

(E) Search the room? Turn to <u>963</u>.

967   Carefully you walk the hallway. Occasionally you glance at the archways and the alcove half expecting to see LaCrossa waiting there. Your major concentration is on avoiding the triangle

(967 cont'd)

stones. Your foot freezes in midair as you almost stagger trying to keep your balance. Is that a triangle or a poorly cut stone?

Roll the dice:

2 to 4, Turn to 942.
5, Turn to 921.
6 to 9, Turn to 949.
10 to 12, turn to 899.

968   Suddenly the room shifts through the labyrinth <u>draining you of 2 manna</u>. It seems impossible to gauge when the shifting will begin. You realize it is time to get out before you are drained further. Do you:

(A) Leave the way you came? Turn to 950.

(B) Walk the bridge? Turn to 975.

(C) Cast a *fly* spell? <u>Mark off 3 manna</u> and turn to 981.

(D) Cast a *reverse* spell on yourself? <u>Mark off 3 manna and the letters GG</u>. Now choose again.

969   In a small chest rests a bundle. You quickly unwrap it to discover a clear vile. Without hesitating you gulp it down and regain up to <u>8 manna points</u>.

Thankful to Elder Edla you wrap it up once again and decide to:

(A) Walk across to an archway? Turn to 939.

(B) Hide and wait? Turn to 920. If you have already hidden turn to 940.

(C) Cast a *reverse* spell? <u>Mark off 3 manna and the letters GG</u>. Now choose again.

970   The Elder's spell crackles deafeningly against your *protective* spell. You try to feed all your power into the spell knowing that everything depends on your ability to cast back his enchantment.

Roll the dice:

2 to 4, Turn to <u>885</u>.
5 to 12, Turn to <u>982</u>.

971   The face comes to life and searches your mind. It stumbles across a dark secret of yours and pulls back in revulsion. The face strikes out with a mind blast.

Go to the Enchantraen table that follows and roll one die. Check off the damage boxes on your score card.

ENCHANTRAEN

Roll		Damage
1	--------	0
2	--------	1
3	--------	2
4	--------	3
5	--------	4
6	--------	5

If you expire your *amula* sweeps you away and you turn to <u>840</u>.

If you live you stumble back through the archway in utter pain. Turn to <u>950</u>.

972   Suddenly the door on the right swings open. You expect to see LaCrossa. A black cloak swirls into the room.

No wait! It's not a cloak. It's thick black mist lapping through the air. Inside the archway, shrouded in the black stuff stands a ghastly vision. A red demon with wings that wave back and forth in the mist.

The creature's stomach has rotted or perhaps it was slashed open with a sword or dagger. Its intestines dangle, licked with tiny blue flames that dance around the hanging mass.

Its foul mouth opens, "You have been waiting for me?"

Do you:

(A) Dive for another archway? Turn to 949.

(B) Answer, "Yes"? Turn to 902.

(C) Attack with a *binding* spell? Mark off 1 manna and turn to 978.

973   As soon as you lean over the pool a frail voice comes forth.

"What do you wish good wizard from one as meager as myself."

Surprised you immediately formulate an answer.

(A) "I wish you to defeat the Penoi LaCrossa and bring him hither." Roll the dice:

2 to 5, Turn to 986.
6 to 12, Turn to 997.

(B) "I wish for little else than cool drink and safe passage." Turn to 991.

974 You concentrate on the reshaping of the ceiling. Arranging and rearranging the very essence of its support.

Roll the dice:

2 to 11, turn to <u>976</u>.
12, Your spell fails! The Penoi smiles and retaliates. If <u>GG</u> is marked turn to <u>918.</u> If not turn to <u>885</u>.

975 You test the bridge first and find it to be sturdy. You walk clumsily across trying to gauge your pace as it sways beneath you. You are almost across when ...

Roll the dice:

2 to 4, Turn to <u>989</u>.
5, Turn to <u>983</u>.
6, 7, turn to <u>949.</u>
8 to 12, Turn to <u>996</u>.

976 The ceiling collapses as 20 cubic feet of mud-like plaster splatters around the Penoi. He is partially buried as he struggles to break free. Then you cancel the spell. The mud reforms into solid rock and holds the Penoi fast.

He curses as you cross the room towards him. He tries to bite your hand as you reach to smash his *amula*. This time you have beaten the Elder! Turn to <u>935</u>.

977 You have entered one of the many endless hallways of the labyrinth. There are multiple archways lining the walls that lead to several rooms. You feel particularly uncomfortable here knowing LaCrossa could charge out of any one of them at any time. At the far end of the hallway you see a symbol. In the poor lighting you cannot make it out.

(977 cont'd)

Do you:

(A) Turn and go out the archway you entered? Turn to 951.

(B) Duck through the first archway you come to. Turn to 949.

(C) Walk part way in until you can make out the symbol? Roll the dice:
2 to 8, Turn to 994.
9 to 12, Turn to 979.

978 You call the magical blue light to your fingertips. As it forms around your hands you turn to aim it towards the demon.

In the blink of an eye the demon retaliates before you can cast it. Your legs buckle beneath you. As you tumble down you feel the earth tremble. Fire races up your spine. You attempt a *counter* spell but the pain stops.

Go to the Enchantraen table that follows and roll one die. Check off the damage boxes on your score card.

ENCHANTRAEN

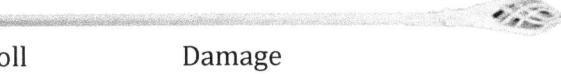

Roll		Damage
1	--------	2
2	--------	3
3	--------	4
4	--------	5
5	--------	6
6	--------	6

(Continued next page)

(978 cont'd)

If you expire you manage to break your *amula* before you pass out. Turn to <u>840</u>.

If you live you feel yourself tumbling through the magic's of the labyrinth once more. Turn to <u>950</u>.

979 You cautiously walk the hallway keeping an eye on the archway. A shadow leaps from your right. A giant serpent-man charges into the room. Before you can stop the ancient savage a spear is thrust at you. The tip explodes.

Go to the Enchantraen table that follows and roll one die. Check off the damage boxes on your score card.

ENCHANTRAEN

Roll		Damage
1	--------	0
2	--------	1
3	--------	2
4	--------	3
5	--------	4
6	--------	4

If you expire your *amula* is also broken. Turn to <u>840</u> knowing you have been defeated not by LaCrossa but by the Elder's ancient enemies.

If you live you dive through an open archway not wishing to waste your energies on this savage. Turn to <u>950</u>.

980   You enter a small 10 foot by 10 foot room. In the middle of the room is a strange Diaz. It looks as if it is a complex calendar surrounded with magical symbols and spells. In the center is a kindly carved face.

Quickly you avert your eyes. You felt the face attempting to control you. Do you.

(A) Avert your eyes and walk to the far archway? Roll the dice:

   2 to 7, 10, Turn to 949.
   8, 9, 11, 12, Turn to 951.

(B) Look again at the Diaz? Roll the dice:

   2 to 9, Turn to 992.
   10 to 12, Turn to 971.

981   As the spell envelopes you, you become weightless. Jumping with confidence you easily glide across the chasm. You near the far side when …

Roll the dice:

2 to 5, Turn to 989.
6 to 12, Turn to 949.

982   Your chest heaves in relief when you see his spell thrown back. The spell strikes the Elder and ripples against his innate magic resistance. LaCrossa is caught off guard as the *binding* spell starts to dissipate but then forms and holds. Losing his balance the Penoi tumbles down into the chasm.

You turn away as the first wave of serpent folk attack. When you look back the Elder is gone!

Somehow his *amula* must have broken saving him from a terrible demise. You wipe the sweat from your bow realizing you have won! Turn to 935.

---

983   You feel the bridge start to give way. It isn't breaking but the bindings seem to have come loose. You guess that this is another of the labyrinth's guards to stop all but magic-users from crossing.

You have plenty of time to cast a *fly* spell provided you have the manna to do so. If you don't, you decide to break your *amula* before you let those creatures below tear you apart. Do you:

(A) Have the manna to cast a *fly* spell? <u>It takes 3 manna</u>. If so turn to <u>981</u>.

(B) Smash the *amula* in defeat? Turn to <u>840</u>.

984   At the far archway across the rope bridge the Elder suddenly enters. You both see each other at the same time. You are both standing just out of spell range. As he looks around to assess the situation you decide to:

(A) Go back through your archway? Turn to <u>951</u>.

(B) Use an illusion of your own on the serpents below to hopefully call them to your bidding? <u>Mark off 4 manna</u> and turn to <u>985</u>.

(C) Cast a *reverse* spell around yourself? <u>Mark off 3 manna and the letters GG</u>. Turn to <u>989</u>.

985   You aim your illusion at the serpent folk. You want to fool them, not LaCrossa.

Roll the dice:

2 to 11, Turn to <u>999</u>.
12, Your spell fails! Turn to <u>989</u>.

---

986   The pool's depths seem endless. The waters boil and the room steams. You back away from the pool prepared for the worst. In moments something bobs and splashes at the pool's edge.

It's LaCrossa gasping for air. Without a second thought you stoop and grab his *amula*.

"Nooooo," he gurgles and grabs your hand. His grip is strong but you feel your wrist starting to give way. With your free hand you smash the Penoi's *amula* and he fades. You got him! Turn to 935.

987   LaCrossa cannot be seen. Do you:

(A) Cast a *detect* spell to search the area for a cache or the Elder? Mark off 2 manna and the letters HH. Roll the dice:

2 to 5, Turn to 962.
6 to 9, Turn to 995.
10 to 12, Turn to 998.

(B) Hide and wait for LaCrossa? Turn to 956.

(C) Walk across the bridge? Turn to 975.

(D) Fly across the chasm? Mark off 3 manna and turn to 981.

(E) Cast a *reverse* spell on yourself? Mark off 3 manna and the letters GG. Now choose again.

(F) Physically search your side of the cavern? Turn to 993.

988   Mark off the letters HH. You leave no rock unturned on your side of the cavern. You also search the cavern walls on the far side with your eyes.

(Continued next page)

(988 cont'd)

Roll the dice:

2 to 6, Turn to 923.
7, Turn to 887.
8, 9, Turn to 927.
10 to 12, Turn to 984.

989   If HH is marked turn to 949.

LaCrossa suddenly leaps into the air and rockets across the chasm towards you. You guess by his speed that he reinforced his *fly* spell with a *time* spell to give him such incredible quickness. You attempt to protect yourself but you seem as if you are moving in slow motion. Curse that hell-spawned dog! He is casting a spell yet another spell.

Roll the dice:

2 to 7, If GG is marked turn to 970. If not turn to 885.
8 to 12, He fails and you dive through the archway to safety. Turn to 950.

990   You have just entered a small cavern room. A spring of water trickles from the ceiling and splashes into a clear pool. There is an archway just to the left. Do you:

(A) Examine the pool? Turn to 973.

(B) Leave through the archway? Turn to 949.

991   You feel compelled to bend down and drink deeply. When you do so you are indeed refreshed and have regained up to 4 manna points. Thanking the spirit of the pool you know it is time to continue through the labyrinth. Turn to 949.

992   The face comes to life. You feel its presence racing through your mind. It pleasantly settles on a single one of your thoughts then pulls back. The face returns to stone.

The Elder Edla has reached out from the past and healed all your wounds and restored all your magic.

With words of thanks you cross through the next archway. Turn to 950.

993   Mark off the letters HH.

You scan the far side of the cavern as well as search your side. You turn over rocks and look behind the boulders. At one time you come too close to the chasm and lose your foothold sending down a small avalanche of rocks.

Then …. Roll the dice:

2, 3, Turn to 962.
4 to 6, Turn to 995.
7, Turn to 984.
8 or 9, Turn to 968.
10 to 12, Turn to 998.

994   Cautiously you enter, glancing at each archway for a trap. You glimpse at the symbol until you realize what it is.

It's a healing symbol. Quickly you walk the hallway and touch it. All damage done to you up to this point is immediately healed. You stay long enough to smile but quickly exit out of this otherwise dangerous hallway. Turn to 949.

995   There it is! Just before the bridge is a small bundle hidden beneath a rock. Quickly you unwrap it to discover a small clear vile inside. You drink it down and regain up to 8 manna points immediately. You praise Elder Edla and rewrap the vile and placing it beneath the rock.

(Continued next page)

(995 cont'd)

As the power flows into you, you decide to:

(A) Walk across the bridge? Turn to <u>975</u>.

(B) Fly across the chasm? <u>Mark off 3 manna</u> and turn to <u>981</u>.

(C) Hide and wait for the Elder? Turn to <u>956</u>.

(D) Cast a *reverse* spell? <u>Mark off 3 manna and the letters GG</u>.
Now choose again.

996 The serpents below look up in unison. You cannot be sure what they see but you dive for cover anyway. A volley of spears and arrows follows.

Go to the Enchantraen table that follows and roll one die. Check off the damage boxes on your score card.

ENCHANTRAEN

Roll		Damage
1	--------	1
2	--------	2
3	--------	3
4	--------	5
5	--------	5
6	--------	6

If you expire you manage to break your *amula* before you totally go unconscious. Turn to <u>840</u>.

If you still live you count your blessings as you tumble through the next archway! Turn to <u>950</u>.

997   The water chokes and gurgles. You sense that it is attempting to comply. In desperation it reaches out to find the power it needs to struggle on.

It drains you of 3 manna! In the end it gurgles and becomes still. You talk to it but it doesn't answer. You leave disappointed through the next archway. Turn to 950.

998   The Penoi is not here and you are unable to locate the cache. Below the serpent folk work steadily. Do you:

(A) Fly across the chasm to the far archway? Mark off 3 manna and turn to 981.

(B) Walk across the rope bridge? Turn to 975.

(C) Cast a *reverse* spell on yourself? Mark off 3 manna and the letters GG. No choose again.

(D) Hide and wait? Turn to 956.

999   You dare not attempt to counter the labyrinth's illusion. Instead you simply add to it. You visualize a staircase brilliantly lit at the top leading directly to the Penoi.

The serpent folk stop their labor. When they see their ancient enemy, an Elder standing before them they charge. Elder LaCrossa is astonished when the first volley of spears and arrows strikes him. Apparently LaCrossa doesn't see your illusion because he seems more than puzzled when the foul creatures run towards him through midair.

He tries to disbelieve the whole thing as an illusion against himself.

The second volley hits him. Gasping now the Penoi rolls trying to escape through an archway but does not make it. His *amula* breaks and as he fades away he hears your laughter. He realizes it was you who defeated him. Turn to 935.

1000 The flames burn to incredible heights. Soon the pain is gone and the night becomes silence. Looking down at your feet you realize that you have been pushed out of the pentangle.

You collapse when you realize that it is over. You lost!

The game is over Enchantraen and you were defeated. Take courage however. In this High Fantasy world you can always erase the marks on your character sheet and start again.

1001 You spur your mount on always heading to what you believe to be Jerican. On through most of the next day you race as the sounds of pursuit disappear behind you.

Your mount stumbles and goes lame. You shoo it away in another direction to throw off any pursuit. On you walk until up and over a hill you spot it! Turn to <u>201.</u>

1002 "The wizard disobeyed our order once and ran away from us," says a soldier.

"For that wizard you will be forced to give up a magical item," says a judge.

Remove one of the following from your character sheet.

(A) Shefast – check the gone box.

(B) The Pearl Godstone – erase the mark on <u>P</u>.

(C) Your Charmed Warning Stone.

(D) Any of the magical items obtained at the magic shop. If it's the *Incantation of Knot* erase the mark on K. If it's the *Vessel of Calming* erase the mark on <u>V</u>.

"Are there any other crimes?" asks the Judge. Turn to <u>438</u>.

1003   By now you have grown used to it, but as it collapses its unnatural power vanishes.

The rainbow is collapsing and the *Challengings* are over!

"It's too late," you involuntarily cry.

You begin to sink to the ground when a familiar sensation floods over you. Jenevan is calling through your mind-link. Since the quest is over you concede to allow her to pull you back to Arcania with a *return* spell.

The blackness engulfs you and the dizzy, falling feeling begins. While traveling through the void plane you allow your thoughts to drift.

"What could I have done to hasten my quest? Did I really ever have a chance? How could I have failed?"

Stone becomes solid beneath your feet. Your thoughts crystallize and you finally submit to the thought that the quest is over.

If T is marked roll one die:
1 to 3, Turn to 1012.
4 to 6, Turn to 1007.

If K is marked turn to 1012.

If W is marked turn to 1007.

If none of the above are marked turn to 1008.

1004   The binding hits and wraps the figure securely, sending it tumbling to the ground.

"I hope this isn't going to get kinky," chuckles the bound figure.

(Continued next page)

(1004 cont'd)

"Remain silent," you order as you begin to search the figure.

You discover that the figure is a harmless wizard from Goldchester, a friendly town in the West.

You ask the wizard to excuse you for your reaction but tell him you cannot be too careful in the wilds.

As you cut the wizard free he tells you his name is Sluss. He asks you if you are Enchantraen and you reply that that is your own business and return his question with another.

"Where are you headed?" Turn to <u>306</u>.

1005 Shefast tears at the clouds in answer to your summons. Down the lightning races, shattering the barn's roof and striking the old woman. She staggers and the barn is instantly filled with the smell of burning flesh.

With the sheer effort of her demonic will the fire goes out!

You gasp at the power that must have forced its way into her soul. With a smile, her eyes meet yours. As she leaps for you, you fully realize your peril. You turn ... to <u>571</u>.

1006 As you struggle through the porthole you begin to chant the words to a spell that might save you. You know that it will take the spell awhile before it works. That delay could mean your death.

You sense the archers taking aim at your exposed end.

The pearl comes to life once again. You are propelled forward just as the arrows whistle overhead. When you hit the water you feel your spell accelerating in speed. <u>Mark off 4 manna</u> as the arrows sizzle around you. Turn to <u>785</u>.

1007 Your head stops spinning and your eyes clear. The light growl of a panther causes you to lift your head.

(1007 cont'd)

Jenevan is tied to a chair. A strange glaze is over her eyes. Beside her is an aetherial panther and the ghostly image of Benolic flutters through her body.

"It seems I was not the only mistake you made along the way," comes the thin voice. "You are a pathetic sight wizard."

Slowly you rise. This was the man who was outside your tower when you first started this quest.

"What would you have of me Spectre," you say in hushed tones.

You are unconcerned about the answer. You are just trying to buy time.

"Your soul, peasant of Nautpolis," the Spectre begins but you shut the words out. You may have lost the quest but there is still plenty of life in you. You have no intention of losing everything now.

Any action you take will be chancy but you cannot afford to wait for the Spectre to make the first move.

Do you:

(A) Cast a *light* spell on Jenevan? If it works it will vanquish Benolic and the panther. <u>Mark off 1 manna</u> and roll the dice.

    1 to 8, Turn to <u>1010</u>.
    9 to 12, Before you finish your spell turn to <u>1009</u>.

(B) Grab a magical dagger next to you on the table? You would have to fight both of them but it could be your only hope.

    As you grab the dagger the panther springs for you.

(Continued next page)

(1007 cont'd)

Benolic however chooses a different attack. He wretches at the soul of Jenevan and by doing so tugs at your own. This weakens you and thus gives strength to the panther's charge.

Go to the Enchantraen table that follows and roll one die. Check off the damage boxes on your score card.

ENCHANTRAEN

Roll		Damage
1	--------	1
2	--------	2
3	--------	3
4	--------	4
5	--------	5
6	--------	5

If you expire turn to 1009. If you live fight back!

Go to the Enemy table that follows and roll one die. Check off the damage boxes on the Rogue's Gallery score card.

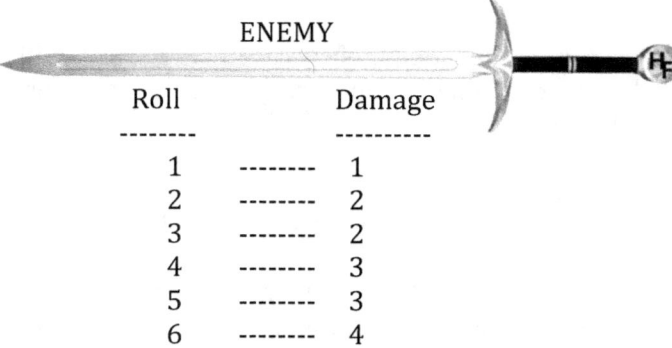

ENEMY

Roll		Damage
1	--------	1
2	--------	2
3	--------	2
4	--------	3
5	--------	3
6	--------	4

If the panther dies turn to 1011. If it lives go back to the Enchantraen table.

1008 As yours eyes refocus you see Jenevan silhouetted against the fireplace. Her giant form and slowly moving wings are comforting to see after the trials you have been through.

"There is no shame with the effort you made."

"Thank you, Jenevan" you say. "I don't need coddling now. I am a war-wizard."

"Of course, I know," she smiles.

Slowly you go to the stairwell and ascend the stairs to the towers top. Looking over the curtain wall you search for the last traces of the glittering rainbow.

"It will come again," you whisper.

You realize in your heart that when it does you will take up the challenge once more. Yes, you will play the game, but next time, yes... the next time...

THE END

1009 The panther leaps for you and its claws pass through your body tearing at your soul. After a long hard fight you realize the ultimate defeat is upon you. As Enchantraen the war-wizard you will walk these grounds no more... until the next game.

THE END

1010 When Benolic sees what you are up to he reacts immediately. As Jenevan chokes, you feel the pressure mounting in your own throat.

You will not be defeated. Through a contortion of sheer will, you complete the spell.

(Continued next page)

(1010 cont'd)

Light bursts from Jenevan's body. Benolic and the panther scream out their undead pain and their souls vanish. You are temporarily blinded by your own spell.

Turn to 1008.

1011 With a final stab at the panther you feel its unnatural soul drift back to the netherworld. A second surprise comes to you. As the panther vanishes, Benolic begins to stagger.

Apparently the panther was Benolic's familiar. Just as Jenevan is yours. Benolic raises an aetherial hand trying to kill Jenevan. His eyes drift your way as a smile crosses your lips. Benolic steps back. The bluff works and for fear of his unnatural life vanishes in a dark flash.

Turn to 1008.

1012 "Perhaps next time I may be of some assistance," comes a voice in the corner of your own study.

It is Benolic the man you met at the beginning of your quest.

"I still believe you can do it."

"Thank you, but leave me now" you reply even before your senses have fully recovered. As he and his panther walk out you ...Turn to 1008.